THE SILLA
PROJECT

Other Books by
John C. Brewer

MULTIPLAYER
THE MULTIPLAYER SAGA, BOOK 1

and coming soon

VIRIDIS
THE SHRIVELING

NON-PLAYER CHARACTER
THE MULTIPLAYER SAGA, BOOK 2

www.johncbrewer.com

ATTENTION: PlotForge books are also available in electronic format for most popular reading devices. For volume discounts on eBooks and paperbacks, please visit www.plotforge.com.

THE SILLA PROJECT

JOHN C. BREWER

For Steve,

Campout?

[signature]

PLOTFORGE, LTD.

The Silla Project
ISBN: 978-1-937979-06-5
LC Control Number: 2012913972

Acknowledgement

This book has been many years in the making and it would be impossible to thank all the people who helped in one way or another. There are those who offered support at tough times, like Heather and Temple Estopinal, Jim Ashburn, and Kim Daugherty; you will never know how much your encouragement has meant to me. Others gave of their time and talent such as Terry Frakes and Paul Shanley. My wife April, and sons Joseph, Benjamin, and Daniel have been unwavering in their support and have tolerated my long hours holed up in my basement office. My writing partner, Terri-Lynne Smiles provided the critique and editorial talent that matured this work from a manuscript to a product. And then there are the many people from authors, to bloggers, to travelers, to defectors who have worked, often putting their lives at risk, to extract information from North Korea. Without them, this would be nothing more than guess work. And of course, the indomitable scientists and engineers from the Manhattan Project to today, who through diligence, hard work, and curiosity, not only uncovered the hidden secrets of the atom, but have provided America's first line of defense for nearly 70 years. All of you have my sincerest respect and thanks.

For

the beleaguered people
of the Korean Peninsula.

1

Clink!

The sound came just after a flash of blue light stabbed through the wet forest night. Dr. Rhee Sun-yi peered out from behind a thick berm of earth. To his side, on leaning, wooden tables, portable data gathering instruments blinked and hummed. Somewhere behind him a Geiger counter crackled. It had burst into static at the flash but was now slowing along with his pulse. Every time they did a drop, his heart pounded in his chest so loud he could hear it in his ears. This experiment was not his idea but came directly from P'yongyang.

"One more time," he muttered, and wiped a sheet of sweat from his forehead. He clicked on his flashlight and stepped out from behind the embankment. A half-dozen men in white lab coats followed him across the muddy ground to where a short tower was erected in the middle of a clearing. Around the perimeter, armed guards patrolled with flashlights that cleaved the evening mist like swords.

Rhee stopped a few feet from the *Canglong* – a short tower of girders about four meters high. A narrow tube ran down the center, and a few centimeters below it was a small plutonium sphere with a hole through the middle: the target. Anything falling through the tube had to pass through the hole in the plutonium target. Beneath it, on the ground, was a metal pan.

Rhee's flashlight flickered and went out. He tapped the chintzy metal case and the bulb warmed to a dull, red glow. "Nothing works in this place," he grumbled to himself.

Beside him, an assistant used tongs to remove a sizzling-hot pellet from the metal pan: the *slug*. Under the ruddy light of Rhee's flashlight, the shiny nickel coating on the slug glowed orange.

Rhee pulled a set of calipers from his lab coat and measured the plutonium marble.

"Shall I return it to the drop carriage, comrade doctor?" asked his assistant.

"Not yet." Rhee turned and called into the darkness. "Comrade, Kim. Was that the last trial with the 115 gram slug? The full three meters?" He spoke like a native but his accent was distinctively Russian.

Another man emerged from behind the wall of earth carrying a clipboard. Rhee aimed his flashlight in Kim's direction. It was barely bright enough to reveal him. They could not even afford batteries here. It was worse than the Soviet Union, thought Rhee. Even at the end.

Kim Sun-gun was thin and wiry with dark eyes and thick black hair. And though he was over 20 years younger than Rhee, he looked the same age, his skin prematurely aged from a combination of nicotine addiction and years of privation.

"Yes, comrade doctor," he said. "We have completed the 88 gram slug as well."

"Then we will do the 145 gram next," said Rhee.

"We do not have one, comrade," Sun-gun answered.

Rhee stood for an instant in silence. "I instructed the metallurgy division to produce a 145 gram slug," he growled.

"The fabrication group needed a large sample to work with casting techniques, comrade."

"Casting," Rhee spat. "Pak Myong-whan is a Party cadre who gets what he wants." He turned away, muttering to himself. "Just like in the Soviet Union." He spun back toward Kim Sun-gun a moment later. "Don't they know that nothing will happen without our studies? *Nothing!*" But everyone just stared at him blankly.

"Very well," he sighed. "We will go to the 181 gram slug and begin testing at three meters."

Kim Sun-gun retreated to the berm and returned a moment later, struggling with two cases marked with radiation symbols. He was trailed by heavily armed, well-conditioned, and much better fed State Security Administration soldiers.

Rhee eyed them ruefully. The SSA was no different than the GRU. Or the NKVD. And just as stupid and lazy.

Kim set the cases down near the base of the gantry. He removed the lids and into the first case he placed the 115 gram slug, a glistening sphere less than an inch in diameter, then took out the new one which was only slightly larger.

Rhee placed it carefully in the drop carriage, then his assistant took hold of the rope and pulled it up into the tube, ready to be dropped again.

Rhee stopped him before he'd raised it a foot. "Wait!" he cried. "Wait." Between his shoddy glasses and his underpowered flashlight, it was difficult to see clearly, but Rhee knew what to look for. Exactly as he'd feared. The nickel coating on the target was beginning to blister. He pulled a screwdriver from his pocket and touched the bright strips peeling off the surface of the heavy, metal orb. Beneath the thin curls, the dull gray plutonium was already beginning to oxidize into a greenish powder.

He was just saying, "I guess we are done for the night," when a faint click and a soft whooshing sound reached him. Out of the corner of his eye, Rhee saw something fall from the tube. *The slug!*

Three thoughts spun through his head. Rules which had been drilled into him long ago from his first days in the Soviet Navy.

Time? *Too long.*

Distance? *Too close.*

Shielding? *None.*

At the instant the slug entered the hole through the target, the plutonium assembly became supercritical, unleashing a flood of neutrons and gamma radiation. There was a bright blue flash and a metallic taste flooded Rhee's mouth. An intense wave, like heat but with no warmth, blasted him. Somewhere behind him Geiger counters burst into static. He cried out, stumbling backwards, hands batting the air.

The slug passed on through the target and the nuclear chain reaction died. An instant later it landed in the pan with a clink.

Rhee collapsed to his knees, trying to remember who and where he was. His head and arms were on fire and his face felt like it had been smashed into a red hot frying pan. His skin had already turned a putrid violet color. Shadowy forms clustered around him shouting and pointing and waving their arms. He tried to answer but his mouth would not work. He knew he should be in pain, but that part of his brain had already shut down. Only the region that registered fear was still working and it was in overload.

He fell slowly backwards until he lay flat, staring upward, his body wracked with convulsions. The last image impressed upon his scorched retina was of the Canglong looming over him with stars twinkling all around.

2

Camera shutters clicked around the packed courtroom as Mitch Weatherby, dressed in the standard issue orange jumpsuit, was escorted in by two big bailiffs. His family was in the gallery along with the few friends who would still admit they knew him, but Mitch avoided their gaze. He sat down at the table where his attorney mumbled empty words of encouragement. Mitch didn't hear them. His mind was on the desperate thoughts that had emerged in the cell where he'd spent the six weeks since he'd been found guilty. He had nothing to live for.

In that cell awaiting sentencing, Mitch saw that his whole life, since earning his Ph.D. in physics, had been one downward slide, dumping him into the abyss of the past year. His reason for working so diligently toward that degree was stripped from him first. The United States wasn't designing nuclear weapons anymore so he would never have the chance to fulfill his dream of seeing his work in action. Government cutbacks and the environmental devastation of his profession made it an impossibility. So he'd spent years of this life huddled over a computer, working with equations and running simulations that ultimately meant nothing. The only bright spot of his life, his only salvation, had been Beth. And now she was gone, too. Along with the God who'd forsaken him.

The judge appeared and brought the court to order. On the front of the podium hung the Federal Seal, and the Great Seal of Arizona. Peering down from on high, the stern, gray-haired man asked if Mitch had anything to say. He knew what the judge wanted: an apology for his crimes. He was supposed to grovel and beg forgiveness in hope for a lighter sentence. But Mitch just shook his head. He couldn't grovel when he'd done nothing wrong. He wasn't the one who'd stripped the last meaning from his life. But neither the judge nor the jury had listened to him during the trial so what was the point or saying anything now?

The robed man frowned, pushed his glasses up and cleared his throat. "Mr. Weatherby, rise and face the court." Mitch's six-foot frame stood slowly. His dark eyes were sunken, but there was a fire in them still. He waited, knowing this was it. An opportunity for the world to make sense again. The last chance to awaken from the year-long nightmare that wasn't his life. A chance for God to prove there was still something in the world called *justice*. The judge gave him a piercing stare, and still, Mitch waited.

"Having been found guilty of high crimes against the people of the United States of America through due process and by a jury duly appointed by this court. And having failed to express remorse for such crimes or acknowledge the legitimacy of these proceedings, you will now be sentenced according to your deeds.

"For the two counts of manslaughter, the court hereby sentences you to ten years incarceration in a Federal Correctional Institution for each count."

Mitch had known this was coming but it didn't make the sword that pierced his heart any less painful.

"For the crime of possession of controlled nuclear materials, the court hereby sentences the guilty party to five years incarceration in a Federal Correctional Institution."

Twenty-five years. Mitch thought the guilty verdicts would be the worst things he could hear. He had prepared himself for this. Gone through his reactions a thousand times. But it was like getting shot in the stomach over and over. The chance to regain any sort of life was closing.

"For the crime of conspiring to construct and use a destructive device, five years incarceration."

Thirty years.

"For the crime of conspiracy to assemble a nuclear device, an additional ten years of incarceration in a Federal Correctional Institution."

Forty years.

"For the crime of improper use and storage of nuclear materials, two years.

"Forty-two years, until such time as Mitchell Weatherby has been fully rehabilitated and can return as a productive member of society." Mitch stood numb. And then the judge took away his final shred of hope – a minimum security facility. "The initial facility of confinement will be the medium security, Federal Correctional Institution, Terminal Island, Los Angeles, California, internment to begin effective immediately." The gavel sealed his fate. A death knell for him and the God who'd abandoned him – or had never existed at all.

Mitch would die in prison, the remaining shreds of his life stripped from him like skin from a dead deer. He would be seventy-eight years old when he was again a free man. His mother, weeping over the Bible she held in her hands, would be long gone. His brother would be gone, too. His sister in her late seventies. His niece and nephews unknown to him. He couldn't meet his family's eyes, staring instead at the worn Bible in his mother's hands. Forty-two years. He'd be forgotten by everyone, especially the God he'd once worshipped.

He had two minutes to say goodbye to his family and friends. He seemed to hear his attorney bellowing something about an appeal and being outraged. His former preacher tried to lead a prayer but no one listened. His brother might have hugged him and he thought his mother kissed him but he wasn't sure of anything that happened after his sentence was read.

In a small room, using fingers that had gone numb, he changed from his bright orange jail clothing into ill-fitting prison garb and uncomfortable shoes. He tied them with fumbling hands under the intense glare of federal marshals. New photos were snapped of Mitch holding a numbered placard, then two marshals pulled him away from the photo booth and hustled him onto an elevator. At the bottom, they hauled him onto a waiting bus and manacled Mitch to one of the seats. It all seemed... not like a dream… it seemed like it wasn't him at all.

"If you need to crap, or take a leak," growled a burly marshal, "raise your hand. We'll get to you soon enough. We got a long drive, so keep your trap shut and your eyes front."

Mitch was sitting on the right side, about halfway back. A few other prisoners were in front of him, spread out on both sides. A marshal sat across the aisle and another sat in the front. The marshals were armed. He was chained. Desperation ripped at his soul. This can't be happening, he thought, as his body filled with cold, wet concrete.

He glanced around again at his fellow prisoners with their dull eyes and slack faces. He wasn't like them. And that difference, his mind and his dignity, no one could take away from him. He needed to remember that or else he might as well go for the marshal's gun and eat a bullet.

The bus pulled out and made for the interstate. Prisoners peered out the windows as the beautiful Arizona countryside streaked past. Their last view of the outside world for decades.

Terminal Island in Los Angeles was a good four hundred miles away. Straight across the Colorado Desert on I-10. But Mitch knew nothing about the place. "Excuse me, sir," he asked the Marshal seated across from him. "Can you tell me about Terminal Island?"

The marshal jaws, which had been mangling a piece of gum, stopped. He slowly turned his head and Mitch knew instantly that he'd made a mistake. A few of the other prisoners snickered. Mitch heard someone behind him whisper, "*Dumb-ass noob.*"

"You got some kind 'uh problem, chief?" asked the marshal.

"No, sir," Mitch replied with lowered eyes. "No sir."

"You think I'm some kinda tour guide or something? Here to answer your stupid ass questions?"

"Uh, no sir. I – I just thought –"

"You just let me do your thinking for you, boy." His voice rose. "Just shut your pie hole or I'll lock your sorry ass in the john for the rest of the trip! You got that?"

By now Mitch's face was on fire but all he could do was answer, "Yes, sir."

Mitch expected it to end there, but the marshal stood up in the aisle, stuck his prominent gut out and leaned his broad, heavily mustached face down to Mitch's so close he could smell wintergreen and cigarettes. He grabbed Mitch's mouth between a thick finger and thumb and wrenched it painfully around. "Maybe you didn't hear Marshal Reed when we drug your sorry ass on here. We Don't Want No Talkin!"

"Yes sir," Mitch grunted, trying to sound compliant, but the rage inside him was so powerful it threatened to burst his heart.

The marshal's face twisted into a scowl of hatred mixed with garbled cursing. "Prisoners these days think they own the place. If I had wanted you to talk, I'd have told you to talk." He slapped Mitch on the back of the head so hard he saw stars. The man's hand was like iron. "You better think about doing as you're told because your new boss at *The Island* ain't gonna be a nice as me!"

Mitch dropped his eyes and remained silent as the bus rolled on. Several hours west of Phoenix, just after dark, they left the interstate and turned south into the deep desert at Quartzsite, Arizona. A dusty, forlorn blip on the map in the middle of a sprawling wasteland of sand, rock, sage brush, and towering cacti. An hour-and-a-half later they rolled up behind the Federal Building in Yuma, Arizona. It was nearly nine o'clock and neither the prisoners nor the guards had had anything to eat. One by one, the marshals stood the prisoners up and locked them together. The marshal turned to Mitch. "You ready to get something to eat Mitchelle?" he laughed, swearing liberally.

The name stunned Mitch, and he didn't reply quickly enough so the marshal hit him in the back of the head so hard it knocked his glasses off. "When I ask you something, you damn well better answer, girly! I said, are you ready to get something to eat?"

"Yes sir," he choked, his head ringing again. He tried to stoop and pick up his glasses, but they were chained like slaves, making it impossible. This must be what Joseph had felt like when his brothers sold him into slavery, Mitch thought. Exactly like it. The government Mitch had worked for, the country he'd sworn to protect, had betrayed him. But Joseph enslaved in Egypt had more of a chance than Mitch would have in a Federal Penitentiary.

Forty-two years? He couldn't take this for even forty-two hours. He gave himself two weeks. Two weeks before someone killed him, or he killed himself.

"What's the matter, Mitchelle?" The marshal picked up Mitch's glasses but didn't give them back. "Tell you what. If you're a real good girl, you can have 'em back after supper."

Mitch tried to keep his eyes down as they ate in the Yuma County Jail. The few times he looked up he caught other prisoners leering at him. Half way through the standard issue meal, the marshal gave Mitch's glasses back to him to "Pick out his new boyfriend."

After they'd boarded, three new prisoners joined them and took seats in the rear.

"Chickie," called the marshal. "You ready to go?"

"Yes sir," Mitch grunted through clenched teeth.

"Can the rest of us go now?"

There was a smattering of laughter.

Mitch's head was filled with thoughts of killing the marshal. Getting his hands on the man's fat throat and crushing his windpipe. "Yes, sir."

"You like me?"

"No, sir."

"You're learnin'. That's good. You'll learn somthin' new tomorrow, too! How to bend over!" The marshal and the other prisoners roared with approval.

The bus pulled away from the courthouse in the dark and crossed into California a few minutes after. The sign at the border read, *Welcome to California, The Golden State*. His former life, all he'd striven to achieve, his years at Los Alamos National Laboratory, all of it, was gone. Mitch's feeling of impending doom swallowed him. Thoughts of prison filled his mind. Locked up year after endless year, raped until he was an AIDS-infected husk. Whatever else happened to him in there, he swore, it would not be that. He would die fighting before he lived on his knees. And he would join Beth that much sooner. He whispered a silent prayer into the darkness, knowing it would be ignored like all his others. There was no God.

A hard blow struck him on the back of the head, and Mitch was overcome by rage. "What the hell is your problem!" he snapped, and the marshal went berserk, bashing Mitch who tried to sit and take it, but by the fourth blow he was cowering to fend off the blows with his chained hands. It only enraged the marshal all the more. He grabbed Mitch by the hair and jerked his head back, then sent a vicious backhand crashing across his face.

"*Stupid* worthless whore!" He screamed in Mitch's face, then feigned another blow. Mitch flinched and the marshal laughed wickedly and faked again. "They are going to wear your ass out!"

Mitch fell back in his seat. His glasses sat cockeyed on his face. Blood poured from his nose so that he could barely breath. His face was throbbing. His head was spinning. He couldn't do this. This couldn't be happening. He wasn't a criminal.

The marshal returned to his seat, and Mitch stared out the greasy window into the night. Through his smudged lenses, Mitch could just make out the constellation Cygnus. Many a night he had spent on the hill behind his house looking at these very same stars with Beth at his side. They'd done that the night before – before the end. And twenty-four hours later, she was dead and he was accused of attempting to build a nuclear bomb in his basement. Nothing made sense anymore.

A loud bang from the rear of the bus interrupted his thoughts. The bus began to slow suddenly when Mitch noticed the engine had stopped running. The marshal who'd beaten Mitch stood and began to protest when there was another sharp bang, a flash, and a tangy smell. The oversized man looked down to find a hole, big enough to throw a basketball through, where his heart and lungs should have been. For an instant, he and Mitch made eye contact, then his head fell into his stomach and he dropped to the floor. Mitch was struck with a sudden satisfaction, numb to the screaming around him.

The head of the marshal in the front seat disintegrated next, leaving his body with an arm still raising a microphone to where his mouth used to be. The marshal in the back of the bus lay slumped across a prisoner, screaming, his legs beating the air like the tail of a fish being scaled. More cannon shells cut the driver in two. His legs remained securely buckled in place, feet still on the pedals, while the upper half tumbled down the stairwell and wedged in the doorway. It didn't scream for long.

The bus rolled to a stop on a long gentle rise, began to roll backwards, then lurched to a halt. Just as quickly as it had begun, the screaming stopped and it became deathly quiet. Black suited figures, nearly invisible in the darkness, surrounded them outside. From the rear of the bus, a triumphant Hispanic voice burst out in laughter. "Time for me to go, ladies!" In the dim running lights, Mitch saw he was one of the prisoners who joined them in Yuma.

The door in front pried open and two figures entered, dressed head to toe in black and with night vision goggles over their eyes. Their posture and swagger told Mitch that the dark bulk in their hands were weapons.

One prisoner was busy in the aisle fishing the key from a dead marshal. He raised it to free himself just as one of the ninja-like intruders snatched it from his hand. A third figure entered the bus with authority and raised his night vision equipment out of the way.

The prisoner with the Hispanic voice stopped laughing. "Ramone?" he questioned.

The leader of the group pulled out a photograph and moved down the aisle, shining a red light on the picture, then on each man in turn. He stopped at Mitch and carefully pulled off his glasses, then compared the photograph to Mitch's blood streaked face. "Mitchell Weatherby?" he asked in an Asian-accented voice.

Mitch nodded and croaked: "Yes."

"Come with me," he said and unlocked Mitch's chains.

Mitch stepped over the body of the fallen marshal with his mind teetering between wild disbelief and sheer terror. The leader took out another photograph and used it to select the man with the Hispanic voice. "See you later," the man sneered to the other prisoners as they led him off. "Told you I was headed home." He nodded at Mitch. "Who is this bitch?" As they left, more black clad figures entered, heavily armed.

Once outside they hustled over to where a van sat with the engine running. They threw the Hispanic man in. Mitch could hear him complaining from inside. The sound of heavy blows silenced him.

The black-clad leader turned to Mitch and said in a polite but hurried voice, "Dr. Weatherby, what is your social security number?"

"My social sec –"

"Quickly!" demanded the stranger. "Time is short."

"Um, uh." He was having trouble thinking. "It's uh, four-eight-eight, one-two, two-oh, eight-five."

"You must undress as quickly as possible," hissed his rescuer. "Everything must come off. Underwear. Socks. Everything. Quickly."

He was given a new set of clothes while, nearby in the darkness, another man, either unconscious or dead, was being dressed in Mitch's clothes.

"I'm sorry, comrade, but we need your glasses." He held his hand out but Mitch hesitated. "They can be replaced. You cannot."

Mitch handed them over.

"Do you have any jewelry?"

Mitch removed his wedding ring and watched them put it and his glasses on the other man. Whoever he was, Mitch thought, he was about to die in Mitch's place. He surprised himself by being relieved at the thought and wondered how this carnage could possibly be the answer to his prayer of deliverance. It couldn't be.

A helicopter flew low over a ridge and landed on the side of the road a short distance away. Dust and sand blew into the air and Mitch had to stop buttoning his new shirt to cover his eyes. The second it touched down, he and the Hispanic man were hurried aboard even as the sound of gunfire rang out from the bus. The helicopter engine spooled back up with a whine and the aircraft rose into the sky amid swirling dust and the pungent smell of jet exhaust, leaving their rescuers on the ground below. With a roar, it sped south over the ridge and disappeared into the desert, headed toward Mexico just a few miles to the south.

Mitch looked back once and saw the bus burst into flame, filling the desert night with a hellish glow.

3

Mitch bolted upright. His skin was damp with sweat. His heart pounded in the intense darkness. Ever since his conviction, he'd been tormented with nightmares. He reached upward, feeling for the rack of his cellmate, but his hand met nothing but empty space. A thrill shot through his veins. "Where am I?" he whispered. But in a nauseating flash, he remembered. The attack on the bus. The helicopter flight and transfer to the float plane. The nighttime rendezvous with the ship. He felt his face. His lips and nose were still swollen and tender. It hadn't been a dream. But it couldn't be real.

Mitch could just make out the muffled thrum of machinery buried deep within the bowels of the ship. He could also hear the slap of water. He groped about the cabin searching for a light switch. Something fell over with a clang. He pulled up short, expecting to hear hammering on the door. But there was nothing. He felt for where he thought the porthole must be, found an opening through which a damp draft poured, and stuck his head through.

Outside he discovered a stout wire screen. Thoughts about notes in bottles evaporated. And who would find them, anyway? And would he want them to? No matter what was happening to him, it was better than Terminal Island, of that he was sure. Craning his neck revealed only the clean lines of a modern ship. Foam shone dimly against the darkness of the ocean, fanning into a broad wake. It did tell him one thing though: his cabin was on the port side.

Squinting into the sky, he could just make out fuzzy blobs of light. Without his glasses, he could only vaguely make out a group of stars off the port-stern, not far above the horizon. The central star in the constellation was a large, dim reddish blob. But even vision impaired, Mitch knew it was probably Antares in Scorpio. They must be headed northwest into the open sea. That meant the United States was hundreds of miles off the opposite beam of the ship and every instant sliding further behind. He knew without a doubt that he would never see it again. His stomach heaved at the thought and vomit poured from his mouth. He wiped his mouth and lay back down, afraid not to pray and afraid of what to pray for.

Sunlight was shining through the porthole when Mitch awoke. His stomach was a cave but a quick look around revealed no food in the small cabin. He stared out the porthole at the shadow of the ship on the water stretched long and dark in the early morning light. He could smell the stale vomit from earlier and it threatened to turn his stomach again so he pulled his head back in.

The room was sparse, with a bed, a small table, and an ancient TV along one wall. A bookcase stood on the other, and a metal locker rested next to the door. The walls were bare except for two portraits hanging in a row beneath the porthole. He leaned in close to see who they were. The massive glasses and wild hair in the first portrait were unmistakable: Kim Jong-il – leader of North Korea. Mitch's heart skipped a beat. Next to him was his father and predecessor, Kim Il-sung. His blood turned to ice, and he knew last night's prayers had been misplaced. God hadn't saved him from prison. He'd sent him to Hell.

A knock on the door froze Mitch's thoughts. He glanced around but there was nowhere to hide. More staccato raps echoed into the room. "Yes. Who is it?" he answered.

"Dr. Weatherby?" came a voice through the heavy steel door. "May I come in, sir?"

"Uh, sure," Mitch answered, half-expecting to see a man with horns and a pitchfork open the door.

On the other side wasn't the devil but the man who'd led him to his room the night before. "*Anniyong haseyo*," he said with a shallow bow. "Are you well? I trust you are rested from your journey?" His English was perfect; his voice, deep and rich.

"I suppose," Mitch answered every nerve on edge. This guy was a North Korean!

"I hope you find the accommodations acceptable. We try hard to make our guests comfortable."

"They're fine, thanks." He responded stiffly, his body about to snap with tension.

"Last night was a bit confusing so you may not remember meeting me," the man said, extending his hand. "I am Lee Song-nam. Please, call me Lee."

"Mitch Weatherby," Mitch said, taking Lee's hand. "But you already seem to know that."

Lee frowned. "Before we get any farther, Mitch, let me extend to you my deepest sympathy on the murder of your wife. Her death was most unfortunate. Most unnecessary."

Mitch frowned, too. "Thank you." He didn't trust this guy. And being called 'Mitch' by a complete stranger, someone who'd abducted him, was just – wrong.

"No doubt you have many questions," Lee went on. "Not the least of which is who we are, and why you are here. All will be answered in time. And please, don't think I'm being evasive, but first things first. Being spirited away in the middle of the night as you were, you have come to us with only the clothes on your back." He smiled and looked Mitch over. "And of course, your new pajamas."

Mitch tried to smile but it made his nose hurt. "Better than jail."

"Good." Lee smiled and chuckled. Everything he did seemed choreographed down to the minutest detail. "In the locker, you will find a change of clothes. If they don't fit, let me know."

"Thank you, again," said Mitch. He opened the locker and glanced inside.

"*Kam-sa-ham-nee-da*," replied Lee, in a tone suggesting Mitch should try it.

"*Kam-sa-ham-nee-da*?" Mitch repeated.

"Perfect! You have learned to say *thank you*."

"In what language?"

Lee just smiled. "Breakfast in half-an-hour. Until then, make yourself at home. Take a shower. Get comfortable. You've been through a great deal. So get used to your room. I do apologize for your not being allowed to leave it. Believe me, it is for the *safety* of both yourself and the crew."

Lee paused. "Before I go, is there anything I can get you before breakfast?"

Mitch decided to find out if he was serious. "My glasses were taken from me last night. Is there any way I could get something to help me see a little better?"

Lee reached into his shirt pocket and produced a pair of glasses with heavy black rims. "Try these."

Mitch put them on and the world snapped into clarity. He realized that the man calling himself Lee had excellent teeth, slightly wavy hair, and fine lines around the corners of his eyes. His expression was softened further by gold, wire-rimmed glasses that gave him a kindly, professorial look. He wore a comfortable pair of western-style cotton pants and a button up shirt with long sleeves. Nothing like Satan at all. The only peculiarity of his dress was a small round button he wore over his left breast. It had a tiny picture of Kim Il-sung on a red background. Then again, this might be exactly how Satan dressed. But why would Satan give him glasses?

Lee laughed. "Of course, we anticipated this need." With a deep, polite bow, he went to the door. But before he left he turned and said, "*Tashoe bopsheeda.* See you soon."

"*Ta-shoe bop-shee-da,*" Mitch repeated with his own clumsy bow.

"Excellent!" He disappeared and locked the door behind him.

Lee's expertise in the Korean People's Army was in psychological warfare. Brainwashing. But Lee didn't think of it that way. He considered it the truth. He was firmly dedicated to the truth of the Juche Idea and took every opportunity to teach others. And the major knew full well that if he was unable to turn Mitch, his superiors would not stop at using cruder methods. Whatever else Major Lee was, he was not a cruel man and hoped Mitch would recognize the truth without drastic measures. After all, to win another's mind with reason was the Confucian way. And Juche presented an advanced scientific process for such tasks.

Lee climbed a ladder and took a few twists and turns until he arrived at his superior's stateroom where he knocked on the door.

"*Tu-ro-ka-yo*," came a strong voice, and Lee opened it. Inside was a stern looking, uniformed man watching a TV monitor. It was Colonel Phoung Jin. Mitch was preparing to take a shower and when he began undressing, the colonel courteously flicked off the monitor.

"Comrade Major," barked the colonel. "How is our guest?"

"Confused. Relieved. Frightened. Perfect."

"Does he know yet who we are?" asked the colonel. "Where he is going?"

"He is a weapons designer. There are pictures of the Great Leader's on his wall. It is a puzzle he should solve quickly."

"Initial assessment?" asked Colonel Phoung.

Lee put his hands behind his back and strode across the cabin in thought. He stopped at the porthole and gazed through it for a moment, then turned back to Colonel Phoung. "He is vulnerable. It is obvious that he finds his new accommodations much preferable to his old. When I handed him his glasses, I thought he would kiss me. It remains to see what his patriotic state is, but by continually reminding him of his dead wife and of his exploitation by the imperialists, my guess is that he will agree to help us."

"Concerns?"

"Only those we have previously discussed. Weatherby is an intellectual. And a scientist. Unused to being ruled by his emotions. While that will make him easier to win in the short term, it could pose problems as his intellect begins to reassert control. But when he comes to see the crimes of his imperialist homeland, his intellectual honesty will demand he face them. And, of course, when he comes to understand the Juche Idea he will never want to leave."

Producing glasses like that had been a real shock. At best, Mitch had expected some loaners which would give him a terrible

headache. To get a pair of glasses of the correct prescription was…
spooky. It made him wonder how much they knew about him.
How long had he been watched? What did they know about this
family? His friends? They'd probably read about his trial in a
newspaper or on the internet and decided he'd be useful if
convicted.

He thought about Lee's advice and took a shower. The luxury
of a private bathroom had never felt so nice. He looked into the
mirror. The heavy, black-rimmed glasses and swollen nose and lip
made him appear every bit the nerd one would expect a nuclear
scientist to be. But Mitch Weatherby didn't fit the usual stereotype.

Fifteen minutes later he emerged clean, refreshed, and better
than he'd felt in a long time. A very long time. The prospect of not
going to prison and avoiding what would happen there had lifted
his spirits, even if it was at the hands of the North Koreans. He
dressed and, with his new glasses, explored his room.

The TV looked like one Mitch's grandmother had had when
he was a kid. The channel selector was missing and a metal plate
had been riveted over the hole. He sat down in the high backed
chair in the corner of the room and examined the bookcase. He
was surprised to find a number of his favorite physics,
engineering, and mathematics textbooks there. Books he had used
in his job on a daily basis. A chill ran up his spine as he wondered
how they knew. He pulled out a copy of *Neutron Physics* and
flipped through it. How he had loved Los Alamos. He never
looked at it as designing weapons. Rather, it was the perfect blend
of theoretical and experimental physics. The ultimate synergistic
device, honed and fine-tuned since the end of World War II,
providing the first line of defense. But … He closed the book and
thrust it back on the shelf. The nation he thought he'd been
defending didn't exist anymore. The God he'd worshiped his entire
life had remained silent while his life was shattered. Had either of
them ever been real, or where they just useful ideas? Like Lenin
had said, 'The opiate of the masses.'

Confirming his suspicions as to his abductors, he found a
small blue copy of *On the Juche Idea*, by Kim Jong-il. Other titles
by each of the Kims were on the shelf too. There was no Bible,

Mitch noticed. Would Lee give him one? He doubted it. Would Mitch read it if he did? He doubted that, too.

He pulled out the copy of *On the Juche Idea*. It was about the same size as a pocket-sized, New Testament once given to him by his mother. And at the bottom of the front cover written in gold letters was the word, *P'yongyang*. Just inside was a picture of a plump, smiling face with curly black hair tossed into a stylish coiffeur. 'The Dear Leader, Comrade Kim Jong-il,' it said beneath it.

He flipped the book open and began reading at a section entitled, "Originality of the Juche Idea." It spoke of something called Juche which placed man at 'the center of everything' and called him 'the master of the universe.' There was also a lot about the popular masses, the working class, and a materialistic dialectic. It all sounded very communist. Very Soviet. Very un-American and definitely not Christian. He was reading about something called *Chajusong* which seemed to be related loosely to the western idea of a soul, when Lee returned with breakfast.

"I hope you're hungry," he cooed. "I've brought scrambled eggs, bacon, toast, milk, coffee, and fresh fruit."

Mitch was ravenous. "Sounds good."

Lee placed the tray on the table and produced a copy of the *New York Times*. It was the national edition, slightly worn and a week old.

Mitch thanked him for everything then Lee left him to eat in privacy. Mitch watched him go, thinking that his assessment of North Koreans may not have been completely accurate. Perhaps they weren't the devil after all. Good treatment. Good food. A newspaper. *An American newspaper*. He wouldn't have expected that after what he'd always read about them. But he'd read about himself in the press and none of that had been true, either.

Mitch read the paper as he ate. The same maddening, mundane minutia which mesmerized Americans. Politics. The economy. The environment. After what he'd been through, the daily drivel that used to rile him had become pointless.

*

Over the next few days, Lee appeared in the morning with breakfast and returned later to collect the tray. Lunch and dinner were much the same. The only other signs of activity came in the afternoon when music filtered down from somewhere up above. But Lee never told him what the military sounding marches signified, and Mitch was mostly left alone, giving him time to heal, although the turmoil within him only grew. Praying didn't seem to 'work,' whatever that meant. Instead of feeling calmer and closer to God, he wound up thinking about Beth. Or about getting closer to North Korea with every passing second, and what he would do when he got there. He assumed the North Koreans were after him to build an atomic bomb. There was no other explanation for his being here, although he wasn't sure why they needed him.

North Korea had tested bombs, successfully, but they seemed to have gone to a lot of trouble to procure his services to create something they already had. And while the thought of creating a device for part of the Axis of Evil initially turned his stomach, the more he thought about it, the more he couldn't think of a reason not to. Everything he'd believed about America had turned out to be one gigantic lie. From his unjust incarceration, to a 750 billion dollar bailout for wealthy bankers. All that crap about freedom, liberty, and justice he'd learned in school was just propaganda, little different than the vapid mush he found in his Korean library. The only difference was that American politicians knew that if you kept people fat, dumb, and happy, the majority wouldn't care what happened. Bread and circus. Consumers to line pockets of the wealthy industrialists who funded the campaigns of politicians. So America offered two party-sanctioned candidates while North Korea offered one Party-sanctioned candidate. Maybe that meant the U.S. system was just twice as bad.

He went through the books, over and over, to stave off boredom and came away with several recurring themes in the Kims' writings: First, the Koreans, specifically those in the north, were the world's most noble, privileged race and were eternally lucky to have peerlessly great leaders. Second, the Americans and their imperialism were the source of all the problems in North Korea and the rest of the world. And third, there was no God, and religion had only ever been used to control people. Mitch gave a grim smile to that one. Maybe the Kims had gotten one out of three right. He'd been on his knees every night since Beth's death and it had changed nothing. He wasn't going to play that fool any more.

4

Four days in, Mitch was sitting in the chair by the porthole, once again reading *Kim Jong-il: The People's Leader* since he was in no mood to read about neutrons. In the middle of the tale of how the Dear Leader, as a result of "his manifold love and concern for the peasants," dealt with a cooking oil shortage in Sakju, there came a knock on the door. He glanced at the clock. It wasn't feeding time. The knock came again.

"Come in," he called, no longer expecting the devil. The door swung open to, once again, reveal Lee standing in the doorway.

"*Annyong haseyo*, Mitch. Enjoying the book?"

Mitch leaned forward and stretched. "A little unbelievable."

A smile broke out on Lee's face. "Yes! The life of the Dear Leader *is* unbelievable."

"That's not really what I meant."

"Well, what did you mean?"

"Reads like propaganda."

Lee sat down on the bed. "Why do you say it reads like propaganda?"

"For one thing, cooking oil was invented long before Kim Jong-il was born. I don't really see why his, what did they call it –" He opened the book and scanned the page.

"On-the-spot guidance?" Lee suggested.

"Yeah. Sounds to me more like all the corn had been carted off by the collective. All Jong-il did was return some of it."

"That is the Juche way. Everything that is grown is collected by the government, then redistributed fairly. That is why, in Choson, there is no hunger."

Mitch frowned, remembering stories about famines and floods that seemed to sweep across North Korea every year. "I've seen a lot of pictures on the internet that say different."

Lee frowned back. "Now that *is* propaganda. Those pictures are staged by puppet stooges in South Korea to try and discredit the Worker's Paradise."

This went against everything Mitch had ever heard. "But aren't we sending North Korea food aid?"

"You mean, the war reparations your country is finally repaying? Let's save that for a later discussion. I've been giving you a chance to decompress. You've had a difficult year and sometimes a little isolation is just what the mind and body need to begin the healing process."

Mitch agreed. "You're right. But I was starting to get a little bored." He held up the book he'd been reading but Lee failed to understand the gesture.

"Then I have come just in time! Tell me, what do you think of your treatment so far? Is it what you expected? We know how Americans feel about us."

Mitch smiled and returned the book to the shelf. "Well I'm not in prison. And nobody's shooting at me, or beating me up. But…" He motioned with his hand as if to indicate the vessel, "…I wouldn't mind knowing where I am. And where I'm going." He paused, then said, "And why." He suspected, of course, but wanted to hear it.

"Mitch, you are on board the Democratic People's Republic of Korea vessel, *Tong Gon Ae Guk Ho*; *Socialist Patriot of the East*. You were rescued from the clutches of the imperialists by elite members of the Korean People's Army and are being taken to Choson, the Democratic People's Republic of Korea. You probably know it better as North Korea."

Mitch raised an eyebrow as Lee made no attempt to hide it, contrary to his evasiveness up to now. But Mitch didn't know whether to be relieved or more afraid. "I'd guessed as much from the reading material and the pictures on the wall."

"So you recognized the *widaehan suryong*. Good!"

Mitch shook his head. "Wee-da – what?"

"The Great Leader. And his progeny. Peerlessly great leaders, iron-willed, brilliant commanders."

Mitch nodded cautiously. "Right. Kim Il-sung," he pointed. "And that's Kim Jong-il, right?"

"Yes. The Great Leader Comrade Generalissimo Kim Il-sung and the Dear Leader Comrade Generalissimo Kim Jong-il. I see that this concerns you."

"Of course, it concerns me! Our countries are technically at war. And I see a lot of things on the news that make me wonder if your leadership is completely… sane."

Lee gave him a knowing smile. "Let me ask you something, Mitch. During your trial, it was reported that you were a religious extremist building a nuclear bomb so you could detonate it in Washington DC during the President's State of the Union Address."

Mitch's eyes flashed. He stood up stiffly and walked to the porthole, his knee groaning from where he'd injured it falling down the stairs that night over a year ago, The night his life ended. His shoulder still sore from the bullet that shattered it as he fell. His heart still broken from what they'd stolen from him. The ocean, like his mood, was gray beneath an overcast sky. A north wind was blowing, pulling the waves into white caps. This wasn't the way his life was supposed to have unfolded.

"Was that true, Mitch? Any of it?" Lee asked again.

Mitch stared out the window and ground his teeth together. Seeing his wife die in his arms. Waking up in the hospital the next morning chained to his bed. Being arrested. Getting fired from his job. Losing his security clearance. Convicted of something he never did.

Lee answered for him, "These same people that murdered your wife and destroyed you seek to destroy us. All that you know of us – of our nation – comes from that same source. All of it."

Mitch chewed his lip in silent, burning rage. They had called him a 'religious extremist.' Painted him as some kind of Bible-thumping, gun-toting, right-wing fanatic. But he still couldn't figure out how any of this had happened. He'd done nothing. Yet… here he was.

Lee rose and came up behind him. "The United States is not what you believed, Mitch. Your being here should be evidence in plenty. And my country is not what you think either." Lee placed a friendly hand on Mitch's shoulder. Mitch looked at it uncomfortably. "Mitch? Can we agree on that point? Isn't it possible that you might have been wrong about us, too?"

Red flags shot up all over the place. He knew what Lee was trying to do. Finally he spun around. "What do you want from me, Lee? Why am I on this ship? Just say it. Now."

"You are a brilliant man, Dr. Weatherby. A man who possesses special talents. Special training. Valuable knowledge. A man whose worth is not understood or appreciated by his homeland. Who was betrayed by his country. You have been saved from a life of imprisonment and the horrors it would bring to help us build an atomic bomb."

Ice slid through Mitch's veins, yet his face grew as hot as if he were staring at an expanding nuclear fireball. Nausea welled up inside him, just like when he was sentenced – a shot in the gut. He'd prepared himself, but hearing it made it so real and immediate. He'd thought the last shred of his life had been taken in that courtroom, but he'd been wrong. He'd still believed in the evil of America's enemies. He still *did* believe it. But maybe that was just propaganda like everything else. But what else did he have? What was left to take away from him? It was like Beth was dying all over again.

Lee sat back down on the bed. "I am glad to see this troubles you. I would lose all respect for you if it did not. You are a man of great honor and integrity and we are not asking you for treachery. It is not something we believe in, even if it helps us. Traitors can never be trusted by either side. And you are thinking this is treason; I would too. You are an honorable man, we know that. We would have no interest in you if it were otherwise. But treason, Mitch, treason can only come from a man with a nation. And the nation to which you gave your allegiance does not exist. Maybe it did once, I do not know, but not now. You have no country to betray, Mitch, only an idea of a country. But that country betrayed you when it murdered your wife, then destroyed you to save itself.

It was your nation that committed treason, Mitch. Not you. You will remain forever innocent of treachery."

Mitch felt heat rising up the back of his neck and the breeze coming through the port hole did not cool it.

"Multi-path effects, Mitch," Lee said sadly. "Multi-path." Mitch spun around and stared at Lee. "The mountains caused their GPS units to malfunction and they brought them to the wrong place."

"I tried to tell them," Mitch whispered. No one had listened to him. No one. Not even his lawyer. Finally, someone who understood. Who believed him!

"I know, Mitch," Lee said softly. "I know. But they refused to listen. And Beth, she just happened to get in their way. Then, when they realized their mistake, they had to silence you."

"Yes. They wouldn't listen to me," Mitch croaked. "They wouldn't let me talk." The rage he'd felt at being brushed aside, at being called a liar, at being silence by security regulations, flooded his veins like gasoline. Hot tears stung his eyes and he wiped them away.

Lee went into the bathroom and emerged with some toilet paper. It was coarse, like burlap with tiny slivers of wood in it. He handed it to Mitch. "There is no shame in your tears. The only shame is that you were unable to shed them until now."

"So what if I refuse to help?" Mitch said, forcing himself to cool down. These people were not his friends, even if they'd saved him. He needed to remember that. He crumpled up the toilet paper and threw it away. "What then? You kill me?"

"I hope that is not your answer," said Lee. "You would condemn our nation to everlasting division. And Mitch," he threw in, "I think you should consider what we went through to get you here. As you might guess, it was not easy. And it was *not* cheap. I think the fact that we saved you from an American prison should be worth something! After all, you were innocent."

"I didn't ask you to do it."

"Would you like to go back?"

Mitch crossed his arms and looked up at Lee. "So what are you telling me will happen if I refuse?"

"You won't," Lee stated. "Just give us the chance to make our case to you in full before you decide. After that, if you say no, we will set you on the border of the country of your choice."

"With no passport and no money?"

"You would not be in prison. You would be free to chart your own course."

"Why do you need me? You already have nuclear weapons."

"And how would you know that?" asked Lee.

"Your country tested one a few years ago."

"Did we?

"It registered on seismometers all over the world."

"Hmm." Lee was suddenly evasive. "Perhaps the test showed the West what we wanted the West to see."

"You don't have nuclear weapons?"

Lee smiled. "I didn't say that."

"So that cooling tower in Yongbyon?"

"A cooling tower is not a nuclear weapon, Mitch."

North Korea, Mitch knew, had claimed to halt their program a number of times. And amazingly, each time, the U.S. had taken them at face value, and had even started building them two light water reactors at Kumho'ri. The images on Google Earth showed that the project wasn't completely dead even after they had claimed to have weapons, then promised to halt their program again. It was exactly as Mitch and many others had suspected. The North had no intention of giving up their nuclear weapons program, ever. And frankly, why should they?

"Okay then, let me ask you this. Why do you want them?"

"Want what?"

"Nuclear weapons. To attack the United States?"

Lee laughed. "Of course not! That would be folly! We would be utterly destroyed. Your country has submarines, aircraft, ICBMs. Thousands of warheads. Thermonuclear weapons that we could never hope to match! And you can shoot missiles down."

"Sort of," Mitch said and frowned. He looked back up. "So why do you want them?"

Lee thought for a moment. "Have you ever been stung by a wasp, Mitch? A large one?"

"Yeah."

"Did it kill you?"

"I'm here aren't I?"

"But you avoid wasps? With this threat, the U.S. will not dare to attack us ever again."

"*Attack you?*" blurted Mitch. "The U.S. doesn't want to attack you!"

Lee frowned and shook his head sadly. "Perhaps if Mexico harbored thirty-five thousand Chinese troops, hundreds of tanks, thousands of artillery pieces, nuclear weapons, and airbases within twenty miles of the U.S. border you might feel differently."

Mitch tried to counter. "You have a point, but those troops are purely defensive. The United States has never had any design on attacking North Korea. I mean, why would we want to?"

"Come to my country, see what we are up against. You will see the *offensive* forces aligned against us from the United States and her puppet governments in the Republic of Korea, and the Empire of Japan. It has always been so in Korea. Peaceful Korea, land of morning calm, lying between ambitious neighbors. We have been invaded and raped by foreign powers hundreds of times throughout history. Why should we feel that anything has changed when your nation stages war games on our very borders?"

"Those war games," said Mitch matter-of-factly, "are to prepare for the invasion of the South by the North. It happened once and it could happen again."

Lee gave an exasperated sigh. "Choson is a peaceful country, Mitch. We have *never* attacked anyone. It was the South, armed and trained by the United States that attacked us. Secondly –

Mitch's jaw dropped. "You've got to be kidding me!? It was the North that attacked the South!"

Lee just looked at him. "Mitch, I live there. My grandfather died in the war. Are you familiar with the *Team Spirit* military exercises held jointly each year between your country and our oppressed brothers in the South?"

"We never attacked you guys. You attacked the South!"

"In direct violation of the 1953 armistice, which spells out exactly how many foreign troops can be quartered on each side of the DMZ, the U.S. deploys over one hundred thousand additional combat troops in simulated assaults and amphibious landings on Korean beaches. They march inland, toward the DMZ, supported by American combat aircraft and warships. They dig-in only four kilometers from my country." He held up four fingers on his hand. "Four kilometers, Mitch! That's less than two and-a-half miles. Every time this happens, we wonder if you will stop at the DMZ or if this is the year we are again plunged into war."

"Oh come on, Lee. Your people don't really believe that the U.S. is going to attack. It is the avowed policy of the United States never to be the aggressor nation."

"Mitch, how can you say that?" Lee erupted. "Look around the world. How many times has the United States attacked first?"

"We've never attacked first."

Lee guffawed. "Your army is occupying Afghanistan even as we speak! They just left Iraq."

"We were attacked. What were we supposed to do?"

"You weren't attacked by Iraq or Afghanistan, though I understand why your nation invaded there. The Taliban was out of control. But your country had no business in Iraq. You found no WMDs there. No nuclear program. No chemical weapons. No link with al Qaeda."

"Saddam moved the weapons to Syria."

"You can't move a containment vessel, Mitch."

"Well it's a war on terror," Mitch reminded him with a shrug, suddenly feeling very uncomfortable. "And Iraq was the front line."

"It is the front line because you invaded. Just as in Vietnam and Korea. And Panama, Grenada, Cuba, Libya, Somalia, Sudan, Bosnia. In the last hundred years, the only time the United States has been directly attacked, other than nine-eleven, was by the Japanese in World War II. And at the time, Hawaii was not even a state!"

"Well, everything you mentioned was in response to direct threats to our –"

"Threats! See. Even you admit it! *Threats.* Threats to American interests. Yet *we* are threatened every single day in ways you cannot imagine!"

Mitch tried to think of something to say but his mind was an empty cavern. This was supposed to be a simple argument. He felt like he was on trial again, helpless, and like then, everything he thought he knew was wrong. "It's different," he finally blurted.

"*No different!* Your nation brought the world to the brink of nuclear war in 1962 because the Soviet Union placed a dozen nuclear missiles in Cuba, ninety miles from the United States. Your nation has stored hundreds of nuclear weapons in South Korea for half a century, two miles from my country. Apparently the United States can go anywhere in the world and attack whoever it wants for any reason while tiny Choson is just supposed to accept nuclear bombs, aircraft, and troops only miles from our border!"

Mitch plopped into his chair confused and frustrated. How he had learned to hate the government while awaiting trial, confined to his house with an electronic ankle bracelet to track his location. Unable even to visit his beloved Beth's grave. Unable to mourn her death. And then convicted and cast into jail to await sentencing. Every semblance of truth stripped away. Caged like an animal. Why he was defending them now he didn't know, perhaps it was just habit. But there was one thing that he did know, and he let Lee know it. "A lot of what you say about America, and about how I feel about her is true. But I can see what you're doing. I know what you're trying to do to me. You're trying to brainwash me."

"Brainwash?" Lee erupted. "The *truth* is brainwashing?"

Mitch's gaze roamed the steel bulkheads of the cabin, lingering on the silver light streaming through the porthole. Helplessness overwhelmed him like quicksand. God. Country. Loyalty. Honor. Even history. Were they all lies? "Maybe I've been brainwashed all along," he finally said slowly. "Maybe we all are."

5

"Mitch!" came an urgent whisper. "Dr. Weatherby! Wake up!" Someone shook him gently.

"Lee?" he said, fighting off sleep. "What's –"

"It's okay, but you need to get up. We are leaving the ship."

"Tonight?" Mitch answered, still groggy.

"Yes, tonight! Get dressed!"

Topside, there was no moon and it was utterly black. The ship rocked gently, silent but for the slosh of wave against hull. There was a tangy, wholesome sea smell. Mitch shivered in the cool air as his mind shed the remnants of sleep. And as he stood facing the unknown, he asked himself the question that had plagued him since his abduction – since his rescue. Would he help them? Every time he said, 'no,' rage welled up inside him so that he threatened to drown in it. But every time he said, 'yes,' he was wracked with guilt. He simply couldn't get past the Axis of Evil. Helping them went against everything he knew, whether it came from his family, the news, or the constant security briefs at Los Alamos. And despite the fact that America had turned out to be a lie and his faith had turned out to be useless, he couldn't shake the feeling that, if he helped them, he'd burn in the lowest pit of Hell for all eternity.

The faint beating of helicopter blades and the cool sea air pulled him out of the spiraling angst. Regardless of what he decided, he'd be on a helicopter in just a few seconds. The alternative was to throw himself into the sea. The sound grew slowly louder until, the deck of the ship lit up like an airstrip. And it wasn't empty. No less than a dozen men in red-tinted goggles sprang into action.

As soon as the ship's lights blinked on, the lights of the helicopter came on, too. It came in slow and touched down on the deck between the two cranes. Mitch and Lee raced across the deck and, with his heart in his throat, Mitch climbed into the waiting aircraft. As soon as they were strapped in, the helo rose into the air and, when it was clear of the cranes, the ship disappeared back into darkness. He'd been on board for two weeks to the day and once again, was being whisked away toward the unknown with nothing but the clothes on his back.

As they flew, Mitch stared down at the complete darkness below. The only feature he'd seen since taking off was a faint line of surf as they crossed from sea to land. Since then, nothing but a black pit beneath the beating rotors. It reminded him of a photograph that had been circulating for years on the internet. A nighttime picture of eastern Asia taken from space with brilliantly lit South Korea at the bottom, well lit China above and to the left, glowing Japan to the right, and a black hole where North Korea was. There were no lights below them, not even a campfire.

His eyes kept searching until they grew heavy. The change in the sound of the engine roused him sometime later and he looked out the window to see the outline of a wide, mountain-rimmed valley coming up to greet him out of the early morning dawn. Filling its floor was a dreary, gray city of squat, lifeless buildings. A moment later, the helo touched down and he was greeted by the smell of raw sewage, fish oil, and aviation fuel.

Two gaunt, machine gun-toting soldiers saluted Lee and shouted some words in Korean. Mitch and Lee followed them across the tarmac to a jeep-like vehicle with an open cab. Lee and one soldier sat up front. Mitch sat in the back where the other soldier trained an assault rifle at his chest and stared with blank eyes.

The engine sputtered to life with a strong, stale, fuel-oil smell and the truck rattled off the tarmac into darkness spouting smoke. They drove past guard towers, barracks, and lines of military vehicles, but it was a blur to Mitch. They stopped at a strip of small bungalows, barely discernible in the darkness. Lee and the humorless soldiers led Mitch inside, where he collapsed onto a bed with stiff, prickly sheets.

*

Mitch wondered why Beth was on the bus with him. He liked that she was there, sitting across from him smiling, but there was something not right about it. She shouldn't be here. He had the same feeling about himself. This wasn't right at all. He tried to stand and found that he was chained in place with handcuffs. A rush of panic shot through him and he looked back at Beth to find she was smiling at him. Her lips moved and he knew she was saying, "I love you," but no sound came out.

He pulled at his chains and glanced out the window. They were driving through a desert that seemed impossibly bright. He glanced around the bus and saw people he didn't know with dark faces and fierce eyes, and up front, above the driver, were two pictures but he couldn't tell who was in them.

Then, it was night and he knew it had been a long time. They were in darkness and in the sky were huge, fuzzy stars shining like headlights, but illuminating nothing. Except he could still see Beth. Her face was beautiful but pale as moonlight and her lips were red like blood. Dead eyes stared out at him and he suddenly knew why she shouldn't be on the bus with him. A nauseas feeling spread through his gut but his arms had suddenly become very heavy. He pulled at the chains but they weren't the little silver chains of before, but huge steel links, like a ship's anchor chain. Around him were clustered other dead people, dead but still alive, like zombies. He looked down at himself to see that he was dead, too. His hands were decaying and dirty brown bone glared through gaps in his skin like torn cloth. Mitch knew it should hurt but he felt nothing, still struggling with the confusion with why he was here and wondering if his hands would heal. But before he could finish the thought, everyone was screaming. He heard gunfire and explosions and flame and the screams rose in intensity. Beth, in the seat across from him was screaming through her bloody mouth at him to get off the bus, to get away, and all the strange people he didn't know added their cries to the mounting discord. But he couldn't move. He was bound in place by chains with links as large as car tires. The red flames drew closer and when they touched him, Mitch awoke.

Sweat soaked his skin and had wicked into the sheets of the same bed into which he'd collapsed the night before. His heart was racing, but over it, he could still hear the shouting from his dream. He shook his head, only to realize that he was fully awake and the sound was a voice coming over a loudspeaker somewhere outside, a breathless announcer who never seemed to stop. He couldn't understand a word, but knew exactly what the frantic woman was saying: it was a call to arms. Then the music started. John Phillips Sousa on steroids. He lay in bed reliving the dream over and over, if only to see Beth's face, alive and in motion.

After a full hour of the music, there was a knock at the door. He pulled himself from bed, and stumbled through the dim, sparsely furnished apartment until he was standing at the door wondering how the universe had conspired to land him here, in the middle of the Evil Empire. They would ask him today. Ask him to help them build a nuclear weapon. What would he say? Was he ready to die? Ready to join Beth? Part of him yearned for the peace of death. Yearned to stand before God and demand to know what was going on. But was he ready to do that for the lie of a nation that had killed his wife and set off the chain of events that had landed him here, staring at the door. His fate lay beyond. He had to open it.

It was Lee, of course, with a frugal breakfast of gooey rice, wilted kimchi, and some sort of dried flesh. Afterwards, Lee and two soldiers drove him to a drab, concrete structure identical to everything else on the base. On the outside wall, above the doors, towered a ten-foot high portrait of Kim Il-sung. When Mitch and Lee walked in to the lobby without their weapon-toting escorts, two female soldiers in high-collared, green tunics jumped to their feet and issued a steady stream of Korean. Obviously, they demanded papers because Lee produced a stack of documents. Some of them bore Mitch's picture and it made him feel very uncomfortable. How long had they been watching him in America?

Mitch cast about nervously. The wall bore portraits of the Great Leaders exactly like the ones on the wall of his cabin on the ship. Around the room hung more pictures of Kim senior and son.

The TV, festooned with archaic rabbit-ear antennas, played grainy parade footage complete with patriotic march music and stills of Kim Il-sung. Magazines with glossy pictures of Kim Il-sung, as if he were still alive, lay neatly arranged on the table. He glanced over to find the lady soldiers glaring at him. Surreal didn't fit. There was no word that he knew of to describe the fact that he was standing here, processing through security at a secret North Korean nuclear facility. Even more astonishing was that part of him didn't even care. A part that he'd felt atrophying while he'd rotted in jail in Santa Fe. The same part that had finally burned up on the ship coming over here, leaving but a puddle of bitter, black, ooze. All that he'd believed in was now concentrated in that putrid slime. Beth had told him to run. But he was trapped as securely as he'd been in the dream.

"First, we go to meet Pak Yong-nam," Lee finally said, stepping away from the counter and jolting Mitch from his daze. He handed a badge to Mitch who woodenly pinned it on and followed Lee into a long corridor lined with Kim Il-sung in paint, photograph, and sculpture. Mitch stopped.

"What is it, Mitch?" asked Lee.

"Is this all Kim Il-sung?"

"His life and exploits took many forms," Lee said proudly. "Wise philosopher," he pointed to a photograph of Kim in a Mao suit. "Brilliant, iron-willed commander." Next to a picture of him in fatigues. "Victorious general. Elder statesman. Teenage partisan. He was the greatest man of all time. You and I are privileged to have shared the world with him." He stared with adoring eyes at a granite sculpture. But all Mitch could think of was a trip to Europe he and Beth had shared years ago. They'd gone to the Vatican and he'd seen a hall like this except the icons were of Jesus. Kim Il-sung, the Jesus of North Korea. He couldn't make it fit.

"Dr. Weatherby," said a thick-bodied man, as he rose from his desk chair. Behind him, on the wall of his office hung the familiar Great Leader portraits. Apparently every room in the country had them! The man's accent was strong but he was easily understandable. "Pak Yong-nam, Minister of Atomic Energy

Industry." He had fat lips and eyelids, was short in stature with broad, powerful shoulders and no neck. He was clad in a charcoal gray Mao-suit with a tiny Kim Il-sung pin over his left breast, just like Lee's. Mitch bowed to him as Lee had instructed and Pak motioned to the chairs. "Sit down. Would you care for something to drink? I believe Americans drink coffee, don't they?"

Mitch settled uncomfortably into a plain, metal-framed chair, scarcely believing where he was, and plagued by remnants of the dream that refused to leave him. "I'll have a cup, thanks."

Pak said something into his seventies-style intercom and a few moments later his secretary, a beautiful Korean woman dressed western fashion, appeared with several steaming cups on a tray.

"Thank you." He took a sip. It tasted like brewed sawdust.

"So," boomed Pak, lighting a cigarette. "Tell me about your journey." Lee pulled out a cigarette and lit up, too. "I imagine you were surprised when the shooting began."

A shadow passed across Mitch's face as the smoke tickled his nose. It wasn't a pleasant memory. And though this Pak seemed cordial, a cold shiver passed through Mitch as he instinctively knew that before him was a man who could smile and torture at the same time. Like the judge who had sentenced him. "I can't really say that I enjoyed it, but I didn't want to go to prison."

"Certainly not, since you were innocent. And now you are here."

Mitch shifted uncomfortably in his seat. "And now I'm here."

"Major Lee tells me that the passage was pleasant."

Major? Mitch nodded. "Yes, sir." He took another sip of his coffee, just to be polite.

"You have questions," said Pak. "Good. That is why you are here today. To get answers. Do you have any questions you'd like to ask us?"

Mitch looked into Pak's eyes. "Only one."

"And what is that?"

"What happens if I refuse?"

Pak didn't even blink. "Yes. Major Lee has told me of this. Like him, I would be concerned if this was easy for you. Dr. Weatherby, Juche seeks not to compel, but to inspire. So, my answer would be, don't decide until you have seen what we have to show you." He glanced down at his watch. "It is time."

Moments later, Mitch was seated in a smoke-filled, poorly lit conference room somewhere in the heart of North Korea with a dozen people staring across the oblong table at him. This was worse than standing before the Honorable Nelson Park having his sentence read. At least then, he'd known the rules and his role, even if none of it made any sense.

Mitch was seated at Pak Yong-nam's right hand, which he didn't know how to interpret either. Was he really Pak's right hand man? Were they just being polite? Did sitting at someone's right hand even mean anything in North Korea? Across from him sat a kindly looking old man with wispy white hair and beard and fragile round glasses. He looked like Confucius himself and Mitch might have thought him wise but for the Kim Il-sung pin on his tunic. In addition to several other Koreans, or Asians, was a European, and another man who looked like Saddam Hussein in his prime. The entire back wall of the room was a large map of Korea, sans DMZ. If the size of the star was any indication, P'yongyang was the capitol of the unified peninsula. Portraits of the Great Leaders, hung above the map, presided over the room.

"We are all here," Pak began. "Our new friend does not speak Korean or Russian. So, until he and Dr. Tarasenko learn Korean, we will use English."

"When in Rome," said the European-looking man, "do as the Romans. Unless of course, you are entertaining Visigoths." He had a Russian accent.

Pak looked at the man and nodded. "Thank you, Comrade Tarasenko." He addressed the group. "As you all know, since our Chief Scientist, Rhee Sun-yi, died a year ago, our progress on Project Silla has been delayed. We have made advancements in some areas, but in the all-important design and testing, were are stalled.

"After the accident," he continued in his heavy accent, "by direct order of the Dear Leader, Comrade Marshal Kim Jong-il, I directed Colonel PhoungPhoung and Professor Yang to identify a candidate for his replacement. Someone with skill and experience in nuclear warhead design. A person who could begin where Doctor Rhee left off. " He turned to Mitch who felt his face go hot. "He has arrived."

Mitch saw the surprise in their expressions and realized that nobody knew who he was or why he was here. Only a hateful looking army guy and the gray headed old man didn't seem shocked. And the European. He had a head of wild brown hair shot with gray and his eyes sparkled behind thick lenses. Mitch liked him instantly – maybe just because he wasn't Korean.

"Allow me to introduce," Pak said with relish, "Doctor Mitch Weatherby. From the United States."

Expressions changed again, this time to terror. Especially the only woman in the room. At the mention of the United States, her look went, from what appeared to be the ubiquitous North Korean scowl, to outright revulsion.

"For over ten years," Pak went on, not acknowledging the hostility in the room, "Dr. Weatherby worked at the Los Alamos National Laboratory, designing and testing nuclear weapons for the imperialist aggressor. He has a Ph.D. in neutron physics from the University of New Mexico. And he has now, along with Dr. Tarasenko and Dr. Jabril, offered his services to the land of the Juche Idea."

Mitch looked up in surprise, but Pak simply blew out a thin stream of bluish smoke. "Dr. Weatherby, let me introduce those assembled here this morning. Major Lee you know already."

"Of course," Mitch acknowledged, trying to steady his voice, reliving his nightmare as if it were happening now. Beth was right; he should run, but how? *What was he doing here!?*

"Seated across from you is Professor Yang Song-jin, former head of the Yongbyon College of Physics and head of our Theoretical Division at Sagi-dong. He is chief scientist of Silla -14." The professor bent forward so that his thin, gray beard touched the table. Mitch had an instinctive liking for the old man. Something in his eyes. Sharp but kind. It quelled the mounting panic, at least for the moment. "At his side is Maxim Tarasenko." The European man nodded. "And Chun Hyon-hui. Both from Sagi-dong."

"Pleased to meet you," announced Maxim. But the woman grew only more fierce. She stared at Mitch with cold, hard eyes and he gasped. Jade-green. He'd never seen an Asian with green eyes before. They were beautiful, even as they tried to kill him with a glare.

Mitch's heart started to pound and the edges of his vision began to turn gray, as Pak went on to introduce a half-dozen others but their names all sounded the same. He'd never fainted in his life but knew that's what was coming. With great effort he breathed deeply and began to master the pounding in his chest.

"At the far end of the table," Pak went on, "is Colonel Phoung Jin of the Korean People's Army, chief of security at Sagi-dong."

"And this," Pak finally said, "is Khadir Jabril, fissionable materials and separation." Saddam Hussein's look-a-like nodded with a look of contempt that was second only to Hyon-hui's.

Mitch looked dizzily at the dark heads around the room. His vision threatened to tunnel but he pushed it away, at the same time hoping he'd have a heart attack and die, right then and there, solving all his problems at once. Here he was at a high level meeting with North Korea's most brilliant engineers and scientists. The enemy. The heart of the Axis of Evil. This was Hell. He was dead and God had sent him to Hell. What had he done to deserve Hell? He felt a rising panic and an intense urge to crawl under the table, or scream, or maybe just start drooling so they would think him nuts and take him out and shoot him. But he did none of these things.

"By order of the Dear Leader, Comrade Marshal Kim Jong-il," Pak went on, "Comrade, Doctor Weatherby will be assuming the role as chief scientist of Silla-14."

Hyon-hui leapt to her feet and unleashed a torrent of Korean that needed no translation. Mitch recoiled in shock. Pak snapped at her and Hyon-hui's words ceased abruptly but not willingly. Torment coursed through her as if facing two irreconcilable imperatives. Pak stuck his chest out and stared at her until she sat and dropped her own eyes to the table.

"Now, Comrade Weatherby," Pak continued, cutting his eyes at Hyon-hui, "Comrade Professor Yang will provide us with a summary of our work at Silla-14"

The Professor looked calmly across the table at Mitch. "Good to have you with us, Comrade Weatherby."

Each time, that word, *comrade*, was like a blade to everything he believed, and Mitch wondered if the old man could tell he was about to lose it. God, he was an American! He couldn't be here – helping these madmen! He'd taken oaths to safeguard nuclear information. And these were the worst of the worst. At least, that's what they'd told him. How he wanted to be back at Los Alamos with Beth at his side. His life was not supposed to have turned out like this. He had planned it out so carefully. If he helped them, somehow he was sure he'd be condemned for all eternity. 'Condemned,' he heard a voice in the back of his mind say, 'by a God that didn't exist…'

Professor Yang went on, oblivious to Mitch's inner tumult. "As you already know we have been conducting research into building a nuclear device for several years now. As you in the West guessed, this technology is based on the fissile isotope, plutonium-239. For a long time, this work was confined primarily to Yongbyon. We have … "

Yongbyon! Mitch thought furiously, looking for some piece of ground to stand on. Something solid. Something that made sense. Anything. He had to get under control, if only to escape later. The professor guy had said Yongbyon. It was where the North did their nuclear research. Mitch had seen pictures of the place at Los Alamos. Had, along with others, analyzed them for the International Atomic Energy Agency, trying to figure out what the North was up to. Is that where they were? Yongbyon? But the last time he'd asked a question he'd gotten beaten senseless. But he had do know. "E – excuse me," Mitch blurted, and flinched, but everyone just stared at him.

The professor stopped. "Yes, Dr. Weatherby?"

"Where are we? I, uh, just assumed I was in Yongbyon but you just –"

"Ah!" Professor Yang smiled. "A good guess, but no." He shuffled over to the map and lifted his arm to a black dot not far from the Chinese border. "We are here in Kanggae." Next, he pointed out the capitol P'yongyang far to the south, the nuclear site of Yongbyon just north of P'yongyang, and the DMZ. "We have not used the reactors at Yongbyon since eighty-seven."

"Yongbyon's been closed since nineteen eighty-seven?" Mitch exclaimed, forgetting himself. "There's no way!"

Everyone laughed and Professor Yang said, "No, no, no. Juche 87."

"Juche 87?"

"The era of Juche begins on the Great Leader's birth," Pak explained. "April fifteenth, 1912. So it has been shut down since nineteen ninety-nine, when our former chief designer, Rhee Sun-yi, recommended we break up the concentration at Yongbyon and move the separate efforts around the country for security. Unfortunately, he was killed in an accident last year."

"So that cooling tower you blew up in Yongbyon? It was…" Mitch's voice trailed off as he realized just how misinformed the West was about the North's nuclear program. The committees at Los Alamos that studied North Korean nuclear assets had missed all of this.

"Unused," Pak said, with a satisfied grin. "Across Choson are seventeen Atomic Energy Research Institute locations, each working on a separate part of Project Silla."

Something inside Mitch clicked. He'd asked a question and received what appeared to be an honest answer. That hadn't happened… since the night Beth died. Over a year. No one would answer any of his questions. They'd treated him like… an animal. Yet here, at one end of the Axis of Evil, they were treating him as an equal. His eyes scanned the assembled scientists as Professor Yang pointed locations out on the map. Only the woman and the Iraqi seemed to harbor ill will toward him, at least openly. In America, on trial, he'd been the subject of widespread hatred and protests.

He found himself spellbound by the white headed-professor, marveling at how thoroughly everyone in the U.S. intelligence community had been duped by these people they considered 'idiotic fanatics.' He glanced around the room. At this gathering, only the strange woman fit that description. Indeed, nothing was left at Yongbyon! Radiological metallurgy was at P'yongsong. Radiochemistry at Nanam. Hydrodynamic test facilities at a different location in P'yongsong. Uranium mines in North Pyongyan Province. Gaseous diffusion at Pakchon. Plutonium production at Yujin-dong. Mitch almost wanted to laugh. At Los Alamos, they'd made fun of the North Koreans for being stupid. But they weren't stupid at all. They were smart and serious and clever. And they were treating him with more respect than his own countrymen had. Mitch felt his will begin to slip but he didn't fight it. What was the point?

"We call this, the Silla Project," Pak added proudly. "After the Silla kingdom that first united our peninsula over fifteen hundred years ago."

"The principal sites," Professor Yang went on, "are Silla-10, the breeder reactor and separation facility, Silla-17, the uranium processing and gaseous diffusion plant, and Silla-14, the warhead development effort at Sagi-dong." At the mention of the last city, Professor Yang's finger pointed to a spot, deep in the northern mountains, east of Kanggae.

Pak took over as Professor Yang hobbled back to his seat. "That is why I asked these other men to be here today. Hyon Chol-hae is chief engineer at Pakchon. Khadir Jabril is chief engineer of our breeder reactor and reprocessing plant. Professor Yang, Maxim Tarasenko, and Chun Hyon-hui are all leading scientists at Sagi-dong."

"And what's at Sagi-dong?" Mitch asked, thoroughly confused but at the same time, strangely mesmerized. "I'm sorry, but the names all sound so similar to me."

"Sagi-dong," the professor answered with a coy smile. "It's like Los Alamos in nineteen forty-two. Think of yourself as Oppenheimer."

Whether or not Yang had intended it, Mitch was stunned by the comparison. Oppenheimer was Los Alamos' greatest legend and a personal hero of Mitch's. What they were doing here was just like the Manhattan Project that he'd led over half a century ago. They'd even named it the same way – *The Silla Project*. And Oppenheimer, a great physicist and leader, had ultimately been destroyed by the same system that had crushed Mitch. Pilloried for daring to think that nuclear weapons might just be too terrible for man – any man – to possess, let alone make *more* powerful, he'd been unfairly stripped of his security clearance and set out to pasture. Just like Mitch.

It suddenly dawned on Mitch that the kinds of ideas that had condemned him – politics, history, religion, ethics, sociology, economics, law – were all, to borrow Kepler's phrase, *a cartful of dung.* Unprovable and meaningless. Abused and misused at the whims of the powerful. But physics was the same everywhere – whether at Los Alamos, or here in this room, or at the center of an exploding star. There was no difference in Korean physics, or American physics, or physics on planet Vulcan for that matter. The thought struck him as deeply profound and his mind clung to it like a shipwrecked sailor seizes a bit of flotsam.

"So why plutonium?" Mitch asked, as the long-dormant scientist in his brain suddenly reasserted with such force that it surprised Mitch, himself.

Everyone looked at him. "What?" Pak replied.

"Why are you basing your nuclear weapons on plutonium?"

Khadir Jabril snickered. Hyon-hui balked. Everyone glanced around confused.

"As I'm sure you know," the professor began hesitantly, "plutonium-239 has a much lower critical mass than does U-235. The minimum dimensions and weight of the bomb can be made smaller. While uranium-235 is an effective nuclear explosive, and in some ways more readily available than plutonium, we are still struggling with compressor seal and permeable barrier failures at the upper end of the cascade in the gaseous diffusion plant." He paused waiting for Mitch to jump in, then continued. "So we moved away from highly enriched uranium to plutonium-239. The breeder reactor is being designed to operate on uranium enriched to twenty-three percent, and the reprocessing facility is nearly complete."

A new voice entered – a deep voice with a heavy Persian accent that condescended to Mitch as if he were a first year grad-student. "Separating plutonium from the uranium source is a relatively simple, chemical reduction procedure, Mister Weatherby. It is complicated only by the presence of radioactivity. There is no technology to be invented in the design of the equipment, such as they are facing with the compressors and the barriers. Do you understand now or do I need to simplify it further?"

"There are other options," Mitch replied. He'd dealt with blow-hards like this before. Los Alamos was full of them.

"Options?" Pak asked. "Go on."

"I don't like plutonium," Mitch stated flatly, remembering it had been Beth's concern for the long term effects of the nuclear waste that first really opened his eyes to this fact. "Its nuclear properties are excellent. A six kilogram critical mass is hard to beat. With four pounds of Delta-phase you can get twenty kilotons. But it's dangerous and difficult to work with." He shot a look at Jabril. "Its chemistry and metallurgy are a nightmare. It has five separate crystalline phases at room temperature. The nuclear waste from processing is terrible and storing it safely is just about impossible. And this is a small country. The stuff is just plain bad and if you use it you'll be sorry. I can tell you, the United States," he glanced at Max, "and Russia, are paying the price now." Max nodded in agreement and Mitch paused, realizing he was actually talking to these people. But he couldn't stop himself. Nuclear physics was his passion and it had been ripped from him. Just like Beth. Just like his freedom. Perhaps he could guide these people, and not reveal anything classified. At the very least, keeping more plutonium from entering the world would be a way he could honor Beth's memory. Until he thought of some way to escape. Or something.

"Well then, do you have any suggestions for the enrichment facility?" asked Pak, sounding irritated by Mitch's attack on their entire industry.

"No, I'm afraid not. Gaseous diffusion isn't my specialty. And if I can help it, I don't go near a separation plant. Mister Jabril probably appreciates that." Mitch actually knew a great deal about gaseous diffusion. He smiled at himself inwardly. By giving them knowledge in one area they'd not questioned weakness in another. This might work.

But Hyon-hui, who had been growing more agitated, could no longer contain herself. "So why do you tell us this if you have no suggestions," she spat. "Perhaps Professor Yang has overestimated your worth to the Silla Project."

Mitch wondered if she was actually a scientist capable of independent thought, or just a commie stooge that spouted commie slogans when you pulled the string in her back. "There are other options, Miss Chun, besides uranium-235 and plutonium-239."

"Neptunium-237?" Maxim exclaimed. "The critical mass is over a hundred kilos."

"No. Not 237, though both our countries have detonated 237 devices. No. I'm talking about uranium-233."

"Two thirty-three?" Pak asked in a way that made it clear he'd never heard of it. "But I..."

Max glanced quizzically over his glasses. His tousled head of prematurely gray hair and thick lenses made him look a little comical.

Professor Yang nodded, staring intently at Mitch. "Yes, comrade minister. Another uranium isotope. It is bred from thorium the same way plutonium is bred from uranium."

"Why have I never heard of this?"

"Contamination," Jabril stated disdainfully. "After time, any device made from U-233 will be lethal from ten meters. We conducted tests with it and found it to be unsuitable. It is possible that Los Alamos did not get that far."

Mitch ignored him. "There is the 232 issue. But there are ways to deal with it."

"Tell me more," demanded Pak. "What is the two-thirty-two issue, professor?"

"Uranium-233," Professor Yang began, "is created when thorium-232 absorbs a neutron of moderate to high energy. Actually, it first becomes thorium-233 which has a half-life of –" He paused in thought.

"Twenty-two minute, beta decay," Mitch answered easily. Nothing secret here. They could find all this on the internet or in any basic radiochemistry text.

"Thank you, Doctor Weatherby. It decays to," he glanced at Mitch – obviously searching his memory, "palladium-233, I believe." Mitch nodded. "The 233 isotope of palladium has a half-life of 27 days."

"Correct," said Mitch, impressed. The old guy probably hadn't studied 233 in decades.

"Then decays via a beta emission to uranium-233 which, is quite fissionable by thermal neutrons. In fact, it has a very favorable neutron spectrum if I remember correctly, and the neutron number is higher than for uranium-235. Critical mass for a bare sphere is only about sixteen kilograms."

"You can get about twenty kilotons from six kilos with an efficient compression system," added Mitch, and cringed inwardly. That may have been classified. He'd have to be more careful.

"Why is this the first time I'm hearing about this?" Pak growled, seeming to grow larger and darker.

"Because it's not practical!" Jabril thundered and brought a fat fist onto the table with a thud. "In one year, a critical mass of U-233 will emit one hundred REM per hour at a distance of three meters. Technicians would die just being around it!"

"Perhaps Dr. Weatherby wishes to poison our people," said Hyon-hui bitterly. "That would be very much in character for an American. After using biological weapons in the Vict –"

"Not now comrade," Pak growled, and turned back to Yang. "I don't understand. Does the U-233 have a short half-life?"

"No," the professor went on. "Two-thirty-three has a half life the same order of magnitude as plutonium. Around sixteen thousand years. The problem is a side reaction in the breeding process. Around one percent of the thorium-neutron reactions will be of high enough energy to result in the formation of thorium-231. The thorium-231 has a separate decay chain ending with a decay from thallium-208, to lead-208. This decay emits a 2.6 MeV gamma ray. Quite lethal. The small percentage of U-232 in reactor bred U-233 slowly decays causing the level of thallium-208 to increase over time. The level of radioactivity emitted is unacceptable from safety considerations."

"Is there no way to get the uranium-232 out of the uranium-233?" Pak asked.

"Of course not," Jabril insisted. "You could build a separate gaseous diffusion plant but with the isotopes separated by only one AMU, it would have to be ten times the size of our current enrichment plant. We are wasting our time with this, minister!"

"There have been many advancements in the past few years," Mitch said.

"Such as?"

"At Los Alamos we conducted studies using lasers for isotope separation."

"AVLIS," Professor Yang commented. "Atomic Vapor Laser Isotope Separation; I have heard of it."

"As have I," Jabril added, expressing intense fatigue with the whole subject.

"That was just experimental, wasn't it?" asked the Professor.

"No," Mitch replied. "It worked so well we designed a prototype plant using a tunable, organic dye laser to selectively ionize isotopes which could then be electrostatically culled from the metallic vapor. It's in the public domain. Just Google it."

"On an industrial scale?" the Persian asked in disbelief. "You lie! That is impossible."

"We were about to begin construction on a manufacturing plant when Congress pulled the funding." Mitch remembered it as the time *everything* went to pot and he and his colleagues were downgraded from weapons designers to programmers. Not long after he'd joined as a new Ph.D. The golden age of Los Alamos was already a memory and Mitch had failed to achieve the one real goal – or obsession – he'd had in life: a nuclear test.

"How long will this take?" asked Pak. The look in his eyes betrayed a keen interest.

"That depends. How far along is the breeder? How far along is the separation facility? Do we have a ready supply of thorium and a means to refine it?"

"The chemistry of thorium is similar to that of any of the lanthanide series," said Professor Yang. "The reprocessing facility should not need any major changes and the process should, in fact, be simplified. The breeder will only require redesigned fuel rods. And thorium is readily available from our own monazite sand deposits along the Yellow Sea. In fact, the Soviets mined it there in the 1960s for this very reason."

"And your payoff will be…" Mitch nodding, knowingly. "Great," he added, realizing they probably didn't follow that cultural idiom, but hoping that somewhere Beth was nodding her approval. "Without all that plutonium chemistry and metallurgy to deal with, it'll be like going from analog to digital. And a bare, spherical critical mass is only sixteen kilograms. A well-designed core is only about eight. Smaller than my fist." He held it up, pretty sure that those numbers were not classified.

Pak broke into a smile. "Yes. Yes. A new approach is exactly what this project needs." He glowered at Khadir Jabril. "Clearly, our plutonium effort is stalled. Comrade Weatherby, you will return to Sagi-dong with Professor Yang. In one week's time, I want a full report on what will be necessary to switch to this uranium-233. Until then, all other work is to be frozen."

6

Mitch was dressed and ready when Lee arrived after the ritual music ended. After yesterday's meeting, Mitch's felt better, if better was the right word. The enemy wasn't what he thought, and part of him wondered, were they still the enemy? He felt like a character in a movie who'd showed up to fight the bad guys only to realize the good guys were actually the bad guys and he'd been one of them. And there was clearly nothing for him in America. There, he had been disgraced and humiliated. Everything had been taken from him. But as strange as it sounded, there might be something for him here. He had no intention of breaking the oath he'd taken by revealing anything *else* that was classified. But he was fairly certain that he wouldn't have to. Maybe only telling them public domain information would be enough? Besides, Lee had been absolutely right. The idea of North Korea attacking America with a nuke was pretty ridiculous, and they sure weren't going to use it on their own soil – and they obviously considered South Korea their own soil.

Major Lee took him to the cafeteria where they found the rest of their party just sitting down. "Good morning, Mitch," the Russian said, when Mitch arrived with a tray carrying rice and... something else. It might have been animal, vegetable, or mineral. All Mitch could tell was it was brown and fibrous.

"Maxim, right?" said Mitch.

"Max, okay?"

For some reason the Russian made him smile and he liked that. He turned to the woman who had been in yesterday's meeting, noticing that in a different setting she might have been pretty – if it hadn't been for the hard glare marring her face. "Good morning Miss –"

"Chun," she barked, destroying any hint of beauty.

Mitch bowed awkwardly. "Professor Yang."

"Sit down, Doctor Weatherby," the professor invited kindly. "Do not let Miss Chun frighten you." He glared at her in a fatherly sort of way, and she responded by dropping her eyes, but her demeanor made clear the invitation was not hers. "She forgets that political ideology should never supersede good manners." At these words, Hyon-hui's green eyes shot up at the old man, and for a split-second, Mitch thought they held fear. But it didn't last. She grunted and swirled her food with her chopsticks.

Mitch shrugged. "They've forgotten that in America, too."

When they'd finished their breakfast, Pak, the neckless man who'd run yesterday's meeting, and Colonel Phoung escorted them to an enormous Mercedes Unimog fitted with a passenger module. Mitch eyed the oversized 4x4.

"You are surprised to see such a vehicle here?" said Pak.

"Didn't really expect a Mercedes in North Korea. Figured Russian, or Chinese."

"American will not trade with us, so assumes the whole world will not trade with us. We have diplomatic relations with every civilized nation on earth. I have a Mercedes, too, you know?"

"Really," Mitch said coolly, not sure what else to say.

"Yes," Pak went on proudly. "CLK 430 convertible. A gift from the Dear Leader, Comrade Generalissimo Kim Jong-il. It is red."

"Nice car, comrade," replied Mitch.

"Did *you* have a Mercedes in America?"

Mitch shook his head. "Nope." Pak grinned and started to say something but Mitch kept talking. "Just a Ford and an ol' Toyota. My wife's BMW." He winked at Max. "A Cadillac. A Corvette. A boat. Couple of motorcycles. Personal watercr –"

"Enough!" barked Pak. "We go!"

The Unimog had two rows of large utilitarian benches facing each other, where Mitch was seated directly across from Chun Hyon-hui. He did his best to look out the window but each time he turned back, his eyes naturally fell on her, often to be met with a spite-filled narrowing of her almond-shaped green eyes. She looked to be around thirty and was wearing a white shirt and a dark-blue, knee-length skirt that did little for her figure. The heavy shoes she wore did even less. But he found her strangely compelling. Maybe it was her unusual eyes. Or her legs. Nice legs. Maybe the best he'd ever seen. No doubt from all the walking. And starving.

They left Kanggae's industrial valley and almost immediately entered a wild land of rushing streams and mists that clung to heavily forested hills. Tiny villages clustered at the feet of mountains that sprung steeply out of the ground to climb to dizzying heights. A greasy layer of smoke spread just above the rooftops of the villages. They met no cars, but passed an occasional ox cart – something Mitch had never imagined still existed. And the road deteriorated, making the need for the Unimog apparent. If not for the colorful propaganda billboards in each village, they could have been bronze age settlements.

At a muddy crossroad, soldiers checked their identification, then they continued their journey, deeper into the folded countryside, where the fields were untended patches of thick, brown clay and the hills were covered with dense forest. Mitch made out a few pitiful peasants, digging in the bare fields with their hands or sticks. Some walked along the edges of the forest collecting branches. Every now and then, a peasant with a large sack on his back could be seen trudging across a field trailed by children collecting acorns. Each mile seemed to slide farther into the past, and before long all signs of modern civilization disappeared. Yet, they were stopped time and again to have their papers examined at checkpoints in the middle of nowhere.

"Why don't they use tractors?" Mitch asked, staring out across a particularly large, field dotted with tiny peasants.

"We do not need tractors," replied Lee. "The peasants love the land. They are part of it. Bound to it with the love of a thousand generations of Koreans. And they will fight for it."

"It is the Juche way," said Pak. From his reading on the ship, Mitch knew there wouldn't be any further answer. He tried something else, just to break the silence.

"What do those little pins mean?" He pointed at the one on Hyon-hui's shirt. It was round, about the size of a nickel, yellow with a red rim, and had a tiny picture of Kim Il-sung. "Everyone's wearing one. Except Max. Hyon-hui's is yellow with a red band." He glanced around. "Everyone else's is just red." Hyon-hui stabbed him with her eyes but her cheeks flushed and she quickly lowered her head as if he'd pointed out a pimple on her unblemished face.

"They denote political status," said Lee. "Red is a member of the Korean Workers' Party. Yellow is a non-member. The red band denotes a probationary member." Hyon-hui shifted on the bench.

"So, you have to wear that?" Mitch asked.

"Why would anyone not want to?" spat Hyon-hui with a vicious tone. "It is an honor."

Mitch abandoned his attempt to talk, and they rattled along for hours until reaching a worn-out village straddling the road. At the edge of town, Mitch saw a billboard that showed a single hand with an outstretched index finger superimposed on a map of the Korean Peninsula. Lee told him the Hangul writing said, "Korea Is One!" Soldiers armed with Kalashnikov rifles and wearing heavy fur hats checked their papers before letting them pass. From there, they turned south and began slowly winding their way up the side of a broad, tall mountain to their destination: Sagi-dong.

Much like Los Alamos in the United States, and Arzamas 16 in Russia, Professor Yang told him the Sagi-dong area had been selected for its remoteness. The site itself was an abandoned coal mine below Wagal Peak which the 3rd Engineers Bureau had spent several years hollowing out for use as a lab.

"The perfection of it," Professor Yang continued, "is that the south side of Wagal Peak is still a functioning coal mine. We can bring in heavy machinery and supplies from the south side, and transport them via tunnel to the north side. But more important, we did not have to improve the road." As if to make his point, the Unimog jolted to the side as it navigated a deep rut. "It is bright, new roads that always bring the satellites."

"As you know," Pak jumped in, "evidence of construction, even if only a child in a sandbox, brings spy satellites and we are accused of an arms race."

Mitch said nothing. He'd seen such photography when consulting for the International Atomic Energy Agency. And Pak was right. So much as a spoonful of turned earth attracted the CIA. But he was fairly certain that this place hadn't been on their list.

The road climbed for a few miles, leveled off, and the truck ground to a halt at yet another checkpoint. Mitch twisted around in his seat to look out the window at a cluster of drab, concrete buildings through the trees ahead. They looked as though all color had drained from the world and it was left only in shades of gray and brown.

"Sagi-dong?" he asked.

"Yonjom-dong," corrected Pak.

The village was little more than a mud street lined with simple concrete-block structures. One of the buildings was larger than the others and on its façade hung a large portrait of Kim Il-sung. Before it stood a tall flagpole with the DPRK colors flapping in the breeze against a clear blue sky. Surrounding the building was a high chain link fence with barbed wire looped over the top. "What's this place?" asked Mitch, but everyone looked straight ahead, as if they could not see the building at all.

As they left Yonjom-dong, the valley walls leapt up on either side of the road and a rushing mountain stream tumbled down amidst trees that grew thickly along its bank. Where the walls came together in a narrow crack in which the stream and the road competed for space, stood a four-foot, finger of stone; a *changsung* with a grotesque face and weathered Chinese characters that had served as a marker to this hidden valley for a thousand years.

"Shangri-La," Mitch whispered as they passed through.

"Where?" Hyon-hui demanded to know.

"Shangri-La," Mitch said, more loudly. She shook her head. "You know, from *Lost Horizon*." Everyone looked at him blankly. "James Milton?" Mitch added but they remained clueless. "It's uh, not important." He wondered what else they'd not heard of.

Silver light poured from beyond the gap, and they emerged into a wide valley. Mitch peered through the dirt-streaked window to barbed wire and guard towers that protected only more colorless concrete buildings and a dismal street that sloped gently up a narrow, flat-floored valley. From their midst a tower rose, taller than the rest and somehow sinister. The dark bulk of a mountain rose up behind, rocky and forested. They ground to a halt and machine gun toting guards spilled out of a concrete blockhouse. This was not Shangri-La.

The guards searched the occupants and after scrutinizing their papers, walked them through a heavy steel turnstile and a metal detector where they waited as the Unimog itself was searched top and bottom and brought through the gates. They climbed back inside and sat. And sat.

Out the window Mitch could see a tall barbed wire fence with guard towers spaced every quarter mile or so, completely surrounding the town. He thought how cruel and paranoid these Koreans must be, until he remembered that early stories of Los Alamos painted a very similar picture. Maybe Koreans weren't so different.

Minister Pak grew tired of waiting and set about explaining how Sagi-dong was laid out. The 'Y'-shaped valley oriented downhill like an arrow. In the right branch was a residential section with apartments and small bungalows. The left hand branch held a small collective farm. And the lower section, that was in front of them, was the administrative area. The lab itself was completely underground, below Wagal Peak and the entrance was at the vertex.

One of the soldiers returned and gave them leave to go on. Pak nodded curtly out the window as the Unimog rolled into the lower leg of the 'Y'.

"This is First Street," he announced. He continued, pointing at buildings on either side, all constructed from monochromatic concrete, naming them as they passed. Security. Army Depot. State Security Administration (SSA) Headquarters. The Juche Study Center. Korean Workers' Party (KWP) Headquarters.

The only colors were the propaganda billboards and posters and the lavish KWP building, a traditional oriental building with sloping rooflines and gracefully sagging ridges. Out front was a fountain and statue of Kim Il-sung, and behind was a large, grassy field with a reviewing stand, bounded by a small lake with a large bronze statue standing before it. After taking it in, Mitch's attention drew back to the enormous flag flying in front of them. It was solid red with a yellow symbol reminiscent of a swastika.

"What's that mean?" asked Mitch, pointing at it.

"The symbol of the Party," answered Pak. "Pen, hammer, and sickle."

"Korean Workers' Party," grunted Hyon-hui with an attitude that said he should have known that.

"For the worker, peasant, and intellectual," added Lee. "The elements of class struggle."

They arrived at a large guard tower at the spot where all three branches of the 'Y' came together. A circular road ran about its base and all of Sagi-dong's streets flowed out of it. Mitch stared up the road to the densely packed residential section, then back to the administrative area, then over toward the barren ground of the collective farm, and was struck by one fact: other than the guards at the main gate, the town was completely deserted. He was about to ask where everyone was, when his eyes caught on something out of place. Rising from the lifeless muck of the farmland was a heavily built, concrete structure. "What is that?" he asked.

"The Explosives Facility," Hyon-hui answered proudly. "I designed it.".

They crossed the farm on a narrow concrete road and came to the south edge of the pond where a small bridge spanned the stream that flowed through the collective farm. Out in front was the larger-than-life bronze likeness that Mitch had seen from the other side of the parade ground. The image stood proudly, commanding his forces. In his left hand was a pair of binoculars. His right hand rested on a holster.

"The Great Leader, Comrade Generalissimo Kim Il-sung," Pak announced, but Mitch already knew the image well.

Against the valley wall behind the lake, a double row of villas, nicer than any anything he'd seen on the drive here came into view. With modern styling, metal roofs, and an abundance of windows. they looked more like an exclusive community in Los Alamos. In front of one sat a red Mercedes convertible, as out of place as Mitch Weatherby at a secret North Korean nuclear laboratory. They stopped in front of it.

"My Mercedes," Pak proclaimed lovingly. He opened the door and dropped to the ground. "I will see you at eight o'clock tomorrow morning." He nodded to all of them, but Mitch thought his gaze lingered on Hyon-hui with a look that was… hungry. A shadow passed over Hyon-hui's face. Mitch felt his muscles tighten, but everyone else pretended not to notice, remaining silent until Pak slammed the door and the tension passed.

The Unimog continued around the lake and back toward the main tower. That same time loudspeakers sprang to life as they approached.

"You will be staying in the visitors compound," Lee informed him, ignoring the cacophony. "All foreign personnel live there."

"Like me," said the Russian.

"How many foreigners do you have working here?" Mitch asked.

"As of today," Max answered, "two."

They circled the main tower once and headed toward the entrance to the lab. People were now issuing out of the tunnel opening, with the end of the day having been announced by the loudspeakers. But before they reached the entrance, the Unimog stopped at a row of two-story brick apartment buildings that stood with the cooperative farm as a backyard. Surrounded by a low fence, they had an inner-city look.

"This is where we get out," Lee said.

"I'm going on to the lab," said Max. "I have simulation results I need to check on. I'll stop by later."

"Need some help?" Mitch asked, wanting to do something that was familiar. These surroundings had taken that away from him again.

Max brightened and he shot a questioning glance at Lee. "What do you think?"

"Tomorrow perhaps," Lee said. "We need to get Dr. Weatherby settled in."

Mitch nodded and the lump in his throat expanded. He glanced uncomfortably at Professor Yang and Hyon-hui, then clambered out and spun around, trying to appear up-beat. "See you guys-"

Hyon-hui jerked the door shut in his face.

"Don't pay any attention to her," Lee told him as the Unimog pulled away. "A contentious woman."

Mitch swallowed heavily, turned around and gazed up at his new home. "Max lives here too, huh?"

"In the apartment just below yours. And I live next door. So if you need anything..." Mitch just stared at his surroundings wondering if Lee guessed at his discomfort. "Let's go have a look," Lee suggested kindly. "I think you will be pleased."

They showed their identification and papers to a guard who let them through the gate. Lee opened Mitch's room at the top of the stairs without a key.

"No lock?" Mitch noticed.

Lee swelled with pride. "There is no crime in the DPRK. We are all equal. There is no reason to steal."

More propaganda? Mitch wondered. He'd find out soon enough.

Mitch's new home was a fifteen feet by thirty foot cinder block box that had been painted white to make it more pleasing. The living room, with its tiny, table-top television, coarse sofa, and desk, was defined by a shabby partition, bearing pictures of the Kims, that stretched three-quarters of the way across the room. On the other side was a small bed on a sturdy, metal frame. Two narrow doors in the bedroom led to a bathroom and a tiny porch. Mitch turned the faucet handle and clear water gurgled out. Better conditions than Los Alamos scientists in 1942.

"There is food in the refrigerator," Lee said, glancing inside. "We will keep it stocked. Place your garbage in the waste bin at the far end of the complex." He headed to the rear, reciting details about clothing and laundry.

"A lot nicer than a Terminal Island cell would have been," said Mitch, forcing a smile.

"Glad you approve." Lee turned and started toward the front of the apartment with Mitch following. "Take the rest of the evening to relax. Take a shower. Watch TV. Get something to eat. You may explore the town if you like."

Mitch trailed him aimlessly through the door, spiraling emotionally downward as he faced the prospect of being alone. The streets were now filled with people on foot – people he didn't know and probably couldn't even speak to since he knew no Korean. Watching them made Mitch feel more abandoned. "Looks like everybody's headed home."

Lee shook his head. "They are going to their study sessions."

"Oh. Saturday night?"

"Every night."

"*Every night?*"

"Except Sunday, of course. Remember one of the three main tenants of the Juche philosophy: place the main stress on ideology."

"They study every night?" Mitch asked. "For how long?"

"Two hours."

"*Two hours?*" he exclaimed. "When do they get anything done?"

"Using Juche methods their productivity is doubled." Lee gave him a fake smile. "I must be off, Mitch, to my own study group. I have been away too long from my studies of the Great Leader's wisdom. It is good to be home, huh?"

"Home was never like this," Mitch mumbled, watching Lee make his way down the stairs leaving him alone outside his new apartment in the middle of the most secret city in North Korea. Mitch looked out over the darkling valley. Red tinged clouds drifted above, catching the last rays of the sun. A breeze that smelled of pine drifted across the valley. Below, communist scientists and workers swarmed about in the deepening twilight. Bathed in the sunset, they looked like ants. Red ants. He stood there leaning on the rail for a long time, not knowing what to do. Longing for anything familiar. A fleeting urge to pray ran through his mind but he rejected it.

Venus came out first, just above the rim of the valley to the west. After that, Spica in the southeast. Ursa Major, high in the north. Familiar shapes. He tried to find comfort in the thought that these were the same stars he'd always known but it just made him feel worse. Homesick for a life he'd lost a year ago. Darkness poured into the valley like water until the only thing still lit was the Kim Il-sung statue bathed in white light down by the lake.

Mitch slunk back inside and wandered into the bathroom, a strange, one-piece casting with everything molded from a single piece of shiny plastic. He stopped at the mirror. The despair and hopelessness that stared back at him was almost unrecognizable from that of the cocky scientist he'd once known. He wiggled his nose, and pushed up on the tip. It was still tender and stiff. Whenever he smiled or squinted, he was reminded of it. Reminded of standing before the judge, being beaten by the deputy. Of the confusing kidnap, or was it an escape? And he was reminded of everything that had come before. His eyes fell to his chest. He pulled his shirt aside and ran his finger across a thin, red scar that reached from the top of his collarbone almost to his nipple. Fragments of the shattered bullet still hurt at times. How had God let this happen? He'd done everything he was supposed to do. What had he done to deserve it? Or was this just some major screw up on God's part. He'd gotten the wrong guy, just like his country got the wrong house, shot the wrong people, framed the wrong man. None of this made any sense!

A panicky feeling gripped him and Mitch stepped back from the mirror. "*No...*" he groaned in a shaky voice. "No." Bit by bit, a crack widened in his mind. He tried to close it but before he could get it under control, he was sitting on the floor with his knees drawn up to his chest sobbing, cursing God, country, and his own existence. He'd never been given the chance to grieve for his wife. Never. He'd never been alone.

And the fact that he was being watched now didn't enter his mind.

7

Hyon-hui watched the American slide from his seat and drop to the ground. He turned to beguile them with soothing words and a poisonous smile but she slammed the door in his face. "Bastard *yang-kee* jackal!" she spat.

"I think Comrade Chun likes him," Max teased.

"You are a bastard, too!" she snorted and kicked at him. "He is a murderer, from a nation of murderers. Have you forgotten what he did at Sinchon?"

"Sinchon?" Max and the professor replied together.

"I think this is his first time in Choson," added Professor Yang.

"They are all the same, Comrade Professor. Thirty thirty-five thousand of us died. They are *all* guilty."

Max shook his head. "Guilty of what? He just arrived."

"They aim to enslave all of the Earth!"

"The whole planet?!" Max laughed. "I think the devil is not so black as he is painted."

"More of your Russian proverbs?" snapped Hyon-hui.

Max laughed. "So what happened at Sinchon?"

"Atrocities," Professor Yang said sadly. "Committed by the Americans during the Victorious Fatherland Liberation War."

"That was over sixty years ago!" Max exclaimed. "Dr. Weatherby wasn't even born yet!"

"It does not matter," Hyon-hui shot back. "He is an American. They are all guilty. If I live for one thousand years, I can never forget the screams of the children as the fires consumed their tiny bodies."

Max was confused. "You weren't there either. You're even younger than he is!"

"I was there in spirit! You must visit the *Sinchon Museum of American Atrocities*. They show a motion picture of the Sinchon Massacre directed by the Dear Leader, Comrade Marshal Kim Jong-il. It is called, *We Will Never Forget the Evil American Atrocities at Sinchon*. I heard those screams in my sleep for a year."

"Catchy title," Max joked as the Unimog rolled to a stop, and in an instant, he regretted it. The terror in Hyon-hui's eyes had shrunk her from the hard young woman he knew to a vulnerable girl, forced to witness an overblown dramatization of the horrors of war. Bastards, Max swore silently to himself in Russian.

Outside the vehicle, people emerged from the tunnel lab entrance after a long day. They formed up and marched along the road in orderly columns. They had probably all seen that same movie. Had they become numb to its effects, or were they as terrified as the brilliant young scientist beside him?

"Well I, for one feel that Doctor Weatherby's idea to shift to uranium-233 is brilliant," remarked the professor, breaking the awkward silence. "A workable solution to many of our problems that does not require the development of new technology."

"The metallurgy and hydrodynamics would certainly be easier to model but nuclear properties of 233 are puzzle to me," admitted Max. "Cross sections. Neutron numbers. Fission spectrum. There would be much to do."

"Treachery!" seethed Hyon-hui. "Treachery to bring our entire nuclear industry to its knees. What happens when the need to separate the 232 arrives? What then?"

"If we limit the neutrons during the breeding process to mostly thermal, under point-two MeV, then that will limit the 232 production to a fraction of a percent," assured the Professor. "And if it comes to it, we will shield our weapons as Comrade Weatherby suggested. Or store them in a shielded area. At least until we develop our own laser separation. Hot nuclear weapons are better than no nuclear weapons."

Hyon-hui started to say something but Professor Yang cut her off. "It will give us time, Comrade Chun. And time is what we have the least of."

She closed her mouth and stared forward, lips pressed tightly together.

Max opened the door. "Professor, Comrade Chun, *dos ve danya*."

"What are you going to look at?" the professor asked curiously.

"I left a simulation running the day-before-yesterday. Neutron diffusion in Fermi gas with no velocity constraints."

"Did you find the problem in the elastic collision model then?"

"You can't hide an awl in a sack," he said, and climbed out.

KWP headquarters was *almost* the finest building in town, second only to the hall where the Peoples' Assembly met. Well-tended, landscaped lawns and shrubbery flanked a fountain in the center of a broad circular drive that was backed up by a sculpture of Kim Il-sung meticulously extracted from a single block of red granite. The building itself, as well as the adjoining study center, was of cast and shaped concrete carefully painted to look like arching wooden timbers. Gracing the front between heavy rectangular columns was a six-foot tall painting of Kim Il-sung, who smiled at the picture of himself that adorned the front of the Army depot across the street.

Like everyone else, Hyon-hui and the professor bowed to the granite statue then went into the marble-tiled atrium. Professor Yang spotted a colleague and headed off to see him. At the desk, Hyon-hui showed her KWP membership card, national identification card, Party Cell card, and residence papers. The Party Cell, Political Security Department kept track of attendance but more importantly, food ration coupons were distributed after the meeting.

Just inside the auditorium, Hyon-hui nodded to acknowledge Pak Yong-nam who stood with Kim In-taek, the son of a P'yongyang Party Assemblyman. In-taek's grandfather had been a partisan who'd fought shoulder to shoulder with the Great Leader himself so had risen quickly since his admission to the Party at the minimum age of eighteen. In his mid-twenties, he was already the General Secretary of the local Party Cell.

"Comrade Chun," said the handsome young man, whose looks were lessened somewhat by the permanent sneer sculpted into his features.

Hyon-hui stopped with a shallow bow to both men. "Comrade Secretary. Comrade Minister."

"I have received word that there is some kind of small problem with your paperwork," said Kim. His concern appeared genuine. She glanced at Pak but he looked away. "I will check with the Party Membership Committee in P'yongyang. But it does mean more delays."

Hyon-hui's stomach dropped. "Thank you, Comrade Secretary," she answered, careful not to look too disappointed. She bowed to In-taek again and pushed past him only to be followed by Pak. He herded her into a corner.

"Another problem with your membership status?"

Hyon-hui kept her eyes straight ahead, avoiding the gaze that made her feel unclean. "Secretary Kim said he is going to check on it."

"I may be able to help. We should discuss it later. Perhaps at my villa after the meeting?"

Her heart froze. "Why can we not talk about it now?"

"Such matters are far too sensitive." He looked her up and down with greedy eyes, "We could have dinner. I can give you meat."

A nauseous feeling swept through her innards. Meat was all too rare these days but Hyon-hui didn't think that was the kind he meant. "I, I cannot," she blurted. "As you know, my mother is old. And, and I, I must go to her. I have to cook dinner and, she will be wanting to see me. She is old. And feeble. I have been away for too long."

"Your mother," Pak parroted with a bitter light in his eyes. "Your mother's counterrevolutionary tendencies are well documented, Miss Chun. It would be unfortunate if her behavior interfered with your revolutionary aspirations."

"I am sorry, Comrade Minister." She hung her head and pushed past his broad shoulders.

She found a seat next to Professor Yang who had already slipped in. Without his sponsorship, she'd have never come this far toward becoming a Party member. Since she'd first arrived at Yongbyon the professor had been almost like a father to her. They'd always known her chance at Party membership was a long one. And she'd come so close. Too close to give up now.

"Is everything alright" Professor Yang whispered.

Hyon-hui looked straight ahead. "Of course."

"Hyon-hui?"

She glanced over her shoulder. They were a little early and the big assembly hall was still over half empty. But whispers could find the wrong ears. And while Professor Yang was her sponsor, he was also a Party member. She reconsidered. "I am fine. It was a long journey."

He looked at her hard. "Is Comrade Pak –"

"It is that American pig, if you must know!" she suddenly hissed to cover her discomfort . "He thinks he is so much smarter than us stupid, backward Koreans! How I despise him. All of them!"

Professor Yang's eyes lingered on her for a moment before finding the front of the room.

After singing the national anthem, the first order of business was the induction of three new members. One was a teenage boy, just out of Sagi-dong High School, the son of a uniformed, SSA major. The next was an attractive woman from Radiological Safety. It was rumored that she'd slept with Pak, Kim In-taek, and others. And there was a technician from Sariwon who worked in the Electronics Group. Hyon-hui watched, helpless and frustrated. If only she could have the kind of ideological purity that the Great Leader demanded, they would have to let her in. She would have to try harder.

The inductions were followed by a public denunciation. A technician in the electronics department had slaughtered and butchered his family's pig without permission. He had been caught when a school teacher reported the rosy, plump cheeks of his children to the Security Bureau, for which she received a commendation. Now, standing before his peers, he was harangued by a Public Security Ministry officer for stealing from the popular masses. The remainder of the meat had been confiscated by the Pork Purchase Office.

The meeting was long and centered around the scientific development of the Juche ideology by the Dear Leader, Comrade Marshal Kim Jong-il, and its systemization as *Kimilsungism*. It was much different than the non-Party, Neighborhood Unit gatherings she had once attended. They were filled only with Party directives and encouragement toward ideological purity. But here, they were studying the actual theory of *Kimilsungism*. It was most exciting.

Hyon-hui was an expert on *Kimilsungism*. She'd read Kim Jong-il's hundreds of works countless times and devoted much time imparting his words to memory. Words that spoke of the equality and dignity of men and women, and their filial devotion to a Great Leader. For Juche, as the philosophy of independence. And the hatred of all imperialists, especially Americans, who deny the masses of their *chajusong*.

But tonight she was having trouble concentrating. She kept finding herself thinking about the young lady from Radiological Safety. She had actually been inducted as a probationary member *after* Hyon-hui. And now she was getting her solid red pin! So instead of considering Juche she debated with herself. Go to Pak's house? Or go back home and wait? It would just be one night. Or maybe two.

She glanced over at Pak and caught him looking at her. He wasn't so terribly unattractive. And even if he was married, his wife was in P'yongyang. She managed a weak smile and saw his eyebrows lift.

The residential section of Sagi-dong was always a mixture of sound and smell, light and shadow. Comforting in a way. Warm yellow light filtered through the shades of the tiny concrete bungalows. Close to the hydroelectric plants on the Chosin and Pujon Reservoirs and at Lake Nangnim, Sagi-dong had more electricity than most places in the country. Citizens were permitted the burning of a 40 watt bulb until ten o'clock at night provided their shades were drawn. And it gave the town a warmth that didn't exist elsewhere.

Row upon row of the identical houses marched by as Hyon-hui walked home, cursing herself for her decision. All she would have had to do is give in to Pak's request. It was just one night. Or maybe a few. And she would be standing there where that other woman was tonight. But now she was that much farther from her life's desire.

The scent of garlic and pepper and fresh, steamed cabbage from personal gardens drifted on the night air. A thin layer of fog hovered just above the roof tops. Somebody coughed in the darkness. A wet, hacking cough. A baby weakly cried. A door closed. But there were no other sounds. And over all there was a sense of watchfulness. And fatigue.

Hyon-hui turned at the street and faced the front door of her home. Golden light shown around the jamb and the sound of utensils told her that her mother was already preparing dinner. From the smell, kimchi, rice, and bean paste. Like the night before, and the night before. It gave Hyon-hui comfort. Her mother might be a hindrance to Hyon-hui's political aspirations, but she was the only family Hyon-hui had ever known. And it was good to be home.

8

Mitch woke with a start. He swung his feet to the floor and rubbed his eyes. The TV was showing a still picture of a glittering waterfall. In the upper right corner of the screen was a digital clock at 10:05. Weird music was playing. There was a knock on the door. "Just a minute!" Mitch stumbled to the door and jerked it open to find the Russian standing there.

"Dr. Weatherby?" said Max. "May I come in?"

Mitch sniffed and opened the door wider. It was black outside and damp. "Sure," he muttered.

Max looked embarrassed. "I saw the light on. I am sorry if I woke you." He started to turn away.

"No, no. Don't worry about it," Mitch replied, clearing his throat. "I was just, uh, crashed on the couch."

"Crashed?"

"Asleep."

"Ah." Max stuck his hand out. "You can call me Max."

"Yeah, I remember," he replied, taking the Russian's hand. "And call me," he yawned widely and covered his mouth with his hand. "Excuse me. Mitch." He shut the door and they stood facing one another. Mitch wondered why he was here. "Can I do something for you," he finally asked.

Max held up the sack he was carrying. "I thought you might like some dinner. I haven't got Pizza Hut, but it may keep us alive, eh?"

Mitch's attitude softened. "Sorry about that. Please, come in."

"*Harasho! Harasho!*" Max bubbled suddenly. "I also bring you this as a, uh, how do you say? House heating present?" He pulled out a large bottle full of clear liquid.

Floating inside it, Mitch realized with a shock, was a long, black snake with its head at the top, mouth open, tongue lolling out. Mitch winced.

"*Baem Sul*. Adder Liquor," Max shrugged casually, "Not as good as vodka but better than Korean water, eh?"

Mitch hefted the bottle and looked closely. "What kind of snake is it?"

Max lifted his glasses off his nose and peered closely at the reptile. "A dead one. I hope."

A smile split Mitch's lips. A smile that quickly grew into an uncontrollable laugh that went on a touch too long.

A confused look crossed Max's face. "What is so humorous, comrade?"

"Oh, Max, you don't know how long it's been since I laughed. Oh, that felt good. Let me get a couple of glasses."

"Excellent. I judged you correctly. I'm a good judge of men."

Mitch rummaged through the cabinet and produced two smudged tumblers while Max screwed the top off the bottle. "You must be careful, these tops leak," he said and poured up two big glasses. "I learned the hard way and wasted a perfectly good half-liter. Or perfectly bad. Depending on how you view this poison."

Max held his glass up. "To the West and the Uncle Sam," said Maxim vibrantly.

"To the East and Mother Russia," replied Mitch. They clinked their tumblers and took a shot. A few seconds later, Mitch grabbed his head and abdomen and wheezed, "You sure this stuff ain't radioactive?"

"Nyet," Max rasped and held his glass up to the light. "But I am still alive. Just sterilized."

Over the food Max had brought, they talked about the lab and the people Mitch had met. Mitch kept wanting to ask him about working for North Korea, but he decided not to bring it up. When they were done with the kimchi and rice, Max produced a small chess set. "Do you play?" he asked Mitch, lighting up a cigarette. His first of many.

"All my life," Mitch answered. He didn't smoke but preferred Max's company to clean air.

"Dr. Rhee and I used to play in the evenings as we discussed nasty theoretical problems of nuclear physics."

Mitch didn't miss a beat. "Lee and I used to play on the Tong Gon as we discussed nasty theoretical problems of Kimilsungism."

Max chuckled. "Comrade Mitch, one fisherman sees another from afar, eh?"

"What's that mean?" asked Mitch.

"You and I, we are of similar mind. Strangers, in a strange land."

Max opened with his knight's pawn.

"So tell me, Max, what brings you to the DPRK?" Mitch asked. "Or are things really that bad in Russia?"

Max leaned back in his chair and took a long drag on the cigarette. "Have ever you heard of Chechnya?"

"Down by the Black Sea. In the Caucasus. Shoehorned in between Kazakhstan and Azerbaijan."

"Very good. Well I am from Chechnya but ethnic Russian. My family had been there since the eighteen hundreds. First working for the Czar, then for the Party, then for… whoever is in control of Russia today. Chechnya's been trying to gain independence ever since the Soviet Union dissolved. Moscow never has liked the idea."

Mitch nodded. "I remember. 'Bout the same time Los Alamos tanked."

"Tanked?"

"Fell apart."

"Hmm. Then you know that in Chechnya there is ongoing civil war? Putin says Russia won the war but I guess the Chechens didn't hear him, at least some of them, because they are still fighting today." Max took a long, deep drag on the filterless cigarette and blew the smoke out in a stream. "My sister Olga," his gray eyes were glassy and staring, "Murdered while out with friends. Raped." Max bowed his head and crushed out the cigarette, sniffed and wiped his eyes. "And my mother. Blown up. Terrorists? Russian soldiers?" He shrugged. "Who knows? Nobody cares. When powerful people are quarreling it is the commoners that suffer."

Mitch just stared, wondering if he'd ever be able to speak so casually about what had happened to him. To Beth.

Max took a big swig of Baem Sul. "I was not there when it happened. I was working for *the motherland*." There was scorn in his voice. "My country. My *Rodina*," he sighed heavily. "Russia is now run by oligarchs who kiss the ass of American capitalists and buy futbol clubs in England." Max sighed heavily, lit another cigarette and moved a chess piece. "So, you have heard of Rhee Sun-yi?"

Mitch nodded. "The guy I'm replacing, right? Korean guy."

"He was Soviet but he was ethnic Korean. His family immigrated to Russia during the Great Patriotic War. I worked for him at Arzamas-16. You know this Arzamas-16?"

"The Los Alamos of Russia."

That got a smile. "We prefer to say that Los Alamos is the Arzamas of America. I worked for him there until he was killed in an airplane crash. A few years later, he sends for me. With my family dead, the decision to come was not so difficult."

"Guess the plane didn't crash after all, huh?"

"No, it crashed," said Max, and blew out a stream of smoke. "Dr. Rhee just wasn't on it."

Mitch realized what Max had just said. These North Koreas did what they had to do. Had they killed Rhee? Mitch had to know. "So, what happened to this Rhee?"

Max studied the board. "He was working one night, testing. They were measuring neutron multiplication values using a ballistic tower. Dropping plutonium slugs through a subcritical target."

Mitch whistled and shook his head. "Ballsy. We haven't done an experiment like that in forty years."

"Neither have we. For reasons that are all too obvious. Rhee was examining the target when the slug fell from just a few centimeters. I heard it from Kim Sun-gun so I believe it. A good man. Excellent scientist. You will be working with him."

The thought made Mitch's stomach hurt. "What a way to go."

"I watched him die in the infirmary. Over a thousand REM. He just…" Max swallowed heavily and licked his lips "… dissolved."

It hit closer to home than Max could have ever expected. Mitch's own father had died of radiation-induced leukemia only a few years prior. "It sounds like he was a close friend."

"He was –" the Russian paused for a moment, staring into space, " – my only friend. He was also the only person in North Korea with expertise in core design. And no one else here has participated in a real nuclear test."

"Well, I don't think anyone knew I was coming." Mitch forced the last of his Baem Sul, down with a grimace. It really was terrible liquor but Mitch didn't care. "And I don't think everybody's real happy about my being here. Including me."

Max leaned back and blew out a stream of smoke. "Then you should fit right it. No one here is happy about anything. Including me." He grinned. "But what are we to do?"

Mitch split the last few drops of Baem Sul between their glasses. The snake was now a heap of black coils piled in the bottom of the bottle. "That Korean girl. The one who rode up here with us today."

"Chun Hyon-hui?"

"Yeah. *Comrade* Chun. She doesn't like me too much, does she?"

Max laughed. "She does not like Americans. But she doesn't like anybody. Not unless you are a KWP cadre."

"Cadre? What's that?"

"A leader in the Korean Workers' Party. She's trying to become a member. You saw her pin." He shook his head disparagingly. "Very political. Very difficult. Especially for woman. Sometimes they have to give up a lot. Too much. To men like Pak."

Mitch felt his face flush. "You don't think she's, you know…?" His gut tightened.

"Screwing Pak?" Max shrugged. "Could be. I have seen it happen with Russian girls."

"She's not one hundred percent Korean, is she?"

"I have heard that her grandfather was a Red Army soldier. Russian perhaps."

"So what's she do?" Mitch asked.

"Chemist. Works with explosives. And she is very, very good. One of the best I've seen. Especially so young. She has developed methods for mixing and casting lenses, and ensuring quality-control that are better than what we had in Soviet Union."

"Must be Juche," Mitch said.

"Juche!" Max smiled. "*Da!* That must be it." They both laughed.

"Still," Mitch said, now curious. "First female explosives expert I've run into."

"Believe me, it suits her temperament. She is also an excellent theorist and has contributed in developing our equation of state for explosives in the hydrodynamic simulation."

This made Mitch even more curious. "I'd like to see what you've come up with. The equation of state for the explosives is always guess work at best.

"Exactly. A major source of error in simulations." Max moved a chess piece and put Mitch into check. "So, what about your life?"

Mitch eyed the board and frowned. But not because of the check. How much should he say? He got out of check, but not far. "Born and raised in Los Alamos. Grew up listening to stories of my dad going to nuclear tests. Studied my little butt off to do what he did. Then, as soon as I get my Ph.D. they shut down the entire development and test division. The only real dream I had in this life was to see a nuclear detonation." He drained the last of his booze. "I hate computers."

Max scowled. "You're as bad as Professor Yang. Despises computers. But he is brilliant. If he had been trained in the Soviet Union, he would have a Nobel Prize in Physics. Maybe two."

"He seems like a decent guy," Mitch commented and was glad the conversation moved away from his past.

"He is head of the Theoretical Division. But he's also high-ranking in the Korean Workers' Party so is often away. Still, he and

Pak, they do not see eye to eye. Yang is, how you say, old school. Pak is…"

"New school," Mitch supplied. "Now that guy is a major-league ass-hole. I wouldn't –" Max started waving his arms wildly and Mitch's voice trailed off. "What is it?" he finally said.

Max glanced around nervously. His eyes scanned around the room until they located a pad of paper and a pen sitting on the desk. He went over and hastily wrote a note that he stuck in Mitch's face. *Even walls may have ears.*

A feeling of dread descended on Mitch at the sight of those words. The half-inebriated Russian quickly rose and nearly fell over, then got his balance, but remembered to tear off the top two sheet of paper and stuff them into his pocket.

"I better be going," he said, anxiously. "Early bird gets the worm. You know there's a ten o'clock curfew? I am past it. Good thing that I am just downstairs. *Dos ve'danya*, Mitch."

9

After a month in the country, Mitch was adjusting to "the Juche way of doing things" although he had yet to get an explanation of exactly what that meant. Still, despite the knee deep political bureaucracy to wade through with every request, he was actually working. Physics was still physics, immutable and constant, and after a year of having his life jerked around by opinions and interpretation, it was liberating. And even more importantly, he was needed. Badly. They treated him well, and so far he hadn't been asked to reveal anything classified. These people were *not* the people being made fun of by late night talk-show hosts in America. They were industrious, hard working, eager, intelligent. As long as he didn't dwell on the ever present propaganda, it was almost a pleasant place, aside from the monotony of the food. And it kept him so busy he didn't have time to think about Beth – at least not as much.

The scientists and engineers were technically competent. Far more than Mitch would have expected. In fact, at first, he couldn't figure out, why they needed him at all. But as he toured one group after another and was briefed by their leaders, the picture became clearer. Structurally, the North Korean program was a disaster. For every scientific group, there was a political oversight group. Experimental results had to be passed through these POGs, where they would often be held up for days before going to the experimentalists who'd asked for the tests. Improved theoretical models had to take the same torturous path. And it served no purpose except to remind everyone that Party members, and its members only, controlled the state and everything that happened. Of course, there had been people like this at Los Alamos, too. Bureaucrats who protected their turf to lock up a share of next year's budget, while contributing only obfuscation and confusion. While America and North Korea were different in many ways, the way people behaved was chillingly similar. In the end, Mitch concluded, it was because both had people in them. And where there were people, there was corruption, malaise, and neglect. This made physics, in Mitch's mind, superior to people in just about every way, and superior to any of the disciplines that claimed to study people.

Having determined the problem, his first order of business was to completely restructure the program, exactly as Oppenheimer had done at Los Alamos. But his first meeting to discuss it was a disaster, with Pak Yong-Nam opposing his every recommendation, just because he had the authority to do so. It was not until Professor Yang told him what motivated Pak – finishing the project so he could return to P'yongyang – that he was able to push through any of his ideas. And now, four weeks after he arrived, Mitch was setting the final division leaders in place, replacing the bureaucrats with competent scientists.

"Who's next?" asked Major Lee, standing outside the entrance to the labyrinthine lab that lay beneath the mountain.

Mitch had saved this one for last. He wiped a sheen of sweat from his forehead and gazed toward the brown explosives building sitting in the middle of the collective farm. Surrounded by a tall, electrified fence, it looked like the Plutonium Facility on Pajarito Road in Los Alamos, and the dark clouds filling the sky made it seem particularly evil. "Chun," he said despondently.

"Are you certain you should do this?" asked Lee, and glanced nervously at the Explosives Facility.

"She's the best chemist in Sagi-dong." If Mitch hadn't known better, he'd have thought Lee was nervous. "Are you afraid to go in the Explosives Facility? I can assure you it is safe."

"No, no, no, it's not that!" Lee's face twisted into a scowl. "She is not one of us, Mitch."

Mitch knew Lee didn't even use this tone when he spoke of Americans, yet everyone seemed to use it when referring to Chun Hyon-hui. Given her technical acumen and intense, annoying, patriotic zeal, it was baffling. "How could she not be one of you?"

Mitch questioned back, hoping to get to the Explosives Facility before it started raining. "She was born and raised here."

"Certainly, you have noticed her eyes," Lee said as if it was obvious. He trotted to catch up with Mitch. "Koreans don't have green eyes, Dr. Weatherby."

"What does eye color have to do with anything?"

"Everything!" Lee exclaimed. "Her grandfather was not Korean. She tries to make up for it by displaying revolutionary zeal." He chuckled. "But nothing can replace genetic purity. She knows this. Her behavior is… pathetic."

"Seriously?" Mitch laughed. The notion was ludicrous. There were immigrants of all kinds working at Los Alamos. And Mitch didn't know where anyone's grandparents had been from. "What does it matter where her grandfather is from?"

Lee gave him a steely stare. "This is not a laughing matter Dr. Weatherby. Ideological purity is central to the Juche Idea. She is just fortunate that her impure blood is Russian and not…" he cast about until his eyes landed on Mitch, "American or Japanese. She would not be here at all."

"I'm American," Mitch replied, feeling an unfamiliar sense of pride.

Lee suggested some of Kim Jong-il's writings on the subject and they hurried the rest of the way in silence. For days the dark clouds had been gathering, warning of the coming monsoons. The storms could not be far now.

Hyon-hui pecked out a report on a typewriter in her office. Official pictures of the Great and Dear Leaders hung on the wall behind her. Her hateful attitude toward Mitch had not wavered, but for some reason that he could not fathom, when he looked in, he smiled. He rapped on the door jamb. "Annyeong."

Hyon-hui brushed her velvety black hair aside with a swipe of her hand and her green eyes turned to flame. "Your Korean is terrible."

Mitch bowed awkwardly and shuffled inside. "Miss Chun, can I talk to you for a few minutes?"

She lowered her head back to her work. "I am busy."

"Yeah. I can see that. What have you got there?"

She rolled her eyes with an audible sigh. "I am writing the weekly report for the Experimental Division which I am to submit to Kim Jun-mo by –" she glanced very deliberately at her watch, "five o'clock."

Mitch nodded, noting she had about an hour and a half to finish it. "Well, I'll try not to keep you too long. Comrade." He sat down in the chair facing her desk. Her eyes screamed disapproval but she said nothing. "You may have heard that we're reorganizing the lab."

"As if there were something wrong with the current organization."

Mitch smiled politely. "I just don't feel that a political oversight committee is necessary for an experiment."

"And why not?"

"Because there's nothing political about the fission cross section of plutonium-239."

"I didn't say there was."

Mitch cocked his head to one side. "But you just –"

"I don't need a *yang-kee* to interpret me!" she spat so hard that Mitch recoiled. "It is the Taean Work System," she said, deriding him with her voice. "Industrial concerns are to be guided by Korean Workers' Party committees. Senior cadres assist junior cadres in solving problems using the principles of Juche. It is the most scientifically advanced manufacturing system in the world."

Mitch was long weary of Juche and scientific. "This isn't manufacturing so, we're replacing it with the Los Alamos System."

Hyon-hui nearly leapt from her seat. "*Does Minister Pak know of this? Has he –*"

"Not only does he know about it," barked Mitch, cutting her off, "we've already replaced all the division leaders and created a couple of new ones."

Her lips became a single thin line. "You are here to replace me! I know that you fear me because of my loyalty to the Great Leader, Comrade Generalissimo Kim Il-sung, and now to the Dear Leader, Comrade Generalissimo Kim Jong-il. I assume you are filling all the positions with American and Japanese sympathizers!"

Mitch stared for a moment, thinking of what Lee had just told him. Did Hyon-hui really understand what people thought of her? He'd have felt sorry for her had she been a bit more civil. "Look Miss Chun, I don't know who sympathizes with whom, but we're going to be creating a separate division for explosives. It's going to encompass not only the Explosives Facility, but detonators, detonating circuits, diagnostic methods –"

"And who is to head it?" Hyon-hui spat. "Syng-mann Rhee? George Bush?"

He tried not to look at her eyes. They were large. Clear. Almond-shaped. Feminine. "No," he said, shaking it off. "I was sort of thinking that *you* might be the best choice. *Comrade*."

"Well I am not going to just –" Her face suddenly went blank. "What did you say?"

Mitch wondered what Lee, standing in the door watching, thought of the look of astonishment on her face. Did he find it pathetic? "Of course, you'll remain over the Explosives Facility as well. It's going to be a big job."

Her scowl faded and the hate drained from her eyes casting an unwelcome spell over Mitch. "*Me?*" she said in a soft but wary voice. "Why me?"

Mitch knew that, for the first time, he was seeing the true Hyon-hui. He tried not to fixate on her eyes and wound up staring at the Great Leaders on the wall behind her. "Because you're the best we have at what X-Division is going to do."

"And what is that?" she asked, still in shock.

"Blow things up. I've talked to your group and they all point to you. Not to Jun-mo. I've looked at your work and you're an excellent empirical chemist. Of course, the job is –" Mitch's voice trailed off. She was sitting with her mouth half-open, sort of mouthing words. "What's wrong? Miss Chun?"

"… just so unexpected," she stammered, having unknowingly dropped her ideological wall.

Mitch liked this Hyon-hui. "Do you think you're up to it?"

The fire returned to her eyes but without the malice. "Absolutely."

"Okay, then. We're going to be developing some technologies that you haven't used before but I know your people can handle it if they work hard."

"They will work hard." Fear suddenly came into her eyes and she actually drew inward. "What will Kim Jun-mo say?"

Mitch knew enough to know that the fear was real and marveled at the spectrum of emotions running through this poor woman's body in the last few minutes. Everyone seemed to be afflicted with this paranoia. "I'm going to recommend to Pak that he be shipped out of here since, despite his supposed Ph.D. in Chemistry from Kim Il-sung University, I have yet to figure out what he *is* good at other than making everybody around him miserable."

Hyon-hui, veering into yet another emotional alley, and cowered as if to ward off invisible blows. "Dr. Weatherby," she squeaked. "*No!*"

Mitch smiled. "Don't worry. You didn't say anything. I thought I'd have a meeting tomorrow afternoon," he continued. "Talk to –"

"You can't have it tomorrow," Hyon-hui interrupted, now turning pale.

"Why not?

"Friday Labor!" she exclaimed, and Mitch scowled. "You don't approve?" Her belligerence was back. They'd come full circle. She was like a machine with buttons. All Mitch had to do was press. "Friday Labor is the essence of *Kimilsungism* in which the members of the Party serve and mingle with the people. How else can an effective bond be forged between the popular masses and the Party?"

"Now that you mention it, that ain't such a bad idea," he said. "I know some American bureaucrats who could use a few days of scrubbing toilets. I'll get back to you on the meeting. Until then, you better finish that report. Just don't put too much effort into it. No use killing yourself for a guy who's gonna be planting rice this time next week."

Mitch scheduled the meeting for Saturday morning. He rose before the loudspeakers came on. Staring out his window, the valley was still dark and heavy clouds obscured Wagal Peak. Mitch cracked the window of his apartment and listened to the gentle hiss of the falling water. The rain had finally come and, he'd been told, would be here for a while. In the dim light, it was peaceful but, as he listened, his former life – seeming almost like a dream now – came flooding back.

He forced himself out of bed to stop the despair that came with thinking about how easy and happy his life had been, and how he'd been abandoned by everything he thought true. His stomach growled but his pantry contained only bean paste and rice cakes. The refrigerator was little better; a container of kimchi and a few cans of Ryongsong beer. Mitch took four of the cakes, rationing them so he'd have something to eat that evening. Sitting down in his underwear in front of the TV, he squeezed the gray-brown paste out onto the quarter-inch thick discs. A poor substitute for the peanut butter he craved. The TV finally warmed up and he watched grainy P'yongyang parade footage emerge from the snow. The propaganda truly was everywhere.

He finished his 'breakfast' and switched off the TV. In the silence, the image of his dead wife leapt into his mind. He was never really free of it but at times the memory of Beth was almost something he could touch. Thunder rumbled in the distance. The speakers blared to life. He dressed, put on his government issue plastic poncho, and stepped outside. Water pouring off the eave soaked his shoes in seconds. An instant later, Lee stepped out wearing his happy face.

"Good morning, Mitch!" He smiled and pointed. "Be careful or you will get your feet wet!"

Mitch stood in the splashing water and stared out toward the dreary, gray town, watching the rain fall and collect in big brown puddles. A few people were already headed toward the lab, head down, water dripping from their slickers. A lone jeep drove up the street, its headlights stabbing through the rain. He wanted this nightmare to end. He wanted to kill himself. Perhaps when he returned to his room later today.

"A bad day in the Workers' Paradise is better than a good day anywhere else," Lee chirped.

Mitch swallowed the lump in his throat. "Max tells me this could last a while."

Lee looked at the sky and squinted. "Monsoons begin early."

"The rice will like it," Mitch droned, eyeing the paddies that Friday-labor workers had planted yesterday.

"If it is not washed away like last year." He looked at Mitch. "Are you okay?"

Mitch closed his eyes and just stood there with the water pouring over his feet. He couldn't believe he was here. Couldn't believe his wife was dead. Couldn't believe he was actually working with North Koreans. Helping them build a nuclear bomb. He'd tried to pray a few times, but when he asked God for guidance, he received nothing but stony silence. There was no salvation.

"*Mitch?*" Lee asked again.

"Let's go," he answered and strode into the rain.

They trudged to the lab entrance, a yawning black hole bored into the side of the mountain and concealed by a colossal steel door suspended on pins the size of small tree trunks. Inside, the tunnel was lined with yellow tile and sloped upwards to keep water out. Every fifty feet or so hung a propaganda poster and loudspeakers played revolutionary music 24 hours a day. Armed guards patrolled endlessly. After some fifty yards, the tunnel leveled off briefly then plunged downward at a steep angle for almost a quarter mile. By the time it spilled out into the main corridor, they were nearly 400 feet beneath the level of Sagi-dong with hundreds more feet of rock on top of that.

The main corridor was over a quarter mile long and arched high overhead. Brilliant arc-lights suspended from tile-covered rock above illuminated the hall in a harsh light. Propaganda billboards told the story of Juche and patriotic music echoed around the hall in a cacophony of echoing chords. On either side of the main shaft, dozens of halls split into the rock at right angles.

They had once been coal seams but now housed departments and lab facilities. Even more than the advanced state of their nuclear program, Mitch was awed and terrified by the scale and ability of the sappers who had constructed this incredible warren about which the West knew *nothing*. They'd been fools at Los Alamos, thinking they could discern the inner workings of a society like this from a few high-resolution satellite photos.

When they arrived at the conference room deep in the heart of the lab, Mitch's feet were freezing and everyone was smoking. He'd already spent a lot of time in this room, sort of the nerve center for the entire operation. The large portraits of Kim Il-sung on every wall and propaganda posters everywhere had become nothing more than background to Mitch. He wondered if it was the same for everyone else. Like fish in water, they didn't even know it was there unless it was missing.

Mitch squinted through the cigarette-supplied haze as people filed in. He recognized most of them even though half their names were still a blank. Lee went over them one by one as they entered.

"Kim Sun-gun," said Lee, "engineering. Yi Kang, test. Sun Ok-li, engineering..." So far, about the only names he had down were Max, Pak, Professor Yang, Hyon-hui, Lee, and Kim Sun-gun, whom he called, "Sonny."

Sonny had been a pleasant surprise. It was hard to tell how old he was. His skin was bad and his angular cheek bones almost cut through the leathery coating. But his eyes were bright, his mind keen, and he had an intense curiosity about the West. He constantly asked Mitch questions about America but Mitch was careful about answering them. Lee had warned him that North Korea was not America and Mitch didn't want to get anyone into trouble. But Sonny pressed all the more.

"Howdy, Mitch!" said Sonny, using one of the words Mitch had taught him. "What's the word for today?"

Mitch thought for a moment and said, "*Pwn*."

"Poon," said Sonny and the fine lines around his eyes creased into a million spidery cracks.

"No, pwn, as in bone. Or own. Or stone. It means to completely overcome somebody. Crush them at a game. Total victory."

"Ah," said Sun-gun smiling. "Pwn. I shall pwn Max at chess."

"In your pathetic dreams," said Max.

"What is tomorrow's word?" asked Sun-gun. If he'd been a dog, his tail would be doing damage.

"Eager," said Mitch and turned to his mounting audience. At ten after eight the room was nearly full. Mitch coughed and rubbed his eyes to see through the smoke. "*Cho-a-yo a-chim,*" he said in greeting, standing up before them. It was supposed to mean 'good morning' from two words he'd strung together from his phrase book. But it wasn't a phrase they used and they just looked at one another. Even Sonny seemed confused. "Thanks for coming," he added nervously.

Professor Yang, Max, and Sun-gun were sitting near the front next to Pak Yong-nam. Around them was a sea of thirty or forty Asian faces. Hyon-hui was not there. "Anyone seen Comrade Chun this morning?" he asked. "No?" That was weird. She was usually early, deriding Mitch even before he had said anything.

"As most of you know by now," Mitch began, "Silla-14 is being reorganized. While the Taean System might work well in many situations, it doesn't seem to be optimal for an effort such as this. The work is just too technical to lend itself to analysis through purely philosophical methods. Our goal in doing this is –"

The door opened and Hyon-hui staggered in. She was pale and barely able to walk, like she'd run a triathlon the day before without having trained. Everyone turned and gaped. Everyone except Pak. Mitch could have sworn he smiled. She hobbled across the room and collapsed into a chair.

"As I was saying," Mitch stammered. "Our, uh, goal in the reorganization is primarily to increase the efficiency of information exchange between the various divisions, streamline their areas of work, and hopefully, improve the ability of management to direct and focus various efforts. Some of the things that the Taean System wasn't handling too well, but that the Los Alamos system handles very well."

He slapped a hand-drawn transparency on the overhead projector showing their new workflow. "Now the heart of the Los Alamos system as applied to nuclear weapon design is simply this: Theorists develop mathematical models of the system using their best understanding of the physics. Engineers use their specifications to build devices. Experimentalists test these devices and pass the results back to the theorists who use them to refine their models."

Mitch went on, reorganizing the three existing divisions – Theoretical, Experimental, and Engineering – to five *Critical Assemblies* aka Gadget – a name borrowed from the Manhattan Project – *Explosives* or X, *Theoretical* (T), *Physics and Research* (PR), and *Chemistry and Metallurgy* (CM).

Mitch would head Gadget Division, aided by Kim Sun-gun, studying the rapid assembly of fissionable materials into supercritical masses. He went on to explain each of the remaining four divisions and their leaders. "And from now on," Mitch continued addressing this new group, "if we need a number, we measure it." A few eyebrows raised, but no one challenged it. Mitch felt relieved since this helped him avoid revealing anything classified. He'd been prepared to defending his edict by reference to their superior Juche methodology, but it wasn't necessary.

In addition, there was a list of important technical items that needed to be addressed, everything from upgrading their Van de Graff particle accelerator to determining the fission spectrum of uranium-233 from thermal all the way out to two million electron-volts. It was a daunting technical challenge, but with the new organizational approach Mitch thought they were up to the tasks.

Besides the restructuring, Mitch instituted a change that was to have an even farther reaching effect. A Local Area Network, in which test and simulation results in Portable Document Format, would be made available to *everyone*. This was a break, not only with the previous paradigm, but with North Korean culture in general, in which everything was compartmentalized. Fortunately, all the necessary software could simply be downloaded by the Internet Espionage Committee in P'yongyang.

"Any questions?" Mitch asked his stunned listeners.

"What about political oversight?" growled Kim Jun-mo. He had been Hyon-hui's boss and was one of the highest ranking Party members in Sagi-dong. With his slicked back hair, sloping forehead, and thick lips, he fit the stereotypical communist bureaucrat only too well. And he was not happy about losing the explosives division.

"Of course," answered Mitch. He had anticipated this but wondered if his offhand remarks were responsible for Hyon-hui's haggard state. "You will be in charge of the Political Oversight and Operational Planning Division, POOP."

Jun-mo nodded gravely. "And what does POOP do?"

Mitch crossed his arms and shifted his weight from one leg to the other in an effort to not grin at his cleverness. "I see POOP division in uh... It doesn't directly contribute anything, being purely political in nature as I'm sure you understand, but it is important in that it, I, uh –" He looked over at Pak and said, "Minister?"

"POOP is necessary," said Pak Yong-nam, "for ensuring that the proper revolutionary spirit is displayed by the workers, and for guidance in employing Juche methods. With this mindset, creativity will be enhanced and *chajusong* will be secured by the masses."

"There you have it," Mitch said. "You're in charge of POOP."

Jun-mo grinned fiercely, seemingly appeased, and the scientists launched into a detailed discussion as to when they might be able to provide a prototype gadget and how they would test it. At first people were hesitant to speak. But slowly, they began contributing ideas until, at one point, with the exception of Hyon-hui who remained silent, they seemed to actually have fun. Something Mitch had never seen any of them do before.

Foremost on everyone's mind was when would enough uranium-233 be available to make a bomb? There were more practical questions as well. How long would it take to measure the cross sections and neutron spectrum of the uranium-233? When would the high explosive implosion system be ready? How long would it take to develop the new diagnostics for G and X divisions. Would they use boosting or a modulated neutron initiator?

They went clear through lunch when Mitch's stomach growled and he suspected he was not alone. Since Mitch had arrived at Sagi-dong, at his urging, Pak suspended Kim Jong-il's, 'Let's-eat-two-meals-a-day' program, so lunch was once again legal. The scientists filed out, discussing the program excitedly.

"Well organized," Professor Yang told Mitch, on his way out. "More creativity than I have ever seen from them."

"People will surprise you when you give them the chance," Mitch replied.

Pak stopped next to Professor Yang. "A year is too long," he said. "I want a test by next spring."

Typical, Mitch thought. Los Alamos managers were not much different, so he was already used to dealing with it. "We're going to need at least ten kilograms and it's going to take that long just to get the 233 from Yujin-dong. That pushes things back to June at the earliest. And it's going to take several hundred full-up RaLa shots to get the implosion system tuned." Pak glowered but Mitch ignored it. "There's a lot to be done between now and then. Our simulations need improvement." He caught the sight of Max's face out the corner of his eye. "Theoretical still hasn't found the problem with the neutron velocities."

"Then why," Pak exclaimed, "have you taken everyone off development for the next two months?"

"Comrade Minister," Professor Yang said gently, edging into the space between Mitch and Pak. "I am very much in favor of Comrade Weatherby's plan. Expend resources to build our test infrastructure now in order to reduce development time in the future. We need both the cyclotron and the Van de Graff to measure the cross sections of 233 accurately. Especially the low energy range. So a new tank has to be built for the Van de Graff accelerator for neutrons above one million electron volts. The cyclotron graphite pile needs to be enlarged for thermal studies. The data acquisition network needs to be upgraded for faster response times." Professor Yang put his hand on Pak's shoulder and gently steered him away, still talking.

"We're going to have trouble with him," Mitch muttered to Max.

"Thanks to God for Professor Yang," replied the Russian. Sonny stood to the side, looking on curiously.

"So what's wrong with your neutrons?" asked Sonny.

Max huffed in frustration. "I have been through the equations," he wrung his hands and blurted something in Russian. "Thousands of times! Almost the entire division is working on it! Even Professor Yang. But more axes doesn't always fell the tree faster."

Mitch scratched his head. "I'll try to give it some time but I don't know if –"

"You have enough to do, Dr. Weatherby," said Sonny. "Perhaps I could look at it."

Sonny was a brilliant, if somewhat inexperienced physicist, so Mitch okayed the request. Besides, he was right.

"And while you're at it," Mitch leaned in close, "any idea what happened to Comrade Chun?" She was only now struggling out of her chair, shunned as usual by everyone.

Max shrugged. "Perhaps she's sick."

"She wasn't at Friday labor yesterday," added Sonny. "We usually work in the library."

So that was it, Mitch thought to himself. Firing Jun-mo. Insulting him. Installing Hyon-hui. The bastards. "You all take off. I think I know what happened."

Hyon-hui was just pushing herself up on unsteady legs when Mitch got to her side. "Miss Chun. You okay?"

"I thought you were leaving with Max," she snarled, but it seemed forced. It always seemed forced.

"As chief scientist, I'm interested in knowing what's going on with my division leads. Are you sick?"

From the look on her face, she seemed ashamed of something. "*No!*" she spat, but didn't stop. "I am not sick."

"Sit down," Mitch said.

She ignored him and kept shuffling toward the door.

"*Please.*"

Her eyes began to flame but Mitch ignored them.

"*An-ja-se-yo*," he said firmly and made his way around the table and pulled a chair out for her. That his Korean was getting better seemed to make her angry. Nevertheless, she sat down and Mitch pushed her chair back in, trapping her. "Now," he said plainly. "I can't have my division leaders in a catatonic state. So what happened?"

She said something under her breath.

"What?"

"Friday labor," she said again.

"Sonny – I mean, Sun-gun said you didn't make Friday labor yesterday."

She hung her head all the more. "I have been reassigned to the collective farm."

"*You* were out there yesterday?" exclaimed Mitch, remembering the hunched over forms of the workers, knee deep in mud from dawn to dusk.

"Yes."

"Is this because of me? Because I replaced Kim Jun-mo?" She didn't answer. "Well who reassigned you?" Still she said nothing. Just stared at her hands. Mitch remembered Pak's look when Hyon-hui came in. "Did Pak have something to do with it?" More silence, though her expression changed. "Aren't you going to let me help you?"

"I don't need help from a *yang-kee*," she snarled.

"Okay, then, you can go." She started to get up. "But you have to go home."

"*What?*"

Mitch knew that many of these scientists were already malnourished from the ongoing famine. This kind of exhaustion, with their third-world sanitation, could easily push Hyon-hui's compromised immune system over the edge. "I said, go home. If you don't get some rest, you're going to get sick. So go home, and get some rest. By Monday, you'll be ready to work again. And by Friday, I'll have this whole thing taken care of."

"You shall not tell me what to do!"

Mitch bent low over her shoulder. This was the closest he'd been to a woman in a long time. Remembering his wealth of programmed buttons, his resolve stiffened and he whispered into her ear. "If I see you up here again, before Monday, I'm gonna tell Pak that I heard you calling Kim Il-sung a son-of-a-bitch." She went pale and her lips trembled. Mitch found the response amazing. And sad. But useful. "Good," he whispered. "We understand one another. Wait here."

Ten minutes later he was back with a guard who he bribed to drive her home in one of the golf cart-like buggies used by security. Hyon-hui opposed him at every step, but by the time he had her seated, he could tell her wrath was even more forced than usual. Mitch's anger was not. He was going to find the bastard that had done this and make sure it didn't happen again.

Mitch found Pak in the cafeteria eating with Professor Yang and a cadre of assorted hangers on. "Why has Miss Chun been moved to the collective farm?" Mitch asked as he walked up. Everyone stopped eating and stared at him. Mitch felt his face flush but it wasn't from embarrassment.

"Why would I know?" Pak shrugged and scooped a pile of red kimchi into his mouth. "Perhaps the peasant woman prefers her own kind?"

Mitch ignored the insult. "I think it may be politically motivated."

Professor Yang seemed to tense. Pak's lackeys grew visibly uncomfortable. "Political motivations are of prime concern in the DPRK," said Pak.

"I think it may have something to do with her replacement of Kim Jun-mo as head of X. Or maybe something else. Perhaps you know something she might have gotten into trouble for?"

"Dr. Weatherby," Pak replied, an icy quality entering his voice. "This is a Korean Workers' Party issue. If Miss Chun has been under-performing perhaps she is being given a warning. It is no business of yours."

"I guess you're right," Mitch said offhandedly, remembering Pak's buttons as well. "I could care less about Comrade Chun. But –" he paused for an instant, "I thought you might."

Pak looked from side to side to his buddies and smiled. "Why would I care about what happens to Comrade Chun?"

"Well everything we do depends on perfecting the implosion system. And she's the only one around here who *really* understands this stuff. If she's sick, or exhausted, she can't work on it, and we'll all be in Sagi-dong that much longer."

Pak's smile disappeared. "You're saying it will push back the schedule?"

Mitch tried to look like he didn't care. "Christmas. At the earliest.

"Christmas?"

Mitch had forgotten they didn't know what Christmas was. "December."

"*Six months?*"

Mitch nodded and stood up. "I've heard it's cold here in winter."

"Dr. Weatherby!" spat Pak.

Mitch whipped back around. "Sir?"

"I would be careful if I were you. We are not Americans. Intimidation will not work on us."

"This isn't intimidation. Americans don't work that way."

"No?" Pak fired back. "Then exactly what are you trying to say, Dr. Weatherby?"

Mitch's jaw tightened as he stared into Pak's eyes. "Simply this. There are things to be done and any scientist who is tired or sick will make it take longer. It isn't a threat, but merely a question." Mitch paused as the tension in the room rose. "How long to you want to be in Sagi-dong, Comrade?" he asked, before turning on his heels and striding out.

10

Mitch drew two circles on the chalkboard, one inside the other. "This," he said, pointing at the smaller circle, "is the pit. A subcritical sphere fissionable by slow neutrons: plutonium-239, U-235, U-233, whatever. For tomorrow's test it's going to be an aluminum sphere a few inches across. And this," he now pointed at the outer, bumpy circle, "is our layer of high explosive lenses. When the H-E is detonated," he drew another diagram, "it crushes the pit." He clapped his hands together and the fifty or so scientists in their standard conference room jumped. "Reducing its size by about eighty percent. The density goes up and the pit becomes highly supercritical." He drew a third picture. "Not for long, generally less than ten microseconds. But that's long enough to spawn a hundred generations of neutrons and liberate a few hundred kilotons of energy. Boom."

"Implosion," Pak replied as if he understood it well. "Simple." Mitch knew enough to be cautious in his reply. It was late summer now, and in the weeks since reorganizing the project, they'd made excellent progress, with all the top scientists, including Hyon-hui, assigned easy Friday Labor duties. But the Theoretical Division was still no closer to solving its problems with the neutron diffusion model, and even if they had, Mitch didn't want Pak expecting everything to continue to go so smoothly.

"It's not   simple," Mitch told Pak. "It'll only work if the collapse is spherical and symmetric. And that's *not* simple. The pit must collapse as a perfect sphere. Perfect. If it doesn't, you're going to fizzle. So if all the detonators don't go off within a few nanoseconds of one another, the collapsing shock will be unsymmetric and the pit will not collapse."

"A billionth of a second," Pak said slowly. "It amazes me that we can even measure something that fast. But Juche does allow greatness."

Mitch wanted to roll his eyes at the mention of Juche, but he smiled instead. He did that a lot, and reminded himself that putting up with that nonsense was better than getting raped in prison. "And our design has thirty-two separate lens elements. So that's thirty-two separate detonators and thirty-two separate wires. And if the lens shapes aren't correct to within micrometer accuracy, or the explosives aren't absolutely pure and homogeneous in the parts per billion range, or if anything is off by the least little bit even if it's a symmetric collapse, it won't be spherical and we won't see any compression. So we need to test it and see if it works. The problem is, everything interesting happens inside an opaque, expanding cloud of detonating high explosive and there's really no way to look inside it. Which is why we use radiolanthanum. This is more a test of the RaLa method than a test of the implosion system because we won't see symmetry *or* compression tomorrow."

"The detonation system has been developed using Juche principles," Hyon-hui sniffed from the other end of the table. "Our computer simulations are in excellent agreement with our two-dimensional lens tests and the tests of our individual three dimensional lenses show uniform, spherical wave fronts emerging from the lens bases. There is no reason that it shouldn't work."

"Nevertheless –" Mitch replied, ignoring her indignation, " – explosives behave quite differently in a system than they do individually."

"We have utilized only Juche methods in our design and all of our technicians have the proper revolutionary spirit and a strong socialist red-flag ideology. It will work."

Mitch smiled. "Glad to hear it." He glanced at Pak. "But from what Professor Yang's told me, there haven't been any full-up tests like this in a while, and those were inconclusive since the response time of the detectors was too slow. The implosion system is the hardest thing to get right. First we'll try to get symmetry, then we'll go after compression. So when we have a successful RaLa test, the rest is details."

"The first pancake is always a blob," said Max and everybody glared at him. "Everyone knows that. It always takes... a..." his voice trailed off. "The first pancake?" Then he frowned.

"I get it," said Mitch, and looked down the table at the head of R-Division's Instrumentation Group. "Mr. Ri, how are the new gamma-ray detectors?"

Ri Chun-sop's accent was thicker than most. He was virtually incomprehensible. "They... okay, Comrade. We calibrate all using Cobalt-60 source. Response time, zero point two microseconds. Counting yield, about one hundred twenty to one. Install counters at RaLa site this morning. Will calibrate for uniformity with one hundred forty tomorrow."

"Very well. Mr. Kim, is the lanthanum extraction ready to go?"

From the other end of the table, Kim Dae-jung, group leader for CM-Division's Radiochemistry and Source Preparation, nodded in the affirmative. "Yes, Comrade Doctor. The barium chloride arrived from Yongbyon last night. The amount of iron and phosphorus is higher than we would like. Probably from irradiation of stainless steel bottle. I tell them use nickel bottle but they not listen. Might slow down rate of precipitation."

"Well it is what it is. Sonny, any changes since we talked yesterday?" Kim Sun-gun was heading up the radiolanthanum test procedure.

"No, Comrade. The aluminum pit was delivered from CM-5 today and we'll pack it in explosives tomorrow morning. We are ready to pwn."

Mitch smiled at his attempt. "Any problems?"

"I still don't like the tool for inserting the screw. We tested it again this morning and made some modifications but..." he shook his head. "Nobody could get it screwed in in under two minutes. We're going to have to come up with something better."

Mitch agreed with a nod. "Not acceptable. A kilocurie source would kill someone." He thought about canceling the test but they had all worked so hard to get this far. "If it comes to it," he said instead, "I'll screw the thing in by hand, myself.

"Miss Chun," Mitch motioned toward where she was sitting across from him, "X-Division's implosion system?"

She just glared at him.

"Okay then. Miss Chun here says the implosion system's ready to go so this time tomorrow, we can start thinking about designing the pit."

It was almost time for their study sessions as they got up to leave, but Hyon-hui stopped him by the door. "You yang-kees are so arrogant," she spat, obviously trying to attract attention to her revolutionary zeal. "How you can be so certain that my Juche design will fail must be a result of your imperialistic, racist tendencies. Always, you Americans are thinking you are superior in every way."

Mitch endured her attacks on a daily basis and usually ignored them just to save himself the trouble. But he was in no mood to take her 'red-flag' ideology today. "Miss Chun, my certainty that *our* implosion system's gonna fail has nothing to do with America or North Korea or politics in any way. It's based on my experience that these things simply don't work right the first hundred times. Theory, component testing, and simulation are helpful, but in the end, the final designs are always cut-and-try. Like Max said, the first pancake is always a blob." Even as he said it, he realized he'd been too polite again, just inviting the counterattack.

"North Korea?" she said disdainfully. "As if there is a South Korea? There is just one Korea, Dr. Weatherby. *One!* Why you legitimize the puppet regime of capitalist flunkies is beyond my capacity to understand. And to insult me by doing so in this way? Are all Americans such barbaric racists that they have no civility? Is this why you still keep slaves?"

"Slaves?" Mitch laughed, amazed at how her conversations would wander suddenly into totally unrelated areas. He considered explaining how slavery had been abolished over one hundred fifty years ago when he realized there might be a better approach. "Racist, Miss Chun? In all the time I've known you, have you," he looked around the room, "or anyone here – ever heard me make a negative statement about Koreans, North or South?" He paused for a moment but she didn't reply. "Or a racist statement of any kind? At the same time, every statement I have heard *you* make about Americans is nothing but racist. So who is the racist, Miss Chun? Me? Or you?"

"Ah! See. You now think all Koreans are racists!"

"Unbelievable," Mitch grumbled and started to turn away.

"That is the way of Americans and all imperialists," she cried to everyone else, but they all turned away. "When they are wrong, they attack. Attack! Attack! Attack! I will not play this imperialist game! And tomorrow – tomorrow we will demonstrate the superiority of the Juche Idea!" She turned and stormed out.

"*Bitch!*" Mitch snapped at her long black ponytail.

Max came alongside him, an unlit cigarette hanging to his lips. "She is making her bed carefully," he said. "Tomorrow she will lie upon it." He flipped open the top of his lighter and it started playing a cheesy, electronic tune.

Mitch jumped. "What the crap is that?"

Max hurriedly lit his cigarette and snapped the lid closed, cutting off the sound with a smirk. Mitch stood staring at him. He puffed to get the fire going, then said sheepishly, "Song of General Kim Il-sung." He held up the lighter and there on the side was a picture of the dearly departed Party Chairman. "My old lighter failed. It was between this one, and the Kim Jong-il variety."

Mitch laughed. "Yeah. They're all pretty ugly if you ask –"

"*Never*," exclaimed Lee, coming up behind him. "Never insult the Great Leader again!"

Mitch's face went hot with embarrassment. "What? What did I do?"

Lee glared at Mitch angrily and everyone stared at them. "He is the greatest man who ever lived," growled Lee. "And I will not allow him to be spoken of in that fashion. Do you understand?"

"So you glorify him on a lighter?"

"*Do you understand?*" Lee snapped louder this time.

"Yeah. I guess so."

"I demand an immediate apology."

"An apology?"

"*Apologize!*" snapped Lee.

Mitch glanced at Max. "Is he kidding?"

"Don't make an elephant out of a fly, Mitch," said the Russian cautiously.

These proverbs of Max's were getting a little old, but the meaning of this one was clear enough. "Okay. Uh, I'm sorry. Just a little humor about Max's lighter."

"Many things are the subject of *jokes*," Lee said menacingly. "The Great Leader, Comrade Generalissimo Kim Il-sung is not one of them. Ever. *Ever!*"

Mitch strode down the long, dark tunnel to Test Site One on the East side of Wagal Peak. The entire mountain was honeycombed with old mining tunnels. Behind him two technicians pulled an old mine cart along at the end of a fifty foot rope. Geiger counters popped, and crackled, and echoed down the tunnel. The technicians tried to look brave but each time the detectors burst into static they winced.

"Don't worry boys," Mitch said pleasantly. "We're far enough away." But it didn't convince them.

The RaLa firing site was in a deep hollow on the east side of Wagal Peak, above Lake Nangnim, sparkling far below. To the south was the Chosin Reservoir, mostly hidden behind a spur of the hills. To the east and north lay rugged mountains as far as the eye could see. A haze born of late summer and the humidity of monsoon rains hung over the land giving everything a smoky look. As they emerged from the tunnel, the early September sun beat down mercilessly, and flies and mosquitoes buzzed in the sticky air.

The cart creaked to a stop beneath a heavy wooden A-frame and, with a block and tackle, the technicians raised the 300 pound lead container that held the barium-140. The stuff had only a twelve day half-life and produced a steady stream of powerful gamma-rays. A piece the size of a grain of sand could kill a man in a few hours.

One of the technicians pulled the lead crucible beneath a covered pavilion that was separated into two halves by a thick concrete wall that ran down the middle. On one side were glass beakers pre-filled with reagents, a centrifuge, and other lab implements. On the other were levers, buttons, switches and several television monitors, looking suspiciously like a chemical separation facility described in great detail in a Los Alamos Technical Report from the forties that had been briefly declassified and placed online during the Clinton Administration.

Mitch, Max, Professor Yang, Sonny and the others watched from a distance while the chemists, working safely behind the concrete wall, separated the radioactive lanthanum from the barium. They started with a thick, greenish syrup. An hour later they had a fine, white, lanthanum powder they compressed into a tiny pellet no larger than a BB.

A wiry technician emerged from the shelter holding the tiny lanthanum source tip suspended at the end of what they called, the 'fishing pole.' He placed it inside an ionization chamber to be assayed and the tall technician took the reading from a meter.

"One hundred twenty-seven curies," he announced.

Further down the dell, a circular concrete pad about twenty feet across formed the actual test site. Spaced evenly around its perimeter were eight, thick concrete posts, like the *changsung* at the mouth of the valley except that each of these held a gamma-ray detector. Over the center of the pad a dark-gray ball about a foot across sat atop a short post. Its surface was tiled with the diamond-shaped fast explosive lenses of the implosion system. Several of the lenses were missing from the top, revealing the shiny aluminum pit resting at the center like a cybernetic brain. A mass of detonation wires sprouted from the ball like hair and were gathered together into a thick, multicolored bundle that draped to the ground and disappeared into a steel pipe.

The concept behind this kind of test was, like the concept for the weapon itself, fairly simple. The radioactive lanthanum in the exact center of the aluminum pit emitted gamma radiation evenly in all directions. So the detectors placed around the test site, since they were evenly spaced, were all receiving the exact same amount of radiation. But when it was detonated, the aluminum pit in the center would be crushed. As it collapsed and the density of the aluminum increased for a few milliseconds, the amount of radiation absorbed by the pit would increase so the detectors would record less radiation. If it collapsed evenly, the amount of radiation emitted would decrease smoothly and all the detectors would record the same amount. If it didn't collapse evenly each of the detectors would capture a different record.

For now, a lead-impregnated curtain shielded the front of the gadget. With the help of a mirror, the two technicians had already lowered the lanthanum pellet into a small hole drilled in the top of the pit and were reaching over the curtain, trying to start the screw that was to plug the hole.

"You were right about that tool, Sonny," Mitch said, watching them struggle with the unwieldy implement. Behind him, everyone gasped when, without warning, the taller technician reached in and started the screw with his fingers.

"No!" Mitch exclaimed. "Son, get that idiot out of here. He's just pegged his exposure for the year. Hyon-hui, he's yours."

"That's too bad," replied Sonny. "He was one of our best lab techs."

After the screw was in, Hyon-hui came forward and gently tapped the last few dull, gray lenses into place.

Mitch pulled out a long checklist and carefully marked off the items one by one.

The scientists and technicians retreated up the tunnel to a hollowed-out chamber into which the recording equipment and test electronics had been stuffed. At present, it contained considerably more people than it had been designed to hold and the odor did more than just tickle Mitch's nose.

"What took so long," Pak snapped when they arrived.

"The stainless steel bottle," replied Mitch. "The phosphorus in the steel combines with lanthanum to make lanthanum phosphate, which in a water solution forms a thick gel. It makes filtering the precipitate slow. They were supposed to ship in a nickel bottle but they ignored it." Pak just grunted. Mitch always over explained everything to Pak so he would stop asking questions. It always worked, just like a Los Alamos.

"Okay," Mitch said. He was a lot more nervous than he liked to admit, even to himself. "Checklist complete?" he asked.

Hyon-hui handed him a clipboard. He looked it over, signed off on it, then handed it to Professor Yang who put his signature on it, too.

"Comrade Chun, arm the circuit," Mitch said, to Hyon-hui.

She carefully armed the firing circuits and checked the voltage on the capacitor bank. "Charged," she said, and glared at him.

Her steely glare calmed him. He almost hoped the test would fail. "O'scopes ready to trigger?" He asked Sonny.

The young engineer glanced at each of the indicators "Triggers ready."

"Detectors?"

"Uniform," Sonny replied, checking gauges hooked directly to each of them.

"I'm going to count backward from ten," Mitch said, sensing the hesitation. "When I get to zero, you push the button Comrade Chun. Okay?"

Hyon-hui nodded. "Okay, Dr. Weatherby." Sweat was beaded across her smooth forehead.

Mitch opened his mouth to say 'ten' when Pak blurted out, "For Choson and the Great Leader Comrade Generalissimo Kim Il-sung!" For an instant everyone just stared at him.

"Right…" Mitch said. "Ten… nine… eight…"

Hyon-hui wiped a bead of sweat from her forehead. Max closed his eyes.

"Seven… six… five…" Pak licked his lips expectantly. Professor Yang covered his ears.

"Four… three… two…" Mitch crossed his fingers.

"One…zero!"

Hyon-hui's finger pressed down on the big red button.

Whoom! The muffled sound of the blast reverberated up the long dark tunnel. Dust popped from the floor and detached from the ceiling to drift slowly through the room. Everyone stared intently at the small, blue, oscilloscope screens as they drew their captured images from memory. Everyone stared but they said nothing.

"What? What is it?" exclaimed Pak. "Was it a success?"

Mitch glanced at Hyon-hui but what he saw gave him no pleasure, as he felt the excitement drain from the chamber.

"Pwned?" said Sonny gloomily.

"No symmetry," Mitch said, leaning in to point at the scopes. "If it had been symmetric, all the traces would look the same since the gamma rays coming from the radiolanthanum at the center would be uniformly attenuated by the isotropically compressed pit material. You can see here, they don't. And see how all the traces drop off at twelve microseconds? That means the pit was destroyed and the lanthanum dispersed across the site. If the implosion is highly symmetric, the pit usually stays in one piece. This high signal here on seven is probably a lanthanum particle deposited on the sensor window. Should fade in a day or two. We'll have to analyze the data to determine the detector simultaneity though just looking at it here, it seems to be quite good."

Pak was glaring murderously at Hyon-hui who glanced about like a cat thrown into traffic.

"And," Mitch went on, standing up straight and brightening his tone – this needed damage control, fast – "it also means that our RaLa diagnostic works. Well done Miss Chun. Good job people. Good test. Good test. Like a well oiled machine. Can't wait for the next one." The dozen scientists and technicians crowded into the room didn't know whether to smile or cry, and from the look on Pak's face Mitch knew they were about to get chewed out.

"Comrade Chun's implosion system has failed?" he growled as if on cue.

"It's our first pancake," Mitch replied. "The diagnostic worked. Nobody got hurt. That's a success."

"She *has* failed," Pak shouted, his face grim and condemning. "*Failed us all!* Failed to apply the Juche method. Months of work and millions wasted! Through," he waved his hand in her direction, "gross incompetence by this half-breed!" Hyon-hui's head dropped. Everyone else looked away, motionless and silent.

Mitch held his emotions in check. "Look, I told you that the first implosion systems were going to fail. It's an iterative process. It isn't an exact science. And it doesn't respect ideology."

Pak glared at Mitch. "Can you write a report that makes this look like a success?" he asked. "Despite Comrade Chun's failure? One that I can send to P'yongyang?"

"It *was* a success," Mitch asserted. "Just getting eight o-scopes to trigger together is a challenge!" He knew that he was protecting Hyon-hui, but he also knew that he was telling the truth. They had met all their objectives.

"Just make sure you don't mention this half-breed in the report," Pak snarled, shot a poisonous look at Hyon-hui, and stalked out.

"Outstanding work everyone," Mitch announced, slapping backs and intentionally overdoing it. "Outstanding. Make sure that data gets recorded. Get your reports in by tomorrow afternoon so we can post 'em on the network. No later! And everybody needs to read 'em! Everybody. Good job."

Mitch found himself alone for the long walk back up the tunnel. Everyone else had gone already, scurrying off to prepare their reports. In the solitude came memories of Los Alamos and his old life. Celebrating accomplishments, even minor ones with friends and colleagues. Going home afterward to his warm home and lovely wife. But that was no more. He was here, alone, condemned to this hell hole for the rest of his life. Anger and despair swept through him like a storm.

He stopped at the sound of a shuffle in the gloom. There next to the track was Hyon-hui, standing at a dim spot between light bulbs. Mitch stiffened, knowing she'd probably picked this spot to lie in wait and accuse him of sabotage.

"What do you want?" he said in a baneful tone.

"I," she began, not meeting his stare, "I wanted to apologize for my behavior yesterday. It was inappropriate and counterproductive."

Mitch's eyebrows raised, but he was in no mood to talk. "Thanks," he said simply and started back up the tunnel.

"Dr. Weatherby," she said again in a softer voice. Despite himself, he turned back toward her and saw an expression that had never graced her face before, at least not around him. "Why do you do this for me?" Her green eyes sparkled like emeralds in the half-darkness, and his anger faded. "You make me a division leader. An opportunity not often granted to a, a non-Party member and, a woman. You had me moved back to the library for Friday labor. You do this even though I do not treat you well. And today, you defend me before Comrade Minister Pak. I do not understand why you do this."

"Well," he stammered, trying to figure out exactly why he was helping her. At the very least, it was the way he'd been raised. It was the Golden Rule he'd learned as a child. The way, he'd been told, Christians were supposed to act, though seldom did. But how could he explain that to her? He couldn't even get a Bible, and wasn't sure he wanted one anyway. "You are the most qualified," he finally said. "There's a job to be done. And I don't see that it would help if I answered your belligerence with more of the same. Sort of like the way our two countries have acted over the past half century. Maybe if one had responded to threats with something other than threats, things might be different." His stomach growled loudly, in protest to the dwindling protein of their diets, and he grinned. "And then, maybe, we wouldn't be so hungry this afternoon. Good test," he told her again, and headed up the tunnel, once again alone.

11

Mitch looked at his plate in disgust. Among the tendrils of pickled, peppered cabbage lay dismembered, suction-cupped tentacles each about the size of a pinky. He fought to maintain his appetite as he looked up at Max.

"Better than *Pizza Hut* in Moscow, eh?" Max said sarcastically and swallowed one of the rubbery octopus tentacles whole.

"You know, Max," Mitch sighed. "If I had just gone to prison, I'd be eatin' good today. Have cable TV. A hot shower twice a week. Shame. But those dang gooks just had to have my help."

Max chuckled as he picked up a a stiff, roll-like thing and rapped it against the table. "Have you noticed? The bread tastes like sawdust."

"And the consistency of a block of wood. I've noticed."

The American and the Russian, artifacts of a Cold War in which neither had participated, sat surrounded by propaganda posters and other scientists and technicians, eating their kimchi and rice in it's last conflict. Sipping green tea. Soup had recently been banned from their diet by Kim Jong-il on advice from Party leaders that it caused more frequent trips to the bathroom and a related decrease in productivity.

"Do they have to make it so hot?" asked Mitch, fanning his mouth as he swallowed the mouthful of pickled cabbage.

"Burns at both ends doesn't it?" the Russian chuckled.

Mitch patted his stomach. "I bet I've lost fifteen pounds since I got here."

Max held out his hands where his gut used to be. "At Arzamas-16 they would not recognize me now. They would think I was a prisoner from the Great Patriotic War!"

"I'd just like to get some decent food," said Mitch. "Some wholesome, substantial food." His eyes glistened. "A peanut butter and jelly sandwich." Then they went flat. "Kimchi and rice. Gets a bit dull even if it promotes," he squelched a burp, "active bowels."

"What is wrong with our food?" came Hyon-hui's voice from behind. "Always it is something with you."

Mitch stood up. "Please, sit down, Comrade Chun," he said with overt pleasantness. They'd sat together almost every day since the first RaLa test. And argued. This, Mitch knew, was the reject table, even if Hyon-hui didn't even realize it. She thought she was getting brownie points for confronting the imperialist bastard, but he and Max were the only people who would talk to her.

"Why do you stand when I sit down or enter a room?" she asked. Of course, her questions were just more accusations.

"Just the way I was raised," Mitch said, picking at his food. "A man stands when a lady enters a room. And if there aren't enough seats, he gives up his own."

"Women in your country are not even allowed to vote."

Mitch didn't even raise his head. "Whatever."

Hyon-hui gave Mitch a defiant, "Humph!"

Max kicked him under the table and when Mitch looked at him, he tossed his head in her direction and winked.

Mitch flushed. "Max! Not now," he hissed.

"I must go," the Russian announced suddenly, rising to his feet. "I have efficiency simulation running in three dimensions. And high hopes for a solution."

"Ah!" Mitch started to get up. "I'll give –"

"No, no, no," urged Max. "Finish your meal. You can stop by when you are done. Besides, I must first visit bathroom."

"Hope everything comes out all right."

"Yes, the simulation –" Max stopped and his eyes suddenly sparkled. "Ah, you make a joke." He turned and bounced off.

Mitch sat hunched over his tray, picking at his cabbage and tentacles. "Miss Chun," he finally grumbled, "I know you're trying to get into the Party so you've got to be all anti-American, but I'm going to spell it out for you as plain as I can." He looked her in the eye and spoke quietly. "You're not fooling anyone. The rest of these guys are laughing at you behind your back. You wanna rip the U.S., you go right ahead, but don't do it around me, 'cause you sound like a fool."

She stared right back, unblinking. "If America is such a wonderful place and North Korea is so terrible, why did you leave? Why don't you just go back to the family you abandoned you imperialist pig!"

Mitch stared for a moment as her words burned into him, then he dropped his head. "I have no family to go back to," he said quietly, almost to himself. "My wife was murdered by the government. We had no children." Tears of rage and grief welled up in his eyes as fast as he could wipe them out, and he was powerless to stop them. How had this happened? Why was he here, arguing with this Korean scientist who hated everything about him for no reason. He leaned over his kimchi and fought to master himself. "Just get the hell away from me," he choked out.

He thought she had left from the silence. He wiped his eyes again, knowing he looked like a fool, and knowing there was no one here that cared, when a voice said softly. "I am sorry, Dr. Weatherby. I did not know." She was still here.

"It doesn't matter anymore," he growled, "I've got nothing."

"Dr. Weatherby," she said more insistently but in that same gentle voice. "I am sorry. You will come to my home tonight. My mother and I will cook you a meal that may be more to your liking."

He glanced up to see if it was a joke or a trap, then looked back down, embarrassed by his bleary eyes. "I, I don't know what to say."

"Say, yes. It is my way of thanking you. For everything you've done for me. Could you arrive at my house at eight-thirty?"

He nodded. "Yes."

"Will Major Lee be coming?" she asked.

Mitch shook his head. "He's in Kanggae for the week."

"Then, I will see you at eight-thirty," she confirmed, then rose and walked away.

*

"How'd the sim turn out?" Mitch asked.

Max didn't answer immediately but typed a few key strokes and hit the 'enter' key. "What kept –" He pulled up short. "Comrade?"

"Please don't call me that, Max."

"You look sort of, pale."

"Well," Mitch began, feeling a little funny. "I, uh – Miss Chun and I had a discussion on philosophy, or ideology, or –" he frowned. "Something."

"Well, I know how that turned out."

"No. She, uh," he scratched his head. "She invited me to dinner with her and her mother tonight."

Max's eyes shot opened and appeared even larger magnified by his thick glasses. "Asked *you* to dinner?"

"Yeah. At her house."

"Are you going to go? Because if you don't I will be glad to take your place."

"Well, of course I'm going. You kidding? She said she was going to cook for me!"

"This is weird, Mitch. Something is not right here. Perhaps it is some kind of a trap by the SSA or something? The KGB used to do that sort of thing. A loyalty test of some kind. How did this happen?"

"I don't know. We were arguing one minute." He stepped in to Max's office and sat down. "She called me an imperialist pig. I told her to shut up." He skipped the part about his momentary breakdown. "Next thing I knew, she's inviting me to dinner." Mitch paused, thinking. "You know, Max," he continued, "I think she works at looking *hard*. I think she could be a lot prettier than she is."

"Comrade?" Max's tone suggested much.

"Give me a break," Mitch retorted. "It's just dinner. She just… has a nice smile, that's all."

"Well, I have never seen her smile. But her legs make me smile."

Mitch snorted. "I just don't know what to think. And stop calling me comrade. I hate it when people call me that."

"Russians smile always. It's a choice. One of the few things we have that our government can't take away… comrade."

"Speakin' of what we have left, what do we have? How'd the sim turn out."

Max rubbed his forehead. "The same."

"We have to get this thing working. We're gonna really need it soon."

Max shrugged. "Yes, the scythe has hit a stone."

"Where do you get all these proverbs?" Mitch exclaimed. "I feel like I'm talking to a Chinese sage."

Max laughed. "My grandmother. She was very wise. But she had to be."

Mitch leaned back in his chair and rubbed his own temples. "Okay. Let's back up. We got a neutron velocity problem. We know that. Things are going too fast. So what have we checked?"

"Everything," Max exclaimed. "You and I. In this same office."

"Well then, let's go over it again."

So they rolled up their sleeves and delved into the equations, going in detail over Max's notes, sifting through every derivation, backtracking to first principles.

"Where'd you get that equation?" Mitch asked three hours later. His finger stabbed at a long, complicated series of numbers and symbols scrawled in Max's notes and on the board.

"What, this one? The multi-velocity equation?"

"Yeah. It looks… I don't know. Where'd it come from?"

Max looked at the notation in his notebook, then went over to his filing cabinet and emerged with a stapled report. He handed it to Mitch.

"Multi-Velocity Kim-Bok Neutron Diffusion Calculations? Atomic Energy Research Institute, Yongbyon 1984." Mitch flopped it open and scanned through it, then stopped cold. "Yongbyon my ass. This is one of those POOP Division makeovers."

"You recognize it?" Max asked.

"It's a Los Alamos technical report from the early fifties. They must have downloaded it when it was declassified. Supposed to be

'Multi-Velocity *Serber-Wilson* Neutron Diffusion Calculations.' Bob Serber was one of the unsung heroes of the Manhattan Project." He flipped to the bibliography and scanned it and began shaking his head. "Bogus. All bogus."

"Check my equation. Maybe there's a problem with it!"

Mitch thumbed through the document until he came to the equation in question, a complicated, four term expression. Along with other formulas and parameters, it made up part of an iterative algorithm that could be used to predict the distribution of neutron velocities given a specific set of initial conditions. Mitch stared at it, comparing it with the equations that came before and after, flipping backward a few pages, then forward. Reading, then scanning. Finally he shook his head and flipped the document to Max. "It's wrong," he said in disgust. "The third term should be negative."

"Wrong!" Max rifled through the pages for himself. He finally looked up, embarrassed. "I'm sorry, Mitch. I should have caught that."

Mitch just shook his head, stunned, but not surprised. "Not your fault, Maxim. Not your fault. No reason for you to suspect there was an error. You're not supposed to have to rederive equations in peer-reviewed papers." His voice rose dramatically as the futility of this overwhelmed him. "That's their point. But when those morons in POOP were Juche-fying it, they transcribed the stupid thing wrong! Cost us – what's today?"

Max looked at his calendar. "September 12."

"Cost us five months. *Five Months!* That's Juche for you!"

They sat there stewing. Both of them. Mitch glanced at his watch then rose to his feet. "I'm going to go tell Professor Yang about this before he bugs out." The last few words rolled off his tongue in increasing derision.

"So what time is dinner?" Max asked.

"Eight-thirty. I don't know these people. Except that they're idiots. Anything special that I should, or shouldn't, do? Don't want to offend anyone."

Max shrugged. "I don't know them, either."

"I don't even know if it's a 'date' or what?"

"You could ask Professor Yang."

"I'm not gonna ask him. He's like her dad or something."

"Well," speculated Max, "it is not typical for a man to be asked to the home of a woman. Even in Moscow. Perhaps even in America? I don't know Korean dating. And what is a date for us might not be a date for a normal person. You can know only after you get there. If she has made herself beautiful, it is a date. If not, it is just dinner."

"Well then I guess I'll find out. Don't wait up for me." He disappeared out the door but a second later, he was back. "Where does Comrade Chun live?"

12

It was a drippy late summer walk. Puddles and little creeks had turned the roadsides to mud. One look at the collective farm and Hyon-hui's heart sank. The rice that she'd worked so hard to plant during her brief time assigned there was mostly washed away. The same thing must be happening all over Choson. How could this happen? What was wrong with the Juche principles that they couldn't stop the predictable monsoons from destroying their source of food?

She stopped in her tracks and glanced furtively around, worried that those around could see the thoughts in her head. *This* was why she wasn't a Party member, she scolded herself. She tried to keep her thinking pure. To maintain nothing but the proper Juche ideals in her head. She knew, from the time she was a small child, that those principles were the pinnacle of mankind's accomplishments. Yet all too often, a bad thought would creep in. A question. She shook her head quickly to knock it away. She must try harder. She bent her head lower to the ground and hurried up the road, determined to keep her thoughts pure.

At home, she removed her drenched shoes at the door and looked their home over for neatness. Timeless traditions guaranteed that everything was in order. Still, she straightened a small blanket on the back of the couch, then swept the floor while she hummed the tune to *Sweet Home*. Satisfied, she retrieved twenty Chinese Yuan from the jar. It was much more valuable than North Korean Won and illegal to possess. But everyone had some. She'd been saving hers for six months. She squeezed it in her hand, as questions threatened to rise in her head again. No. This was how everything was done. It must be part of the Great Leader's plan.

She adjusted her government issue, yellow, plastic slicker, and splashed back out into the gray afternoon, making for the state-run food store at the center of the housing area. Inside, samples of everything were on display in glass cases. Rice. Soybean paste. Corn meal. *Kimchi.* Lots of kimchi. Assorted vegetables, all wilted. No meat at all.

"Don't you have anything else?" Hyon-hui asked the grim-faced lady behind the counter.

"Everything we have is what you see," she answered, her eyes glancing off of Hyon-hui's Party pin. Hyon-hui knew all too well the probationary pin had no clout.

"Everything? But there is nothing!" she exclaimed.

"You might have heard," the attendant snapped, "there is a food shortage."

Hyon-hui knew there must be more. Pak and Kim In-taek surely had better fare. Pak was fat and he didn't get that way only by looking down her dresses. Why did they get to... Stop, she ordered herself, taking a deep breath. If only she were a member of the Party she might have more luck. But she had brought the Yuan for a reason and it was time to use it. "Look, I am entertaining a Party cadre tonight," she said quietly after the last customer had left. "He is expecting more than rice and bean paste. And –" she hesitated for a moment. This was new to her but she'd heard rumors of how such transactions happened. "There might be something extra in it for you."

"What do you mean?" It was stern but interested. A practiced response.

"What do you have?"

"Perhaps, your cadre would like a nice, fresh chicken?" the woman whispered.

Hyon-hui hid her excitement with a half-scowl. "That might do. How large?"

"One point three kilos."

"So small? How much do you want for it?"

"One hundred won."

"*One hundred won?!*" Hyon-hui hissed. "For a scrawny bird like that? That is more than a month's wages!"

"One hundred won. And I will include some fresh carrots."

"Three hundred fifty grams of fresh carrots and red peppers," Hyon-hui replied.

"What do you think," the woman responded indignantly, "that I have my own garden? One hundred ten won for the chicken, the carrots, and the red peppers. Two hundred grams of each."

"For one hundred Won, I want three hundred grams of each, the chicken, plus a bouillon cube."

"Three hundred grams?" hissed the woman.

Hyon-hui flashed the Yuan and the woman's eyes followed it. "Three hundred grams of vegetables, the chicken, and a bouillon cube for one hundred twenty Yuan. "That is my final offer."

"Two seventy-five grams."

"Two-eighty."

Her countenance fell but Hyon-hui knew she was doing better in this deal. "Very well." She went into the back and returned with an almost frozen bird with everything except feathers and a head, the carrots, the red peppers, and a bouillon cube. And she threw in a tiny bottle of ginseng extract. The label said it was made in Kaesong and improved virility. Hyon-hui blushed when she read it.

By the time she got home, it was nearly four o'clock and the nightly Juche study session was only an hour away. She prepared the chicken and vegetables for what was one of her favorite dishes, *Sam gae tang*; baked chicken stuffed with rice and carrots in a thin soup. She prepared everything then left a note for her mother to cook it when she got home from the laundry where she worked.

As Hyon-hui walked back through the rain for the fourth time that day, this time joined by Sagi-dong's teeming masses, she found her usual patriotic fires strangely banked. Indeed, the majority of her thoughts were occupied with trying to figure out why she had just spent a month's salary on dinner for a man she barely knew. And an American aggressor at that! Her mind sped through a laundry list of his crimes as defined by the Party. One at a time they shot through her head. Capitalist, imperialist, warmonger, murderer, baby killer. She almost laughed when the last thought took its turn. Dr. Weatherby, a baby killer? It didn't fit.

In the shadow of the guard tower, she halted mid-stride. *The 'Drink-No-Soup' directive!* She was violating it! She turned and started almost running back home. but it was over a half-mile away. She glanced at her watch. She would only be on time at the Juche study center if she turned back for the assembly hall *now*. And tardiness was not tolerated, she turned back toward the center of town. But what if it were discovered that she had made soup? It was well known that the SSA conducted searches when residents were at the study sessions. They might find the soup!

"I'll just tell secretary Kim when I get there," she said aloud, trying to calm her nerves. "I'll just tell him that I forgot. No. He'll ask why I'm cooking. He'll ask where I got the chicken!"

In anguish, she turned back up First Street, "I must get back home and pour out the soup before anyone finds out!" She went three steps, and stopped again. "Sweeps are rare," she said to herself. "It has been nearly a month since I have been inspected." She turned, then stopped again. "But what if the clerk at the store reports the bouillon cube? Or if the SSA walks by and smells the food." A final glance at her watch. There was no time. She whipped around and headed back toward town, knowing this would go on her record. How would she ever get into the Party if she couldn't even follow the Dear Leader's commandments?

The Juche session was typical; punishment and reward. Revolutionary zeal and the scientific theory of Juche, usually Hyon-hui's favorites. But this evening, she couldn't make herself care about Juche at all. And she kept thinking about that American! This was the second time he'd ruined a study session for her. But try as she might, this time, she couldn't get mad about it.

It was quarter-past-eight as she approached her house, and the aroma of chicken was spilling into the street. People stood in their doorways with their noses in the air. She burst through the door and surprised her mother who was standing at the sink.

"Hyon-hui, what is this all about? The chicken? And this note?"

"I can't talk right now." She checked the stove. "Good, you started the chicken cooking. When will it be finished?"

"Are you going to tell me what's going on?"

She glanced at the clock. "I've got to get ready. He'll be here soon!" Hyon-hui rushed into the back, forgetting to remove her shoes, and wondering why her heart was beating so fast.

"Hyon-hui!" her mother followed her, more curious than ever. "What are you talking about? Who is *he?*"

"Mother, will you prepare drinks and set the dinner dishes out? I must get ready. And pour out the soup. I forgot that –"

"I'll do no such thing. That campaign is the stupidest thing I've ever heard."

"Mother!"

"Absolutely not!"

Hyon-hui didn't have time to argue. "Okay. It'll be okay as long as we don't eat it. No rule against making it." She stepped into the bathroom.

"I heard you say *he*," her mother called again.

A moment later, Hyon-hui flung the bathroom door open and flew to the closet. She found a brightly-colored silk dress of a beautiful, deep emerald and put it on, examining herself critically in the small mirror. When she pulled out her mother's makeup, the older woman snatched it out of her hand.

"Hyon-hui, tell me immediately what is happening!"

She stopped for a moment and took a deep breath. "Mother. My supervisor is coming to dinner tonight. I invited him today at lunch. We must receive him with utmost respect. He is the lab director."

The old woman smiled the smile of a mother who had forever feared her daughter would become an old maid, then suddenly finding she is engaged, and assisted with the make up. The two of them stayed busy until there was a knock on the door and they both looked up.

"That's him!" said Hyon-hui excitedly, brushing damp tangles from her long dark tresses. "Get the door!" she hissed to her mother, and ducked into the bathroom.

13

Mitch was apprehensive about bribing the guard but, as Max had pointed out, there was no North Korean phone book. He nervously tapped at the wad of cash in his pocket while he slowed in front of the guard shack at the entrance to the residential area. "Use small bills," Max had told him. "Lots of them."

"*Shin-boon-chung!*" barked the guard. He was the same one who had taken Hyon-hui home from the lab when Mitch had ordered her to rest. He'd seemed like nice guy.

Mitch showed him his identification as he'd requested and said in his best Korean, "*Tong-mu Chun Hyon-hui, a-nae-hal-soo-ee-so-yo?*"

The guard said something Mitch didn't understand, but Mitch was ready for that and showed the guard something he did understand. The cash. Mitch cringed, but the guard took the bills without a word and stuffed them into his pocket. Mitch tried again to ask for directions in Korean but the guard stopped him.

"You little better, but hurts my ears still. Engrish prease!"

Five minutes later, Mitch stood in the rain, facing the dark structure where the guard had directed him. The street was deserted and, but for the number next to the door, the buildings were identical. Like a street from a *Twilight Zone* episode. He sighed. Since he and Max had discovered the source of the neutron velocity error that afternoon, he was less enthusiastic about this 'date' and was looking forward to sticking POOP's bungle in Hyon-hui's face. "What do you think about your cadres now?" he thought to himself. "And the Juche way of doing things?" Maybe even admit that POOP had an entirely different meaning in English. He knocked on the door.

An old woman opened it and bowed low. Mitch knew she must be Hyon-hui's mother as she had the same green eyes and looked even more Caucasian than her daughter.

"*Anniyong hasimnika*," he said with a bow. "Chun Hyon-hui?" he asked loudly.

The old woman frowned and said something in Korean, looking none too friendly. Her face was stern and heavily-lined from a life of hard work. Her long black and gray hair was pulled tight into a bun on the back of her head. Mitch stood uncomfortably, thinking he should turn around and leave, when Hyon-hui appeared. Or someone who looked like Hyon-hui, but not at all the same person.

"Welcome to our home, Dr. Weatherby," Hyon-hui said graciously and bowed low, beckoning him to enter. "This is my mother. Chun Sup-suppie. She does not know any English." She turned to the old woman and introduced Mitch in Korean. He heard the word 'American' and the old woman's eyes grew wide as saucers.

"Pleased to meet you, ma'am," said Mitch with a bow. He noticed Sup-suppie's cotton split-toed slippers and realized he was still wearing his shoes – his muddy shoes – inside their home. "Uh, I'm sorry," he mumbled and slipped his loafers off to rest in a pile in the entryway.

The old woman bowed again, spoke a few words, and went into the kitchen to remove dinner from the oven. Mitch offered to help, and although the older woman couldn't understand him, she waved him away, trying to hide the tears that now wet her cheeks. He shouldn't have come, he thought to himself. He'd been rude and upset Hyon-hui's mother.

Hyon-hui didn't seem to notice. She hung his wet slicker up to dry, distracting Mitch from the woman in the kitchen. He'd always known Hyon-hui had captivating eyes and shapely legs, but this beauty was totally unexpected. He swallowed and held out a small package.

"I brought this for you," he stammered, suddenly nervous. "and your – your mother."

"*Kam-sa-ham-nee-da*." She bowed again, and Mitch wondered if this could be the same woman he'd fought with almost every day.

"Smells good," he said, forcing himself not to stare. "Is that chicken?" His stomach growled as he breathed in the aroma.

"Yes," she laughed, and looked inside the bag to find a bottle of rice wine. "Thank you, Dr. Weatherby." She bowed again and went to pour him a glass. Mitch watched her go, following her bare feet across the floor with his eyes. Thoughts of bringing up POOP evaporated.

He forced his heart to slow a little and explored the room. Though not as well built as his own room, and clearly much older, it had a woman's touch that made it infinitely more livable. He found the pictures of the Kims on the wall, of course, and a large bookcase filled with Party literature from the P'yongyang Publishing House, by the looks of it, well read.

The standard TV – Japanese design and manufacture with a North Korean nameplate and tamper resistant seals – stood against another wall. Mitch had learned from Max that all televisions were modified to receive only authorized frequencies and then sealed. If the SSA found that someone had opened a case during one of their surprise sweeps, bad things happened to them.

Hanging on another wall were pictures of family. A distinguished gent wearing a horsehair hat and smoking a long, thin pipe. Several men wearing the traditional white overcoat or *turumagi* flanked by women in long flowing robes. Youthful photographs of Hyon-hui's mother – who had been beautiful, too – and childhood photos of Hyon-hui. She had looked like a boy. Was even dressed as a boy. Among the photographs was also a faded black and white picture of a Caucasian man wearing the uniform and broad-brimmed hat of a Soviet Army officer.

"My grandfather," Hyon-hui said over his shoulder, startling him. She handed him a glass of wine. "He was a captain in the Red Army. I never knew him."

Mitch took the glass and their fingers touched. Hyon-hui looked away embarrassed. "Dinner is ready," she said and gently led him to the table by his hand.

"It is our custom in the home to bow to the *widaehan suryong* before our meals," said Hyon-hui. The three of them turned and bowed their heads toward the south. When they'd finished, the old woman said something.

"My mother wants to know if you have any such customs in your land?"

Mitch nodded. "Yes ma'am, we did in my home. We pray before meals."

Hyon-hui relayed Mitch's comments, then took some from her mother. "My mother wants to know what is your god called?"

"Called?"

"His name."

"Oh. We, just call him, God."

Hyon-hui translated then replied. "She wants to know," Hyon-hui said, uncomfortably, "if you would do this pray, to this… this, *god.*"

"Okay." Mitch swallowed feeling awkward, knowing he hadn't prayed since that day in the conference room. Physics was his religion now and his political ideology. No interpretation, just logic. It was either correct or incorrect. But how could he say no to this? He took the hands of Hyon-hui and her mother who looked at each other and clasped hands. With bowed head, he muttered a simple prayer which Hyon-hui translated. When finished, Mitch noticed that the green eyes of Hyon-hui's mother were moist again but it didn't seem to be from anger. He remained silent for a moment, feeling the emptiness inside him left by the prayer – or maybe just pointed out by it. A ritual from a former, happier life, but one that made him long to feel connected again.

Mitch enjoyed the dinner even though Hyon-hui kept telling him not to eat the soup, and didn't touch hers. Mitch ate all of his, as did her mother, and couldn't figure out what the problem was. The soup was delicious. The chicken was a bit chewy and Hyon-hui kept apologizing, but Mitch hadn't had any meat in weeks. Throughout the meal, Mitch kept catching himself looking up at Hyon-hui. Sometimes she would be looking at him and they both smiled shyly and looked away, like a silly teenagers. But it made Mitch feel good.

When they were finished, Hyon-hui asked him to stay a while. Mitch gladly accepted and started to clear the table, but Hyon-hui's mother shooed them out of the kitchen. Hyon-hui turned on the television and 'Ms. Chun' brought them more rice wine. Despite the three presets, there were only two stations, one very snowy, the other less so. Hyon-hui chose the one with the best reception. "This is broadcast from Kanggae," she told him. "The other station comes from Wonsan. Much farther away. Many mountains between."

Mitch thought about telling her what TV was like in the United States. Hundreds of channels but nothing worthwhile on any of them. But how would she interpret that? He already knew there was nothing on North Korean TV that wasn't related to Kim Il-sung or Kim Jong-il in some way. What would the idea of a sit-com, or worse, reality TV mean to her?

She began translating the program for him, an installment of a biography series about Kim Il-sung; episode 63 of 410. This one was set during the Korean War era. Sup-suppie tiptoed in a few minutes later, kissed Hyon-hui on the forehead, thanked Mitch for the wine, and disappeared into the back.

"I don't think she likes me," Mitch whispered.

Hyon-hui turned to him. Her face was just inches from his. It made his heart ache. "Why do you say that?" she asked.

"Well when you told her I was an American, I think it upset her."

"Yes, that was strange. And when you performed your ceremony also. She doesn't usually act that way."

"She must really hate Americans."

Hyon-hui blushed then shrugged. "We don't talk about it much. She and I don't really see things the same. Politically."

Mitch cocked his head, deliberately and smiled. "She's even more hardcore than you? Is that possible?"

Hyon-hui frowned and smiled at the same time. "Patriotic zeal is important. But no. She is… the other. She had a hard childhood. I am one quarter Russian. She is half. It made life very difficult for her. There is some bitterness I think."

"So tell me of yourself, Dr. Weatherby," Hyon-hui asked, pulling her feet up on the couch. Her eyes were shining and her face smooth like a porcelain doll. Her hair was a black ocean of liquid silk spilling over her shoulders. Mitch knew he could be swept away by that ocean if he wasn't careful. And he wasn't sure he wanted to be careful.

"First off," replied Mitch, "Don't call me Dr. Weatherby anymore. My name is Mitch."

She tried it out a few times. "*Meech. Meech?*"

"Close enough."

"So, where does Mitch come from?"

"Well, I was born in Los Alamos," he began, then went on to tell her about his former life. His father was a nuclear physicist like himself, and began working at Los Alamos in the late 50s. "When they weren't quite as careful with things." His mother was a high school physics teacher. He had a brother Steve – a lawyer, two years older – and a little sister Traci, three years younger, a doctor. High school valedictorian, Sigma Cum Laude, B.S. Physics, UC Boulder, Ph.D., New Mexico. Refused numerous postdocs and an assistant professorship to go to Los Alamos. His life's dream was to see an above ground nuclear test. His father had died of leukemia just a few years after Mitch arrived to work at Los Alamos. "Same time the bottom fell out of the nuclear industry," he said with bitterness. "My mom was alive when I… When I left. I guess she's still in Los Alamos." He began looking for a way off the subject that was killing the pleasant buzz from the meal and the company.

"You were married?" Hyon-hui asked before he'd found one.

He closed his eyes for a moment, but didn't answer. "So what about you?" he asked. "Your grandfather was a Soviet officer. Your mother, I know." He paused waiting.

"That is my other grandfather," she said, pointing at the picture of the man in the horsehair hat. "My father worked in coal mines, over in South Hamgyong Province, near Hamhung. He was killed when the mine he was working in collapsed."

"I'm sorry. How old were you then?"

"Five or six. I don't remember much except that he would come home with a black face. It frightened me."

It was Hyon-hui's turn. Twenty-nine years old, born near Hamhung. Since her mother was a half-breed they had existed at the lowest tier of the North Korean caste system. At the top, she explained with envy, were the true converts of the Revolution; the loyal. Second, those who were wavering. Last, the hostile. By virtue of her mother's impure blood, they had been officially registered with the Public Security Ministry as *jeog-ui*. Hyon-hui casually described horrible living conditions, back breaking toil, and an older brother who died of strep throat when he was ten. It was, she told him, almost impossible to move from one cast to the other. "But one day," she continued as if nothing were wrong with the picture she was painting, "I took a test in school." It identified her IQ as somewhere above 180. Their life improved. Ultimately, she attended Kim Il-sung University. It was her dream to return there some day as a professor and teach chemistry and Juche to the up-and-coming generation.

Mitch had no idea what to say so he went with, "So how about you? Ever been married?"

"No," she laughed, her smooth cheeks turning slightly pink.

"What's so funny?"

"You know no one would ever marry me."

Mitch felt that familiar heat rising up his collar but refused to let it ruin the evening. "That's the dumbest thing I ever heard. These North Korean boys are real idiots. You, you're, you're absolutely beautiful, Hyon-hui." He flushed, having said more than he intended.

She blushed profusely and stared at the floor. "No, no," she finally stammered. "No. Thank you, but no. I am not. No one would marry me. No Party member would want children with my genetic material. And would never marry a non-Party member so, I have accepted that I will never marry. Never have children. It is a sacrifice I must make in order to become a member of the Korean Workers' Party."

Mitch couldn't see the logic in any of this. Hyon-hui, dressed like a normal person instead of a Party member, and with a smile on her face, was stunning. He'd been here long enough to understand her desire to be in the KWP, but he'd also been here long enough to know that it was the KWP that was killing their nation. A strange and totally unexpected thought careened through his head like a full battleship salvo. Could he escape this brutal place and take Hyon-hui with him? One look at her clear, almond-shaped eyes told him she'd never leave. But it didn't matter anyway. There was no way to get out. North Korea was larger than Terminal Island but it was even more impregnable.

"You said earlier today," Hyon-hui said with veiled curiosity, "that your wife… that she died. What happened?"

All thoughts of escaping with Hyon-hui evaporated and he was suddenly wracked with guilt for having entertained the idea, even if accidentally. Mitch glanced at the clock on the wall and swallowed hard. "I got to get going."

Hyon-hui grabbed his hand. "*Mian.* You do not have to answer. Do you have to go?"

Mitch recognized the first word as an apology. He squeezed her hand and held on to it. So warm and soft. His voice grew thick. "You know how Colonel Phoung hates it when somebody gets caught outside after curfew."

She nodded in agreement. "I am sorry, Mitch. I hope I did not spoil your evening. I meant nothing."

He looked at her and smiled. "I know. And believe me, you didn't spoil it. It's been wonderful. Thank you."

They went to the door and stood, facing one another. Mitch realized they were still holding hands. He liked it. Never wanted it to end. Then felt guilty but didn't let go.

"Thank you so much for coming, Mitch."

"Thank you for inviting me Hyon-hui. With all due respect to Max, it's the nicest evening I've had since I got here."

"What about Max?"

"He said he'd come tonight if I didn't want to."

"So you wanted to come?" she asked hopefully.

"Is that a trick question?"

"What?"

"I wanted to come. And he did, too. So I put him to work."

"Mitch, that is cruel. Max is such a nice man."

"Cruel? Are you kidding? We solved the neutron velocity problem this afternoon. He's testing it right now."

"Congratulations!" Her face lit with a lovely smile. "What was the problem?"

Mitch stood in the opened door staring into her beautiful green eyes. "Sign error," he finally said. "Just a simple little sign error." He let go of her hand and slipped into the darkness.

14

It wasn't raining in the morning and, to Hyon-hui, the sun seemed brighter and more radiant than ever before. Puddles lined the road and glistened in the morning light. Waterfalls cascaded down the walls of the valley and mingled with the stream that flowed through the village with a cheerful rush. Wildflowers opened and soaked up the sun, smiling happily into the cloudless sky. Hyon-hui grinned at everyone she saw. It wasn't proper to do so, but she could scarcely help herself. Incredible, she thought, what a little protein will do. She couldn't remember the last time she'd smiled simply because it was sunny.

She glanced at herself in a puddle as she passed, straightening her hair in the reflection. She smiled again, surprised at the act and how she felt. Strange. Somehow, lighthearted. As if nothing mattered anymore. Not the Party. Not the Silla Project. Not reunification. Not even, dare she think it, the *widaehan suryong*. Stop thinking like that, part of her brain screamed. But she didn't want to stop. Something was different and she liked it.

She said, "*Anniyong hasimnika*," to the guard at the outer door and presented him with a deep bow. He looked at her strangely, glanced at her badge, and waved her through. At the bottom of the tunnel, she frowned at the anti-American propaganda poster, wondering why Mitch was so different than the country he came from. She gave a ringing, "*Kam-sa-ham-nee-da*," to the attendant who passed out the dosimeters.

Inside, the tunnels didn't seem as grim as usual and there was a spring in her step as she strolled along the narrow, empty corridor to her office. She began humming a tune and spun like a ballerina into her office where she stopped cold. Seated at her desk was Chairman Kim In-taek.

"Good morning, Comrade Chun," he said with ghoulish delight.

Hyon-hui's smile disappeared and the lighthearted joy caught in her throat. "Comrade Secretary –" she stammered and gave a terse bow. "To what do I owe the good fortune of your visit?"

"Please come in, Comrade. Sit down." He sat fingering something. "You seem in good spirits this morning. Perhaps a revolutionary thought has caused your mind to reflect on the Great Leader with uncommon joy?"

"Yes, Comrade Secretary. Thank you." Her mind raced. Why was he here? Did they know about the chicken? The soup? Or worse, what she'd been thinking.

"You seem nervous. Does my presence surprise you?"

"Of course not," she lied. "I am always delighted to see a Party official."

"I came by this morning to make sure that you were not about to do something that would be counter productive to your career in the Party."

She finally saw what In-taek had been toying with as its face flashed in her direction. A badge with a blue background! The badge of a non-Party member. It shook her to the core. "I… well… I don't know," she stammered. "I don't know what that would be. My loyalty is unquestioned as it always is." They knew! They were random, unpatriotic, impure thoughts, but somehow they knew!

"Let me ask you a question, Comrade. Suppose two apricots are picked from a tree. One is rotten. Full of worms and putrid disease. Fit only to be eaten by pigs. The other is plump. Juicy and sweet. Ripe and ready to benefit the body. Fit for the Great Leader. Perfect in every way. If they are placed together in a sack, will the ripe make the rotten good?"

Hyon-hui looked at the floor and answered quietly. "I am not a piece of fruit, Comrade Secretary."

"Just answer the question, Comrade."

She gave the only answer her years of Juche training allowed her brain to form. "I'm not a piece of fruit. Fruit does not have a brain, Comrade Secretary. Fruit cannot reason and understand the truth of the Juche Idea. Fruit is not endowed with *chajusong*."

"Nevertheless, the spread of impurity is much more difficult to control than is the maintenance of that purity. For this reason, the *widaehan suryong*, Kim Il-sung has taught us that it is safest to avoid impure thoughts entirely."

"What is all this about?" she asked, controlling the quaver in her voice.

"You have to ask, Comrade? After what you have done?"

Hyon-hui's mind raced. "What is it that – what, that I have done, Comrade Secretary?"

"The American, of course! Do you really feel that it is wise to entertain him in your home?"

Hyon-hui's stomach dropped out. This was about Dr. Weatherby? He'd been so helpless and kind. Everything the Party wasn't. She swallowed the thought. "He was hungry, comrade secretary. And lonely. I do not know what has brought him to Choson, but his heart is choked with despair. Is it wrong that I have done this? Are we not the Land of Eastern Courtesy?"

In-Taek fingered the little badge in his lap. "I admire your spirit, Comrade. And appreciate your loyalty. But what do *you* think is best? What would the Great Leader, Comrade Generalissimo Kim Il-sung, have thought?"

She swallowed again. She had worked too hard. Waited too long. Her own happiness was not important. "The American means nothing to me," she stated, feeling the words rip in her gut, despite reminding herself that it was true.

He smiled with a Confucian nod. "So far, your loyalty to the *widaehan suryong* and to the Party has been without question. It has even been suggested by an influential Party member that you attend the Cadre School in P'yongyang. A hostile has never done that before." His eyes bored holes in Hyon-hui and he said quietly, almost to himself, "Perhaps a demonstration of your loyalty?"

"Demonstration, Comrade?" she asked.

In-taek ignored her and his voice took on a condescending tone. "If you have feelings for this American, I can appreciate that. After all, real Koreans find the thought of fraternizing with a teekee such as yourself disgusting. But even half-breeds desire companionship I suppose. Just remember, anything, anything at all, that lessens your revolutionary fervor and commitment to Juche, and to the *suryong*, is dangerous. American, Korean, or otherwise. We must each remain fully committed and galvanized behind the monolithic ideology of the Party. There is no room for anything else."

"I understand, Comrade Secretary," she replied, stinging from the affront. "As I said, my ideology remains firm and is unmovable."

He stood up. "So, I can expect you to offer a testimonial at the Study Session tonight?"

"But it is n –" she stopped short when his eyebrows went up. "Yes, Comrade Secretary. Proudly."

"Perhaps you should prepare a short lesson on the evils of capitalism and the way in which warmongering U.S. imperialists and Yankee bastards have exploited and enslaved our brothers in the South and threaten us with colonization."

Hyon-hui stood and bowed, the blackness of her life having returned to fill her soul. "It will be my greatest honor."

"Good then. We will not be needing this, yet." He slipped the badge into his pocket.

After he was out of sight, Hyon-hui looked down at the probationary badge pinned to her shirt. It had taken her entire life to get this far. Daily struggle. She removed it and looked at it intently. She knew every line on that face. From her youth it had been omnipresent. Even in the crib at the government daycare facility she'd attended. She had no intention of changing that pin for anything but a solid red one. "*I am red*," she said, wiping the tears that gathered in her eyes and cursing her impure thoughts. "*I am red. I am red. I am red.*"

Mitch was awake for over half-an-hour before he realized that he hadn't thought about Beth. She was usually at the forefront of his mind, but this morning she wasn't and he felt guilty. Then, when he realized that the guilt for having not thought of her seemed forced, he felt guilty about that. In the end though, he found himself excited about getting to the lab because he knew he would see Hyon-hui. Which made him feel guilty.

He took a shower and combed his hair, put on his best khaki pants and a white shirt, ate breakfast, and headed out the door, humming to the accompaniment of the daily dose. When he got to his office – a concrete lined nook, deep under Wagal Peak – he went around leaving notes and rounding up the key people for an early meeting. So, by nine o'clock, their regular conference room was filling with smoke, and except for the lack of donuts and the brooding presence of Pak Yong-nam, it could have easily been Los Alamos in 1943. And Mitch was Oppenheimer. With a sexy Asian babe as his girlfriend. He looked at the pictures of the Great Leaders on the wall and winked mischievously.

"So how was last night?" Max asked, arriving a few minutes before the meeting started.

"Pretty good," he answered, glancing toward the door.

"Pretty good? Is that all you are going to tell poor Max? Pretty good."

"Well, I didn't kiss her, if that's what you asking. But we had a nice time. Ate some chicken."

"*Chicken!*"

Mitch nodded. "Tough bird but I wasn't complaining. Met her mother."

"So how did she look?"

"Pretty old. I guess she's probably late sixties, early –"

"Not her mother! Comrade Chun!"

Mitch nodded, thoughtfully. "Date. Definitely a date."

"I don't like you anymore."

"Her mother's free."

"I hate you."

Mitch smiled a shy grin. "It's not like she wants to marry me, Max. I think," he lowered his eyebrows in thought, "I think she just felt sorry for me."

"Then I shall start complaining more often," Max said and nodded toward the door. "I see your shadow is back."

Mitch looked up. Lee waved with his characteristic toothy grin. "Fun's over," said Mitch. "Back to totalitar-reality."

Hyon-hui was right behind him and Mitch's heart skipped a beat. Though she looked no different than any other day, she was far more beautiful than he ever remembered. He gave her a subdued wave and a grin. She looked away and he knew instantly that something was wrong.

"Who can understand the nonlinearities of a woman's mind?" Max said with a shrug.

Lee made his way around the table. When he got to Mitch, he bowed.

"How was Kanggae?" asked Mitch as if he cared.

"Revolutionary," replied Lee. Then asked, "What were you doing at Comrade Chun's house last night?"

Mitch wasn't really surprised. "Nice to see you, too."

"Were you not at Comrade Chun's house last night? Why were you there?"

"That's none of your business."

Lee was unfazed. "Actually, it is my business."

"If you must know, we were plotting the over –" Max shook his head furiously, and Mitch remembered the lighter and shifted his thoughts. " – population of neutrons versus time. The Juche session interrupted our efforts, so we worked late over dinner."

"In the future," Lee told him, "make sure you obtain a permit."

"I need a permit for a date?"

"No. To go into the residential section. And you might want to consider how your presence might affect her." He went and seated himself.

"You're a *chyort* fool, Mitch," said Max quietly. "Plotting the overthrow of…? You might have sent her to prison for that."

Sonny walked up. "What is today's word, Dr. Weatherby?"

"Why are you so interested in our words?" snapped Mitch. "You planning a visit?"

Sonny laughed nervously. "No, of course not. It is just a hobby of mine."

"Okay then," Mitch announced. "How about fubar?"

"Fubar," repeated Sonny. "And what does it mean?"

"It means something that's broken. Fu – fouled up beyond all recognition."

Max scowled. "Don't you mean fuc –"

"Close enough," Mitch shot back.

"So Max's simulation is fubar?" Sonny asked, innocently.

"Actually, no," Mitch said, cringing. "Max's sim pwns." He brought the meeting to order.

"Good morning, ladies and gentlemen. I consider this, the first true meeting of the Gadget Design Committee. And thank you all for coming given the short notice. Before we get started, I have some good news to report. Yesterday afternoon, Comrade Tarasenko solved the neutron velocity problem. I think." He turned to Max. "What'd the sim show last night."

Max cleared his throat. "I cannot take credit for finding the problem," he said. "It was actually Dr. Weatherby that found the-" he cleared this throat, "error. I fixed it, recompiled, and submitted the job using the baseline simulation initialized with data from the nominal dispersions we ran at the beginning of August. This morning," he smiled, despite himself, "I can report the sim is no longer-" he glanced at Mitch, "*fubar*, that velocities, even at the upper end of the spectrum, agree with the experiment to ninety three percent."

Everyone cheered.

"But don't forget to post the error on the network," said Mitch, trying not to smile. "And everybody, make sure you check the bug-board and correct your own copies of the paper.

"So," he went on, "now that that's *finally* finished, we can roll up our sleeves and get down to the business of building our gadget." Mitch always used the word gadget. It was what his heroes had called the first bomb at Los Alamos.

"As all of you know, it's a lot more than just a ball of slow-fissionable material coated with high explosive. To get maximum efficiency, we need to exploit every physical principle we know to help hold the pit together for a few more microseconds." Mitch opened his arms to the group. "So where do we start?"

They spent the next four hours talking about how to build a nuclear bomb and the different options available to force more yield from the same amount of fissionable material. Over the many years in which American, Russian, British, and other designers tested these devices, tricks were learned to increase yield while at the same time making the whole package smaller and lighter. Ways to vary the geometry and composition of the nuclear material, arrange and detonate the lenses, reflect escaping neutrons back in, take advantage of the physics of shock waves, and introduce or increase the amount of neutrons present in the core at the time of initiation. These tricks, as well as data, such as critical masses and neutron numbers, became arguably the most closely guarded secrets of the cold war. And Mitch divulged none of them. He didn't have to.

Through a combination of previous espionage and declassified Los Alamos reports, the Koreans already knew how to build a nuclear bomb. It was the process that had caused them so much trouble. That, and the chronic famine. And the energy shortage. And political interference at all levels. And the lack of infrastructure. And international sanctions. And orbiting spy satellites. What they needed wasn't a brilliant scientist, but an effective administrator. And that is where Mitch was so valuable. Not because his intellect was far beyond the Koreans – it wasn't – but because he wasn't hampered by a lifetime of creativity-stifling bureaucracy. At least Los Alamos' bureaucracy didn't squash creativity as completely as did Juche.

So in the end, the meeting finished with the design of a new process. It would start with a series of computer simulations by Max's group to explore the performance of various pit designs. Promising designs would go to Hyon-hui's explosives division to be tested using high speed photography, RaLa, and other diagnostic tools. The information gained through testing would then be passed on to Professor Yang's theoretical physicists who would use the data to adjust their models. They would then send their refined mathematical models back to Max's group where the process would repeat starting with more simulation studies. It was the Los Alamos model and it had been repeated all over the world, and now it had come to North Korea.

15

October 10th, the anniversary of Workers' Party of Korea, began early with patriotic music and inspirational speeches in every village and town broadcast over the national public address system. People gathered at local squares for group calisthenics and mass adulation exercises, followed by ideological training sessions where the popular masses learned of the wise life and great deeds of the Great Leader, Comrade Generalissimo Kim Il-sung.

In Sagi-dong, as elsewhere, a dozen probationary members had their life's dreams fulfilled with the award of full Party membership. Hyon-hui was among them. She accepted her red pin and took her oath under the tearful gaze of Professor Yang. She would never know that he had expended significant political capital in pushing her application beyond Pak's stalling tactics. And while her loyalty test – shunning Mitch – had helped her Party status, the guilt of what she'd done to him gnawed at the pit of her stomach. But it had been worth it, she said to herself a thousand times a day. She was red.

Mitch and Max sat in the audience as guests of the Sagi-dong Party Cell. Hyon-hui stood proudly as Kim In-taek removed the old badge and pinned on the new one with the solid red background. But as he stepped away, Hyon-hui felt empty. Indeed, the entire ceremony and the oath was anticlimactic and hollow somehow. Yet, she smiled. They all did.

The highlight of the day was the Party parade. Wearing their best Party clothes, the Party members put on their Party medals, and marched around Sagi-dong singing Party songs carrying gigantic red Party flags emblazoned with the Party symbol. They ended in a field behind Party headquarters goose-stepping past a reviewing stand of onlooking Party cadres. To the music of a brass band blaring patriotic Party tunes, they shouted militant Party slogans at the top of their Party lungs. Those sad unfortunates *not* in the Party had the privilege of lining the street, cheering triumphantly and waving miniature DPRK flags. As evening fell and the fireflies came out to play, everyone settled in to watch artistic Party performances of Party songs and Party dances given by local Party members.

The overdose of planned patriotism and structured zeal revived Hyon-hui's enthusiasm, or at least her sense of accomplishment, for this, the best day of her life. And her new political status only energized her the more toward the success of the Silla Project. She was filled with pride to prove her worth to the Party and to the nation, and she had work to do. Pak had demanded a report on X-Division's status be delivered to him first thing in the morning.

On her way to the Explosives Facility after the festivities, Hyon-hui gazed across the collective farm's rutted sea of mud to the apartments where Mitch lived. A warm light shone from his window. He and Max were probably playing chess. For a half-second, she thought about going to see him. But there was a guard at the entrance on the other side. And guards in the tower looking down. And patrols. And she'd didn't have authorization. And no money for a bribe. So she hurried on. "I am red," she said. "*I am red.*"

Yet, as if her thoughts had been known, headlights of a vehicle popped on, stopping her short. Hyon-hui held up her hand as the form of a man approached, silhouetted by the headlights. From his outline, it was a soldier. Hyon-hui glanced at her watch. It was only 9:30. She would receive a warning, unless they really could read her thoughts. She pushed that idea away.

"Annyong-haseyo," she said nervously and bowed when he drew near.

"Comrade Chun?"

"Yes," she answered, surprised that he knew her by name.

"Come with me."

Her breath caught in her throat when she got to the jeep and the door opened. She froze as her blood turned cold. Inside sat an SSA man, uniformed in black.

"Where are you taking me, Comrades?" she asked in a trembling voice. The soldier didn't answer as he shoved her in. She'd just been inducted into the Party. What could she have done? Then a thrill of excitement shot through her veins. A secret initiation! That had to be it. It was the only explanation.

She peered out the window as the vehicle made its way up to the villas and stopped at one on the upper road. Hyon-hui instantly recognized the bright red convertible in the driveway. "Comrade Minister Pak's residence?" she stammered as the cold fear crept back. "Why are we here?"

They didn't answer, just hauled her out of the jeep, took her to a side door, and knocked. It opened and a shaft of light spilled out revealing Pak in his white shirt and black pants. His red Party tie hung loose around his neck.

"Comrade Chun," he said in a silky tone. "Won't you come in?"

Before she'd had the chance to respond, she was pushed through the door and Pak closed it behind her. Her eyes darted nervously around the room. It was dim but she could see that the floor was carpeted richly. There was a large, flatscreen TV set and a stereo with huge speakers. Down a short hallway, Hyon-hui could see an unmade bed in the room beyond.

"Comrade Minister Pak," she said with a stiff bow.

His eyes danced over her and she noticed that his shirt was unbuttoned half-way down, and she could smell the alcohol on his breath. "Relax," he said smoothly. "Can I get you a drink?"

"No thank you, Comrade. I was just on my way to the Explosives Facility and –"

"You don't have to work tonight," he interrupted with a wave of his thick hand. "This is a big day. You're in the Party. Time to celebrate." He walked over to a counter and Hyon-hui heard the clink of ice. Then a pouring sound. Music came on. Strange, techno-pop with English lyrics, unlike anything she'd ever heard. When he turned around, he had two drinks.

"Comrade Minister," she said more anxiously this time. "I, I do not think I should be here."

"I think you should," Pak replied, holding out the glass. "Take it."

Hyon-hui stared at it with wild eyes. "Why am I here, Comrade Minister?"

Pak took a swig of his drink and stared at her greedily. "Where else would a beautiful, new Comrade be on her wedding night?" He started swinging his hips rhythmically.

Nausea swept through her stomach. She took a step backward and glanced at the door. Perhaps she could make it... "Comrade. Please. I – Please, just let me –"

Pak lunged forward and grabbed her by the neck. The glass he'd been holding fell to the floor and spilled on the carpet. Hyon-hui tried to scream but his tongue invaded her mouth. She gagged and tried to get away but his grip was like a vice. Just when she thought she would suffocate, he released her. She staggered backwards choking.

"Better than that bastard, imperialist American," he said with a wicked laugh.

"But I –"

"Half-breed, yang-kee lover, bitch!" he growled. "You don't get into my Party without going through me."

"Please," she pleaded. "Just let me go. I will tell no one. Just let me go. *Please*."

Pak advanced until she was pinned, his hot breath on her face – alcohol and cigarettes. His voice came low and menacing. "You *will* keep your mouth shut. Because if you don't, I'll kill you and your bitch mother. Now we're going to do this. And you're going to like it."

16

One of the things Mitch soon discovered was that, while they understood the theories, the Koreans had very little experience working with critical assemblies. The accident with Dr. Rhee was but one example of this and there was no way Mitch was going to let them work with pure materials and risk repeating that tragedy. A pure, sub-critical system can be driven to a runaway chain-reaction by something as small as moving the pieces a millimeter closer together. Or placing a cup of water two feet away so that a tiny fraction more of the neutrons are reflected back toward the system. And the change happens so fast with a pure system, and can be so extreme, everybody in the vicinity could receive a lethal dose of neutrons and gamma before it could be shut down. Several scientists had died in the U.S., and many more in Russia, Max told him, from accidents such as these. So when the first shipments of uranium-233 arrived from Yujin-dong, Mitch had no intention of letting anyone form a critical mass with the pure metal. Instead, he had the Chemistry and Metallurgy Division do the same thing Los Alamos had done a half century before: grind the uranium into powder, mix it with melted plastic, and mold it into tough, one-inch blocks. Not only did it make the uranium safe to handle, but with the high hydrogen content, it only took a very small amount of uranium to build a critical assembly, which also made it less susceptible to an accident. So when he was ready, Mitch and Sonny invited everyone to their lab to construct North Korea's first, U-233 nuclear reactor.

For the demonstration, Sonny had designed a table with a trapdoor above a basin filled with a neutron-quenching solution of cadmium. If their experiment began to run away, a switch connected to a neutron counter would open the trap door and the pile would fall into the bucket bringing the chain reaction to an abrupt halt.

So like children playing with blocks, Mitch and Sonny, wearing heavy lead-impregnated aprons, began stacking the tiny cubes as Max, Professor Yang, Hyon-hui and others watched from twenty feet away. Max had used his computer models to predict that the finished structure should be a cube five blocks on a side, or 125 blocks overall. A little over one and-a-half kilograms of uranium distributed throughout the plastic. One by one, they placed the blocks and listened to the clicks from the Geiger counter come faster and faster.

By the time they were on the third layer, everyone was about to snap with the tension. "You know," Mitch said to calm them. "This is really no different than Enrico Fermi's first reactor at the University of Chicago. Just a lot smaller since our uranium is pure. Fermi was using natural uranium, of course. My dad used to tell me stories about Fermi and –"

"*You knew Enrico Fermi?*" Sonny blurted and took a step back.

"My dad went to the University of Chicago."

Sonny started shaking with excitement. "*Your father was a student of Enrico Fermi?*"

"Yes, he was." Mitch placed another block on the pile and the clicks from the counter came a little faster. He caught Hyon-hui's eye. She was standing in the back with the same empty expression she'd had since her induction into the Party. Not like when she ignored him after their date. This was different. Darker. Something was wrong. But Sonny's exuberance drew his attention away from her. Something always did, and she seemed to want it that way.

"It is such an honor to work with you, Dr. Weatherby," Sonny sputtered. "A student of Enrico Fermi! That is pwn!"

Mitch laughed at his misuse of the word, but didn't correct him. "Not me, Sun. It was my father. Fermi died twenty years before I was born." He didn't tell them that, at the age of fifty-three, Fermi had died from stomach cancer most likely brought on by exposure to radiation. Even at the time, Fermi knew the risks of his work but felt that the danger was justified by the importance.

The Geiger counter crackled and Mitch looked down at the growing pile, just a few feet from his own stomach.

They kept stacking but Sonny kept asking questions about Fermi. Mitch told them about the time before the first nuclear test at Alamogordo when Fermi was taking bets on whether or not the chain reaction would spread to the atmosphere and destroy the planet. Or the time he stopped in his battered old pickup truck and joined a group of boys in a game of baseball. And his impromptu estimate of total yield by tossing a handful of paper scraps into the air and seeing how far the Trinity blast pushed them back. Sonny's eyes shone with delight and Mitch wondered if it was a good idea for him to be hearing this. Mitch had no doubt that Lee would have stopped him, but he was afraid to come into the room.

At row five, they stopped talking. Just twenty-five more blocks and their micro-reactor would be critical, meaning it would be producing as many neutrons as were escaping. They placed the center block of the last layer in place first, then worked their way outward. The neutron counters threatened to explode into a hiss, and as they died down, Pak walked in.

"Good afternoon, Minister. Glad you could join us," Mitch said, trying to sound casual as the counters slowed. He glanced around ready to make another joke to break the tension, but saw Hyon-hui's face as Pak's eyes mentally undressed her. Rage threatened to shoot through Mitch's veins, as his mind made assumptions about both of those looks. His fists clenched as Pak looked back to him, and the tension in the room grew higher, as if he and Pak formed their own critical assembly, ready to burst into an uncontrolled chain reaction. You can't assume anything about these people, Mitch reminded himself. They don't make sense. He exhaled slowly.

"Are you okay, Comrade?" Sonny whispered.

"Fine," Mitch muttered. This was a dangerous experiment. He needed to stay focused. The counters crackled and thoughts of Fermi's death intruded.

"Go on. Go on," Pak instructed him.

"We haven't gone critical yet," Mitch told him through almost gritted teeth. "All you missed were some stories about Enrico

Fermi." Mitch watched him cross the room where he took his place in front of the others. Hyon-hui cringed and shrank further to the back. Mitch stiffened, but all he could do was turn back to the growing pile. Something was going on between them. It had started on Party induction night. Max had told him women sometimes had to –

The hiss of the counters as Sonny placed the next block brought Mitch back to his senses. A mistake could unleash a dangerous burst of radiation. The counters in the room popped and crackled as they placed one block after another. But each time, the clicks would die off. In concert with the radiation detectors, the tension in the room was rising to climax. As was the temperature. And the odor. And Mitch kept imagining strangling Pak with his bare hands.

All the while, Sonny babbled on about Fermi's first reactor. Compared to the tiny cube on their table, a mere five inches on a side, Fermi's first reactor had been over twenty feet on a side and weighed nearly 400 metric tons. The difference was that Fermi's reactor had used natural uranium, that contained only a tiny fraction of fissile U-235, while Mitch's pile used pure U-233 metal combined with hydrogen moderating plastic. Sonny even knew it was called Chicago Pile-One. Usually these people wouldn't even acknowledge things that weren't invented in North Korea.

The combination of topics was enough to drive Mitch mad. With each pop of the counters he knew that hundreds, perhaps thousands of neutrons and gamma rays were passing through their bodies. Then there was Pak, leering at Hyon-hui. And Hyon-hui looking as if…

Mitch felt Sonny nudge him, and he snapped back again. There was but one block to go.

Mitch raised his head and looked at his audience. "Professor Yang," he said, "would you care to place the final cube on the pile?" The old man lowered his head sheepishly and started to step forward.

"I will do it," interjected Pak, stepping out in front of him. "It is my program."

Mitch felt heat rising up his neck as his teeth ground together. This was the last straw. He was about to contest the fat Party boss but Professor Yang stepped back into line. "Yes. Yes, that would be best," the old man said, clearly disappointed, but halting Mitch's outburst with his eyes.

Pak lifted his chin and strode confidently toward the pile. When he was a few feet away, the clicks from the counters around the table burst into a loud hiss. Everyone ducked. Pak froze and swayed as if he was about to faint. Mitch and Sonny leapt back. Just as suddenly, the clicking died away.

"Dae-jung!" cried Mitch to one of the other scientists, fighting the nausea in his gut as mental images of Fermi's stomach cancer filled his mind. "Check the counter!" But he already knew they were okay since it hadn't triggered Sonny's trap door.

"Negligible, Dr. Weatherby," the scientist said with a wobbly voice. "Everyone should be alright. But Sun-yong is going to be angry when she gets the dosimetry."

The scientists were regaining their composure although any chance of lightening the mood was gone. Pak's face was gray, he was trembling, and there was a small wet spot in his groin area. His hands moved and clasped in front of the spreading stain as Mitch locked eyes with him for a split second.

"This is an excellent example," Mitch announced, in a quavering voice, looking back to the others, "of how a hydrogen-rich moderator in close proximity to a near critical mass will drive it to chain reactions. Minister Pak, please step closer. Slowly, this time."

Pak inched forward and at a few feet, the popping from the detectors started to inch upward. "A few minutes ago," Mitch went on, "Sonny and I were standing close, too. Now that we've moved back, Minister Pak isn't having as much of an effect. The hydrogen and carbon in our bodies is reflecting just enough neutrons back into the pile to drive it to criticality. Max probably didn't take that level of hydrogen into account in his calculations. Let's try somebody with less hydrogen."

They tried several other people but Pak was the only one who would set it off that way. He couldn't even get close. And though no one said so, everyone knew why. Fat has more neutron-moderating hydrogen in it than any other tissue in the body and Pak had plenty of it. Everyone else was rail thin. So in the end, it was still Professor Yang who placed the final block and brought the first u-233 assembly to a controlled critical mass. The radiation counters went to a steady crackle and, depending on the objects Mitch brought close to the small pile, he could control the rate of fission with amazing precision. Pak inched to the back as the scientists were focused on the pile, keeping his hands over his crotch until he finally snuck out the door.

When they were finished, Sonny scampered around the lab with a huge smile on his face shaking everyone's hand. If he'd had a tail, Mitch thought watching him, he'd have been wagging it. "That pwned!" he gushed, coming up to Mitch. "A self-sustaining pile, just like Fermi's! We pwned!"

"We definitely pwned." He held out his fist and Sonny bumped it with his own as Mitch had showed him. "But, how do you know so much about Fermi's pile?"

Sonny grinned at Max, standing at Mitch's side, and the Russian raised his hands to defend himself. "But, I was always careful to point out that Fermi was a capitalist stooge." The three of them laughed as the scientists began to file out, but Mitch's eyes fell on Hyon-hui, waiting for the other scientists to leave – avoiding their presence – until she could dart out.

"I know it's time for your study session," Mitch said to Sonny and told him he could leave.

"I should help you put the lab in order first."

"No. I'll put everything away. You go ahead and take off."

"Will you be okay by yourself, Comrade Mitch?"

"Sure. And thanks, Sun. Excellent job." Hyon-hui was almost at the door.

Sonny bowed to Mitch. "Kam-sa-ham-ne-da, Comrade Weatherby. We pwned today, didn't we?"

Mitch had to smile. "Yes, Sonny. We pwned."

Hyon-hui was halfway through the door when Mitch blurted, "Hyon-hui, wait!" She halted and turned reluctantly. "Glad you could make it," Mitch said.

"I was told to come." Her voice was as cold and flat as her eyes.

Mitch eyed Lee who remained standing in the doorway as well. "Don't you have a study session to go to?"

Lee jerked in surprise. "Excuse me?"

"I'd like to talk to Comrade Chun for a minute."

"Go ahead." He didn't move.

"*Alone.*"

Lee frowned. "Why would you want to speak to her alone?"

"No offense, Lee, but she's a lot prettier than you." Lee frowned and ducked out the door.

"Now then." He turned back to Hyon-hui and she was trembling. "You okay?"

"Why do you keep asking me that?" she retorted.

"Because ever since you were inducted into the Party you –"

"I don't know what you mean!" she snapped. "Everything is fine. I don't know what you're talking about."

"Alright. I just –"

"I cannot fraternize with imperialists!" she blurted.

"But –"

"Mitch, I've got to go or I'll be late. Please."

"Wait," Mitch said with more than a note of pleading in his voice. "Can I, uh, see you some time?" He suddenly felt extremely awkward. "Maybe you could come to dinner at my apartment. You're welcome to bring your mom."

She paused and glanced in Mitch's direction but would not look at him. "I don't think we should see each other again, Dr. Weatherby," she said and disappeared down the hall.

Max was standing behind him. "I'm sorry to hear that. I did not mean to…"

"It's okay," he said quietly. "Wasn't your fault." Mitch took a breath, held it for a second as if to speak, then exhaled and stood in silence.

"What is it?" asked Max.

"I'm sure you've noticed her lack of energy lately. We've talked about it before," he said, reminding Max of how the output and quality of lenses from the Explosives Facility has suffered.

"Something's not right there." He scowled, knowing that he could be imagining things with Pak. Maybe this was nothing more than the enormous number of activities in which the Party kept its people involved, everything from calisthenics in the morning, to accordion rehearsals at night – and by all accounts, Hyon-hui was one of the best accordion players in Sagi-dong. And maybe, she'd decided she just didn't like him.

"Food?" Max suggested as another explanation. "None of us are getting enough to eat. I'm having trouble concentrating and I think that is part of the reason at least."

"I don't think so. When Pak is around, it's like –" he cocked his head. "Just watch her face when he comes into a room. Let me know if you notice anything. Maybe it's all in my head," Mitch conceded. "Probably is."

"It is nothing a little *Baem-sul* won't take care of," Max suggested, referring to the semi-poisonous adder liquor. "Or maybe a lot of *Baem-sul*."

Lee bent over the cassette player on Pak's desk, listing to the sound of Mitch's alcohol slurred, recorded voice, with music in the background. "Max. Think we're doing the right thing here?"

Maxim Tarasenko's voice answered. "I believe so. We won't be using a moderated critical mass in the gadget, but it is still instructive. I'm not sure Sonny had ever assembled a critical mass bef –"

"No, no, no," stammered Mitch through the recorder. "No. I mean, helping them build this... this bomb. It's … I don't know. Sometimes, I think maybe we –" There was a pause where nothing but crackling radio music could be heard. When Mitch's voice came back, it was low and serious. "What happened, Max? One minute, I'm getting home from work at Los Alamos. The next minute, my wife's dead and I'm doing hydrogenated 233 studies in a secret lab in North Korea. What would your grandmother say about that?"

The sound of cheesy electronic music from a lighter interrupted the recorded conversation. A moment later, Max's voice said clearly, "*Prishla beda, otvoryay vorota.*"

"Which means?"

"Trouble is here, so open the gates."

Pak punched a button on the tape player to stop it. "Do we still have control of Dr. Weatherby and Dr. Tarasenko?"

Lee was unconcerned. "It was only a matter of time, Comrade Minister. We expected this of course, and I know what to do. We will take the necessary steps to see that he remains pliant."

"See that you do, Comrade Major."

17

The year grew stale and ever colder, and despite the worsening food shortage, Sagi-dong's scientists doggedly pursued their goal. The Critical Assembly group completed their critical mass experiments and moved on to neutron multiplication and reflector studies. The RaLa group was ready for another test, having received several shipments of radiobarium from the reactor at Yujin-dong. But there was bitter disappointment when it showed no evidence of compression. Given the high degree of symmetry, however, Mitch interpreted it as a sign of jetting resulting from overlapping detonation waves. He suspended any more shots until the newly formed Magnetic Group had completed the design of their pickup coil and field generators that would help them diagnose the problem. Pak was furious at the failure and denigrated Hyon-hui publicly.

Lee brought Mitch a copy of a report used in his sentencing. It provided detailed connections Mitch supposedly had to various terrorist organizations, citing these relationships as the source of the radiological materials found on Mitch's property. Covering up their mistake hadn't been enough. The government had made sure he'd be destroyed completely. But he had no anger left, so Mitch redoubled his efforts, burying himself in his physics.

Professor Yang oversaw the Theoretical Division's ongoing simulation development efforts. The Hydrodynamics Group was putting the finishing touches on their first version of the implosion model which simulated the behavior of shock waves and matter throughout the entire implosion cycle. Beginning with the initiation of the detonation wave in the high explosive, it followed the shock wave's growth and progress through this material and into the pit, then employed hydrodynamic principles to model the flow of the pit material under temperatures and pressures normally found only in the core of a star.

At the same time, Mitch had directed Max to look into the behavior of the fissionable pit material under the compressive forces generated by a well-shaped shock. His team's product was to be a detailed simulation of the neutron population: how it begins; how it grows; and how it eventually dies out. It would be used to prevent accidentally creating a deadly critical assembly while assembling the prototype bomb itself.

In the Chemistry and Metallurgy Division, the emphasis was on perfecting techniques for the casting, forging, and machining of uranium. Something they could practice with benign and plentiful uranium-238 since the chemistry and metallurgy were the same as the 233 isotope.

The most visible successes of the program, though, continued to be in the Physics and Research Division. Studies into basic properties and constants continued to move forward, as did the design and improvement of instruments and detectors. On a weekly basis, it seemed, a new detector or improved instrument would roll out of the Instrumentation Group. Mitch knew this was the core of a nuclear program and realized he might have changed the course of the entire nation.

With all this activity, in early December, they again found themselves at the RaLa Test Site. It was an icy, gray day with a light covering of snow on the ground. A clean, cold smell permeated the still air and the boughs of evergreens were dusted with white. Below them, ice on Lake Nangnim stretched from the shore half-way to the middle. Beyond, the rugged, snowy mountains marched into the distance.

An hour before the RaLa test, scientists poured from the tunnel like ants. Their breath came as fog, and snow crunched beneath their feet as they went about their tasks. Sonny and his technicians installed sensors around the test pad. The men from Chemistry and Metallurgy peeled back the tarps covering their equipment and started the radiolanthanum separation, now a well-practiced procedure. Others from the Magnetic Group set up large metal grids on either side of the pit that would be used to create an electrostatic field. By observing the changing field as the metal pit changed size during the test, they could infer the pit's rate of collapse.

The test site was busy and Mitch knew he wasn't needed. His mind turned to food and he rubbed his aching belly. Such a day would be perfect for hunting, he thought, and followed a set of fresh deer tracks in the snow. He'd seen them at all three RaLa sites and, judging from their size, Mitch knew they had to be smaller than the whitetails he'd once tracked in the San Juans above Los Alamos.

The sounds from the test site faded and he found himself alone, outside the wire and fences of Sagi-dong. Doubtless, the nearby forest was crawling with soldiers but at the moment, no one was watching him. It was the first time he'd been on his own since Beth's murder. But he hadn't gone far before he came across another set of fresh footprints. He rounded a boulder and found Hyon-hui standing on the edge of a low cliff, staring out over the snow-covered mountains. An icy breeze hissed over the lip and drew her hair into long black streamers.

He watched her for a moment, frozen in place, until desire overcame fear and he called out to her. She spun around, frightened, then softened when she saw it was Mitch. He pointed at the ground. "I was following these tracks. Professor Yang says they're deer. I used to hunt them in Mew Mexico but they were a lot bigger than these."

Coming up beside her, his breath billowed out in clouds which mingled with hers. "It's beautiful," he said, staring toward the eastern horizon. "Much like my home." Still, she didn't say anything. "Miss Chun?" he asked. "I know you're sick of me asking you this but, are you okay?"

For several minutes she stood, unmoving. Mitch grew more and more uncomfortable with the silence until finally he turned to leave, convinced at last that their relationship was over, when in fact, it had never begun.

"The Party," Hyon-hui said quietly. "It is not... what I thought it would be."

He turned to catch her wiping a tear from her eye. "I take it you don't mean it's better than you expected?" She didn't answer. "Do you want to talk about it?" he asked.

"I cannot, Mitch. I cannot."

He stepped back to her side and the two of them stared into the east. The wind was freezing but Mitch didn't want to leave her. Instead, he kept looking down at her face. "That night," he said, "why did you invite me to your home for dinner?"

"You were alone," she finally said. "Far from home. I was cruel and it hurt you. I thought that is what I wanted. But then… I know what it is to be alone. And far from loved ones." Silence descended again and only the wind could be heard. "Your wife, Mitch, was she very beautiful?"

Mitch's stomach twisted at the question. "Yes," he croaked. "She was very beautiful."

"You loved her very much, didn't you?"

He couldn't bear to look into Hyon-hui's eyes so kept his fixed on the horizon. "Yes. She was the love of my life."

Fingers suddenly intertwined around Mitch's and he felt the warmth of Hyon-hui's hand radiating into his. He stared down in astonishment to see their hands clasped together.

"How did she die?" Hyon-hui asked.

Mitch marveled at the feel of her hand. The touch of her soft fingers squeezing his robbed him of the means speech for a moment. Finally, he took a deep breath and swallowed hard. "We lived out in the country, a few miles from Los Alamos. In mountains not unlike these. The most beautiful place in the world." Mitch was staring outward but his eyes were seeing something else.

"One day, I came home early from work, depressed about the lab. Los Alamos. About my career. They were turning us into programmers. No more physics. Just code. Like Max plays with all the time. Simulations. Beth and I went hiking up in the mountains. We made love. Talked. Made plans. Got home around dark. Ate dinner. Sat down to watch a little TV. Around ten o'clock, we heard something out back. Lot of coyotes around there so Beth grabs a rifle and we go out on the deck to see what it is. She hated those things. Killed one of her horses a few months before and she declared war on them."

He paused for a moment and swallowed heavily. Then went on. "We can't really see anything 'cause it's too dark. But there's a little movement over by the corral. She aims." He stopped talking and his face fell. "I hear this muffled shot, and she collapsed on the deck. There was blood everywhere. She'd been shot through the heart. I got her in the house and there were these guys inside, in black suits. I had a rifle so I started shooting. I killed two of them before they shot me in the back."

Hyon-hui was watching him closely now.

"Government agents," Mitch went on, not daring to stop. "They were at the wrong house. To cover up their mistake, they made it look like I was trying to build a nuclear bomb in my basement. They planted classified data in my house, then said I brought it home from Los Alamos. They buried enriched uranium in my backyard. Made me look like some kind of a terrorist. I was sentenced to forty-two years in prison. When this 'opportunity' presented itself, the words 'yes' and 'no' just didn't seem to make much sense.

He looked over to see her studying him. "Why am I telling you this?" he asked, in answer to her look. He thought for a moment, then swallowed hard. "Because, I thought America – the United States – stood for certain things. Liberty. Freedom. Justice. The kind of stuff you learn when you're a kid and can't give up, even when you know different." He shook his head. "You said the Party isn't what you expected." His voice trailed off and he stood in silence for a moment, but the indignance inside him – rage at the injustice and the untruths – kept growing.

"You want to know why I'm here, Hyon-hui?" he blurted out. "Because everything I believed turned out to be a lie. And that's why I don't feel like a traitor. My country was the traitor. It betrayed *me*, Hyon-hui. I would have died for America. But what I thought existed, was only in my mind. A lie told by the government. And by rich people to suck labor from the masses. The rich take from the poor then pass laws to make themselves even richer. It's all – " He stopped, realizing how much he sounded like Lee. But maybe Major Lee was right.

Hyon-hui shivered, glancing around nervously as if she expected an SSA agent to be hiding behind a rock. But they were still very much alone and she moved close to him. Mitch let go of her hand and put his arms around her.

"Mitch?"

"Yes."

"What if our test fails today?"

"We'll run it again."

"How many times?"

"As many as it takes."

"Do you think Minister Pa –" She swallowed heavily and Mitch felt a tremor sweep through her body. "Pak will stand for another failure? I don't know how much…"

"Hyon-hui, is there some kind of problem between you and Minister Pak? Because if –"

"*No!*" she snapped and pulled away. "There is nothing between us. Why would there be?"

Mitch nodded, but knew he'd touched on the truth. "Okay. I just thought I'd seen a little, I don't know, tension between –"

"I said *no!*" she blurted. She turned away from him and headed back up the trail.

Mitch stood staring into space. He remembered what Max had told him about how some women got into the Party. And the lustful way Pak looked at her during the critical mass assembly. His body tensed and his brain was flooded with an almost uncontrollable rage. He wanted to kill Pak, no matter what it meant for himself.

He stormed back to the test site, where a technician was just removing the radiolanthanum from the separation hut. He checked his pace when he saw the head of the magnetic group. It was their first test and he shouldn't screw it up with his blind anger.

"Any problems?" he asked the young engineer.

"No, sir. We checked the grids a moment ago. Electric field was uniform all the way across."

"Looks good," Mitch commented, trying to sound encouraging as he inspected the magnetic test apparatus.

The radiation from the pit forced the four of them out of the area and the technicians completed the preparations for the test using a much-improved tool to insert the plug. Hyon-hui finished assembling the gadget and they trudged back up the tunnel where the test coordinator went over a checklist, making last minute adjustments and finally announced that everything was ready. As always, there was a countdown, the switch was thrown, and a muffled boom reverberated down the long hole into the mountain. Almost instantly, traces appeared on the scopes.

"Well," said Sonny, neither disappointed nor heartened, "the symmetry at least is good. Detonators are working properly. But these traces are really fubar." Mitch's head spun to look straight at him. The kid would not let it go.

"No compression," said Hyon-hui bitterly. "None at all."

"Jetting," said Mitch gravely. "Look how the magnetic and RaLa traces are out of sync? Tells me that we've got a jetting problem." He bent forward in the dim light. "See this spike," he said pointing to a sharp but short rise on the trace from the magnetic pickup coil. "This is from the magnet at the center getting hit by the collapsing core." He paused and pointed to the traces from the RaLa detectors which began to rise after the magnet spike. "It tells us that the collapse was symmetric. That's good. But…" He moved his finger a little farther down the trace. "This rising signal strength, after the spike, tells me that the surface is continuing to move inward but without compression. The only way the surface can move inward without compression is if pit material is being ejected somewhere." Mitch rubbed his head as he thought. "Let's review the data and we'll figure it out later."

"Why wasn't I informed of this meeting?" Pak snarled as the conference room door banged into the wall and the no-necked minister marched in.

"We have debriefings everyday," Mitch replied calmly. "I wasn't aware you wanted to come to them all."

Pak glared at him. "There was a RaLa test yesterday. What was the outcome?"

"We were just talking about that," Mitch replied casually. He had kept the test secret outside the small, necessary group of participants to avoid Pak's bluster. But now he realized that might have been a mistake. He continued, keeping his tone even. "Of course, you're always welcome to –"

"Another failure?" Pak spat. His eyes shifted slowly over each scientist, only to land back on Mitch. A chill went up his spine, the same chill that had stiffened everyone in the room.

"The magnetic diagnostic worked perfectly. Symmetry was good. As far as –"

"What about compression? Did you see any compression?"

Mitch started to speak, but halted and simply said, "No. We didn't. The magnetic test showed that we've got a jetting problem."

"Jetting?" Pak said calmly, then erupted. "*This is taking too long!* The Dear Leader demands results! Do you know how much money we have poured into this effort since your arrival, Dr. Weatherby? A complete restructuring of the program. Billions spent in U.S. dollars that we do not have. And eight months later, nothing to show for it! Nothing!"

"Nothing to show for it?" Mitch countered. "You have a real lab. You have a test infrastructure. You have –"

"*Do you have my bomb?*" he roared. "*Do You Have My Bomb?*"

Hyon-hui had turned green. The room was staring at them in horror. Everyone except Professor Yang, who was staring at the floor.

"Of course not! It was never scheduled to be ready until this summer. That's six –"

"You have not even achieved compression!" Pak cried. "What is the delay?"

"There is no problem," Mitch answered holding his voice steady. "This is what I expected. Look at the schedule. We're headed in the right direction. In a few more months, we'll –"

"The world is in turmoil, Dr. Weatherby. Your imperialist brothers are marching to war all over the planet. We could be next! I want a bomb! And I want it now!"

"Building a nuclear weapon is a tremendous technical challenge, Minister. We can do this, but it'll take time. It always takes time.'

"I have no doubt about that, Dr. Weatherby. With Juche as our guide, failure is not a possibility." He glanced at Hyon-hui. "I just wonder if all of our division leaders are up to it." Hyon-hui tried to shrink into her chair.

Mitch saw it and a cold hand wrapped around him. His voice grew anxious. "They're up to the challenge. All of 'em. I can —"

"*I* am not so sure that they are, Dr. Weatherby," Pak declared, glaring at Hyon-hui. "G-Division, under your esteemed leadership, has assembled critical masses and conducted neutron multiplication studies. T-Division solved the neutron velocity problem. Research Division has two new neutron sources. The Chemistry Division has made great improvements in metallurgy, purification, and source preparation. But as far as I can see, X-Division has done nothing!"

Mitch spluttered. "That's because the implosion system is —"

Pak cut him off and stared at Hyon-hui. "Why is that, Comrade Chun?" he asked coldly. Why has X-Division failed to produce a workable implosion design? Every division at Sagi-dong has performed flawlessly under Dr. Weatherby's leadership except yours." Condescension dripped like poison from his tongue. "Perhaps your mixed blood has left you an imbecile?"

Mitch flashed to anger. "That has nothing to do with it! The combined RaLa-Magnetic test yesterday shows that the detonator simultaneity problem has been solved. Symmetry was excellent. That was not the case when we started these runs back in August. If anything, it is the technology for shaping —"

"But was there any compression?" Pak inquired.

"That doesn't mean the test was a failure. This is an iterative process."

"*Iterative! Iterative! Iterative!*" Pak burst out, waving his arms and stomping his feet. "Let me tell you, Dr. Weatherby, I am sick of hearing that word! It is no secret that you are protecting Comrade Chun! And it is no secret why you are doing it! I want to see evidence of compression before the end of the year! If, by that time, Comrade Chun has not developed a workable implosion system, I will iterate her out of Sagi-dong!"

"*You must be joking!*" Mitch burst out. "That's less than four weeks and this is going to take another three months at least. We're ahead of the schedule that you agreed to last summer! We weren't even supposed to have the magnetic diagnostic ready until –"

"Exactly what I have been saying!" Pak cried. "All the other divisions are ahead of schedule except Comrade Chun's. You have until the end of the year. If we are not seeing compression by then, X-Division will have a new leader. Four weeks. Until the first of January." He stormed out, slamming the door behind him.

Hyon-hui was pale and trembling, her blank eyes fixed on nothing. Everyone else was in shock. "You heard the man," Mitch spat angrily. He threw his chalk at the board where it shattered and fell to the floor in pieces. "End of December. Thirty days. Keep working."

Hyon-hui rushed from the room. Professor Yang looked up, his eyes were filled with despair. But he said nothing, just turned and left the room.

"Wait until he cools off," Max advised as he came up beside Mitch. "Then you need to tell him that it's not Comrade Chun's fault. She is only casting the lens shapes that we calculate. I would go tell him now, but when he is like this," he shook his head back and forth, "there is no use talking to him."

"You really think that'd make a difference?" Mitch shot back. "Something is going on between her and Pak. Have you noticed it yet?"

"Yes," he said quietly, looking like he wanted to change the subject.

"You think she's screwing Pak, don't you?"

Max shrugged again. "I don't know Dr. Weatherby."

"Dr. Weatherby? You only call me that when you don't want to tell me bad news, Max. So you think she is screwing Pak."

Max nodded. "But I don't think she is enjoying it."

It was too much for Mitch. The heat came up his neck and he didn't even try to force it down. He gave a cry as he laid hold of the overhead projector, lifted it above his head, and smashed it onto the concrete floor with a tremendous crash. The lenses shattered and flung glass in all directions, the metal body twisted and bent into a mangled heap. Max stood, paralyzed. The few scientists in the room froze for an instant and then rushed out. Heads poked in the door, then jerked back out just as fast.

"Mitch," said Max, very calmly. "Calm down."

His entire body was still buzzing but he knew Max was right. But how to calm down? How to accept that the woman he could love was having an affair with someone they both hated just so she could be a member of a political party that cared nothing for her. How? he wondered. HOW??!!

"Breathe," Max said slowly. "Breathe…"

And Mitch did.

Suddenly Sonny was at his side. "Pak is really fubar," he said quietly.

A grim chuckle crawled out of Mitch's mouth. "I'd say you just used that phrase perfectly, Comrade," His eyes searched the door she'd gone through a few moments before. Except for the three of them, the rest of the room was now empty. He looked at the remains of the overhead projector. An entire day was shot. He glanced at his friends. "I'm going to go talk to her."

"Be careful," Max replied. "She may react strangely. I have found these North Koreans can behave very irrationally at times." He glanced at Sonny. "No offense."

"We can be extremely fubar," Sonny agreed matter-of-factly, and Mitch agreed completely.

Mitch arrived at Hyon-hui's underground office to find the door closed. He leaned forward, listening, then knocked gently. "Hyon-hui? You in there?"

"Go away," came a weak voice, so he opened the door and looked inside. She was hunched over the keyboard stabbing at keys. Her face was pale and her eyes were bleary and red. She glanced up at him with the air of a hunted animal, then turned back to her work.

"You okay?" he asked, then realized it was a stupid question. She just shrugged. "Can I come in?" Hyon-hui looked up and helplessness poured from her green eyes like a wave. Mitch entered and shut the door.

"It is hopeless," she choked, trying to stifle her sobs. "How are we supposed to function. No fuel. No food."

"I want you to know I think what Pak did back there was completely uncalled for and totally unprofessional."

She snorted in disgust. "What does it matter what *you* think. Or what I think. He is the leader of The Silla Project. I will respect any decision that he makes, and I will accept it with the proper revolutionary spirit. Juche calls us to display complete loyalty –"

"Cut the crap!" Mitch exclaimed. "You've been acting weird for weeks. It's affecting your work. And that means, it's affecting mine. Now, I want to know what's going on between you two."

"*Nothing is going on!*" she spat. "Nothing that concerns you. Nothing important. Why you would ask, I do not know. There is nothing. Nothing between us, I tell you. Nothing. He has never touched me!"

Mitch froze, his heart pounding. "Why did you say that?"

"Say what?"

"That he never touched you. What did he do to you?" Mitch demanded and he could feel his muscles cramp as they tightened with rage. He didn't need to lose it again. Not in front of her.

"It, it doesn't matter," she stammered. "There is nothing you or I can do about it. You cannot protect me from him, even if you wanted to. I will soon be gone from this place and you will forget that I ever existed."

"You're not going anywhere."

"What do you expect me to do" She said bitterly. "He takes what he wants. No one can stop him."

Mitch slammed his hand on the metal desk as he rose and paced the two steps across the tiny office. This wasn't right. He had to do something – anything – to help her. To stop Pak. He spun around and looked at her tear stained face, and suddenly saw the solution.

"Hyon-hui. We're going to give Pak compression before the end of the year. We can do it."

"If you believe so, you are a fool, Mitch Weatherby," she spat. "You know that we cannot –"

"We're not going to do spherical implosion," he said in a clear, hard voice and she stopped. "We are going to show compression in a *cylindrical* implosion."

"Cylindrical?"

"Pak said he wanted to see compression. We're going to give him compression so he can have his bomb. He never said it had to be spherical."

Hope dared to enter her eyes. "Will that work? I mean, will it result in supercriticality?"

"Oh, yes, it'll work. It's in half our stockpile. The Russians, too. It's a lot easier."

Hyon-hui's almond eyes grew large and round. "Why did you not mention this before?" she gasped. "Why have we gone through all this effort and wasted this time if this is just as good and a lot easier?!"

"It's not quite as good. There is a slight loss of efficiency. A few percent. Plus –" his voice trailed off and he looked away, pain in his expression.

"*Plus what?!*" she cried, jumping out of her chair. "*Why have you waited until now to tell me of this? When it is too late! I am doomed!*"

"*It's a classified system!*" he blurted. "*A top secret design.*" His voice fell and his shoulders drooped as he fell down into the chair. His last pretense of dignity and honor vaporized. "Above TS. Critical Nuclear Weapons Design Information. CNWDI. I took an oath not to reveal it." He said as tears welled up in his eyes. "In all my years, I have never betrayed that trust. Not even once." He looked up at her, searching for sympathy, and became lost in her eyes. "Did you know that as long as I've been here, I have yet to reveal *anything* classified at *any* level. So far, everything has been managerial and open source, except for a few slips. The technical stuff, the RaLa testing, the uranium hydride, it's all open source. *This* changes all that. Now…" he sighed heavily. "I really am the traitor they said I was." He hung his head. "I'm a traitor. Betraying my country… betraying my family… my ancestors… Betraying my God." His voice trailed off as he shook his head sadly. "But I have no choice."

"Don't do this for me, Mitch," Hyon-hui said quietly. "I am not worthy."

"You don't understand, Hyon-hui," he choked looking up into her eyes. "You don't understand." He swallowed heavily. "I won't let this happen to another woman that I –" His voice clamped off. Did he love her? He blinked away tears and said thickly, "I can't go through this twice."

18

"Have you ever done this?" Professor Yang asked with more than a touch of skepticism.

"No," Mitch answered, having come to terms with his treason. It was no longer about him, he decided. His soul was already condemned and there was no way they'd ever let him leave alive. This was about saving Hyon-hui. Maybe, somehow, that would make up, just a little, for his failure to protect Beth. A heavy swallow pushed down the residual guilt. "But it's in several fielded designs and I understand the concept."

"Which fielded designs?"

Mitch paused and answered simply, "I'd rather not say."

No one pressed the issue. They'd become more than just comrades over the past months and knew it was Mitch who had bound them together, not nationalism, or ideology, or even Pak's tyranny. It was about the truth of science. Mitch turned to a blackboard and referred to some drawings he'd constructed before the meeting.

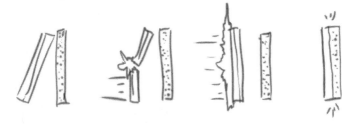

The concept, he went on to explain, was a totally new way to compress the fissionable material based on a technique known as explosion welding, or flying-plate welding. Two pieces of dissimilar metal to be permanently bonded are placed at a slight angle to one another. High explosive is carefully layered on the side of one piece, opposite the other. When the explosive is initiated, a detonation wave travels up the HE, shearing the angled plate and resulting in hydrodyamic flow of the metal. At the point that the entire explosive is consumed, the angled plate is now parallel to the stationary plate and moving toward it a high speed. When the two come together, the metals bond due to the hydrodynamic flow at the surface. The technique could then be easily extended to include two flying plates that bond to either side of the stationary. Of course, in a practical system, the angles tend to be very shallow, almost undetectable to the eye, and the central rod is fatter more than tall.

The scientists were intrigued, but what really got their attention was extrapolating the concept into a full three dimensions. If the stationary plate were actually a cylinder, and the flying plates on either side formed a surface of rotation about the cylinder – a truncated cone – the entire outer surface could be layered in high explosive. If this were detonated along the bottom edge simultaneously, this cone would become a collapsing cylinder, called a *tamper*, that would impact and then compress the stationary cylinder. Fabricate the central rod from a fissionable substance, and it becomes a way to transition from a subcritical system to a highly supercritical system. It becomes a bomb.

Everyone stared in wonder as Mitch's words died to silence. He glanced at Max who gave him a single, perfunctory nod. Both knew what Mitch had just given them.

"Pwn!" Sonny finally exclaimed. "It is so simple!"

"A unitary, symmetric lens," Hyon-hui said in astonishment. "Single detonator." Her brow furrowed. "Placement could cause problems if not carefully calculated."

"But it will not be as efficient," commented Sonny, showing doubt.

Mitch smiled inwardly. This kid was a genius. Too bad he was stuck here. "True. But you can get more compression in 2-D, so you get some of it back."

"But not all," added Max.

Sonny spoke up again. "Choice of the angle could be problematic. If too steep, the bottom will implode first producing a jet from the top."

"True," agreed Yi Tong-whi from metallurgy. "But casting a cylindrical pit, especially if hollow, will be much less complicated."

"And look how much it will simplify boosting," Max suggested. "The entire top is open. Tritium line to center would be very simple. Modulated initiators would be easy to replace and the warhead could be made completely safe by inserting a plug into the center."

"Testing," Hyon-hui exclaimed, "would be simplified as the imploding cone could be directly imaged from above by a high speed camera."

"So would RaLa testing!" added Sonny. "The pit is much more accessible."

"The real question is," said the professor, bringing the younger ones back down to Earth, "how long is this going to take? Is three and a half weeks a realistic goal? And do we have enough energy to do it? I'm not talking about fuel or the power blackouts. I'm talking about food."

"No, it's totally unrealistic," answered Mitch without emotion. "For every reason you can think of. But we really don't have a choice. So we're going to have to stay focused. The bulk of the work is going to fall to X and CM. All we have to do is turn cones. Press lenses. Blow 'em up. It's not like the 32-point system where some of the components have twenty vertices and twelve sides. Some of them curved. As simple as this lens is, X can get started on the one-dimensional case this afternoon. Those tests are small enough that we can run them in the blockhouse at the Explosives Facility."

Mitch set a grueling schedule. Less than a week for the single plate testing. Another week to gather data for the two-sided configuration. This would give time for the machine shop to come up to speed on turning the cylindrical tampers and the test sites time to reconfigure their electrical grids and install high-speed cameras. Max also needed time to transform his spherical implosion simulation into a cylindrical implosion simulation in order to support X-Division in calculating the tamper shapes. In two weeks, Mitch wanted them doing full-up cylindrical tests. But they were going to need dozens of cylindrical tampers to test, which would seriously tax the machine shop. The grizzled old machinist, who could make anything out of metal, assured Mitch that they were up to the task, but Sonny's back-of-the-envelope calculations proved that he was being optimistic at best. Hyon-hui hit on an idea for using pipe as the blanks for the cylindrical tampers, since it would require removing less metal. But where to get the pipe?

In the United States, it would just take a few phone calls to order the necessary materials, or bring in some more theorists and staff up on the simulation effort. But here in North Korea, there were bottlenecks everywhere. Not enough trained personnel. Not enough raw materials. Not enough access to technology. Not enough equipment. But these were the least of their problems, Mitch realized, looking over his technical team. Seventy years ago, Los Alamos had gotten by with equipment far less advanced than the Koreans had access to today. The biggest problem was that there wasn't enough food or electricity. Professor Yang was right, these people were all slowly starving to death. None of them, including himself, were physically ready for the sixteen to twenty hour days an effort like this was going to require – with the Juche study sessions and bitterly cold weather on top of it. They just weren't getting enough calories or protein to bear up under the strain.

But maybe there was something Mitch could do about that, he thought as he watched the gaunt and haggard scientists file out of the room. It was a crazy idea, but with what they were facing, he had to at least try.

Colonel Phoung, Sagi-dong's head of security, frowned. He always frowned, but this was on top of his usual sneer. "A very unusual request, Dr. Weatherby. Very unusual. My first inclination is to refuse."

"Well, we can't go on like this, sir," Mitch pleaded, standing in front of the colonel's desk in the lab security office. Above him, on the wall, hung the usual family portraits. "My people, and yours, are just too hungry. We can't design a nuclear weapon if we can't concentrate."

"And you think that one man – you – can make a difference?" His grim face was even more lined than usual.

"The Great Leader was one man," Mitch answered.

Colonel Phoung sighed heavily. "Dr. Weatherby, do you realize what you are asking? You want me to give you a loaded rifle, and let you disappear into the mountains."

Mitch shrugged. "Well, when you put it like that it does sound crazy. But I didn't want to go alone."

"My men are not hunters. They are trained to defend our homeland from foreign aggressors and imperialist. From *yang-kees* like yourself! They know nothing of hunting!"

"I'll teach them, Colonel. I've been hunting since I was a little kid. All through the mountains of Northern New Mexico and Southern Colorado. Even done some hunts in Wyoming, Montana, and Alaska. Terrain not much different than here. I know there's game up there. I've seen tracks in the snow. There's deer and boar up there."

"How am I going to explain this to Comrade Minister Pak Yong-nam?"

Mitch knew the colonel still wasn't convinced so searched for the man's buttons. They all had them. "You've seen Comrade Pak. He likes to eat."

Colonel Phoung nodded and sighed deeply and then surprised Mitch. "I will consider it, Comrade Weatherby. If there is anyone who appreciates the importance of a full belly to good morale, it is a soldier. And I appreciate your concern for our people. That is the mark of a good officer. And a Party cadre." Mitch caught a queer gleam in the soldier's eye. It lasted only a second, then was gone. "But you must realize, Dr. Weatherby, even if I approve this hunt, any game is the property of the people. I will have to get special permission from the Party. And then, it is likely that we will only get to keep twenty percent."

"Twenty percent?! What happens to the rest?"

"It will be collected by the Party and redistributed."

Mitch felt heat rising up his collar. "You're a man of action, Colonel Phoung, so I'm going to say this plainly. The Party's redistribution system means the cadres receive everything and the people receive nothing."

Colonel Phoung didn't even blink. "Twenty percent is one hundred percent better than nothing."

Two days passed before Mitch heard anything more about his request. The first round of flying plate tests went as planned and they moved on to two-sided testing several days ahead of schedule. The team was running smoothly gathering data and Mitch found himself mostly helping Max and Professor Yang on the mathematical models.

On the morning of the third day, Colonel Phoung appeared at Mitch's door. He had a peculiar habit of appearing silently and one never knew how long he'd been standing there watching.

"I will grant your request," he said simply. "My men are hungry too – as am I – and if you can train them, I would be in your debt. Report to my headquarters this afternoon. I will have two of my men meet you at the front security building at two-thirty. Dress warmly."

*

The sky was deep blue as only a mountain winter can provide. The streets were deserted and the snow crunched under Mitch's insulated boots. It was almost enjoyable. Almost. Mitch spied guards in the towers, watching him. And his stomach ached. He was hungry.

The idyllic setting was further eroded when he was stopped twice, in less than a half-mile, by grim-faced soldiers wearing heavy coats and gray-green fur hats demanding to see his papers. But each time he was released and continued on his way. But as a result, he arrived a few minutes late at the heavy, single story security building. Two young men were waiting in a shoddy North Korean copy of a Russian UAZ-469, like a cross between an old Willys Jeep and a Hummer. As Mitch approached, the older and slightly more experienced looking of the two soldiers climbed out. An unusually tall North Korean.

"You're late," he growled in a thick accent. Both stared at him with mistrust and fear.

"I kept getting stopped by security," Mitch said, his heart racing in their presence. Either of these two would be willing to kill him in an instant, and think nothing of it. What was he doing?

The two soldiers glanced at one another, said something guttural in Korean, and laughed. After double-checking Mitch's papers they climbed in the UAZ and were on their way.

At the gate, they stopped again and presented more papers to a similarly clad guard wearing a shin-length wool overcoat. An AK-47 was slung over his back with a long, curved magazine sticking out of the receiver. The level of "security" did nothing to make Mitch feel safe, but the ice and snow covered drive down the steep road toward Yonjom-dong presented a more immediate threat. But it was beautiful as well. Mount Paektu gleamed white in the distance framed by the steep, snowy walls of the valley. Much different than when he'd arrived in the summer.

They stopped at the Army headquarters building, where Mitch was greeted warmly by the colonel. They exchanged bows, and Phoung led Mitch down a paneled hall leading toward the rear of the building. Soldiers in uniform were all about. A few cast him dirty looks but for the most part they ignored him.

The corridor was lined with the expected propaganda photos. Most of it was Kim Il-sung, but there were also pictures from the Korean War, or as Mitch had learned it was called, The Victorious Fatherland Liberation War. He scanned them casually until one brought him to a dead stop. It was the flag raising photograph from Iwo Jima. Except... He leaned in and looked closer. It was a North Korean flag! And those weren't Marines. One was even wearing a fur hat! They had copied it. Altered it or staged the same scene!

"Jujak Peak," said Colonel Phoung, his voice suddenly thick. "When the victorious Peoples Army crushed the imperialists. It was the finest hour of the 337th Infantry Regiment."

"And this picture was taken then?" Mitch asked.

"Yes," the colonel answered, swelling with pride. Mitch pressed his lips tightly and said nothing. It would do no good.

In the armory, the colonel introduced Mitch to Sergeant Paik, a balding soldier with a broad smile and an amicable manner. He proudly showed Mitch racks of assault rifles, rocket lunchers, mortars, and submachine guns. Large steel shelves held ammo-boxes and flat, wood cases with rocket propelled grenades and mortar shells. The sergeant went to one of the racks and selected a sleek, long-barreled rifle that looked like a stretched AK-47. Mitch instantly recognized the Russian-made *Dragunov* sniper rifle. Sergeant Paik opened the breech with a firm slap and handed it to Mitch.

Mitch examined the rifle with all his experience from hunting in the mountains of New Mexico. It was not the first time he'd held an AK-47-type weapon. It seemed a bit nose heavy and he wasn't very impressed with the trigger pull, but other than that it seemed functional.

The sergeant instructed Mitch in the Juche method for tearing down the rifle and cleaning it. Then he demonstrated the use of a Juche designed stuck-case-extractor which just so happened to have been designed by Kim Jong-il himself, or so the sergeant told him. Finally, he gave Mitch instruction on the Juche method of shooting as outlined and demonstrated by Generalissimo Kim Jong-il's on-the-spot guidance at the 574th KPA unit on April 24, 1997. Mitch listened respectfully.

Finally, Mitch, the sergeant, and the two young SSA soldiers, Private First Class Shim Jae-kee and Private Kim Bok-won, climbed into a truck and drove down a frozen dirt road to a nearby rifle range. By the time they commenced firing, it was on the edge of dusk and the tritium lamp in the scope proved its worth.

As Americans have done for over two hundred years, Mitch demonstrated that mediocre training of conscripts can't replace a heritage of gun ownership by free men. After properly zeroing the scope, Mitch shot inch-and-a-half groups at a hundred meters standing, and four-inch groups at two hundred meters seated. By the time they returned to the UAZ, chilled and stiff, all three had abandoned Kim Jong-il's advice, instead soliciting Mitch's advice on marksmanship.

19

Over the next few weeks, Mitch found himself balancing game hunting with being a nuclear weapons designer, much as he'd done at Los Alamos. Professor Yang not only helped derive the equations for the conical tamper but also gave Mitch tips on hunting Korean deer and the Asian wild boar. During the Japanese occupation of World War II, Professor Yang's father had stalked game to survive. Under communist rule, private ownership of firearms was strictly forbidden so Professor Yang had never hunted, but he fondly remembered the stories his father used to tell him.

The daylight hunting hadn't worked, as Professor Yang had predicted. Five times they'd returned empty handed, because Korean game was primarily nocturnal. Yang warned him that he'd see little during the day other than squirrels, rabbits, and an occasional fox, perhaps even a tiger, but nothing edible. Colonel Phoung however, citing security concerns, was loathe to let Mitch out at night.

But there had been one bright spot in the past week. General Ri solved the main supply problem by obtaining rocket motor cases from a missile factory near Kanggae to use as blanks for the cylindrical plates. And on the weapons design front, as expected, the two-sided flying plate was a mere formality. They quickly moved on to cylindrical flying plates which turned out to be much more difficult. But there, the first test was an impressive failure. Instead of compressing the pit, it created a brilliant jet of molten metal that destroyed the high speed camera in a blinding flash. Later tests moved the expensive photographic equipment to the side and used an angled mirror. Hyon-hui was publicly denigrated for the failure by Pak Yong-nam who promised to have her sent to work a coal mine to die like her father.

They kept trying, but no matter how they varied the cone-angle of the flying plate, it simply would not compress the pit. It would pinch it at a point. Or squeeze it from one end to the other. Or blow it to bits. Indeed, by the end of the second week after nearly a hundred trials, they were no closer to arriving at compression than they had been at the beginning of the week. Why it varied so much from the simple, one-dimensional cases, nobody could understand. Mitch attributed their inability to solve the problem to malnutrition. None of them could concentrate. He was certain the implosion problem was simple and staring him right in the face, and all they needed was a few, good, protein-heavy meals.

And just as they all despaired that things couldn't get worse, Pak announced that instead of two more weeks, they only had one. He would be leaving a week before the end of the year to participate in New Year's celebrations in P'yongyang and would be gone through the middle of January. Anything they wanted to show him had to be ready before he left, and any changes in personnel were to be made then as well. Everyone knew what this meant.

And still if got worse. The supply trucks from Kanggae stopped coming. Not only was the nation out of food, it was out of gas. Party members blamed the imperialists bastards in the West for the oppression. As the food situation became ever more dire, more people became ill. That's when Mitch began thinking of escape. Looking for an opportunity, though there was none. He'd take Hyon-hui with him, he'd decided, half knowing that it would never happen and that the hope was nothing but a fantasy of a starving man.

In the middle of November, several older staff members became ill and died. After that, a key machinist died, and others were weakening. So, with crisis looming, Colonel Phoung cleared Mitch for a hunt the night before their final day of testing. Mitch knew the tests would fail. But it didn't matter, he thought. This was his chance. He and Hyon-hui would be gone by morning.

*

"Hyon-hui."

She looked up from her workstation, took off her glasses, and put on a weak smile. She had resigned herself to her fate. North Koreans seemed good at that, and Mitch wondered if their brothers in the South were as fatalistic.

"Any progress?" he asked.

"None," she answered. "I've been over at Theoretical all day."

"What'd you come up with?"

"Max and Comrade Ho-pyong think it is hydrodynamic. An un-modeled effect. That *is* the problem isn't it? At least all the high speed photography shows the base of the flying plate closing up too fast. And we don't have time to study it properly."

"But we've tried variable angles."

"We've tried everything."

"Yeah. I know it has to be something simple. I just can't seem to put my finger on it."

"So you don't have any ideas, either?"

Mitch shook his head and rubbed his belly. "We've tried all my ideas. Besides, I'm so frickin' hungry all the time I can hardly think." He tapped his skull. "Brain doesn't seem to be working right. I think we need some protein."

"I agree." She smiled weakly. "I guess you'll be up here all night, too?" But Mitch hesitated before answering. "Mitch? What is it?" she asked.

"I'm not going to be up here tonight. I'm going hunting."

"Hunting?"

"Yeah," he said sheepishly. "Colonel Phoung has allowed me to go hunting to try to help with the food shortage."

She cocked her head. "Wh – Why tonight? Wouldn't some other night be better?"

"Yeah. But I've already been up there a dozen times during the day. It was like pulling teeth to get out after sundown."

"*Hunting?!*" she cried. "Does Pak know about this?"

"Of course. He was all for it."

"Are you an idiot?" Hyon-hui shook her head in disgust. "Of course, he is! Don't you see what he's trying to do? He wants us to fail! We've all been trying to get this working and you've been wasting time hunting?"

"We're starving to death in case you haven't noticed, so I'd hardly call it –"

"And all this time I thought you were working!" she snapped angrily. "But you were up there on that mountain. You've been trying to get up there ever since you arrived and you finally got the chance!"

"We have to eat! People are dying, Hyon-hui."

"Mitch, the test is tomorrow! If it fails, I – I – I will be – You can't leave tonight!"

"It's important, Hyon-hui. I have something to tell –"

"So is this! If you had spent more time the last few weeks at the lab we might not be facing this!" Her eyes flashed.

"Look," he retorted, as his own temperature began to rise. "If we don't get some protein, we're not gonna get much farther anyway, walking around like a bunch of burnt-out zombies. Besides, there's something I need to –"

"And your hunting is going to fix all that? You're going to feed the entire town?"

"Would you just slow down for a second?" Mitch hissed. "I need to tell you something. I am –"

"There is no way you can feed the entire town!" she blurted, interrupting him again.

"I'm not gonna' feed the entire town but it's a start! We gotta do something." Mitch's voice started to raise. "I'm not just gonna sit up here and starve to death! What's wrong with you people anyway? You're just willing to sit back and do nothing? I don't get it!"

"Sit back and do nothing?" Hyon-hui shrieked. "It is because of the Americans that we have no food!"

"The Americans?" Mitch laughed. "What can they possibly have to do with it?"

"Ever since the Victorious Fatherland Liberation War, they have been trying to isolate us from the rest of the world. They could not defeat us on the field of battle, so they try to defeat us economically. They would starve children to death and freeze old people just to have our nation. The imperialist aggressors will stop at nothing!"

"If you're out of food and gas, don't blame Americans. Centralized economic planning *always* does this. Just look at the Soviet Union or Europe. The Eurozone is just about dead. The only reason China is –"

"The Soviets," she said bitterly, her voice dripping with venom. "They sold themselves into the slavery of capitalism and see where it has landed them." Her voice swelled with pride. "But the imperialist American aggressors should not hope that Choson will be so easily defeated."

"You really think the U.S. cares about your pathetic little country?" He'd been listening to this since his arrival and was sick of it. "It's smaller than Mississippi. And a lot poorer. You all act like the Korean War ended yesterday and the Americans are over there getting all whipped up in a frenzy to come back over here for round two."

"Well, they are!"

"Hyon-hui, they don't give a rat's ass about this *ttong* hole" Mitch bellowed. "You ask an American about North Korea and they're gonna scratch their head. Ninety-nine percent of Americans couldn't even tell you what D-P-R-K means, and I bet half-of 'em couldn't find it on a map, though Kim Jong-il always gets a laugh on the late-night talk shows. This war is dead and buried for fifty years. You guys are the only ones keeping it alive."

"I thought you were different but you are just like the rest," she shrieked. "They murder your wife and still you attack. Are all Americans so stupid and brainwashed? Is that all your people know? Is that all they think? How can they destroy us?"

"You have got to be joking!" Mitch fired back. "The only reason the world pays any attention at all to North Korea is because you're so psychotic! Listen to you!"

"You lie! All Americans are liars! The Workers' Paradise is the envy of the world. It drives the imperialists mad to know that there are those who would defy them and yet live in peace and prosperity."

"Workers' Para –" Mitch choked. "Prosper – This country is a complete and total joke. The laughing stock of the industrialized world. You have absolutely no idea what's going on outside your borders."

"Our nation has a perfect structure and the people are truly free. Not the false freedom of Capitalism. The slavery of capitalism. Our leader is the most brilliant, iron-willed commander of the age!   Juche-sasang is the most scientifically advanced system of socialism the world has ever seen! We pay no taxes! There are no poor! We have no want! Can you say that about the United States?!"

"Well, I –"

"Everyone has a job, free retirement, free healthcare for life. There is no theft, no murder, no hunger, no rape –" Hyon-hui started shaking all over and her face grew red. With surprising speed, she leapt around the desk cursing him, flailing wildly with her hands and screaming insults.

The attack caught Mitch off guard, and a wicked slap turned his cheek red. He pushed her away and retreated from the office, jerking the door shut in her face. He could hear her yelling and kicking the door as he held it shut. A few heads poked out but did their usual turtle when Mitch finally turned around.

Back at his apartment he choked down two spoonfuls of rice. If she was going to act that way, fine. They could all sit here and rot for all he cared, but he had no intention of starving to death. He dressed and headed for the security building where he was to meet Privates Kim and Shim.

"Plan?" he whispered to himself as he walked. "I have no plan." His brow knotted. He would have to kill the two soldiers to escape. He had no doubt that Shim would gladly kill him, and that seemed to justify it in his head. But the younger of the two soldiers, Private Kim Bok-won, had turned out to be a very likable fellow. He was misinformed and his head was full of mush, but he had a good heart. Mitch had no desire to kill him. And faced with that thought, the whole idea of trying to escape seemed ridiculous and unreal. Still, he had to try. Escape was better than the alternatives of slowly starving to death or more mercifully being killed for failure to produce a bomb.

The walk to the front gate was long and cold and the big portraits of Kim Il-sung on the buildings along 1st Street stared down at him as the thought about the things he'd said to Hyon-hui. North Korea was a joke to the rest of the world, but he had said it to hurt her. And that was the last thing he wanted to do. He'd meant to tell her to be home by ten o'clock, but his anger and frustration with this place had gotten the best of him. Now, she'd be in the lab all night and there was no way he could get her out. Unless he could slip in through one of the RaLa site tunnels. The thought was intriguing but at the same time, he didn't know if he could find the entrances. Or if Hyon-hui would come with him or turn him in.

When he arrived, Mitch was surprised to find Colonel Phoung waiting there with the soldiers.

"Colonel Phoung," Mitch said, bowing anxiously. "You're joining us tonight?" In a strange sort of way, he liked the colonel. Of all the people he'd met in Korea who were in leadership positions, Colonel Phoung was the most genuine.

"No, I am not," the colonel replied. "I have come to see you off and to give you this." He held out a bulky wooden case with Russian and Korean writing on it.

"What is it?"

"PGN-1 night vision scope. For the Dragunov. I sighted it in myself." Their eyes met. It made Mitch uncomfortable but he couldn't look away and he wondered if the colonel could read his mind. "Dr. Weatherby, I expect you to take care of my men and return them to me unbroken. They are like children to me and I should hate to lose one of them."

Mitch nodded, feeling very exposed. "I understand, sir."

"Then good hunting, Doctor. And bring something back with you. I am hungry."

Private Shim turned the UAZ onto the road that ran along the perimeter of Sagi-dong. There had once been a gravel road that connected Sagi-dong with the mining village of Sayang-dong on the other side of Wagal Peak. The year before though, the whole slope had given way under the rains and the little that remained was now virtually impassable, but they pressed on.

The sky was clear when they stopped, and the sun had long since dipped behind the ridge. It would be growing dark soon but a nearly full moon was rising from the other side of the valley. Mitch attached the night vision scope to the Dragunov and pulled his gear from the vehicle. With his rations, and those of Bok-won and Jae-kee, he and Hyon-hui would have food enough for several days along with weapons and warm clothing. And in the UAZ, they could cover some good ground. The only thing he hadn't worked out yet was how he was going to get Hyon-hui out of Sagi-dong. And where they'd go after that. And how they'd actually get out of North Korea. And there was the matter of murdering his companions.

I could kill them now, he thought. They were unarmed and bantering lightly as they readied their packs. Mitch found himself imagining Shim as Pak. Killing Pak would be a pleasure. Mitch checked the magazine. It was filled with jacketed hollow points. He pulled back the bolt on the Dragunov, then let it slide forward slowly, feeding the first cartridge into the breech. He pushed the bolt home until he felt the lugs lock into the receiver, then imagined the dead eyes of the men staring up at him. Their bright red blood spilled across the snow. And the image of it being Pak lying there in place of the soldiers dissolved. And what if he only wounded one of them? Or if the Dragunov jammed? Not now, he thought, flipping the safety up with his thumb. Too close to the road. Not now.

They headed across the north slope of the mountain following a trail that was probably a thousand years old. The sky passed through deepening shades of blue and purple until the silvery glow of the rising moon illuminated the land, blotting out the stars. At a clearing, sweating from the exertion despite the bitter temperatures, each ate a few bites and Mitch told them to wrap their trash in plastic. After everything was cleaned up, he had them climb up into trees to wait.

The spot Mitch picked had been the site of a landslide. The soil was deep and loamy and rotting tree trunks poked from the ground. A hundred yards to the east, they could hear the stream that tumbled into Sagi-dong further down the mountain. Professor Yang had told him, abundant rotting vegetation, a source of water, and deep soil, attracted wild boar.

Mitch could just make out the outlines of his comrades in trees to either side. As always he was between them. They each sat on a folded blanket and for safety had a short piece of rope tied about his waist. Not the best shooting position but the snow-covered field was spread out just below them like a shining, silver sheet, making it easy to spot their prey. If it came.

The frigid hours stretched out while they silently waited, and Mitch's mind turned to Hyon-hui. He stared up at the moon as if began to dip to the west. It was inconceivable that a member of the Korean Workers' Party would ever accept an apology after what he'd said. He imagined the possibility of happier days with her, like one's he'd had with Beth. Picnics. Thanksgiving with his whole family showing up. Maybe Hyon-hui would add Korean dishes to the normal holiday fare.

His mind froze on that thought and he counted on his fingers. Thanksgiving had passed. Tonight was – it was Christmas Eve! His heart ached at the memory of Christmases past. Of watching Beth joyfully sing in the church choir. Of helping her bake cookies. Reading the story of Christ's birth. Of all the traditions he may never hold again. They didn't care here. His comrades didn't even know what Christmas was. It was as gone as his faith. His pain turned to black anger as he dwelled on the cruel twist of fate that had landed him in this God-forsaken place. He raised his weapon and targeted Bok-won's head in the sight. He held his breath, and his finger began to squeeze.

And he exhaled. He couldn't do it.

He lowered his rifle, when a snuffling sound from below drew his attention. The light of the moon, so bright before, was nearly gone. A few flakes of snow drifted out of the intense darkness. Mitch peered down, just making out dark objects against the white field below. Mitch lifted the Dragunov to his shoulder and looked through the scope at the field that now appeared bright green.

"There you are," Mitch whispered to himself when he finally detected movement. Through the scope, something that looked like a cross between a pot-bellied pig and a cat was alternately plowing with its head and scratching with its hind legs as it moved into the clearing. An easy shot. Only about ninety yards.

Then again, perhaps he should take this opportunity to dispatch Bok-won, sitting a few yards ahead of him. These were heathens, he reminded himself. And they'd kill him in a heartbeat if the situation were reversed. He checked on Shim's position. He was behind Mitch but he might have time to get turned around. This wouldn't work. Then a better idea came to mind.

He placed the post sight just behind the grainy, green phosphor image of the boar's front shoulder, and squeezed the trigger. In a thunderous blast, the.30 caliber bullet streaked from the barrel in a flash of white light. The creature leapt into the air a full six feet, squealing and crashed down into the snow. It tried to struggle to its feet once, then collapsed.

Cheers came from the branches of nearby trees and their trunks shook and dropped snow as his comrades moved to climb down.

"Stop!" Mitch barked. "*Jong-jee!* Bok-won, go see if it's dead." A moment later, muffled, crunching steps could be heard approaching the clearing.

Mitch followed his comrade's progress across the clearing with his night vision scope. A solitary green figure, holding his rifle in his hands before him, advanced hesitantly across the opening to where the steaming body of the animal lay. Who should he kill first? He twisted around and the crosshairs in Mitch's scope came to rest on Private Shim, seated in a tree twenty meters away. Mitch could see him following Bok-won's progress. A smile was on his face. Mitch flicked off the safety and placed his finger on the trigger. It was now or never. The pit of his stomach heaved and twisted, and in the back of his mind, Mitch knew this is how Beth had looked to the FBI sniper. He tensed his finger on the trigger.

A roar split the frigid night air. But it wasn't the Dragunov.

Mitch spun around and snapped the rifle down to glimpse a dark mass hurtling across the clearing. The mate of the slain animal. It bore down on Bok-won with terrible speed. The young soldier froze before the speeding locomotive's tusks, sinew and bone. Mitch swung the crosshairs in the path of the onrushing beast but it flashed through the field of view. In seconds, the beast would be on Bok-won, tearing him to pieces.

He switched to the iron sights. They glowed a dull-green from the decaying tritium. He placed them on the animal, moved just ahead, and squeezed off two shots. *Crack! Crack!*

Five meters from Bok-won, the animal stumbled and plowed into the snow, digging through to the mud beneath, churning out great dark clods which flung across the silvery surface. It slid into the diminutive North Korean, sending him spinning like a rag doll.

Mitch knew his chance was gone. "You check on Bok-won," he yelled to Private Shim. "I'll check on the boar."

Bok-won Kim was struggling to his feet when Private Shim reached him. "Comrade?" he exclaimed in Korean, extending a hand.

"Yes," he answered with a shaky voice, trying to laugh now that it was over. He was covered with snow but seemed uninjured. "Can you help me find my rifle?"

Mitch stopped where the big boar lay next to its mate. In the dark, he couldn't tell where he'd hit it or how many times, but it had dropped fast and a powerful gamy smell had filled the air. "He's dead," Mitch called to the others, and saw Bok-won wiping the snow from his rifle.

"You saved my life," Bok-won said gravely as he approached. "I shall not forget it."

"I'm just glad you're okay! That was close."

Bok-won went on bowing repeatedly. "You are the finest marksman in all of Korea. How ever were you able to do it?"

"Just lucky, I guess," Mitch replied.

"Perhaps you can teach the men in my company how to shoot like that? We would be the finest marksmen in the world!"

"We already are," said Private Shim with disgust.

Mitch estimated their first kill, the female, weighed at least 180 pounds. The other, a large, thick, male, was huge and would top the scales at over 300. There was no way they could carry him out by themselves. And certainly not in the dark.

"Make camp," he said to the two Koreans, pulling out a long, sharp hunting knife that shone dimly in the night.

"What are you going to do with that?" Private Shim asked alarmed.

"Field dress it."

"Dress it?"

"Gut it. Cut out the entrails. Can't leave it here all night with its bowels full. Ruin the meat."

"You can do that?" marveled Bok-won, peering over his comrade's shoulder like a child regarding a dead dog in the street. "Will you teach me?"

"Grab a flashlight."

They threw a rope over a tree limb and the three of them hauled the carcasses into the air by their hind legs. As he showed the fascinated soldiers how to field dress an animal, he realized that he was grateful he had not killed his companions no matter how much he disliked them. He wasn't a murderer, and certainly not in cold blood. And he didn't really have an escape plan. Just an escape desire. Acting on it would have only succeeded in getting him killed, or worse.

But something needed to change. The meat would help with the starvation, but they needed a successful test. Hyon-hui's future depended on it. As he sliced into the large boar, he began silently praying that something might happen to give them a successful test, or at least a reprieve. It was the first time that he had prayed since he'd eaten dinner with Hyon-hui last summer. He'd tried a few times but had been unable to... to connect – whatever that meant – and ended up feeling silly, even in the solitude of his apartment. But in the darkness and cold of the Korean night, for some reason, Mitch didn't feel quite so alone. Maybe it was because it was Christmas, or maybe it was because he'd had the chance to commit murder and didn't, or maybe it was just because Mitch was excited about having a successful hunt – whatever the reason – the prayer didn't feel as hollow.

Mitch looked at the shining faces of his two companions and the bounty of fresh meat in front of them, and smiled. A pork barbecue was not only the best Christmas present he'd ever received, it was also the best he'd ever given. And with that thought, a warmth for these industrious, hard working, maltreated people rose up inside him. And as he stood there in the frigid night with snow flakes sifting from the clouds, his chest filled with an inexplicable pride.

They pitched their tent in the middle of the silver clearing not far from where Bok-won had gone down, and climbed inside, nestling deep into their clammy sleeping bags. Of all his time in North Korea, this to Mitch, seemed the most bizarre, and he told them so. Heavily armed, bivouacked with two KPA special operations troopers on the side of a mountain in the middle of the winter. If he wasn't so cold, he'd have sworn it was all a weird dream. Regardless, he was… happy.

Their conversation wandered. Mitch gave his impressions of North Korea, taking care not to be insulting, then told them something of America. Even Private Shim listened, though for the most part, said that Mitch was lying. Especially about the supermarkets stocked with fresh fruit and vegetables. But Bok-won was interested and wanted to see it for himself.

The talk eventually turned to guns and weapons and the Koreans were surprised by Mitch's knowledge of firearms, which greatly exceeded their own. Bok-won and Shim were especially stunned to learn that any American can simply walk into a gun store and purchase a firearm. The reason – something Mitch called *liberty* – they had no grasp of, but agreed that all those guns would make invasion difficult. There was, of course, the obligatory argument about which was better; the AK-47 or the M-16. Which turned into the 7.62 mm bullet versus the NATO 5.56. Soviet armor versus American armor. Soviet planes versus American planes. Mitch mentioned the Iraq war but they had no idea such a war had even occurred, only that the Americans were hopelessly bogged down in Afghanistan which they had invaded for the opium. Mitch let it go.

Private Shim was amazed, most of all, by the fact that Mitch used to make his own ammunition. Mitch's father had done his own reloading as a boy and Mitch picked it up from him.

"Many of the most popular cartridges in the U.S.," Mitch told them, "were derived from the .30-06 just because there was so much of the stuff left over after World War I. Two-seventy. Two-forty-three. Three-oh-eight. You can cut the top off of a .30-06 case, trim it, and make a case for a .45. All you need is a press and a good set of dies. Brass is amazingly ductile and can be easily resized to fit different size bullets. The only thing you need to be careful of is that over time, the case can thin."

"What causes that?" asked Private Shim, enthralled so that he forgot how much he hated Mitch.

"Well." Mitch paused. "Let me see one of your bullets."

Shim handed him one and, with the help of his knife, he wrenched the bullet out of the top and poured the powder out.

"This part here is called the neck," Mitch said, pointing to the top of the case. "This taper under it's the shoulder. Well, when you neck it down with a die," his words began to come more slowly as dissimilar pieces fell together in his mind. "The metal gets thick-e-r – " He stopped in mid-sentence. The vapor from the words he'd just spoken hung like a wraith. "Oh my God…" he whispered.

"What is it!" Bok-won hissed, reaching for his rifle.

"I'm so stupid." He turned slowly to his comrades.

"What are you taking about?" they asked together.

"Don't you see!" Mitch said excitedly. "When you neck down the brass, it gets thicker! You make the radius smaller, the thickness of the walls has to increase! But it increases more at the bottom than at the top! That's it!"

"What does that mean?"

"I can't believe I was so blind! I can't believe we were all so blind!" He turned to Private Shim. "How far is it back to Sagi-dong?"

The soldier nervously stammered through his reply. "It is about four kilometers back to the jeep. Another six back down the road. But we cannot get the boars out –"

"How about straight down the mountain."

They both looked at him like he was nuts.

"How far is it back to Sagi-dong if we go straight down the mountain?" Mitch's heart was thundering and prickles covered his body.

"Maybe... eight kilometers. Why?"

"About five miles. Guys, I've got to go. I've got to go *now*." He began thrashing around in his bag, trying to get out.

"What? Why?"

"No time to explain!"

They tried to stop him. "Dr. Weatherby, it is two o'clock in the morning! The temperature is minus five degrees!"

He was already pulling his boots on. "When I get back, I'll get in touch with Colonel Phoung. Tell him you guys are gonna need some help with those critters."

Within minutes, he was dressed and crawling out of the tent, his escorts still protesting in confusion but not leaving their warm sleeping bags. "Don't leave the meat," he told them again, shoveling rations into his mouth and pockets. "When you guys get back to town, we're gonna' have a barbecue like you've never seen!"

"What is *barbecue*?"

"Tell ya later. I'll see ya when I see ya."

Bok-won and Private Shim poked their heads out of the tent and watched him race down the hillside toward the stream. "Americans are strange," Bok-won said quietly, thinking of the supermarkets.

"They are liars," replied Private Shim. "But, we have meat."

20

Pak stood to the side gloating. The first RaLa test had been a dismal failure. He expected no better of this new set. And there'd been no sign of Weatherby all day. Pak smiled to himself as he scanned the monochrome hillside. Ragged clouds clung to the slopes, sheared by the wind. The whole top of the mountain was shrouded in mist. Somewhere up there, Pak knew Weatherby was stumbling around in the fog, freezing and miserable! He'd made sure Hyon-hui knew what Weatherby was up to, and she'd taken it exactly as predicted: a betrayal of the project – and herself. After today, Hyon-hui would hate the man forever. But it didn't matter since she'd be gone before the new year.

He glanced over at her, readying the shot. He could tell from her expression that it, too, would be a failure. This was going to be so easy. He would be rid of the half-breed bitch permanently, and there was nothing she could do. No way she could implicate him, because no one would ever believe anything she said.

Hyon-hui and her crew loaded the lanthanum into the cylindrical pit and retreated up the tunnel. Pak watched from behind as he followed them. They looked like mourners at a wake. They'd never follow Weatherby again. He'd abandoned them when they needed him most. But he might still be of use. Put him in a cell and torture him for information. Or maybe just for fun. But as a leader, it was over. He couldn't have planned it any better if he'd tried. Weatherby had played right into his hands.

The scientists gathered around the equipment, anxious and uncertain. The countdown commenced, and – *BOOM!* The sound of the blast rolled up the tunnel. Oh, to have had a camera, Pak thought. Just to capture the look on their faces. On her face. One more test and it would be over.

Pak relished in the anguish with which the team assembled the last device at RaLa Area 3. Hyon-hui was gray. Max was frowning. Sun-gun's face – the one Mitch called 'Sonny' – was drawn and pinched. Mitch's failure might even make Sun-gun's planned re-education unnecessary. Professor Yang said nothing. Cho Ho-pyong had the look of a beaten man in his eyes. They grumbled about Weatherby, his failures, and imperialists in general. Hyon-hui especially reviled him, calling down curses on his head.

"Wait! Wait! *Jong-jee!*" came faint cries from the tunnel. Pak turned. They all turned.

"Wait –" came the plea again, now closer. A harsh, croaking shout. A moment later, heaving with exhaustion, Mitch burst from the tunnel, muddy and ragged, wearing a blood-smeared, KPA winter uniform and a fur hat. "Stop the test!" Mitch cried, and fell to his knees in the snow. "Stop the test!"

Nobody moved to help him up and he was forced to stagger to his feet alone. He doubled over and coughed uncontrollably. A wet, sticky, spasm.

Sonny was the first to speak and it was not kindly. "The first tests were fubar!"

Max frowned. "Better late than never, Mitch," he said, then added, "or maybe not," in case Mitch had missed the sarcasm.

Hyon-hui ignored his presence, continuing with her task, while the others gathered around casting stern looks, waiting for answers.

Mitch finally stood up straight. Dressed as a KPA sniper, they looked at him like he was Yi Sun-shin reincarnate – the Korean hero who'd invented ironclads 300 years before the West. But he smiled and tried to laugh, which gave way to a fit of coughing, then back to laughing. "Merry Christmas, Max," he exclaimed. "Merry Christmas!" He stepped forward, hugged the shocked Russian, and planted a kiss on each side of his neck.

"Ugh!" Max grunted and pushed him away. "You smell of blood."

"Sonny, Merry Christmas," Mitch laughed and clapped his protégé on the shoulder.

"You're fubar, Mitch," said the gnarled Korean, flinching away.

Mitch laughed all the more. "You're going to have to stop saying that, Sonny. I should not have taught you that word! Bad!"

"Are you going to destroy something like you did the projector?" Sonny went on. "Have another fit?"

Mitch glanced at Hyon-hui. "Not exactly. Merry Christmas, everyone," he called loudly. He wanted to add a hearty 'ho, ho, ho,' but didn't want to push it too far. "Minister Pak," he bowed deeply, "Merry Christmas, sir."

"You have missed the first two tests already," Pak announced with relish. "You should know that neither resulted in compression."

"Of course, they didn't! They couldn't."

"And this one won't either," Hyon-hui announced bitterly.

Mitch nodded. "Yes, it will." Mitch turned as Soon-young stumbled out of the tunnel. The machinist stepped forward and handed a dull aluminum cylinder to Mitch. It still bore grooves on its outer surface from the lathe. They'd not had time to smooth it.

Puzzled looks spread from face to face and Hyon-hui looked at Mitch in confusion. So did Max. And Professor Yang.

"What is this?" Pak barked, suspicious that somebody had changed the rules to a game he had well in hand.

"The solution," Mitch proclaimed, striding forward. "The solution to our problem. Get that other junk out of there."

The assembly team sprang forward. All except Hyon-hui who stood staring darkly at the ground.

"You see," Mitch explained as they pulled the assembly apart, "I was up on the mountain hunting last night. Killed two huge wild boars, by the way. Gonna' barbecue 'em. Feed everyone in town if we can." The looks of stunned surprise were almost too much to behold and Mitch laughed again. It was Christmas, and he was Santa Claus.

"Me and these two KPA privates were huddled in this tent, about freezing to death. I was explaining how we used to resize rifle brass using a hand press." They were listening intently. "You know. Opening it up. Necking it down." He stared at their blank faces and shrugged. "Maybe not. Anyway, I was visualizing in my mind how I used to do it when it suddenly came to me." Mitch stood up and stepped back for a moment. Everyone stopped and watched him. "When we'd neck down the brass, the wall size got thicker. But because it was conical, it got thicker more at the bottom, than at the top. Just like when this here flying plate closes up. But, and I'm not calling any of you a butt," he held up the cylindrical flying plate. "The base, having a larger initial diameter —"

Max slapped himself on the head. "Thickens faster!" he exclaimed, and let go a string of Russian.

"Give the Roosky a cigar! dT-over-dr is *not* constant, but is a function of height *and* radius!"

It was obvious now and everyone bore the shame of missing it in their own way. Some laughed, some swore. Only Pak had no idea what Mitch was talking about.

"And it's not a linear relationship," Mitch panted, buzzing with excitement. "But varies as the cube of *dr*." He reached in and grunted as he grabbed the naked flying plate, now deprived of its high explosive covering, and lifted it off the test stand. He walked to the edge of a short drop off and with a mighty heave, threw it over the side. With a clash and a bang, it tumbled down the hillside dragging snow and rocks with it. "All of our simulations assumed a constant dT/dr. We didn't even think about it! Probably too hungry. But not only is it not constant, since it is a cubic, it was impossible to get it right with a linearly or quadratically varying angle!" He picked up the other cylinder and held it up for all to see. "The wall of this flying plate, unlike all the others, is thinner at the base than at the top and follows a curve describing a cubic."

This trip back up the tunnel was the opposite of the two earlier in the day. The team was in high spirits. None, though, had ever seen Mitch in as good spirits, despite his rapidly worsening cough. He joked and bantered with his people, telling them of his sprinting decent down the mountain, only to collapse when he reached the Army headquarters. He'd almost been shot before Colonel Phoung arrived and he could explain where his two soldiers were and why Mitch was alone. Throughout the story,

Mitch cast furtive glances in Hyon-hui's direction, but unlike the others, her countenance toward him had not improved. Exhausted and emotionally drained, it was only the adrenaline that kept him going. And it was fading fast.

"Get ready," he said. "In just a minute, we're gonna be done with the hard part."

The countdown commenced and they all held their breaths. *BOOM!* the powerful blast echoed up the tunnel. Bits of rock fell from the ceiling and peppered their heads. The traces on the Tektronix scopes flickered and disappeared.

An instant later, a rousing cheer went up.

"Pwwwwwnnnnnnn!!" cried Sonny.

The eight oscilloscope traces, frozen on the small blue screens as thin, glowing streaks, were perfectly synchronized. Constant until triggered, they dove in unison as the gamma-rays were attenuated by the compressing aluminum. Microseconds later, the rebound of the core was captured as the traces from the gamma-ray detectors rose, then flattened out at a level just under their original value. The pit had remained intact! For the first time ever, it hadn't blown itself apart. Perfect symmetry. When the radioactivity died down, they would retrieve the imploded core, cut it in half, and study the blast symmetry firsthand.

Mitch found himself jumping up and down, and exchanging embraces with Max, Ho-pyong, Soon-young, Sonny, and even Professor Yang.

"Dude, that rocked!"cried Sonny, using words Mitch had taught him. "You totally pwned!"

"We!" said Mitch, grinning broadly. "*We* pwned!"

"Three cheers for Dr. Weatherby!" exclaimed Max.

Only two people stood detached. Pak, on side of the room, flexed his fist while eyeing Mitch viciously. And on the other side, Hyon-hui was wiping her eyes, until, unnoticed in the revelry, she quietly slipped up the tunnel.

Despite his exhaustion and a worsening cough, Mitch attended the party the next night. It wasn't thrown in his honor, but he was the man of the hour having solved The Silla Project's most daunting technical hurdle and provided them with meat. As they shoveled mountains of steaming, barbecued pork into their mouths, it was as if a stifling fog began to lift from their clouded minds.

His belly full, Mitch pushed his plate away, poured down the last of his Ryongsong beer and plopped the can on the table with a smack. He craned his neck and spotted her, seated against the far wall of the dimly-lit community center, just beneath the twin portraits of the Great Leaders, picking at her food. As usual, there was no one near her. Mitch and Max were *far* less ostracized.

Max looked up from his plate, his face smeared with thick brown sauce. Except for his smudged glasses, he looked more like a Mongol horseman in a yurt than one of the world's top mathematical physicists. He saw Mitch staring. "Go talk to her," he mumbled past his food, and shoved in more of the shredded meat.

"I don't understand why she's acting like this. It worked."

Max chewed a thick plug of meat and washed it down with beer. "Ahh!" He looked back up, and let go an enormous belch. "She is embarrassed. She said things yesterday, that –"

"About me?"

Max smirked. "*Da.*"

Mitch chuckled. "Then you don't think she's mad at me? I thought she was mad at me or hated me or something."

"She just feels like an idiot."

"I guess I can see that." Mitch pushed his chair out and stood up.

"You going to finish that?" Max asked, pointing at his empty plate.

"There's nothing on it, Max."

"There's sauce!" answered Max, running his finger across it. "Look at this! Better to die of gluttony than to die of starvation."

"Is that one of your grandmother's proverbs?"

Max smiled. "No, that is one of Max's proverbs." He picked up the plate hungrily and licked it clean.

As Mitch made his way across the room, he was stopped repeatedly by half-drunken scientists and technicians, slapping him on the back. Hyon-hui saw him long before he got there, and watched him apprehensively. She dabbed her napkin on her mouth, straightened her hair, and sat up straight.

"Hey," Mitch said quietly when he stood before her at last.

She stood up without meeting his eyes and bowed. "Hello, Mitch."

"How you doing?"

"I am fine. Congratulations on the test."

"It was a group effort," he replied. "Everyone did a great job. We have a lot to be proud of."

She stood awkwardly, looking at his chest, or past him. Or through him. "Dr. Weatherby, this is twice now that I have doubted your intentions. And yet," her voice trailed off.

"It's okay, Hyon-hui. We both said some things that maybe we shouldn't have. I'm sorry. And, and you can look at me if you want to. I don't mind."

"Asked Sonny about the projector. I had not heard. It is not the kind of news we talk about. That was," she paused still staring at the floor, "because of Pak? What he was doing to me?"

Mitch nodded. "Yes. I didn't want to…" His voice trailed off when he realized he could not lose something he didn't have.

Her eyes started to fill with tears and their gazes finally met. "Why are you always so kind?" she asked. She looked away embarrassed, then unexpectedly stepped forward and embraced him. "*Kam-sa-ham-nee-da*, Mitch," she whispered.

He threw his arms around her and held her tight, feeling her tears soak into his shirt. "Merry Christmas, Hyon-hui," he whispered in her ear. "Merry Christmas."

"Mitch," she said quietly, sniffing and wiping her eyes. "What is Merry Christmas?"

21

Two and a half months is very little time to finalize a design for a nuclear weapon or prepare for a test. Mitch knew this well, especially when the test is one-quarter of the way around the world in one of the most inhospitable places on the planet. Doing both at once on a shoestring budget gave new meaning to the 'speed battles' that North Korean labor leaders waged to complete important tasks.

Pak insisted on a full test of their weapon. Colonel Phoung picked an uninhabited, glaciated, volcanic island fifteen hundred miles north of Antarctica – Heard Island. Probably the best place in the world to test a nuclear bomb if you didn't want anyone to know about it. It was almost perpetually veiled in thick clouds, lay far from shipping lanes, and at that time of year experienced only an hour of daylight. It's far southern latitude also placed it on the edge of detection by America's early warning satellites.

But islands like that were important habitat for seals and other marine life, Mitch told them. Thousands could be sheltering there, and be killed by the test.. As a keen hunter, Mitch had always been concerned about habitat loss and wildlife management. That interest had brought Beth into his life – her work with one of the more rational environmental groups. And what was being proposed now was an affront to everything she'd believed in. Professor Yang understood, and ordered a study that determined that the seal migration left the island practically deserted at that time of year. With that assurance, Mitch approved the location.

They set the date for the 7th of July, the anniversary of the Great Leader's death. Which made logistics almost impossible since they wouldn't have enough uranium-233 until after they left. But Pak would not be dissuaded. That meant in just a few short months, they had to finalize the design and develop the tests and methods to observe the blast so they could determine yield. They had gone from a phase of almost constant research and testing to almost constant meetings.

To make matters worse, by the end of April, the food situation in North Korea had gone beyond crisis. The previous year's harvest had been another failure. Rumors of mass starvation and cannibalism in the countryside reached P'yongyang and the Party leadership moved to suppress them by an energetic TV blitz featuring model collective farms and rosy-cheeked peasants being praised by a plump Kim Jong-il. But even if they never talked about it, the people knew the truth. The ration for Party members of 600 grams of cornmeal a week was down to 400 grams per family. One egg and one deciliter of cooking oil. Besides that, all they had was the half-a-year of food they'd stored up back in October and that was mostly kimchi which had almost no nutritive value. The only thing that saved some were the boars culled by Mitch, and another half-dozen that fell to KPA hunters that he trained.

Mitch and Max ate better than most. Their refrigerators were stocked twice a week with rice, bean paste, and kimchi. Every once in awhile, they had bread and even an occasional bacon-like strip of meat which Mitch always gave to Hyon-hui and her mother. There wasn't even beer to wash down the meager meals, since the grain had all gone to make bread. Mitch often dreamed of peanut-butter, chocolate chips, and too many other things to name.

Not until late April did Juche methods begin to make up the shortfall. It wasn't normal rice, however, that appeared on their tables. This rice was smooth instead of sticky. The papers reported that it was a special variety, genetically engineered to grow fast in the fertile lands around P'yongyang. Mitch thought it looked and tasted a lot like *Uncle Ben's*. And it was maddeningly difficult to eat with chopsticks.

Although they hadn't seen fresh milk in six months, shipments of U-233 arrived regularly. In X-Division, Hyon-hui tested and refined the cylindrical implosion system, making it smaller, lighter, and more reliable. Her experiments were guided by Max's and Cho

Ho-pyong's simulation results from T-Division on how a cylindrical pit should behave under implosion, and what shape it should take to achieve the largest energy release for a given amount of fissionable material. Tall and skinny, short and squat, or something in between.

It was here, more than anywhere else, that Mitch's experience and knowledge was indispensable. While Sonny was a talented physicist and had been trained in neutronics on Yongbyon's reactors, his practical experience was more limited. Mitch tutored him on the black arts of weapons science as the two of them guided Gadget Division. Theory, as Mitch knew well, simply could not replace knowledge gained through a half-century of weapons tests, even if he'd never actually participated in one himself. This would, he realized, be the culmination of his career. Strange that it should occur here.

Sonny, enamored of Mitch, sat at his feet like a disciple absorbing everything Mitch would tell him. It wasn't his fault that he'd been trained at Kim Il-sung University and his physics education was thirty years behind. But he certainly knew his Juche ideology to the letter. Even so, he was one of the few people in Sagi-dong that wouldn't argue with Mitch on every point, assuming that their Juche-based education had to be superior to that of an imperialist. Mitch enjoyed his open-mindedness, and fed him sparingly and very discretely with scientific knowledge of the rest of the world, never forgetting Pak's warning against discussing such matters.

22

A little after a year since Mitch's arrival at Sagi-dong, two Chinese-made buses departed from Sagi-dong's Party Headquarters on the 12th of June, just as the sun was going down over the western rim of the valley. The departure was timed so that the deep shadows in the hollow made observation by the West's myriad of electronic eyes more difficult. And once the buses were out of the valley and snaking along North Korea's winding roads, it would be impossible for them to be followed under cover of darkness, even though, at Yonjom-dong, they picked up an escort of four UAZ-469's each with a heavily armed squad of SSA troopers.

The road wound around the north slope of the big mountain, snaking through narrow valleys terraced for growing crops, but like Sagi-dong's they were hard dirt and fallow. At a crossroads, they turned south and the dark, still waters of Lake Nangnim appeared on their left side, a long skinny finger running north to south for twenty miles. This road was better than the one from Kanggae, surfaced with concrete and wide enough for two vehicles.

It had been a dry spring and a foul smell came off the water's surface. Crumbling docks stuck out over dried mud. The only boat they saw was a disintegrating dinghy 50 yards from the desiccated shoreline, buried to its gunwales in mud. Here and there, on the other side of the road, were a few low concrete hovels tucked away in a fold of the mountains.

Mitch stared out at the scenery, with Hyon-hui beside him. It was his first time off the mountain since arriving from Kanggae last year. But what he saw was depressing. He knew there were economic problems. He just couldn't have imagined they were this bad. Before he left, things had taken a turn for the worse in the United States with rising fuel prices, falling dollars, and gyrating stock markets. But there wasn't a single spot in Mitch's homeland that could compare with this place. And as hard working as he knew these people to be, he began to wonder if the West was actively keeping North Korea down. Until at the top of a pass, above a wooden shack, he saw a large, fully lit billboard showing Kim Il-sung greeting happy school children, and remembered what the real problem was.

They stopped at the shack, where guards came out to check their papers. According to Sonny, who was seated in front of Mitch, they were at the border of Chagang-do and Hamgyong-Namdo provinces. Here, at the top of the pass, it was still dusk, and Mitch could see jumbled peaks, like blocks poured from a bag, leading off to the west. Below them, in the valley, a black tongue of water stretched south and disappeared between two mountains.

"What lake is that?" Mitch asked, remembering something from his childhood.

Hyon-hui jerked at his side and stirred from her doze. "Hya?"

"I'm sorry. Were you sleeping?"

"No. No." She smoothed her hair back. "What is it?"

"That lake, what lake is it?"

"That is Lake Changjin," she answered with a yawn. "Also called Chosin. If you stay on this road, it will lead to Hamhung and the Port City of Hungnam on the East Sea."

"Chosin, huh?" Mitch said.

"You know of Lake Changjin?"

Mitch nodded, and squinted out at the water. "I know of the Chosin Reservoir." In the failing light, its surface was a yawning black void. "My mom's uncle died there."

"*Your uncle?*" Hyon-hui exclaimed. "How is that possible?"

Mitch turned toward her. "We fought a war with you guys. Remember?"

"Why did you never mention this?"

Mitch shrugged. "I never knew him. He was my mom's uncle. Died twenty years before I was born. Billy, his name was Billy. William. A captain in the Marine Corps. He never came home."

"You mean his body is still somewhere out there?" Hyon-hui sat straight up, strangely animated. "I don't understand why you never said anything about this!"

"It never came up."

She looked at him in wonder. "You lost loved ones in the Victorious Fatherland Liberation War, too. I'm sorry, Mitch. For your mother. And your grandmother. I never thought about how others may have been touched..." She trailed off, uncertain what to say.

"Fifty thousand Americans died in the *Forgotten War*," replied Mitch. "Fifty thousand."

As they dropped into the valley, the darkness grew and people on the bus began to nod off, exhausted by the mad dash to reach this point. Mitch and Hyon-hui bumped along for a while until she spoke again. "Mitch?" She leaned in close, and whispered into his ear. With the hissing of air, he almost didn't hear her. "Why did you call it the 'forgotten war?'"

"Because it's been forgotten in my country," he murmured back. "I know the war is still fresh in the North Korean mind, but in America, it's a minor historical footnote between World War II and Vietnam. Nobody cares anything about it and the veterans are just sort of forgotten."

"You said that once before," she replied.

He looked at her. "I did?"

"In my office one afternoon. You said that Americans can't even find Korea on a map. That we were some kind of a joke."

Mitch grimaced. "Christmas Eve. I remember. I'm sorry I said it."

"But is it true?" she asked tentatively. "Is what you said that day true?"

"It doesn't matter," he said but he could feel her staring at him in the darkness, waiting for an answer. He slowly nodded, not knowing if she could see. But she stopped talking, and later, Mitch found her head resting on his shoulder. He glanced down and her eyes were closed, her chest rising and falling to her deep measured breathing. She was beautiful and they'd become close friends struggling through the difficulties of the winter. They all had. But it brought up memories, too. "Beth," he whispered, and touched Hyon-hui's smooth, flat cheek with his fingers. "This isn't how it was suppose to turn out. Not even close."

He had tried praying again, after it seemed God had listened to him that night on Wagal Peak with the two soldiers. There, under the stars, he had felt closer to God, somehow and it seemed that God had heard him, not only feeding them, but saving Hyon-hui. Saving them all. But since then, that wall had risen once again and the fragment of faith Mitch had clung to that night seemed farther away than ever. Bumping along that back road in North Korea his mind searched the universe for some shred of hope, some glimmer of evidence. Something to tell him this was not all just some random spiral into nothingness, but that there was a plan and that somehow he was part of it.

He sighed and leaned his head back and his eyes fell on the twin portraits of the Great Leaders mounted above the bus driver. He searched their bitter eyes, wondering what could have happened to fill them with so much hate. But then again, he was on a bus in North Korea at the beginning of a journey that might change the balance of power in Asia. And he, Mitch Weatherby, had been instrumental in making that happen. Hate? Mitch knew all there was to know about hate. The prayer trying to spark in his mind went cold and dark, replaced by the simmering rage he knew only too well.

Mitch woke up. They weren't moving and a dark shape was moving down the aisle, nudging people awake. He panicked for an instant, thinking he was back on the bus to Terminal Island. It was just for an instant but it was long enough to set his heart beating madly.

Hyon-hui jerked awake next to him. "What's wrong?" she hissed. "Mitch, you're sweating. Is everything okay." She coaxed it out of him then sat in the darkness humming softly and running her fingers up and down his arm, calming his heart and mind.

"Where are we?" he finally said, feeling a bit silly about his episode.

"Smells like the ocean," Hyon-hui answered, breathing in the salt-tinged air. She glanced at her watch. The radium numbers glowed bright green. "Ten-thirty. We must be at Mayang-do."

They settled back into their seats to wait and Hyon-hui once again leaned her head on Mitch's shoulder, as they listened to the sound of their gear being unloaded. He liked the way it felt but knew it didn't mean anything. They were colleagues, friends, and exhausted, and the personal space in Korea was about six inches to begin with.

"I need to use the bathroom," he whispered a few moments later.

"Me, too," said Hyon-hui with a giggle.

"Me, three," whispered Max from in front of them.

A dark figure entered and stood at the front of the bus. He thought of the prison bus again but without the wrenching emotion. Then, too, he'd been headed for a ship, though he didn't know it at the time. Then, too, it had been a member of North Korean Special Forces. This time however, it was Colonel Phoung and Hyon-hui translated for him: "It's time to go," she whispered to Mitch. "And he says we can relieve ourselves off the edge of the pier." And they did. Even the women.

They boarded the Japanese-flagged *Mikisan Maru* which looked like a typical cargo ship. A high, narrow wheel house spanned the entire beam near the bow and, at the stern, lay an even larger structure, but Mitch already knew any similarities to a legitimate cargo ship ended there. Anti-aircraft guns perched atop each of the houses. A large tarp covered the two hovercraft they were going to use to unload equipment at Heard Island, and under his feet, beneath the armor-plated deck, was a floating laboratory equipped for everything from assembling the bomb to measuring the neutron flux a half-mile from the blast. They hadn't told him what this mobile laboratory had cost but from his days at Los Alamos, Mitch could only speculate it to be in the hundreds of millions. Spent while the nation starved. It reminded him of the way Washington levied ever heavier burdens on the people, crushing the economy for both sides, while a privileged few on both sides reaped the rewards. The longer he lived here, the more North Korea and the United States seemed alike.

Once on deck, they followed the line of bleary-eyed scientists through a door in the rear house and down a narrow passageway that emptied into a cramped mess hall. Mitch found Professor Yang hunched at a table.

"Professor Yang, I wondered when you'd turn up," Mitch said bowing.

The old man stood, looking particularly haggard, and returned the gesture. "*Annyong haseyo*. How was the trip from Sagi-dong?"

Mitch shrugged. "We slept most of the way."

The professor smiled and gestured around the room. "It seems everyone else did, too."

"They've worked hard. How about you, sir. Everything ready to go here?"

"I am weary, Mitch. Like never before," he yawned. "But this is exciting. Except for the fissile material, everything is already on board."

"Undamaged?"

The old man nodded. "I inspected it all myself. I have the inventory list in my cabin if you would like to see it."

"Not necessary." Mitch yawned and covered his mouth. "Wouldn't mind getting back to bed myself. Where are we sleeping?"

"I'm afraid the accommodations are somewhat rudimentary. Crew berthing below decks."

They discussed the U-233. Most of it was already in Sagi-dong but they were still waiting for the last shipment to have enough to cast and form the cylindrical pit that would catch up with them in Jakarta. They both knew that should anything happen with the reactor at Yujin-dong, or in transporting the pit, their entire mission would be for naught.

About that time, the last few members of Silla-14 stumbled in followed by guards carrying machine guns. It was crowded and already growing warm and stuffy. The faint smell of garlic and ginseng permeated the steel-walled room and the portholes let in only a meager draft. Mitch assumed they would be given their bed assignments and get some sleep. He was wrong.

Lee, who was never far away, excused himself and made his way to the front of the room, flanked on either side by large portraits of the Great Leaders suspended on the bulkhead behind him.

"Workers, Peasants, and Intellectuals," he began, and the crowd grew instantly silent. Hyon-hui translated, though by this time she almost didn't need to. Mitch recognized the propagandistic speech almost instantly. "Party members in good standing, and ever-victorious soldiers of the Korean Peoples' Army and Navy. Tonight, we begin the last leg of an historic journey. A journey of Revolution embarked upon by the Great Leader, Comrade Generalissimo Kim Il-sung many years ago at Mangyongdae along the banks of the Taedong. A journey with a dream to cast off the yoke of foreign imperialism, and adopt a scientifically perfect system of socialism in which we could rely on ourselves alone. Juche! A communist Revolution without end. Much has happened since those fateful days. Empires have fallen, and new ones have arisen. Through it all, the revolutionary vision of the *widaehan suryong*, his monolithic ideology of Juche-sasang, has remained solid and steadfast. Immovable. It was this vision, his vision of a united Choson that drove the fire of his patriotic, revolutionary zeal and allowed him to endure any hardship in the liberation of his beloved Choson first from the Japanese robber barons, and then from the imperialist aggressors across the sea. To bear any sacrifice. The same vision that has fueled our revolutionary fire. And his philosophy of Juche-sasang that has guided all of our efforts and that will grant us success."

Mitch watched the Koreans around him. They were no longer sleepy. It was as if they'd been activated by some kind of hypnotic word that turned them into political zealots. Hyon-hui was not immune, and even Professor Yang's eyes shone. Besides Mitch, only Max was unaffected.

"He who makes the biggest speeches, always faces the least danger," Max whispered. Mitch nodded, wishing he could have met Max's grandmother.

"Over the coming days, there will be hardship," Lee went on. "And danger. But we will not falter, and we will not fail. And with the nationalistic example of the anti-Japanese, anti-imperialist activities of the Great Leader and of the Party, let us bear our burden so that *we* can endure any hardship, and in so doing, carry forward the revolutionary tradition of the Party, and of the *widaehan suryong*. Comrades of the Revolution – you are the best hope of our nation. Proof positive of the superiority of the Juche ideology as revealed by the Great Leader, Comrade Generalissimo Kim Il-sung, who guides and watches over us still. The best hope to reunite our land under a red-flag ideology. To extend the socialist Revolution and bring the freedom of Juche-sasang to our enslaved comrades in the South, so long oppressed by foreign imperialism. And to once again reunite our land under Marshal Kim Jong-il, lodestar of this century!"

Without warning, the Koreans jumped to their feet and launched into an expertly choreographed cheer. "*Heeeyyyy! Heeeyyyy! Heeeyyyy!*" they shouted, holding their fists in the air.

"Even in Soviet Union it was not so... mechanical," Max whispered, as he and Mitch stood in nervous awe at the cheers of the automatons.

23

The excitement of the scientists to be beyond the borders of North Korea for the first time in their lives dulled as the repetition of life at sea made Sagi-dong seem diverse. They woke to loudspeakers. And each day after calisthenics and political agitation exercises, the engineers and scientists on board practiced setting up their equipment in various labs spread around the ship. Everything from assembling the bomb, to hooking up the data acquisition network, to logging the data and taking it all apart again. Often, they practiced in the dark with flashlights to simulate conditions on Heard Island where there would be little daylight. Technicians continued their never ending task of instrument calibration in the onboard laboratory. Soldiers drilled and exercised on deck, cleaned their weapons, and maintained the tarp-covered anti-aircraft batteries. Mechanics checked and rechecked the engines on the two hovercraft. Procedures were constantly revised and refined, then revised again. And the nightly Juche study sessions continued unabated.

For some, the only positive was the three good meals they were served each day instead of the usual two meager ones. But even that was painful for those who did not acclimate to life at sea. Professor Yang developed an inner-ear disturbance that made him especially susceptible to seasickness, and the brightness of the sun on the water pained his eyes. He remained inside, below deck, most of the time.

The only advantage to not having the completed fissile pit on board lay in disguising the intent of their mission should they be boarded by imperialists. After Jakarta they would finally pass into the open sea. Their cover story, should the unthinkable happen, was a scientific expedition to Antarctica and they had the cold weather gear and temporary shelters to prove it, equipment they would rely on once they reached the frigid shores of Heard Island.

Still, despite the dangers, being beyond North Korea seemed to expand Mitch's mind somehow. He found the smell of the South China Sea, foaming beneath the *Mikisan Maru*, both refreshing and somehow intoxicating. Every night during the Juche sessions, he stood on deck, breathing it in and gazing at the stars. It gave him time to reflect. Mitch's spiritual life had been a key part of his existence, even after Beth had been murdered. In fact, that horrible night had made it had grow even stronger. But despite his knees forming callouses from all the praying, the silence on the other end only deepened, until finally, on the bus, it had evaporated completely, leaving Mitch seeing the world with unfiltered eyes for the first time in his life. And this was it – the sum of his life – here on this ship. His life's work and the only people who cared about him, and most of them only wanted his knowledge. There was no great meaning to life, or justice, or fairness. Nothing at all, except ants scurrying around frantic activity, protecting their colony against others.

Then there was Hyon-hui. The relationship between the two of them had been rekindled after Christmas, but it was different. They were friends now, even though Mitch felt a thrill when she would smile at him. He would wake up thinking about her and then curse himself for betraying Beth. Except the curses had begun to feel forced. More than forced. Faked. The bitterness that had driven him for so long just wasn't there anymore, because he'd let it go with the idea of God. Nothing mattered. Except …

"I thought you would be here."

Mitch turned to find Hyon-hui standing a few feet behind him and a familiar, pleasant warmth spread through him as their eyes locked. "Study session over already?" he asked.

She nodded shyly, staring out at the clear night. The brightness of a full moon lit up the water with glowing, silver radiance so that they could see to the horizon. Off their port beam, the gleam was broken by a dark and bumpy mass rising from the sea with pale yellow lights flickering along its coast like tiny torches.

Hyon-hui pointed at them. "What do you think those are? They seem to be burning on the water."

He looked over at her. The wind was hissing over the bow of the ship, streaming back her long black hair. Mitch remembered the first time he'd ever seen this woman. So bitter and angry, with green eyes that had sought to kill him. Now, those eyes were soft and the face radiantly smooth. "You're beautiful," he thought.

She looked at him in surprise, and Mitch's face burned with the realization that he'd spoken aloud. "I …" he stammered and swallowed hard. "I … what I meant to say, was that, uh, I think those are natural gas fires from oil wells." Mitch quickly pointed to the land mass they'd been paralleling all day. "That's probably Borneo. Indonesia has a huge oil industry."

Hyon-hui had a gentle smile on her lips, and Mitch wanted to kiss them. He jerked his brain back before it betrayed him again, staring up at the sky. "I… I figure we'll be crossing the equator soon if we haven't already," he stammered, trying to sound natural. "Look how high the moon is. And you can't see it tonight because it's so bright but the … uh … the uh …" He swallowed again. "The Big Dipper is on the horizon behind us, and …"

"Mitch," Hyon-hui said, reaching out to stop him from wringing his hands

"Polaris… the North Star… is probably below the horizon by now. And I… I think…"

"*Mitch*," she said more sternly.

"That's Antares, in Scorpio which is just barely above the horizon from North Korea. So, we must've come thirty or forty degrees south for …"

"*Mitch!*"

He looked down, embarrassed.

"Thank you. You are the only one who has ever told me that."

Mitch fidgeted as his face became like molten lava. "Well, I'm sure others have noticed even if they haven't mentioned it," he mumbled. "It's, uh, sort of hard not to. Notice, I mean."

A soft, wry laugh popped from Hyon-hui's mouth. "You are the only person who does not seem to care I'm not full-blooded Korean."

This full-blooded crap always took him aback, but he knew she was serious. "Hyon-hui," he said, gaining confidence. "I thought you were pretty the first time I ever saw you. You remember, I was staring at you?" He smiled at the memory. "I was sitting across from you in that big Mercedes truck when we left Kanggae?"

Hyon-hui's eyes widened. "Is that why you were looking at me? I thought it was because you wanted me dead."

Mitch laughed. "I was looking at you because I couldn't stop, couldn't stop, uh – if you must know the truth, I couldn't stop staring at your legs."

"My legs?" she exclaimed, putting her hands on her thighs as if to cover them.

Mitch nodded. "Yeah. Pretty pitiful, huh?"

She leaned up on the gunwale with him, letting the cool night air course through her hair. "You truly find me pretty."

Mitch's throat grew tight when he realized, for the first time, she'd said it not as a question, but as a statement. "Yes," he squeaked.

She went red to the ears but turned to him anyway. Mitch's heart burst into a gallop. Did she want him to kiss her? That's what her body language meant in America. But this wasn't America. Screw America, thought Mitch. This body language had to be universal. He leaned forward as a hatchway from the pilot house popped open behind them, flooding the deck with bright yellow light. They both jerked back.

"Hello! Is that you, Mitch?" came Lee's voice.

Mitch clenched his teeth together. "Yes, Lee. What is it?" That little creep had been watching them, waiting for just the right moment. He was sure of it!

"I have looked everywhere for you! Comrade Chun, what are you doing here?"

Hyon-hui turned and bowed awkwardly. "Comrade Major." Her voice seemed disappointed as well.

"I thought you would be interested in knowing," he said with a smile, "we are crossing the equator *right now*."

"Yeah, I can feel it," Mitch shot back, as Hyon-hui walked away. "Getting cooler already. Thanks a lot there, buddy."

"No problem."

Mitch didn't have a chance to find out if Hyon-hui wanted him to kiss her. He couldn't very well just ask the next day as he, Hyon-hui and Sonny drilled on assembling the gadget. And that evening, the scientists were confined to their bunk rooms below deck, as the *Mikisan Maru* inched into the port of Jakarta where they would refuel and resupply. The other scientists crowded around the portholes, spellbound by the lights of the city streaming from a million windows, reflecting from the waters of Jakarta Bay in shimmering, wavy lines. And the ships! They had never imagined so many ships could exist. A few suggested that something was up – perhaps imperialist military exercises or the like – because how else could such things exist in a backward nation like Indonesia. Mitch laid on his cot, silently shaking his head. The scientists were seeing the clear evidence of the world outside their beloved "Choson," but failing to reach the obvious conclusion.

They all remained in the stale, stifling air below deck for two days, until Pak Yong-nam and Khadir Jabril, accompanied by a small contingent of Middle Easterners arrived, and they immediately set sail. Mitch knew the large metal suitcase they'd brought on board contained a precisely machined chunk of uranium-233, the size and shape of a hockey puck, and its arrival was a sobering moment for Mitch. Now, they had everything they needed to build a fully functioning 40 kiloton nuclear weapon. If they wanted to, they could have assembled it and set it off in Jakarta bay, vaporizing most of the city. And Mitch had given it to them. He knew it didn't matter – just another ant hill controlling the laws of physics. But a heavy dread grew in the pit of his stomach.

Soon after crossing the Tropic of Capricorn, they came as close as they would to Australia. Though well outside the reach of radar and regular patrol flights, the scientists gazed anxiously skyward, straining their ears for the sound of imperialist war planes. The radar spun non-stop and soldiers were stationed on deck with binoculars. But the only thing they saw were the contrails of jet liners high in the sky. And there were few of those. But those on board the *Mikisan Maru* had never seen so many, and it only added to their paranoia that something was wrong, that America's stooges were watching them. During one of their practice assemblies, he assured Sonny it wasn't true, telling him that if the U.S. knew what they were up to, they would have already been either boarded or sunk. But the thought gripped Mitch's heart. He looked at Sonny's eager face and Hyon-hui's beautiful one and wondered what would happen to them if they were caught. And what would happen to him. He buried the questions he didn't want to face. It was too late to turn back now. And it didn't matter, anyway. Instead, he focused on the assembly before him. Physics was what mattered now and it was the only thing that had never let him down.

The days grew shorter and the water took on an unwholesome feel, changing from a transparent, crystal blue to slate. Choppy waves appeared atop the swells, and the weather grew cold and windy. The *Mikisan Maru* rolled on undulating hills that were as tall as the ship. The scientists donned life jackets and stayed below decks, nearly everyone of them seasick. Professor Yang became more ill, running a high fever that the ship's doctor treated with the few precious antibiotics that they had on board. But not a single Juche study session was missed. For some, it became the only way to track the days.

As one miserable day blurred into the next, Mitch was awakened in the middle of the night. "You are wanted on the bridge immediately," said the soldier standing over him. Mitch rose and dressed, happy to leave the groans of his shipmates all around him. Professor Yang was clinging to a rail in the passageway, having been summoned to the bridge as well. Mitch took his arm and guided him down the dark corridors. They met up with Pak, who was pale and unsteady himself, as they arrived at the bridge. They allowed him to enter first, to find Colonel Phoung waiting, his uniform crisp and neat as always, and his demeanor totally unaffected by the conditions.

"We are ten kilometers from the island, approaching from the north. There are shoals here and here." Phoung pointed at a map, indicating areas northeast of the island. "We will drop anchor in Atlas Cove as planned."

Mitch stared at the map of the island he'd seen many times, and the dread grew. He couldn't escape the feeling that he'd done wrong and was about to do worse. A Bible verse that God would never let someone be tempted beyond their ability to resist and would always provide a way of escape came to mind, and Mitch's lip curled into an involuntary sneer. There had been no escape route for Mitch. None. And that proved there was no God. Yet he could not shove the feeling of dread out of his heart.

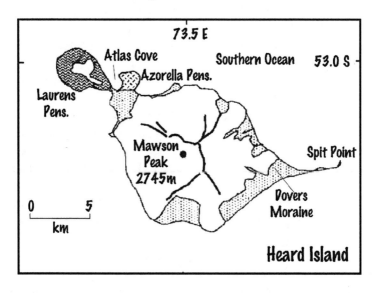

"How long until landfall?" he asked Phoung.

"About two hours."

The sailors picked their way slowly forward using a bathymetry chart that showed the contours of the ocean floor, the depth finder, and a lookout in the crow's nest wearing night vision goggles. Strong currents and shifting winds coming off the conical island made for an anxious and harrowing approach, if they were approaching at all. Big Ben, the enormous volcano forming most of Heard Island swayed back and forth in front of them with the rolling of the ship, but kept its distance. Twice, they had to backtrack and navigate around uncharted shoals that would have sent them to the bottom. For hours, it felt like they hadn't moved, when the rocking suddenly subsided. In the relative clam and silence, the thrumming of the engines reverberated through the hull. The captain signaled the engine room to scale back to one-quarter.

"We're in the lee of the Laurens Peninsula," he announced.

The cone of a short volcano, Mt. Dixon, loomed up off the starboard bow, with its ice-capped head just beneath the dark, swirling clouds. Soon the arms of the Laurens Peninsula and the much smaller Azorella Peninsula reached out and took them into Atlas Cove on a sheet of obsidian.

Pak opened the door and out of the darkness and from all directions, came a strange, guttural barking and growling, accompanied by a strong fishy smell. "What in the Great Leader's name is that?" he exclaimed as the others joined him at the rail.

"Seals," Mitch muttered. This island wasn't empty.

"Fur seals," said the colonel who had scouted the island six weeks earlier. "They gather on the point over there," He pointed out to a dark mass to port that stuck out into the water. "Hundreds of them."

Mitch frowned, his dread growing. "You said there was no seal population."

"Just here," Pak assured him.

"That's not what you said," Mitch reminded him. "How about out on Elephant Spit where we're going to test the bomb?"

"It is miles away. No seals there. None at all," Pak glibly replied.

"You're sure?"

"Yes, yes," insisted Pak dismissively. "Surf and waves are far too great."

Anchor chains rattled from the bow and stern. Within minutes, the soldiers had clambered out on deck and were staring into the darkness. A searchlight swept the shore where dark rocks absorbed the light, and snow and ice reflected it back. The deck lit up as the sailors and soldiers put well-practiced plans into action. Atop the fore and aft houses, anti-aircraft guns were uncovered and missiles were readied for use. They rolled back a heavy tarp covering the two hovercraft which had been stacked for the journey. The crane fired up and soon the top hovercraft was in the water. A dozen soldiers piled in and the German-made Deutz engine rumbled to life. The rubber skirt inflated and the large fan at the rear spun with a whoosh and the big yellow craft crabbed away toward shore. The other hovercraft was lowered from the *Mikisan Maru* and boarded by a second group of soldiers who sped out to sea, making for Spit Bay.

Hours later, as the sun made its brief appearance, the scientists donned their heavy, government-issued clothing and climbed topside to see the landscape of black volcanic rock and glistening ice. Big Ben's volcanic mass towered above them to the south, its sides draped in streaming glaciers, and its summit shrouded in thick grey clouds.

The hovercraft from Spit Bay returned and took aboard a load of supplies and the advance survey team, among them Mitch, Max, Hyon-hui, Sonny, and Professor Yang. As they left Atlas Cove, the sun set and they began 23 hours of night. Once beyond the calm, dark waters of the cove, the waves battered the hovercraft as the icy, seal infested shores of Heard Island slid by.

"It will be the death of us all!" cried Professor Yang, clutching the stainless steel handrails as the craft slammed into a large wave that crashed over the bow. Pak had turned green. And when Mitch was certain the man was about to lose his breakfast all over the rest of them, the waves lessened and the gentle curve of Spit Bay came into view. Elephant Spit, just barely above the waves, stretched out into the darkness to their left and was lost to sight. To their right, the dark expanse of Dovers Moraine at the foot of the mountain rose up. Beams from flashlights and generator-powered lamps shone from around its base.

Black dots sprinkled the shoreline. As they drew closer, Mitch could see that they were seals, elephant seals, stretched up and down the darkened beach, barking at the strange craft and at the people gathering on shore. Armed guards kept the enormous mammals at bay. One of them, a huge beast the size and shape of a Volkswagen bug, lay dead, surrounded by soldiers.

"Pak!" Rage swelled up inside Mitch. "There's hundreds of seals here. Two or three kinds at least, and your men are already pumping 'em full of lead!" he shrieked. "You all lied to me! Told me it was empty just to shut me up!"

Pak looked at him with watery eyes and threw up.

Mitch griped the steel handle until his knuckles turned white as the hovercraft maneuvered up on the shore. This place wasn't what he'd agreed to. He stormed off the craft as soon as the engine idled down and the heavy rubber skirt deflated. What difference did it make, he asked himself. Just more lies on the pile of lies that formed his life. And the seals – what did they know of the ants that were invading? He swore to himself, but knew there was no turning back.

A rocky valley extended for a mile or so inland before glaciers met it and rolled up the side of the volcano. In the other direction, a sloping plain narrowed down to a skinny finger of glistening, black gravel until it was lost in the darkness. Separating the two was a steep-sided, rocky hill, Dover's Moraine; a huge pile of rocks deposited by countless oscillations of the glacier.

The soldiers had been busy. At the foot of the hill, generators were humming as soldiers were erected the base camp made of fabric stretched over a wooden frame. Behind the Quonset-like huts, the skeleton of a geodesic dome emerged. This was to serve as a mess hall of sorts. Around the perimeter, other soldiers were setting up heavy machine guns, recoilless rifles, and mortars.

"Is all this really necessary?" Mitch cried over the generators.

Colonel Phoung appeared out of the gloom. "Our orders are to defend the beach against any and all intruders."

"The seals?" Mitch yelled and gestured toward the spit. "It was supposed to be uninhabited!" But the sound of the generators nearly drowned him out. "Might as well go out to the end of Elephant Spit and see what we're going to be dealing with," he muttered, kicking at the stones. "Anybody seen Sonny? We've got to get that tower started right away." A soldier pointed down at the shoreline, where Sun-gun was throwing rocks at a big elephant seal. "What does he think this is, a vacation?" Mitch said in disbelief. "Get him up here. There's work to do."

"Hyon-hui!" Sonny called excitedly as he puffed back up the shore. "Look at this!" He held out a tiny, green plant with thick leaves, a Kergulen cabbage that grew indigenously on the island. "I bet your mother could make kimchi –"

Pak snatched it out of his hand and threw it into the darkness. "We did not come halfway around the world to make kimchi!" he shouted.

They climbed aboard the hovercraft, which floated down the narrow jetty, sending terrified seals lumbering out of the its path.

"I thought Elephant Spit had no seals," he grumbled again to Pak. "You lied to me! Flat out …"

"Do your job," snapped Pak. "No more talk of seals."

"I can't do this!" Mitch shouted in fury, as he rose to confront Pak. Word rushed from his mouth faster than he could think. "It's wrong. My wife spent her life trying to protect places like this. Protect them from evil people like you! I can't do this to Beth! I won't! I will not!"

A tense silence fell in the hovercraft as Pak's glare hardened. No one moved. No one even breathed, until Professor Yang reached over and put his frail hand on Mitch's arm. "This is no different than Eniwetok, Dr. Weatherby," he said calmly. "Or Bikini. Or Ringalop. Or Yucca Flats. Hundreds of times, your country tested on islands teeming with life. And even underwater."

Mitch opened his mouth to say that was different, but fell back into his seat instead. Professor Yang was right. His father had been at each of those places doing *exactly* what he was doing here – what he'd always dreamed of doing. Dozens of atolls wiped clean of life. Entire reef systems destroyed. He'd never thought about it that way. His life's dream was Beth's worst nightmare. How had he never considered that side of it? Had his own ambitions blinded him that much?

"I have an idea!" Sonny suddenly said. "We'll use the seals as thermal detectors!"

"No!" Mitch cried, but simultaneously Professor Yang exclaimed, "Excellent idea!

"We'll stake them to the jetty just before the blast and they will give us a record of damage all the way down the spit."

Mitch was incredulous. "You can't be serious? Those are living animals! Can you hear what you're saying?"

Professor Yang turned to Mitch with an expression that was no longer sympathetic. "Your country did it with pigs," he reminded Mitch.

"But – but –" Mitch stammered, trying to find a hole in his argument. "Pigs are domesticated." The others stared at him in confusion for a moment, until Sonny resumed the discussion.

"They're going to die anyway," he pointed out. "After the test, we can pick one up every fifty meters or so. The depth of tissue damage from the thermal pulse will provide an excellent record of radiant energy over distance."

"We'll have to kill a few dozen before the test then," Professor Yang added. "To serve as controls."

"The essence of Juche!" Pak declared proudly. "Sun-gun, you are to be commended."

Mitch was appalled – and confused. How could he object? His country had done exactly the same thing. The Americans had even used the scorched and burned bodies of dead Japanese people to measure the radiation output. His stomach twisted in nausea as he watched the seals pass by on the narrow sandy jetty – imagining their blistered, charred remains.

"I've never seen anything like this before," Colonel Phoung remarked, nodding toward the spit of land, in places only twenty feet across. "I wonder how it formed?"

"I wonder how it doesn't wash away," said Mitch, watching the rough water batter the narrow spit. "I hope our weapon doesn't damage it."

"I hope it is wider at the far end," said Professor Yang, wearily. "Or else we may find ourselves looking somewhere else on the island."

"It is," answered the colonel. And as he reported, when they neared the end, the flat strip broadened until it was some 300 meters across. A large, flat, tear-drop-shaped mound of volcanic sand and shale connected to the land by the four-and-a-half mile thread of beach. The hovercraft set down and they climbed out to survey the area. Everyone except Professor Yang who remained inside to rest.

"This is most peculiar," said Sonny, staring back up the isthmus toward the mountain now lost in darkness. "There is a hill at the center. What is that Colonel, five meters above sea level?"

"The GPS unit measures it as seven," he responded.

"The ground seems surprisingly firm," Hyon-hui said, testing the well-compacted sand and shale with her foot. "This should be a good base for the foundations of the tower." Fist-size chucks of black volcanic rock stuck up here and there. She bent down and hefted a piece as large as a frying pan. It was hard and rough with sharp edges. "I wonder how this large a piece got all the way down here?"

Mitch knew they'd been pushed here over eons by the glaciers, but said nothing. He didn't want to be here. The crushing guilt was tearing him apart. He tried to push it away – the memories and the effect of what they were doing now – telling himself it didn't matter. That there was no right or wrong. They were just ants, scurrying in pointless activity. Nothing but ants. But Beth's shining eyes and her beautiful smile wouldn't leave. Tormenting him. Telling him he was wrong. Mitch stared off the very end of the spit into the blackness of a sunless sea. Australia was over three thousand miles away across the most treacherous water on the planet. "What have I done?" he muttered to himself.

24

Over the next few days, the *shot tower* rose from the end of Elephant Spit. That was the traditional Los Alamos name for the tower from which the bomb would be detonated. The corrugated metal shed at the top, that protected the device during assembly and prior to H-hour was called the *shot cab*. When completed it would be almost a hundred feet tall. Mitch had taught them the names, thinking how cool it was going to be to test their bomb. *His* bomb. Now every time he heard one of them use on of the old Manhattan Project words, gadget, shot tower, shot cab, and others – and they used them a lot – it was like a spiritual knife stabbing the heart of his soul. God might not be real but the soul, Mitch concluded, was. And his was dying and lost.

While a team of technicians swarmed over the growing tower, other scientists were hard at work setting up data gathering equipment that would measure everything from seismic motion of the ground, to air pressure, to gamma-ray output. The sophisticated network of ionization chambers, fission counters, and neutron cameras surrounded the shot cab as well as spanning the length of Elephant Spit, crossing Dovers Moraine, and even extending to the *Mikisan Maru*. From the hundreds of sensors, they hoped to gather enough data to get an accurate determination of yield. Or to figure out what went wrong.

To connect all their instruments to the data acquisition network, they laid out over fifty miles of cable and fiber optic line. Their training aboard ship proved invaluable. And of course, all the experiments were calibrated for the expected blast strength as calculated by Max's efficiency calculations. So if Max had made mistakes, all their data would be useless. But Max was supremely confident and not suffering from the guilt devastating Mitch.

Of course, no above ground nuclear test would be complete without an extensive photographic record. To measure the growth of the fireball in its early stages they employed two high-speed cameras. A similar device, except designed to record the wavelength of light instead of images, was used to measure the temperature of the fireball. Both would be carried aboard the *Mikisan Maru*. In addition, each scientist aboard the *Mikisan Maru* was issued a still camera, some digital, some film, and some even sensitive to infrared or ultraviolet light. While most of the scientists were to be stationed on the ship, a small party was to stay on shore on the west side of Dovers Moraine about seven and-a-half miles west of ground zero, where a corrugated metal shed, shielded from the blast by the crest of the hill, was erected.

The scientists and technicians worked sixteen to twenty hours a day in the perpetual darkness. It would rain, then snow, then rain again, then freeze, coating the black rocks with a hard, slick glaze of ice. After a few days everyone was battered and bruised and the infirmary on the ship had treated broken bones and sent the injured back into battle. The wind never stopped blowing. The swells out at sea grew to enormous size and sounded like artillery pounding the beach. The work was so grueling that Pak suspended the study sessions. They ate and crawled into their sleeping bags, too tired to care about the conditions. They fell asleep to the crashing waves, and in their sleep, their breath turned to fog dampening everything around them. They were always cold, always tired and always busy. Of course there was no real reason they were in a hurry. The push was so they would detonate the bomb on the anniversary of Kim Il'sung's death.

On the sixth day, the eve of the anniversary of the Great Leader's death, hours before daybreak, the hovercraft finally brought pieces of the gadget to Spit Point, sending seals and sand flying. Scientists and soldiers, unstable from the pounding of the waves, stumbled from the craft.

"Hyon-hui, Sonny," Mitch said, rubbing his neck, "you all head up into the shot cab. Max and I will load the equipment down here."

Hyon-hui didn't move, but stood silently, staring downward.

"You okay, Hyon-hui?"

She nodded and swallowed heavily. "A little sick from the ride. Give me one minute."

Hyon-hui stood, staring at the ground for another moment, before quelling the nausea sufficiently to ascended the ladder. The tower's base was over thirty feet on a side and the climb long and frightening. The higher they went, the more it swayed. At the top, they crawled inside and Hyon-hui lay beneath portraits of the Great Leaders clutching her stomach. She closed her eyes, but knew she couldn't stop it. She grabbed for the bucket they'd put up here for exactly this purpose, and vomited. After wiping a sheet of clammy sweat from her forehead, she pulled open the trapdoor.

Below, Mitch and Max saw a golden square of light appear high above them. Sun-gun's voice crackled over the intercom. "*Is it ready to go?*"

Mitch patted the first component that lay secured onto a rack, ready for the heavy cable to pull it upwards into the darkness, and punched the intercom button. "Take her away." The generator began to hum from the load that wound the cable upwards.

"You seem nervous," Max said as they watched the component ascend.

"We've never put it together with the real pit before," Mitch grunted. "It could go critical when we're assembling it. It probably wouldn't explode but it would scrub the test. Pak would probably put all of us to death. Or just leave us here."

"It won't," Max assured him. "We measured seven times and cut once."

"Well, if it turns out she made a bad cut," Mitch told him, "just leave me up there and I'll flip the switch myself."

Max cringed. "Don't talk like that. It is bad luck."

"Bad luck?" Mitch replied. "I'll tell you what's bad luck. Spitting on your dead wife's grave."

"Mitch," Max said. "It wasn't your fault. They lied to you."

Mitch gave him a piercing stare knowing the truth. "No. It is my fault. For believing them."

"What choice did you have?" Max asked, as the carriage above them disappeared through the lighted square in the floor and the sound of the motor stopped.

Mitch didn't answer, and Max didn't pursue it. They'd had this conversation before and it always ended like this. Time and again they repeated the process of loading the components and waiting as it rose to the top, until Mitch checked the last one off his list: the pit.

"Looks like all of it," he said turning. "Max, Professor Yang, we'll see you later."

Mitch gripped the bottom rung of the ladder and began his ascent to the top. His own nausea grew as he climbed but it wasn't from the swaying of the tower. He stopped at one point, clinging to the ladder as he gazed at the ground seventy-five feet below. He could just let go. Fall. It would end the nightmare. His hand clenched tighter to the rail, even as his mind said to let go. Had this been the other option all along? If he'd died – killed himself – none of this would be happening. He silently cursed a god that would give him suicide as the only way out, and knew it wouldn't do any good at this point, anyway. He slowly resumed his climb.

At the top Mitch poked his head through to be greeted by the stench of vomit. "Somebody puke?" he asked.

After Mitch translated *puke*, Hyon-hui raised her hand, weakly. "Sorry."

"Do you need to go down?" Mitch asked.

She shook her head. "Let's get started."

Mitch pulled out a spiral bound notebook, opened it, and read the first step for assembling the bomb, just as they'd practiced every day on the *Mikisan Maru*. Bomb case, explosive lenses, tamper, flying plate. Piece by piece, the device took shape under the sharp edged shadows of naked bulbs.

At each piece, Mitch made a checkmark on the list and read the next step. The wind howled around the cab, and sweat beaded across his forehead. Mitch straightened for a moment, and looked at his two companions. "We're ready for the pit," he said.

Sonny opened a heavy case exposing a thick ring of shiny metal. Radiation monitors broke into a static and the two soldiers who squatted at the back of the cab glanced at one another uncomfortably.

"It's okay, boys," Mitch said, but it did nothing to temper their nerves.

"It's beautiful," said Sonny, wiping off a droplet of sweat that ran down the side of his face. Wearing white cotton gloves, he reached into the box and lifted the metal disc, about the shape of a hockey puck but larger and heavier and with a hollow center. Twenty-three pounds of purified, uranium-233. He carefully aligned it with a lip machined into the bomb case and pressed to sink it into position.

Mitch saw the look of horror on Sonny's face as he gently pressed down again with a slight twisting motion. Then he leaned back, his eyes wide with fear. "It's too small."

"*What?*"

"It doesn't fit. It is too small!"

Mitch pressed down on it but Sonny was right, it wouldn't fit. It wasn't much, maybe a sixteenth of an inch, but it may as well have been twenty miles.

"Pak is gonna kill us!" Sonny moaned. "He's going to have us shot!"

"*Hold on!*" Mitch snapped. "Just stay cool." He rubbed the beard that was sprouting from his chin. "Soon-young isn't going to make this kind of mistake. He's too thorough."

"Cool?" Hyon-hui reached out and touched the metal of the pit. "It is too cold," she suggested. "It is warmer in here, and the other equipment has expanded with the temperature."

Mitch nodded. That had to be the answer. "We'll wait a few minutes."

But after ten minutes that felt like ten hours, it still didn't fit. Mitch drew back from the assembly as if it was malevolent. "This is not good."

"This is fubar, Mitch," said Sonny.

"Do we have a way to machine uranium?" asked Hyon-hui.

Mitch shook his head. "No. Need a nitrogen bath."

"What are we going to do?" Sonny whined. "Pak is going to kill us! He'll throw us into the sea. Or have us shot. Or maroon us here."

"No one is going to get shot," Mitch snapped, not believing it. "Now just cool it."

The intercom crackled. It was Pak. "What is the delay?" he asked.

"No delay," Mitch said into the mic. "Everything is proceeding smoothly."

"He's going to have us shot!" Sonny squealed.

"Stop saying that!" snapped Mitch, wracking his brain. "Let's stick it under the lamp. We'll heat it up."

Twenty more minutes seemed like twenty more years, but when Sonny placed it in the gadget, this time it inserted easily into place. Everyone relaxed, but only a bit. The rate of clicks had increased noticeably. Like the pile Mitch and Sonny had built on the table back at Sagi-dong, this could become a reactor too, and if it went critical, it would kill everyone in the room.

Mitch checked it off on the list. "This is where it gets dangerous," Mitch said. "We need to keep an eye on the radiation counters."

Next came the lithium deuteride boosting layer, a ring that sat a few inches outside the pit. It would enhance the explosive force of the bomb but also acted as a neutron reflector. When it was in place, the clicks coming from the radiation counters increased again.

Mitch winced. "Starting to inch up on us here. Secondary plate," he said, and Sonny handed over an annulus of machined U-238 that Mitch placed outside the lithium deuteride layer.

With each new component, the Geiger counter's clicks registered faster, until finally, when the bomb was complete, they had become a crackly hiss. But fortunately, still short of critical. Mitch said a silent prayer of thanks before heading down the ladder.

25

When "The Song of General Kim Jong-il," played the next morning, scientists, soldiers, and technicians rolled out of bed and struck camp while The *Mikisan Maru* pulled out of Atlas Cove and made its way to the shallow anchorage off Elephant Spit. As soon as the anchor was down, the hovercraft began ferrying equipment back to the ship. Not so much as a grain of rice was to be left behind.

Mitch and Hyon-hui stayed on shore to man the equipment, along with Colonel Phoung and a contingent of soldiers. The countdown was started at three hours and Mitch got on the radio with Sonny, who was still in the shot cab, to go over the checklist. The hovercraft, having dropped its passengers on the ship, arrived at ground zero just as they were finishing. The soldiers emerged from the craft and piled the expedition's trash on the ground beneath the shot tower where it would be disintegrated by the blast.

Up in the shot cab, Sonny kissed his hand and patted the gadget. "For reunification," he said. The last thing he did before descending the ladder for the final time was take down the pictures of Kim Il-sung and Kim Jong-il. They had debated long and hard as to whether to keep them in the shot cab so the Great Leaders could oversee the test as a sort of good luck charm. Or if they should remove them to avoid their destruction. Professor Yang ultimately made the call, fearing what might happen should knowledge of willful destruction of a Kim Il-sung portrait find the wrong ears. Careers, and even lives, had been ended over such things.

In the darkness aboard the *Mikisan Maru*, the scientists and crew gathered on the deck, cameras in hand, goggles on head.

Every thirty minutes they released a hydrogen filled Mylar balloon that they tracked with the ship's radar to determine wind speed. Pak paced the deck, eyes burning with a fierce light. Curls of steam rose from his lips with his heavy breath. Every few minutes, he'd charge up to Professor Yang and Max and ask, "Are you certain that we are safe at this distance?" Or, "Are you sure this will work?" Or, "Are there any problems?"

Professor Yang, at the railing with the other division leaders, would nod and calmly say, "Yes, Minister, we are quite safe here," or, "Yes, Minister, it will work," or, "No problems yet, Comrade."

Back at Dovers Moraine, Mitch and Hyon-hui kept one eye on the instruments and another on the pulsing red beacon atop the shot tower. Every five minutes, they checked in with the *Mikisan Maru*. Every fifteen minutes one of the technicians announced the time remaining over the loudspeaker. At an hour, still up in the shot cab, Sonny armed the firing circuits and made his final descent. Soon after, the hovercraft appeared out of the gloom and dropped him off at the bottom of the hill, before heading to the *Mikisan Maru* where it would hide behind the steel hull of the ship.

Staring out into the gloom, Mitch could see the dark spots of elephant seals all along the peninsula, and hoped Beth wasn't watching from somewhere. He tried to count them but gave up after one hundred. He should be condemned to Hell for what was about to happen, but there was nothing he could do. That had moved far, far beyond him.

"Are we ready?" Sonny asked as he strode in the door of the shack, snapping Mitch back to the work at hand.

"Ready!" Hyon-hui called beside him.

Mitch glanced back and forth from dial to gauge. "Ready!" he confirmed. A live video image of the bomb showed that nothing had changed inside the shot cab. "We have continuity to the detonator. Signal from the coil looks good. Electron multiplier tube is steady. Ionization chambers and piezos are clean. Clean enough. The neutron camera is ready to go. Radiation level in the shot cab is normal. Just waiting on meteorology."

After what seemed like forever, the radio crackled. "Winds out of the west at 17 knots, increasing to 37 knots at two kilometers, then bearing toward the northwest. Hovercraft has arrived at the *Mikisan Maru*. Sending out the seal team." A contingent of soldiers was sent out from the ship to travel down the spit. Every hundred meters, they shot a seal and staked its body down with a length of rebar.

About that time, the sun came up. There had been much debate about when to detonate; darkness or light. Some measurements were more accurate at night and there was no doubt that the pictures were more impressive. But with the sun in the sky, the flash of the detonation would be less noticeable to any ships or aircraft in the area. And even someone who happened to see the flash on the horizon would probably not notice the thermal pulse. At night, it would be a five mile tall flare. So the security issue won out and it was decided to detonate at high noon – thirty minutes after sun rise – although at this latitude, that was little more than twilight.

At ten minutes to go, Sonny flipped a switch and started the final automated sequence.

"No turning back now," said Mitch, staring at the red numbers counting swiftly to zero. Sonny and Hyon-hui looked at him, a mixture of nerves and excitement in their eyes.

On the ship and on shore people lifted their goggles, readied cameras, and waited nervously.

"Nine minutes…" said Sonny.

"*Radar reports no contacts in the area,*" crackled the radio.

"Eight minutes…"

Hyon-hui walked out of the control hut and climbed the makeshift steps to the top of Dovers Moraine where the soldiers had constructed a chest-high stone parapet. Though there was virtually no prompt radiation danger at their 10 kilometer distance, they were close enough to receive second-degree burns from the thermal pulse. She stared down the spit at the flashing red beacon on top of the shot tower. The seals that had been frightened away by the hovercraft were returning. Through the gloom she could just make out their dark shapes as faint dots crowded onto the sand of the spit. She knew these seals were important to Mitch, and a queasiness seized her stomach as the moment they would be destroyed drew ever nearer.

Mitch and Sonny joined a moment later, followed by Colonel Phoung and some of his men. Sonny glanced at the stopwatch in his hand. "*Three minutes,*" he said woodenly, into the radio in his other. On the ship, the people heard his voice and a hush settled over those watching.

Mitch thought about the endless accounts he'd read about the Trinity test. Fermi joking about the Earth being disintegrated when he knew full well it would not be. Oppenheimer's chain smoking. Hans Bethe pacing. Richard Feynmann sitting in a car miles away. Groves ready to line everyone up in a firing squad if the test failed. He'd always thought of a scene like that as fun. But now? He couldn't even shake the feeling that Beth was watching him from Heaven, or wherever the afterlife may have taken her. His eyes cast out over the parapet and down the long, thin ribbon of Elephant spit. What was worse, he wondered with a racing heart, the anxiety of whether or not the bomb would work, or the environmental hell he was about to unleash? He was glad that Beth was gone and couldn't see what he'd become, and felt sick for thinking it.

Hyon-hui slipped a slender hand through his arm. "Are you okay, Mitch."

He swallowed heavily. "No. No, I'm not." Professor Yang had once compared Mitch to Oppenheimer, and here, just moments before the test, he was having the same doubts as his legendary hero. Mitch had always thought Oppenheimer had been being melodramatic with his doubts, but standing here looking at the black dots of elephant seals and knowing what was about to happen to them, he understood. He finally understood.

"*Two minutes...*"

A hush fell over the soldiers and scientists on the parapet. No one even moved.

"*Thirty seconds...*" said Sonny into the mic.

They lowered their goggles and crouched down behind the earthen wall. Back on the ship, everyone sat down on the deck with their backs to the blast.

At the last came the calm voice of Sonny, counting down. "... *ship, koo, pal, chil, yook* –" Hyon-hui grabbed Mitch's hand and held it, "*–oh, sa, sam, ee, ill, chee-goom!*" He felt her squeeze.

Through his dark goggles and closed eyes, Mitch saw a brief flash and tasted lead. He opened his eyes and saw the glaciers of Mawson Peak above them shining white in the hellish glow, like a stairway to heaven. He knew that miles behind him a boiling, seething mass, brighter than the sun, was expanding rapidly, consuming all before it rocketed upwards. The initial pulse of light dimmed after a second or so, followed by warmth as the fireball turned from white to yellow. Mitch slowly rose, as the others remained squatting in terror, and peered over the embankment as the fireball grew hotter, and larger, and hotter, and larger. The wind had disappeared and it was as quiet as a still day in the desert. And still it grew.

The million degree fireball catapulted upward at 300 miles an hour, punching a hole through the thick Antarctic clouds. Churning and seething as it rose, the nuclear cloud formed three ice caps in quick succession, each of which was left behind as a shining, crystal bell along the glowing rope-like column. It was just as his father had described. Just as he had imagined. Only bigger. Much, much bigger.

Hyon-hui and the others joined him as the fireball reached its maximum output. The thermal pulse fell on their upturned faces, giving them sunburns, melting the snow, and splintering rocks. All around, the clouds were tinged with every color imaginable from violet through deep red. In complete silence, the fireball rose into the sky, forming a mottled, dirty stalk, sucking up dirt, dust, and water as clouds rushed away from the epicenter revealing blue sky above.

Yet Mitch felt no triumph. No joy. In the roiling blast, he could see Beth with tears running down her face. "Why Mitch?" he could hear her say. "Why?" Spit Point, an unspoiled wilderness, was gone. Most of Elephant Spit was clearly visible under the new sun, a thin ribbon of the purest black dividing the glowing ocean beneath the ascending mushroom cloud. But a mile from the far end, it disappeared into an opaque ball of water, sand, and rock heaved skyward by the blast. But Mitch knew what it was hiding: a quarter-mile-wide crater blasted fifty feet deep into the sand and rock of the ocean floor.

Mitch saw the shock wave coming toward him. Racing across the water like the leading edge of an enormous, expanding bubble. It hurtled down Elephant Spit then crossed Dovers Moraine in a heart beat. Twenty-five seconds after the explosion, a clap like ten thousand howitzers all firing at once passed over them, followed by a powerful gust blowing snow and sand and rattling the tin shack below. Then came a long, rolling, thunder-like boom that echoed off the mountainside.

Twenty seconds later, the people on the ship heard the shock and the professor dropped a handful of paper scraps. They blew back and came to rest on the deck about 8 feet away. "One hundred forty kilotons," he announced confidently.

Huge as it was though, the mushroom cloud couldn't fight the wind. A little over three miles wide and four miles high, it had already begun to tilt away from them. Soon it started to smear out like a watercolor left in the rain and it quickly faded from yellow to orange, through red, and then to a dusky, dirty gray. In less than five minutes, it was all over. The far end of Elephant Spit was gone and all down its length, dark objects lay scattered in the sand. The clouds returned with the hiss of the wind and the crashing of breakers.

Mitch stared down the remains of the spit, his mind seething with emotions no less turbulent than the spectacle he had witnessed. *He* had created this power. And used it to destroy. And in that instant he had no doubt of the depth of his sin, nor of the existence of God, such was the judgment he felt lowered upon him. Not just for giving this power to the paranoid North Korean government, but having accessed the incredible power itself. This was not what he had seen in photographs or video footage as a scientist. Not what his father had told him about as a boy. The reality was outside the capacity of images or language to convey.

This wasn't something meant for the hand of man. A quote that had always puzzled Mitch ran through his head:

> *If the radiance of ten thousand suns were to burst at once into the sky, that would be like the splendor of the mighty one. Now I am become Death, the destroyer of worlds. "*

Oppenheimer's words now made far too much sense. Despite the cheering Koreans behind him, a tear rolled down Mitch's cheek.

26

Professor Yang steadied himself on the wall as he reached out to knock on the door to Pak's stateroom. Something had changed in him over the last month. Some malady that wasn't the same as the seasickness plaguing the rest of the passengers. The cause of that was obvious – the thrashing gale that seemed to be following the *Mikisan Maru* on its homeward voyage. His illness was different, he feared. When they got to P'yongyang, he would have access to doctors who could perhaps diagnose his problem. The vertigo hit again, and he leaned against the door, waiting for it to pass.

"We didn't even want to do a full test," came Pak's voice through the door. "Weatherby said it wasn't necessary. But, if you remember, your organization refused to fund any more development until we demonstrated a success!"

"We wanted to be certain that we were not buying junk again," came a deeper voice. It was Khadir Jabril. "Why do you think the Americans attacked my country? Twice now, we have put your devices in position only to have them fail. Our network cannot risk another failure!"

"Risk?" retorted Pak. "Have you forgotten that we share this same risk? You received the weapon you paid for. Then you paid us to blow it up. Now you can buy another one for a cash payment to me of twenty million Euros, a South Korean passport under the name I gave you, immigration visa to Thailand, and transportation."

"My master will not be pleased," Jabril's voice menaced.

"Then tell him to look elsewhere. Your forms of terrorism have been disastrous," laughed Pak wickedly. "Tell him to be on the lookout for drones." There was a pause and Professor Yang could sense the tension through the door. "It has done nothing but stir the Americans to wrath and turn most of the world against you. Twenty million Euros, no less."

Professor Yang backed away from the door, and stumbled down the hall. "This is not Juche" he hissed to himself, sweat suddenly breaking our across his forehead. "It cannot be," he whispered. "It cannot be!"

A week after leaving Atlas Cove, the weather smoothed and Java's gray-green mountains appeared above the placid, blue waters of the Indian Ocean. Ships of all types and nationalities were around them again as they slipped unnoticed into Jakarta Bay. As soon as they tied up at the pier, Pak disappeared down the gangplank with Khadir Jabril and the other Middle Easterners while the scientists remained, as ordered, below decks, sweltering in the withering Indonesian sun. He returned, alone, late in the afternoon, well after the supplies for the final leg of the trip had been loaded, and the *Mikisan Maru* pulled out almost as soon as he arrived. That evening, he called the scientists to the mess hall.

"Fellow Comrades of the Choson Revolution," he announced, flanked by new, even more glorious portraits of the Great Leaders, apparently installed for this speech. "Today, I informed the Dear Leader, Comrade Marshal Kim Jong-il, of our successful 163-kiloton test on Heard Island. He has asked that I read a statement." He took out a piece of paper and held it up. "It is dated today, the fourteenth of July. 'Scientists, engineers, technicians, soldiers, and sailors of The Silla Project. Comrades of the Revolution. I have been informed of your manifold success that occurred on the anniversary of my esteemed father's passing. It is an auspicious occasion of which the Great Leader, Comrade Generalissimo Kim Il-sung, would have been proud. And it is an auspicious event of which I am both proud and grateful. You have proven yourselves to be of the highest revolutionary order and, imbued with the Juche ideology, have taken us one step closer to reunification with our oppressed comrades in the South. In recognition of this auspicious event, I invite you to join me in P'yongyang for the anniversary of our victory over the imperialist aggressors in the Victorious

Fatherland Liberation War. Congratulations, comrades on a job well done.'"

Everyone but Mitch and Max jumped to their feet, their faces filled with joy. "Long live the Great Leader!" they shouted. "Long live Marshal Kim Jong-il!"

"Mitch! Mitch!" cried Hyon-hui, pushing her way through the crowd. Mitch shot a glance at Max and rose to his feet. "Can you believe it, Comrade?" Her green eyes were sparkling and her lips spread into a broad smile. "P'yongyang! Finally you will get to see everything that our nation represents. Everything which we have strived for! You will finally see Choson!"

In her excitement, she leaned forward and kissed him on the cheek, then shrank away in surprise and blushed. Mitch, who could feel his face turning red as well, opened his mouth, uncertain what he was about to say, when, out of nowhere appeared a half-dozen accordion players bleating out *The Song of General Kim Il-sung*. An instant later, the voices of the scientists lifted up in song. Hyon-hui squealed and joined her comrades.

"Let's get out of here," said the Russian. They slipped out and made their way to the bow of the ship.

"That is so weird," Mitch said quietly, looking up at a half-moon riding off the port beam.

"The singing?" Max asked.

He shook his head. "No. The moon setting to the left! I grew up watching the moon set to the right. Now it's upside down, setting to the left. And I can't tell if it's waxing or waning. And the Big Dipper is straight ahead on the horizon. There's Hercules upside down, and Cygnus over there. Virgo's off to the left. Everything's backwards," He said, working into a rant. In the distance, the sound of the music changed to, *The Song of General Kim Jong-il* with a powerful accordion lead. "And I hate accordions!"

Max raised his eye at the outburst, and Mitch wrung his hands in frustration. "Everything has just gotten so screwed up! Beth being murdered. Me getting sent to prison only to be saved at the last minute by North Korean commandos. I mean, what the heck is that? Who gets saved by North Korean commandos? And now, not only have I betrayed my country, I betrayed the whole planet. Do you remember those seals, Max? Do you?" Mitch demanded. The smell of seared flesh from the destruction at Ground Zero haunted his dreams, but not nearly so much as the shrieking cries of the blind, scorched creatures closer to Dovers Moraine. Those hellish sounds he would never forget – nor that he'd caused them.

"Da," Max quietly confirmed. "I remember. And you had help."

"What the hell are we doing here?" Mitch blasted, casting his arms around in frustration. "Everything around here, everything we've done is evil! EVIL! And if that's not enough, I'm in love with the enemy!"

"I thought as much," Max nodded.

"American nuclear weapons designer falls for North Korean scientist. Ever hear of anything that stupid?"

"Stupid?" Max replied. "Stupid that you love her? Or stupid that she loves you?" Mitch glanced up at him, uncertain what point Max was making. "But I must warn you," he continued. "She loves Kim Il-sung, too. How she would respond if it came down to a choice between the two of you, I don't know."

"I'd never put her in that position, Max. Never."

"You are American," Max said as if it was not obvious. "She is North Korean. She is there already. Have you not read Romeov and Julietski by the great Russian poet, Shakespearikov?"

"Shakespearikov? Are you –"

Max burst into laughter. "*I am kidding, I am kidding!* You Americans are so gullible. But you should consider the story. I would not like to get caught in the middle. Remember poor Tybaltikov? It did not turn out well for him."

"It won't come to that. But have you forgotten what happened to Romeo and Juliet?"

Mitch turned to stare out over the ocean. The sky was velvety black and the moon shone on the water in a wavy line. The smell was clean and fresh and the ship felt solid. Even the taste of the air was sharp. All of Mitch senses seemed heightened, as if he was fully alive for the first time since Beth had been murdered, as if the shock wave of the bomb had shaken him from a long nightmare to finally confront a more confusing reality. Or was it Hyon-hui's soft kiss?

"So what do you think's going to happen to us now, Max? Have we outlived our usefulness?"

"That is a good question, Comrade."

"I never thought about what comes *after*. It's not like we can go home. And keeping us around could prove to be risky. I mean, if we were discovered. If it was found out by the U.S. that I'm here…" A rush shot through his veins and his hair stood on end. *Treason*. The word hung like cement in his chest.

Max nodded in agreement. "I am sure the Russian intelligence serv –"

"There you are!" Hyon-hui blurted from behind them.

Mitch jumped at the voice from the darkness and spun around. "Hyon-hui! You scared the crap out of me!"

"I am sorry," she said with a slight dip of her head. "But why did you leave?"

"I, uh –" stumbled Mitch.

"We, uh –" stammered Max.

"It seemed to be turning into a cultural thing," Mitch finally said.

"And we don't know your patriotic songs," added Max.

"But you will learn them," Hyon-hui pronounced excitedly. "Comrade Minister Pak had not finished his announcement." She smiled and her voice changed to that of a little girl in Santa's lap. "By order of the Great Leader, Comrade Marshal Kim Jong-il, the two of you are to be made citizens of Choson!"

"*What!?*" they exclaimed together.

"When we visit P'yongyang for the anniversary of the Victorious Fatherland Liberation War!" Her face was glowing with glee in the moonlight.

They looked at each other in disbelief.

"What is wrong?" she asked in a puzzled tone. "I thought you would be excited."

"Well," said Mitch, "I, uh – at least that solves the problem of where we go from here. It's just –"

"It is a big step," exclaimed Max, feigning excitement. "Are you certain we are ready for it?" He shot a sidelong glance at Mitch who instantly realized that refusing this honor could be dangerous.

"Yeah. Max and I were just discussing what happens to us now that the bomb is – well, we have a prototype. This is good news. *Great News!*"

27

Since time immemorial, the level of the shallow Taedong River, as far inland as P'yongyang, had been dictated by the tides, making the river unnavigable. Each day a wall of water would course up the river only to drain slowly back out. But as Kim Il-sung had changed Korea, so he had harnessed the tides. Early in the morning, after more than a month of being away, the *Mikisan Maru* was pulled by tugs into the West Sea Barrage's enormous locks. They reminded Mitch of Hoover Dam except four miles long and topped with a gigantic statue of the soldiers who had built it. The West Sea Barrage had transformed Nampo into one of the world's greatest port cities, or so Lee had told him. But Mitch could see that the concrete of the giant locks was already crumbling.

As the ship slowly rose, the nearly deserted docks of Nampo appeared, set against rank upon rank of identical concrete buildings. The streets were empty, and everywhere was filled with a grayish haze and the stench of sewage and rotting fish. It didn't look much like Hong Kong or New York City, or even New Orleans. Mitch's heart sank.

"The Soviets have been here," Max remarked sadly.

A pair of rusting North Korean freighters were tied up at at nearby pier. A child was using the bathroom off the stern of one of the vessels and, at the other end, a woman drew water with a rope on a bucket. Yet next to them, a well-tended ship poured grain into three large hoppers on the dock. A row of large, sealed bags issued from a conveyor on the other end of the hopper, and soldiers were loading the sacks onto trucks and train cars while uniformed women with bayoneted AK-47's kept watch over the operation.

"We have shipped grain from the north and are loading it into cars to be taken across the border to South Korea!" Lee announced proudly. Mitch just shook his head, knowing the grain was aid from the West.

The *Mikisan Maru* docked and Pak and Professor Yang were whisked away from the ship in a big, black, Rolls Royce sedan. The rest of the scientists milled around for what seemed like hours until they climbed aboard buses that sped them out of town on a deserted four lane road. The roadside was lined with large factories, long abandoned. Rusting train cars choked with weeds and crumbling smoke stacks shared the landscape with barren, dry fields spotted with steep, rocky hills. The villages they passed were empty. Only the large propaganda billboards offered any color that wasn't a shade of brown, and even they were drab beneath thick coats of dust.

Mitch stared blindly out the window. The last few weeks on the *Mikisan Maru* had grown increasingly unbearable. The Koreans were absolutely giddy with the success of the Silla Project and the prospect of visiting P'yongyang. Hyon-hui bubbled continuously about the colossal statues and various museums dedicated to "The Great Leader, Comrade Generalissimo Kim Il-sung." She didn't notice his increasing depression. Only Max had some inkling but didn't share the feeling of condemnation that went with it.

Mitch knew he had sinned against God, against man, against his country, against nature, against the Earth itself. He longed for a Bible to read, if only to study the many ways he had transgressed and revel in the descriptions of punishment that awaited him. Dante's *Inferno* would have been even better. But of course there was no Bible here, much less the Medieval poem of death and punishment. Mitch began to half believe that Hell might not be a specific location at all but rather, the absence of God in the soul. To be condemned and yet exposed to the glory of the eternal Father would no doubt sear ones soul as surely as a lake burning with fire and brimstone. So maybe everyone did go to Heaven. Including the souls who should not be there, crawling away from God and hiding in dark corners and alleys in the city with golden streets. Except one cannot hide from the Almighty. A fitting fate for him – a traitor the equal of Brutus, Cassius, and Judas Iscariot. Dante's Satan needed a fourth face.

They rolled into P'yongyang on an empty, thirteen lane-wide boulevard, passing monument after monument to Kim Il-sung. Propaganda billboards were everywhere and enormous Kim Il-sung murals covered the backs of buildings left windowless for just that purpose. The streets were immaculately clean. The grass was green and vibrant. Huge, forty story apartment blocks lined the street. But the sidewalks were empty and there wasn't another car in sight. Still, compared to the outskirts of the city – indeed to anything else Mitch had seen in the country – this was a different planet. No wonder Pak had been itching to get back.

They passed under an arch which Lee told them had been built to commemorate their defeat of the imperialists in the Victorious Fatherland Liberation War. Across the eight lane street sat Kim Il-sung stadium, and in front of it, in what looked like a parking lot, hundreds of people were lined up doing synchronized calisthenics, like the opening ceremonies at the Beijing Olympics.

A lone traffic guard stopped them at an intersection. Mitch peered in all directions. Far away, he saw another vehicle. It looked like a Volvo. Then the perky, blue clad policewoman performed a choreographed, dancelike maneuver, and let them pass. Mitch's skin began to crawl as they passed another square where more people were gathered doing calisthenics like the others. Lee told him they were practicing for the Mass Games to be held for the anniversary of the Victorious Fatherland Liberation War, but to Mitch, they looked like soulless automatons. Soulless, like him.

As the bus climbed a low hill, Lee continued his proud narrative, sounding like a tour guide. "The Mansudae Grand Monument was a present from the nation to the Great Leader on his sixtieth birthday," he recited as the deep-brown of a burnished-bronze figure of the Great Leader emerged in front of them. The frozen figure's right hand was uplifted in friendship. Or warning. It was hard to tell. "It is the largest bronze statue in the world. Over 30 meters tall."

Past the watchful figure, the road curved down a tree-lined avenue, and the bright blue Taedong River came into view on their left. A white spire tipped by a red flame shimmered in the afternoon sunlight on the opposite bank. Huge jets of water arced out of the river to flank the structure.

"Tower of the Juche Idea," announced Lee. "Over five hundred feet tall. The fountains are the tallest in the world!" Mitch gaped, not at the inspiration of the monuments but at the money that must have been spent here as the nation starved.

The bus slowed and entered a giant open space, paved with smooth granite tiles. This, according to Lee, was Kim Il-sung Square. Flanked by massive column-lined, granite buildings covered with Party regalia, the square could easily have held two million people. At the one end stood a magnificent structure like a Chinese palace. The Grand People's Study House, Lee told him. Green tiles covered its intersecting roof lines and multiple floors. Hundreds of columns graced the white granite exterior and, at its feet, sprawled a two-hundred yard long reviewing stand. The other end of the square was open to the view of the Tower of the Juche Idea on the other side of the river. The bus passed through with its occupants glued to the windows like children in a wildlife safari park.

Down a side street, they stopped at the Taegonggang Hotel, a five story, rectangular structure of brown brick with buzzing air conditioners stuffed into its many windows. Mitch and Max were assigned a room together on the third floor, and found it to be clean, functional and smelling of ginseng. They changed into the waiting sets of white shirts, black pants, and red tie and returned to the lobby as they had been instructed. It took forever for the rest of their group to arrive – they had been paying their respects at a room that Kim Il-sung had once stayed in and had been turned into a museum.

Their bus took them to a big building on the riverbank. Unlike most of P'yongyang's massive concrete mausoleums, this one was of traditional oriental design. A luscious smell filled the air making Mitch's mouth water as they wound through a tortuous maze of corridors and winding stairs. Finally, they emerged at a banquet hall that looked out over the Taedong River. Tables were lavishly set for them and a stage stood with waiting instruments. Mitch was surprised to see a Gibson Les Paul guitar, a Yamaha accordion and keyboards, and drums with Zildjian cymbals. Even a Rickenbacker bass. Out in the river, the Tower of the Juche Idea glistened but the rest of the city had disappeared into blackness.

"Professor Yang," Mitch said warmly, after making his way over to where his older colleague was seated.

The old man looked up and his eyes sparkled, but he seemed weak and drawn, almost translucent. "Dr. Weatherby," he said, with a raspy voice, and slowly rose to his feet. "I was hoping you would be here. P'yongyang is beautiful in –"

His breath caught and Mitch turned to see Hyon-hui approaching. She was radiant with shining eyes in a snug, red dress. Mitch could not understand how men could ignore her simply because she was not of 'pure blood.' He remembered the racism in America and the word 'discrimination' that got thrown around so freely. Not that there weren't problems, but seeing the attitude here toward Hyon-hui, he concluded that the current generation of Americans didn't know what the word even meant.

"Hyon-hui!" exclaimed Mitch. "You look lovely tonight." Max, standing at his side, agreed. She bowed awkwardly and those around them looked nervously away. "What's the matter with –" Mitch began, but Max silenced him with a single, quick shake of his head.

"Did they tell you?" Professor Yang asked turning back to Mitch. "I have been selected to be a delegate to the Seventh Party Congress in September."

Hyon-hui's face lit up. "A great honor, comrade professor. There is no one in Choson more deserving." She bowed deeply, but as she rose, Pak appeared behind the professor with an attractive older woman on his arm. Hyon-hui turned pale.

"Comrade Minister Pak," said Professor Yang with a deep bow. He turned to the woman. "Comrade Gyong-hi. It is a pleasure to see you again."

Professor Yang sank into a nearby chair as Gyong-hi smiled and said in perfect English, "And where are you gentlemen from?"

"France," said Pak abruptly, not giving Mitch a chance to answer. "Comrade Chun, my wife, Kim Gyong-hi. Chun Hyon-hui is one of Choson's finest scientists," he added to his wife. "We are deeply in her debt."

"Comrade Chun," Pak's wife said with a bow. "It is always good to see Choson's women playing such a pivotal role in the revolutionary cause. Class struggle is not for men only."

Hyon-hui's eyes lost their luster and her voice caught in her throat. She managed to bow, but that was all.

Pak glanced beyond her. "Comrade Cho!" he exclaimed bowing. Professor Yang struggled to his feet and bowed as well to the particularly dour-looking middle aged man behind them. Pak unleashed a stream of Korean, bowing his head with tremendous deference. Then he turned to Mitch and switched to English in a voice that was strangely subdued. Mitch had never heard this tone. "Dr. Weatherby, Dr. Tarasenko, First Deputy Chairman of the National Defense Commission, Comrade Cho Myong-rok."

So that was it. Pak's boss. "Chairman," Mitch said politely, and bowed to the coldest eyes he'd ever seen. He knew he should say something subservient but just couldn't do it.

"Dr. Weatherby," the deputy chairman replied with thinly veiled hatred. "I am told that your mission south was successful. The *widaehan suryong* has asked that I convey to you his appreciation for your efforts."

A cold chill swept up Mitch's spine at the bomb being attributed to him. "It was a group effort," he said.

Cho nodded tersely and spoke to Professor Yang in Korean. Mitch understood some of what they were saying, and Max seemed to be listening, also. Their names came up repeatedly and confirmed to Mitch that their names were known at the top of the North Korean power structure, making it less likely he could ever sneak away unnoticed.

When it was time to sit, Professor Yang invited Mitch, Max, Hyon-hui, and Sonny to his table. Waiters and waitresses poured out and began taking orders for P'yongyang cold noodle and the band came on stage. The lead singer – dressed in a pink, taffeta prom dress – picked up her mic and the band started to play tunes that sounded like a cross between folk music and a march: *Doraji*, *Hin-nun-duppin*, *We Shall Follow You Forever*, *Our Answer is Bullets*, *Reunification Rainbow*, and other favorites.

The food was good and Mitch ate all of his noodles and about half of Hyon-hui's. Sweet dog tongue was served for desert but Mitch only ate half before learning what it was. Max laughed when Mitch gagged and turned green. When they'd all finished and were sipping their drinks, with many of the men smoking Cuban cigars, the band stopped playing and left the stage. Pak got up and stood before the assembled scientists and technicians.

"Comrades!" he said. "You have done well and because of your efforts the Silla Project is a success, and our country is stronger. Reunification is at hand! Once again, the Juche Idea is shown to be superior!"

Everyone stood up and clapped. He let them go on for a moment, then motioned for them to sit back down. "Your service has not gone unnoticed by the Dear Leader, Comrade Marshal Kim Jong-il. And he has authorized me to tell you that each of you is to receive the DPRK Distinguished Service Medal." They cheered again. "But that is not why we are here tonight," Pak went on. "Tonight, we are going to honor two men, who have helped to make all of this possible Dr. Weatherby, Dr. Tarasenko, rise and come forward."

Mitch and Max glanced suspiciously at one another, before awkwardly making their way to the stage. Mitch's eyes scanned the crowd of Korean faces as he stood unmoving, uncertain what would come next. He knew each of the dozens of people watching him anxiously, had worked with them closely, but now it seemed an unfamiliar, hostile sea. Max, at his side, fretted like an fretful horse.

"These comrades," began Pak, speaking to the audience, "have met with unprecedented hardship in their lives, and have at the last come to grips with the lies of capitalism and imperialism. And, to our gain, they have chosen to make their homes in the Worker's Paradise permanently."

Mitch's heart pounded, wishing he could blurt out that it was a lie. That he could take back everything he'd done for them – take back the bomb. But his rational brain knew he had no other options. His rational side had always known that, which is why he was standing here. No options. God had provided no way of escape. He stared across the heads of the crowd before him, willing himself not to think about it, and to think of Hyon-hui instead. If damnation was his only option, at least Hell had one bright spot.

"They are truly examples of the Juche ideology and as such have acquired some measure of chajusong," Pak continued. "For this sacrifice, and for their participation in The Silla Project, the Dear Leader offers them his gratitude." He paused and licked his lips. "And admits them as honorary citizens of the Democratic Peoples Republic of Korea, and probationary members in the Korean Workers' Party."

The banquet hall went deathly quiet. Food fell out of Sonny's mouth. A man across the room dropped his drink, spilling it across the table. Hyon-hui choked on something.

"Join me," Pak went on, "in congratulating them on this auspicious occasion!"

When he started clapping, everyone in the room, including Professor Yang, leapt to their feet, applauding. Pak produced two probationary pins which he fixed to the shirts of the dumbfounded recipients.

Mitch stood awkwardly before the group. Kim Il-sung's image, burning like a brand on his chest – that was his reward for the atrocity he'd committed on Heard Island, for abandoning his country, for betraying Beth and everything she'd sought to preserve. A beady-eyed devil stared up at him from the pin, gloating over his damnation. He wanted to rip it off, to rewind and take some other path, any other path, but there were none – then or now. He'd been dropped into a funnel and there was only one way out.

Mitch saw Hyon-hui's face with joy radiating from it beyond anything he'd seen. It made his heart ache until it nearly burst. He soaked it in, her beauty, her radiance. The salvation to his damnation. But he was still damned.

*

"This changes everything, Mitch," Hyon-hui burbled, openly clinging to Mitch's arm as he escorted her to her hotel room. "*Everything!* You are a Party member now. Do you know what that means?!?"

Mitch wanted to vomit. And it wasn't from eating dog. "That it changes everything?"

"Yes!"

They stopped at her door and she looked up at him with the green eyes that smote his heart like a thunderbolt. She stood on her tiptoes and their lips met. Mitch put his arms around her, kissing her deeply as he felt her body against his for the first time. Hyon-hui gently pushed him away and they parted for the night.

Mitch staggered through the door of his room and fell against the wall in a daze.

"You look like I feel," said Max from the edge of the bed, his tie in his hands.

"So what happens now?" Mitch shuffled over to the other bed and plopped down, staring at the ceiling. In his mind, he saw Chairman Cho's eyes. They made him shudder. Then he would see Hyon-hui's eyes and feel weak inside, but in a pleasant way. But then he saw the bomb exploding. The roasted seals. A change in the balance of power in the Far East. And Kim Il-sung's face laughing at him from the pin on his chest.

"It's gone too far," Mitch said into the silence. Still, Max didn't respond. "Heard Island. Did you know that was what our... gadget, was going to do?"

"I thought I knew." There was a long pause, then Max admitted quietly, "I'm having nightmares."

"Oppenheimer turned against the bomb after they tested it."

"So did Sakharov. I always thought he was a traitor." Max sniffed back a tear. "My God, Mitch. What have we done?"

"The question is, Max, what are we going to do?"

The glowing numerals on the clock showed 3:30 a.m. Mitch rolled over in bed to the sound of singing. It sounded like children just outside their window. Max groaned and mumbled something in Russian.

But the singing went on until Mitch stumbled over to the window, swearing under his breath, and leaned over the air conditioner to see what it was. Outside, several hundred school children marched up and down the street, rehearsing for something. Probably the Mass Games. A truck followed close behind, bathing them with its headlights. They kept it up until nearly four o'clock, then melted off into the night.

Mitch awoke a few hours later to the sound of "...the U.S. imperialists and their treacherous puppets will pay one hundred-fold in blood for this thrice-cursed crime against the Korean people."

Max had discovered the third house channel on the TV, consisting of propaganda films prepared for the International Festival of Youth and Students.

"Can you believe this *govno*?" said Max.

"You could always *turn it off.*" Mitch said and dove back under the covers.

Max turned up the volume and laughed. "Time to get up, Party member! We're late already!"

Mitch groaned at the thought of wearing that Party pin from now on. God, this needed to end. It needed to end now. But neither of them had any idea how to make that happen without pain. Lots and lots of pain.

Their first activity of the morning was a visit to Kim Il-sung's ancestral home at Mangyongdae. So after breakfast, they spilled out onto Sungni Street, where the kids had been practicing in the middle of the night, and marched off behind two tour guides. The woman was attractive and elegant in traditional dress. The man wore a light-blue windbreaker and looked like a chain-smoking used car salesman.

The day had just enough of a breeze to keep the coal-polluted air from seeming quite so tainted. Not a cloud in the sky. Warm and dry. And only a hint of sewage smell. This close to the Taedong, the drought was less evident with well-watered lawns, fountains, and trees, as well as forsythia and azaleas. Mitch and Hyon-hui held hands, drawing more than a few surprised looks. The night had given him no wisdom, but he knew that he relished the feel of her hand in his. He also knew there was a decision coming, and he wasn't sure he could make the right one. He wasn't sure what the right one was if it meant hurting the woman at his side.

P'yongyang Station, where they were to board the subway, was about half-a-mile from the hotel, more than far enough for Mitch to notice the eerie silence. There were no birds chirping in the trees that grew along the sidewalks. No traffic noises. No people. No cars. And not so much as a scrap of paper anywhere. He started humming a familiar a tune. Hyon-hui gave him a puzzled look.

"*The Twilight Zone*," replied Mitch.

"The twilight zone?"

He thought for a minute then said, "There really would be no point in my trying to explain."

As they emerged from beneath the trees, Max exclaimed, "What's that?" pointing at a dark triangular shape rising high above the skyline. The steeply angled pyramid was covered with shiny windows and towered over everything else in the city.

"That is the Ryugyong Hotel," the guide muttered, and attempted to direct their attention toward a nondescript copse of trees along the road.

Mitch remembered laughing with his colleagues at Los Alamos about the Ryugyong. It had stood unfinished for nearly a decade, marring the skyline of P'yongyang. It was rumored that the concrete at the base was crumbling and the foundation was unstable. Pictures he'd seen on the internet had backed up the claims. Either they had fixed it, or decided to cover it with glass and pretend it had been completed. Mitch decided to test that theory. "Can we go up in it?" he asked with faux excitement.

"No," said Lee firmly. Mitch and Max tried to get more information but neither Lee nor the guide seemed to hear their questions which answered it for Mitch.

Passing through a raised arch with a twenty-foot-tall picture of Kim Il-sung above it, they entered P'yongyang Station, an old style train depot with a circular central atrium. Inside, they stepped onto an escalator, and the female guide beamed proudly at the gasps as they were plummeted downward at a speed that made the wind blow through their hair.

"This was built with all-Korean technology," she announced proudly. Mitch's ears popped twice through the martial music reverberating up and down the green lighted shaft. Max leaned over and muttered that, from the depth, it was probably meant to double as a nuclear bomb shelter. Mitch grinned, looking down at at his feet to hide it. There, cast into the metal step were the words, 'MADE IN SHANGHAI.' So much for all-Korean technology.

"The P'yongyang Metro," the male guide told them with a sweeping gesture, when the escalator dumped them into a giant room decorated with crystal chandeliers and patriotic murals. "This is not only the traffic means but also the place for ideological education," he continued. "Its decoration is depicted artistically so as to convey to posterity the glorious revolutionary history and the leadership exploits of the Great Leader President Kim Il-sung. You see here," he pointed to the mural on the left, "*A Morning of Innovation.*" It showed happy factory workers inventing... something. "And here is *Song of a Bumper Crop.*" Happy peasants, harvesting. "And," he pointed toward the rear of the station, "*Kim Il-sung Among Workers.*"

This was easily the strangest painting Mitch had ever seen. Beneath a mustard sky, the Great Leader was striding forward in a long, brown Drover's coat and a heavy, black fur hat. Around him were adoring men and women from every walk of life, out of place in the industrial power plant with belching smokestacks and transmission lines stretched over their heads like spider webs.

Long, white train cars pulled into the station with a whoosh as Mitch stared at the mural. "That's a German train!" Max blurted out and the guide shot him a quick frown. "I was in Berlin once," he told Mitch. "At a conference. I guess they sold the cars after East Germany collapsed."

"*Comrade*," snapped Major Lee, "please."

"Maybe this is the very one I rode on last time?" he continued, stepping toward the door.

"*Max!*" Mitch hissed.

"What?"

Mitch jerked his head toward Lee who was glaring intently. "*Shut – up.*"

"I have heard that the subway in New York City is quite dangerous," their guide, who reeked of cheap cigarettes, said as they took their seats on the subway. Mitch glanced up at the framed portraits of Kim and Kim glaring down at them. Twin devils guarded this subway. There may be no crime, but sitting on a picture of Kim Il-sung could get you sent to a labor camp. And they thought the ones in New York were dangerous? But the guide's statement had its desired effect.

"Dangerous?" several of the scientists prodded. They loved these sorts of anti-American anecdotes.

"Yes, quite," the guide confirmed. "Fighting and thievery."

"Oh, it's much worse than that," Mitch added and lowered his voice. "They have wars on it." He waited for them to take the bait. He glanced at Sonny and winked, then wondered if Sonny knew what a wink was.

"Tell me of this!" hissed the guide, his hand itching to hold a cigarette. The others crowded in to hear.

"I don't know if I should. Probably shouldn't have said –"

"Please! I must know of this!" exclaimed their guide.

Mitch looked down at the floor of the spotless train. "It's horrible," he finally uttered. "I've been there. Evil warlords control subterranean New York City. Hundreds of miles of subway. Sewer lines. Some dating back hundreds of years. They command vast armies of mutants who –"

"What is a mutant?" hissed the guide. Everyone leaned in to hear and Mitch had to work to keep from laughing.

"A human who has been deformed by chemicals and radiation leaking into the ground from capitalist factories. People with three and four sets of eyes. Extra legs. Long, dog-like fangs. They say that some of them are telepathic and can see infrared." Sonny gazed at Mitch doubtfully, while Max stared at the floor, suppressing a smirk.

The story ended as they arrived at their destination: Rich Origin Station, where the ceiling was held up by marble pillars sculpted to look like torches wrapped in grape vines. As he exited the train, Mitch smiled inwardly, knowing the guide would regurgitate the story as truth every chance he got, and any foreigners would think him a fool.

At Kim Il-sung's boyhood home, they were greeted by a demure woman in national costume. She provided the important details of the Kim theology: born 15 April, Juche 1 (1912), the same day the Titanic sank. Became a revolutionary fighter following the death of his father at age 12. From age 13 on, he *led* the Anti-Japanese Struggle, participated in thousands of battles, won victory against the Japanese, victory against the Americans, etc., etc., etc. Undoubtedly, Kim had been a brave and charismatic partisan leader, but Mitch felt the stories were about like his own tale of the New York subway. And who in North Korea hadn't heard them hundreds of times already?

The tidy concrete and thatched abode, contained photographs of his parents, his executed brother, and his revolutionary cousins. There was also the famed 'Ugly Pot.' The Great Leader's parents were so poor, the costumed woman told them, they could only afford a cooking pot with a lid which had collapsed upon firing. It was from such hardships that the Great Leader developed such a keen dedication to the prosperity of all of his countrymen. Maybe it was true, but it was being twisted to justify making his own people live the same way.

The next stops on the tour were on the other side of town: Kim Il-sung Stadium and the Arch of Triumph, which was three feet taller than the one in Paris. From there, they went on to the Chilgol Revolutionary Site, the Liberation Tower, the Friendship Tower, and the Mangyongdae Schoolchildren's' Palace – a huge, twelve story daycare center. On their way back, they passed a row of gymnasiums and stadiums built for the 1990 South Korean Olympics, which the North boycotted after the South refused an even split. Out in front, large crowds were practicing for the Mass Games to be held the next day at the May Day Stadium on Rungna Island.

Their bus traveled on through town, which Max likened to a Mandelbrot set – a mathematical object whose complex patterns never repeated but looked basically the same no matter how closely examined. Empty streets. Huge, vacant apartment blocks. Lush gardens and parks devoid of any normal daily life. And propaganda billboards everywhere. It felt more like a frozen diorama than a place where people lived. They crossed the river on a modern, four-lane bridge where Mitch got his first look at the May Day Stadium, a gigantic, titanium-domed mothership. Mitch knew the "all-Korean" structure had to have been built by Russian engineers since, at the time it was constructed, the Russians were the only ones who knew how to work with titanium on such a large scale. Nevertheless it was impressive, even from a distance. A few minutes later, they pulled to a stop near the base of the Juche Tower. Everyone climbed out and stared up in awe at the massive white obelisk.

"This is the Tower of the Juche Idea," their cigarette-reeking guide said reverently. "It was built by the Dear Leader in 1982, for the Great Leader, Comrade Generalissimo Kim Il-sung's 70th birthday. It is 170 meters, the tallest stone tower in the world." He looked around until he spotted Mitch. "Even taller than the Washington Monument," he told them, and the style seemed to have been copied from exactly that. The guide went on to recite fact after fact about the honorary structure: it contained 25,550 granite slabs – one for each day in Kim Il-sung's life at age 70; it was surfaced with 70 large granite tiles, and surrounded by 70 granite steps; the artificial flame at the top was 20 meters high and constructed from red glass and gold; the fountains in the river were the tallest in the world. And all of it, he claimed, swelling with pride, was assembled with all-Korean technology by the nation's finest Juche-trained craftsmen.

The enormity of the tower overwhelmed the emptiness of the plaza below. Its base alone was fifty yards on a side. And high up on the tower were two massive, gold Hangul characters spelling the word, Juche. Each must have been fifty feet tall and weighed tons. Everything in this city was of monstrous proportions. Like it had been fashioned by titans for whom money was no object. But in the countryside, Mitch knew people there were starving. He'd seen it. He'd been one of them. The waste and inequity were staggering.

Hyon-hui called Mitch to where she pulled him happily into a niche at the base of the tower and pointed out the marble tiles lining the walls, each bearing greetings from Juche study groups from around the world.

"Look! U.S.A." She pointed to a tile sandwiched between plates from France and Belgium, and read it aloud.

LONG LIVE KIMILSUNGISM
New York Group for the Study of Kimilsungism
April 8, 1979

The guide had followed behind them. "You see," he said joyously. "Juche is everywhere, studied by the masses!"

Mitch bolted from the alcove, telling Hyon-hui it was to escape the cigarette-stench of the guide, but it was just as much to escape his rhetoric. But the guide followed, adding meaningless anecdotes to every trivial detail. A seventy foot-tall bronze sculpture of two men and a woman holding aloft the hammer, sickle, and pen rose in front of them.

"The worker, the intellectual, and the peasant," chirped their guide. "They bring together the symbols of Party unity and class consciousness. And these," he said, turning and pointing to the fountains in the river beside them. "These are the largest fountains in the world."

Mitch bit his tongue to stop from calling out the guide as to what evidence he had that these useless marvels were the best or the grandest, or any other superlative. Or why any of this was important in a country where everyone not living in P'yongyang was starving. There seemed no end to the excess.

Eventually, the group gathered back in the front where a long corridor tunneled into the center of the tower. A dozen of them crammed into an elevator – for 20 Won apiece – and made the rickety ride to the summit. The doors opened and just beyond were a pair of gold doors that the attendant rolled apart by hand. The riders stumbled out of the cramped space onto the parapet of the tower.

The sun was a brilliant ball of shimmering, orange fire suspended just above the city. The huge pyramid of the Ryugyong stood out like a temple to Ra. The twin towers of the Hotel Koryo, their burgundy brick and twin revolving restaurants awash with afternoon flame, rose where their own hotel was obscured below it. Arcing gracefully skyward from the river, the two fountains were a jet of rubies. Just across the river was Kim Il-sung Square and the multiple, sloping, green-tile rooflines of the People's Study House. At the center of it all, the Grand Monument. The blood red sky behind the colossus lent the image a god-like appearance. P'yongyang had been built to impress and it didn't disappoint.

"P'yongyang!" announced their guide, his charred breath nearly flooring Mitch. "And those," he added, gesturing toward the fountains again. "Those are the largest fountains in the world."

Mitch gritted his teeth, knowing he should remain silent, but when the guide began repeating the same details of the Juche Tower's construction on the elevator ride down, he could take no more of the orgy of excess and deception.

"So did you say 25,550 slabs?" Mitch asked, throwing a tinge of doubt into his tone.

"That is correct. One for each day of the Great Leader's immortal life on his 70th birthday. Each is individually numbered."

"Twenty-five thousand, five hundred fifty? You're sure? At 70 years old?"

"Precisely. One for each of his revolutionary days."

Mitch looked down. He was going to put this little commie stooge in his place. When he looked up, he'd added a troubled frown to his face. "Doesn't your calendar include leap years?"

The guide shook his head. "Leap years – what?"

Everybody stared at Mitch.

"There are seventeen leap years in 70 years. So at age 70, assuming the scientifically perfect Juche calendar keeps time in accordance with time in the heavens, he had actually lived 25,567 days." When he was done, he stood there looking smug.

"You're right!" exclaimed Sonny. But their guide just stood with a dazed expression on his face, trying to decipher what Mitch had just told him. No doubt, astronomical motion was not something they'd covered at the P'yongyang Schoolchildren's Palace or the Tourism Academy. All he knew was Kim Il-sung's immortal exploits. The guide's face twisted as he tried to work out some response, knowing there had to be one. Max stared at the floor. Sonny looked troubled. Hyon-hui glared. As the elevator descended, the silence grew heavy, but still, Mitch waited for an answer. The guide, from his frantic eyes, had concluded he was too weak-minded to determine the correct response, and was looking for a way out of his bind without admitting the imperfection of his knowledge of the tribute to the Great Leader. The moment, the elevator stopped and the doors slid open. the guide shoved everyone off and rushed toward the bus to escape his humiliation.

"Are you trying to be funny?" Hyon-hui hissed at Mitch as twilight was setting in. The entire western sky was a brilliant orange, casting the skyline of the city into a black silhouette.

"Funny? What are you talking about?" Mitch asked with a hint of laughter in his voice.

"You know exactly what I'm talking about. Leap years!"

"But they're off by seventeen days. Someone had to tell 'em! We can go dig up some rocks from the river bank and dump them on the steps."

She snorted and turned away, staring out over the river at the Mansudae Colossus. "Can't you see what is around you, Mitch? This beautiful city. There is none other like it. It is all a tribute to the Great Leader, Comrade Generalissimo Kim Il-sung. This isn't *his* city. It is the city of the Popular Masses. It is our *chajusong*. This tower was a gift. Certainly you can understand the spirit of a gift? The actual number does not matter."

Mitch had seen the city. Seen it from the tower above. Seen it from the streets. Seen it on Google Earth before ever coming her. And he was sickened by it. It was nothing but a personality cult that one man and his cronies had funded by foisting a failed social, political, and economic system on a raped populace. And no matter his feeling for Hyon-hui, he knew one thing beyond a doubt.

"I'm not a communist," Mitch said quietly.

"It isn't a communist party," Hyon-hui replied. "It's a Workers' party."

"But your whole governmental system is communist. And I'm not a communist. I was brought up to believe communism was the worst thing possible. I can't get away from that."

"You were also brought up to believe in justice."

"This isn't justice," he snapped back, waving at the grand display across the river. "We were starving at Sagi-dong. Poor old Bao Yan-what's-his-name starved to *death*."

"He did not starve to death, Mitch. He died of influenza."

"Brought on by malnutrition." But Mitch saw the programmed fear leaping into Hyon-hui's eyes as she became aware of the cognitive dissonance that filled all of their minds. He softened. "I just don't think I can be a communist. I know I can't do it. Like, learning to eat sweet dog tongue. Maybe it just too ingrained, but it's wrong for me. Everything I see and everything I am tells me that."

Hyon-hui took his hand. It was so warm and soft in his. She glanced at his Party pin before looking up at him with pain in her eyes. "Does looking at me tell you that, Mitch? Could you do it for me?"

Her attitude towards him had changed drastically since he'd been admitted to the Party. She made no attempt to hide her affection anymore. He was now her one hope at marriage. At children. At a normal life. As normal as it came around here. Mitch tore his eyes away from her to stare out into the gathering darkness, knowing that he couldn't bear to take that hope away from her. Knowing that he could drown in those eyes and forget who he was and everything he knew. And knowing he'd hate himself, either way.

The evening's entertainment was a circus show, complete with a crowd-pleasing skit of a buffoonish GI in olive drab uniform directing South Korean clown-soldiers in a display of gross ineptitude. Mitch gripped the armrests of his seat, offended by the bigotry and disregard for the truth. But these people knew nothing of the truth, or cared nothing for it. A burst of patriotism jetted up inside him, only to be mingled in his mind with the sight of Beth dying in his arms, blood spouting from her chest and mouth, like the twin fountains in the Taedong flanking the Tower of the Juche Idea. Tallest in the world. He closed his eyes and grasped the armrests tighter, nearly shaking as he tried to sort out this world where nothing he knew was true anymore. But it had to be. Deep inside, he knew the truth had not changed. But that didn't tell him what the truth was – or what he was to do now. He needed a choice. Some way to get off this path.

They were taken to the Koryo Hotel after the circus, where some of the scientists gathered in the karaoke bar and others sat in the lounge watching TV. Mitch, Hyon-hui, Max, Sonny, Lee, and their tour guides found a table near one of the revolving restaurant's huge picture windows. Outside, except for the illumination on Kim's statue, not even a light from a parking lot broke the darkness. Indeed, the only way they could tell they were rotating was that the gibbous moon slid by every so often. Once drinks were ordered and quickly dispatched to their table, the tour guides spoke of the horrors of the world outside North Korea: the South Koreans were held captive by their evil government; they had massacred a lot of people in Kwangju in 1980; theirs was a U.S.-controlled puppet state; the U.S. occupation forces murdered hundreds of thousands of South Koreans every year; the National Security Law proves that South Korea isn't a free society; half of their population was infected with the AIDS virus.

Mitch ignored their lecture, watching the moon slide back into view as the restaurant turned. After another swallow of his beer, he stared at the dark blotch of the Sea of Tranquility on its bright face. Apollo's photographs from space, he remembered, had shown that there were no political borders. And even now there were none on the moon. "You can almost see the flags on a night like this," he said to steer the conversation into a less propagandized area.

"What flag is that?" asked the cigarette-smoking tour guide, squinting out into the darkness.

"The ones on the moon."

Sonny laughed as if Mitch had made a joke.

"The moon?" Lee asked incredulously.

"Yeah. Flags. Like the one at the edge of Mare Tranquillitatis."

"Mare what?" said Sonny, his smile dropping into confusion.

"Mare Tranquillitatis," said Mitch slowly but they just stared. "Mare, Latin for sea." He pointed up at the moon. His companions following his fingers to the orbiting rock. "Those dark patches are lava flows but the ancients thought they were seas."

"We know *that*," Lee sneered. "What is this flag you're talking about?"

"There's one at the lower edge of Tranquillitatis. That'd be from Tranquillity Base, Apollo 11. The Eagle. Then there's Apollo 12 at the southern edge of Mare Ibrium. Apollo 13 didn't land, so Apollo 14 landed I think just west of Apollo 12's site. Apollo 15 landed at –"

"Landed?" said their guide dubiously. "What are you talking about, Comrade?"

"Apollo," said Mitch. "You know, *Apollo*?" But they just stared back with blank faces. Mitch glanced at Max who gave a barely perceptible shake of his head. "You guys have never heard of Apollo?" Was it possible that they hadn't?

"No," said Hyon-hui. "What is Apollo?"

"A god from Greek mythology?" offered Sonny.

Mitch leaned back into his chair scarcely believing what he was hearing. How could they call themselves a technological society when they had skipped the greatest technological achievement of the previous century?

"Don't make us play games, Mitch. Tell us what it is," Hyon-hui insisted. He closed his eyes and leaned forward, rubbing his forehead. "Mitch?!" Hyon-hui said again, looking back and forth between him and the moon that was now moving out of the field of view as the room slowly came around.

"Apollo," he began, as if addressing a tribe of Kalahari bushmen who knew nothing of the modern world, "was the name of a U.S. space program that landed men on the moon. There were six landings between 1969 and 1972. Apollo 11 through 17. They left a small American flag at each site."

Everyone, with the exception of Max, laughed. "You're making that up," Hyon-hui giggled. "Nobody's been to the moon!"

Mitch shook his head. "Apollo 11. 1969. Neil Armstrong stepped out and said, 'That's one small step for a man. One giant leap for mankind.' Probably the most well known phrase of the Twentieth Century." They just stared. How could they not know. "Haven't you ever seen the photograph of the Earth taken from Apollo 14?" They hadn't and refused to believe any of it.

Mitch remembered, as they'd been preparing to leave on the Mikisan Maru, how he'd felt the United States and Korea were more alike than he could have imagined. The bureaucracy. The waste. That was before P'yongyang. He'd been a fool to think that, even for an instant. Sure, there were lazy and corrupt administrators everywhere. But the United States, even at its worst, was nothing like this and never had been. Nowhere on Earth was like this place.

At the end of the night, Mitch grudgingly joined in as they raised a final toast, in jest, to the DPRK having landed on Mars to place a flag there – because it was red. But with their glasses raised, Sonny's eyes drifted longingly out toward the moon.

After the long day, Mitch and Max collapsed onto their beds, half watching a TV documentary of how applying Juche methods over thirty years had repaired the devastating environmental damage the Japanese and Americans had inflicted upon Mt. Paektu. Mitch opened his mouth to say something to Max when a swift knock sounded quietly on the door. They looked at one another and it came again, low and frantic.

Mitch half expected Hyon-hui when he opened the door to find Sonny, glancing up and down the hall. "What are you doing here?" Mitch asked as the scientist pushed inside and shut the door behind him.

"Dr. Weatherby," he asked, wringing his hands, "am I a good scientist?"

"What makes you ask that?"

"Just please answer. I must know. Compared to American," he glanced at Max, "or Russian. Am I a good scientist?"

Mitch scratched his head. "Sure, Sonny. You know you're good."

Sonny frowned. "Then how could I not know about this?! Man has walked on the moon. On the moon, Dr. Weatherby! *On another planet*. Before I was born! We cannot send a man to the moon, and we cannot even admit that someone else has. How can we say we are the greatest?" His voice trailed off and a helpless look entered his eyes.

"I don't know what to say, Sonny," Mitch finally said. "I wish I hadn't said anything. I just assumed that –"

"So, now tell me. If I did not know that, if I cannot do those things or even understand how it could be done, tell me how I am I a good scientist?"

Mitch looked at the floor. Max looked away. "Sonny," Mitch finally answered, looking into the man's deep brown eyes, "you're a brilliant young man and possess an excellent analytical mind, but your education is about forty years behind mine. And thirty years behind Max's."

"Hey!" objected Max.

"It's true," said Mitch.

Max's face grew hard and he nodded grudgingly. "Da."

"I knew it," Sonny said sadly. "All I ever wanted was to be a great scientist, like Fermi, or Bohr, or Sakharov. I am nothing but a fool. I am fubar."

"You're not a fool, Sonny. Juche has prevented your country from keeping up with technology. That's all." The look on Sonny's face pierced Mitch's heart and he groped for something to say. "You're a brilliant man and you can still go far."

"*Far?*" he spat, knowing how fabricated the statement had been. "Compared to what? Shall I invent the wheel again and pretend it is unique? The South is so far ahead of us we can never overtake her. And the West. How can Choson be so fubar?" He looked up, his eyes filled with longing. "Tell me Dr. Weatherby," he begged. "Who is this Armstrong? Did he survive the trip? Does he live still?"

Mitch hesitated at the thought he was shattering this young man's life, simply by giving him the truth about the world. He swallowed heavily but had to answer. "He does. I've even met him. He's brilliant, and approachable. And humble."

Sonny stared as the tears collecting in his dark eyes grew into brimming pools, and spilled from his heavy lids. "Tell me more, Dr. Weatherby. Please. I must know."

28

In order of the DRPK's holidays, Victorious Fatherland Liberation War Day is number four. Most hallowed is Kim Il-sung's Birthday. Then his death day. Then Kim Jong-il's birthday. Yet the defeat of the imperialist hordes is considered the nation's defining moment. Entire museums were dedicated to the Great Leader Comrade Generalissimo Kim Il-sung's victory over the imperialist aggressors, and Mitch had been taken to visit every one in P'yongyang. If he heard the phrase "Great Leader Comrade Generalissimo Kim Il-sung" one more time, he told Max he was going to leap from the top floor of the Ryugyong Hotel, which stood across the street from a colossal twenty acre monument whose name sounded like all the others. From less than 100 yards, Mitch could see that even though it was now encased in glass, it was still a derelict, and his guides still ignored it.

Each of the exhibits in the museums they visited documented how America started the Korean War and how North Korea had won it, decisively – without addressing the fact that South Korea was *still* just across the DMZ. This revisionist history was accompanied by lies about how American forces used chemical and biological weapons against dozens of defenseless villages. Mitch saw grade-school children being taught that Americans packed warehouses with women and children and set them ablaze. And how G.I.'s had stripped others and thrown them into freezing water. Maybe America had changed from what Mitch had believed as a child, but it it had never been this. Even Nazi Germany didn't compare with what the North Koreans said about the United States. But it made sense why North Koreans were so terrified of Americans.

The day ended with the Mass Games in the titanium bulk of the May Day stadium. One hundred fifty thousand Koreans packed the arena to watch four hours of choreographed propaganda. Thousands of synchronized participants from old men to children marched, danced, tumbled, and whirled down on the field forming ever-changing patterns of astonishing intricacy. At the same time, up in the stands, twenty-five thousand North Korean youth had put on a show like an enormous LCD display with each pixel being a person holding a colored card. Mitch remembered the Beijing Olympics and how everyone thought it was so incredible. China had nothing on North Korea. With nothing more than colored cards, they displayed detailed maps of Korea, animated dams with crackling transmission lines, armies marching to victory, happy peasants working in fields, P'yongyang with lights twinkling in windows, and image after image of Kim Il-sung, all performed to the strains of militant marches. All it lacked to be complete, Mitch thought, was a nuclear detonation, but the mind-blowing fireworks at the end came close.

And Sonny missed it all. He hadn't appeared at breakfast that morning, nor was anywhere to be found the entire day. The following day he was missing as well, although no one other than Mitch and Max seemed to notice his absence, or acknowledge that he had been on this trip at all. Watching a parade from the grandstands at Kim Il-sung Square, Mitch and Max feared the worst. Their room had probably been bugged. SSA agents had heard everything Sonny had asked, and everything Mitch had answered. Sonny was probably already in jail – or worse.

A sea of people packed tightly in phalanxes with rows and columns, too straight to be human, stretched from the foot of the grandstands all the way to the river, over a quarter mile away. Stoic and unmoving under the boiling sun. Before them, for hour after hour, men and women filed by with their weaponry to the powerful strains of North Korea's most militant songs. Trucks. Tanks. Jeeps. Missile launchers. Navy. Air Force. Army. Rank upon rank, upon rank, upon rank of Party members with their colorful floats and flowing red flags, shouting anti-American slogans. While high above them on a balcony, the reptilian eyes of the Great Leader, Comrade Marshal Kim Jong-il stared out impassively.

Surrounded by scientists from the Silla Project, with Hyon-hui on one side and Max on the other, Mitch looked down on the parade. A sea of Party faithful from across the land. Thousands of women in brown, wool skirts goose-stepped past carrying AK-47's. Trained bitterness filled their faces and he remembered the mushroom cloud rising high above Elephant Spit. The screams of the dead and dying seals. He'd given that power to the man in control of the hate he was watching. Would it just be seals next time?

He glanced over at Hyon-hui. Joy shone from her eyes like the rays of the morning sun. Could he accept this for her? The crazed devotion of the acolytes all around him? If the visit in P'yongyang had shown him anything, it was that he could not believe any of this was real. But could he pretend – for her? Or maybe they could live in Sagi-dong? But live in Sagi-dong forever?

The final parade of troops and military hardware stomped by them as the sun dipped in the sky. In response to some hidden cue, tens of thousands of spectators, the scientists of the Silla Project included, rose from their seats and flowed up the broad concourse leading to the very foot of sacred Mansu Hill. The crowd became a living river, sweeping Mitch along as he struggled to find air that wasn't thick with sweat and pungent herbs and spices. The river flowed up the broad flight of steps that ascended the hill to the grand monument of Kim Il-sung with its massive arm and outstretched hand. There, the river of bodies joined a massive human sea lapping beneath the image. He turned around and looked down the hill at the millions coming to pay their respects. And suddenly, Mitch realized what was about to happen. He'd seen it on the small TV in his apartment. Now, he was about to be part of it.

They came to a stop not far from Kim Il-sung's huge feet and waited. Mitch looked up at the face of the dark colossus looming over him, and his heart began to pound. Ancient names came into his head: Shadrach, Meshach and Abednego told to bow to Nebuchadnezzar's image of gold. It had never been anything more than a children's story to him. Such things didn't happen in real life – or so Mitch had believed. But he had been wrong. The graven image leered down at him and he knew this was his chance – his last chance – to save his soul.

"I'm not going to bow, Hyon-hui."

Her eyes open wide. "But –"

"*I can't!*"

"Mitch, you must!" she hissed in terror. "You are a Party member! There will be a million people watching you! More on TV." She leaned in close, hysteria creeping into her eyes and voice. "Please, Mitch. For me. Do this for us."

He nodded stiffly. "I can't. I love you but I can't do it."

Silence descended. If there had been birds in the trees down by the river, their songs could have been heard. But all the birds had long ago been eaten. The tinkling of fountains in the distance, away down by the green-tiled Study House, drifted up the hill to the supplicating masses. The entire city, indeed the entire nation, held its breath. Before them all, impassive and silent, stood the bronze colossus with the red sun transforming its bronze body into a deep, luminous orange, like a rising mushroom cloud.

"Now I am become Death," Mitch recited. "The destroyer of worlds."

Hyon-hui looked at him. Tears were streaming down her face, and her eyes encapsulated a lifetime of suffering and disappointment culminating in this, her most bitter defeat. Somewhere inside, Mitch remembered Max's words warning against making her choose between him and Kim Il-sung. But he stood firm.

A deep gong sounded somewhere and echoed over the hill. Those in front bowed and the motion spread outward like ripples on a pond. Images flashed through Mitch's mind from ancient stories that he now knew were true. The fiery furnace. The lion's den. Those men had been terrified, too. Just as he was.

"Please God," he hissed. "If ever you answer a prayer, answer this one: *help me stand.*"

The wave of human prostration struck like a shock wave from a nuclear detonation. Out of the corner of his eye, he saw Hyon-hui and Max go down. His face flushed hot, his gut tightened cold, and he stiffened his legs with a grunt. The urge to bow became almost irresistible, as if another force were at work, trying to bend him to its will. The wave moved outward and came to the edge of the plaza then disappeared down the slope of Mansu Hill, traveling by television and radio to the farthest corners of the Hermit Kingdom.

In all of North Korea, the only things still standing were Mitch Weatherby and Kim Il-sung.

At that moment, darkness enveloped the image. Not something Mitch could see, but a presence. It swirled around the idol then flowed downward and rippled over the prostrate masses. Mitch cringed as it approached and squeezed his eyes shut. A stench burned his nostrils. He gasped for breath and opened his eyes but he could see nothing. It was utterly black. He couldn't breath. He was suffocating. "Please God," he cried out. "Save me!"

Beside him, Max climbed, trembling, back to his feet. He clasped Mitch's hand. Hyon-hui looked up at them with loss that far outstripped any anger. A circle grew around them. Loyal subjects backed away as if they carried a pandemic virus. Hyon-hui hesitated for an instant. There was a wild look in her eyes. "Mitch…" she cried, and his heart broke into pieces as she stepped away from him.

Their eyes met for an instant and he said, "I forgive you."

A silence descended over the crowd and the two Westerners found themselves alone in the middle of an expanding circle. Police and security entered the circle and advanced toward them.

"What would your grandmother say now?" asked Mitch, and Max said something in Russian "What's that mean?" Mitch asked.

"You don't want to know, comrade."

29

Hyon-hui rode the escalator up out of Red Star Station, certain that Mitch's description of mutant wars in New York's underground wasn't true. It couldn't be true. A country that could send people to the moon would have solved any such problem. Unless the moon was a lie. She scowled and stared down at the metal slatted step as she approached the top. The moon wasn't a lie. She knew it from the expression on Mitch's face when he told of it. She knew it from the sincerity of his voice. And she knew it from the ideas and methods he'd brought to the Silla Project. The West was ahead of them scientifically. Vastly ahead.

She stepped from the metal tread just before it disappeared beneath the upper landing, and pulled up short at the image that vanished with the step. A man behind her strode off and bumped into her, with a dirty look. She stepped aside for a young lady – probably a Kim Il-sung University student, and then there was an open span on the escalator. She studied the metal steps as the words, "*Made in Shanghai*" vanished with each one. Her eyes widened. They'd been told this was technology and a product of the DPRK. No one had questioned it. No one had noticed the words at their feet proclaiming it wasn't so. Hidden in plain sight. No, not hidden, made invisible by blindness. And why had they bothered to lie about such a trivial matter? She dipped her head and hurried on.

She had been noticing a lot of things in the days since Mitch and Max had been taken away. Like the fact that Sonny had disappeared as well. She'd seen the look on his face when Mitch talked of Apollo. And after Mitch's crime, all the scientists had to participate in several days of ideological refresher courses by Party senior cadres at the Peoples' Palace of Culture. Major Lee tried to couch it as an honor, but Hyon-hui saw it for what it was – damage control. The rallying cries of the Party only left her more melancholy. It seemed as if a piece of her had been deleted, leaving an emptiness that she was at a loss to explain. And Juche only caused the wound to burn.

No one spoke of Mitch or Max, as if they had never existed. Just like Sun-gun. Hyon-hui glanced over her shoulder at the huge triangular colossus rising into the sky a few blocks away. Just like the Ryugyong Hotel. The man and woman who'd emerged from the station behind her were watching her. Everyone, it seemed was staring at her. And the blistering sun beat down upon her like a search light. She put her head down and walked on.

This is why she'd never noticed, never questioned any of it. She'd had her head down. Her entire life, she'd held only proper Juche ideals in her mind, and never raised her head to see that the world around her didn't match. Her cheeks burned at the blasphemy of the thought, and she tucked her head lower so that no one would see. But she couldn't unthink the thoughts any more than she could unsee the words "*Made in Shanghai*." And that is why she was making this side trip to the University. To find the one person she might be able to talk to. The one person who could help her sort it out. After paying Lee a precious thirty won 'processing fee,' he issued papers which allowed her to move unescorted within P'yongyang's city limits for a twenty-four hour period.

She entered the meticulously maintained campus of Kim Il-sung University. There was much she remembered about her time here. Students were sprinkled about, studying on the grass of the central square. No groups larger than two. No discussions. No debates. Just as when she had been here. So different than the way the Silla Project had run after Mitch took over. But the freedoms he had introduced were already disappearing. The thought struck pangs through her stomach, and she lowered her head and hurried across campus to the guest cottages along Pipa Street. The one she was seeking was not hard to find – a cheerful looking place with well-watered azaleas planted out front. But as she approached, anxiety welled up inside her. Maybe she should not have come.

The window turned dark and she thought she saw a curtain drawn to one side, but when she looked again and it was closed. Had someone been watching her? Hyon-hui glanced over her shoulder and in both directions. It was practically deserted but for a gardener trimming the hedges a few houses down. Her breath hitched as he raised his head to look at her. Sweat was running down his cheeks and a grim expression was on his face, but the gardener was the same man who had bumped into her coming off the subway! *She was being followed!*

Hyon-hui froze in terror, staring unseeingly at the bloom on the azaleas. What should she do? If she ran, that would only bring more attention to her. Did they know what she was doing? What she was thinking? A movement from the corner of her eye caught her attention, and she looked to see that the man had resumed his gardening. Her heart slowed as she looked at him more closely. Hadn't the man in the station been wearing a green shirt? This man's shirt was blue, and he was wearing a straw hat. And how could he get there and start sweating so quickly?

"What is the matter with me?" she said to herself. "This is the Worker's Paradise. I have nothing to fear." But the words rang hollow in her chest. She strode down the walk and knocked on the door. She heard a shuffling sound and, a moment later, was greeted by a weakened Professor Yang.

"Comrade Chun," he said, bowing. "Please, please, come in."

Hyon-hui slipped off her shoes and stepped inside with a bow. "Comrade Professor. Thank you for seeing me on short notice."

"It is always my pleasure to see my beautiful niece. Can I offer you something to drink? Some mineral water perhaps? It is very hot and dry outside."

She bowed again. "Yes, thank you. If you will tell me where it is, I would be most honored to get it."

He sat down slowly as if it pained him. "I am tired today. There is a bottle in the refrigerator."

Hyon-hui looked around the room. It was pleasant but simple. A cadre's residence. Nothing fancy. Little adornment but for the photographs of the Great Leaders on the wall.

"Now, what is it you wanted to speak with me about?" he asked, setting down the glass she handed him. "Your message sounded peculiar."

Hyon-hui perched on a cushion and crossed her legs, not knowing where to start. The thoughts in her head were a tangled mess.

"Are you well?" Professor Yang prompted with concern.

Hyon-hui began to nod that she was fine, when the words rushed out of her mouth instead. "It is about Doctor Weatherby, Comrade Professor."

A shadow flashed onto the old man's face and he glanced suspiciously around the room. In a perfectly social tone, he stated, "It is a beautiful day and the fountains are singing. If you will help an old man find his cane?"

"I am sorry that was necessary," he puffed as they strolled among the forsythia lining a side-square. In the center, a fountain gurgled cheerfully and beyond it stood a tall statue of Kim Il-sung looking down in wise contemplation. "Old men must be cautious. Too often, we... become ill." He raised his head and squinted, shielding the brightness of the sky with a pale, bony hand. "The sky is strangely bright," he said, his breath laboring.

"Professor, are *you* well?"

He patted her hand. "That is not your concern, young daughter of the Revolution. I am well enough. And you, too, will be old some day."

She smiled. "I hope."

He took a deep sigh. "I heard about Dr. Tarasenko and Dr. Weatherby. I inquired but," he shook his head, "it is in the hands of the SSA, now. I am sorry, Hyon-hui. I know you had deep feelings for Mitch."

She wiped her eyes. "I am sorry, comrade professor," she said sniffing. "I did not mean to cry."

"It is understandable... Though I am still interested in why he suddenly changed his mind about Choson. Do you know why he would do this? Did he say anything to you? Something perhaps that I could use to help him."

"No. Just that he would not bow. He said he could not bow."

The elderly scientist shook his head sadly. They walked on a little farther until they came to the fountain in the middle of the square. It was surrounded with a low concrete wall that also served as a bench. Around them were the manicured lawns of the university. Professor Yang was laboring so the two of them sat down on the edge of the fountain. Its rain-like noise was soothing in the sweltering heat.

"I did not expect to like him so much. Almost like a son, he had become to me. But the good of all Choson requires unity in action and purity of thought," Professor Yang added sadly.

"But it is not just Mitch," Hyon-hui insisted, emboldened by the masking sound of the water. "It is Sun-gun. Why can we not speak of him? Why do we fear he was taken away because he had learned the truth? Juche is the truth. It is purity. I have always known that. And yet, even our proud minor achievement of the modern escalator was made in China and shrouded in lies. How can this be?"

The old man grew more pale as she spoke. He stared away for a moment as if torn between comforting his protégé or hobbling away to pretend they'd never spoke. After a moment, he looked back at the green-eyed woman. "Your place is not to ask such questions," he said in a kind but stern tone. "The Party provides for a fair and equitable life for everyone. The Party knows what is it doing, even if those truths are not apparent to you."

"The Party is not what I had hoped, Professor," Hyon-hui added.

Professor Yang was taken aback. "You have worked hard to gain admittance to the Party. Harder than most. Party membership will ensure you a good life. You are disappointed by that?"

"The Party does not ensure a good life, Professor," Hyon-hui responded and began to break down. "I do not know what to do. It is terrible and has tormented me so. I live with it day and night and am ever terrified. I cannot go on like this!"

"What are you saying?" he asked gently. "Tell me, and I will do what I can to correct what has gone wrong." He placed his hand tenderly on her wrist.

She forced herself to stop crying. When she began speaking again, she was staring down at the concrete bench, her hair hanging down in front of her face. "Minister Pak," she whispered.

"Minister Pak?" he asked. "I cannot hear you, Hyon-hui. What about Minister Pak?"

"Minister Pak," she sniffed. "He – He – He raped me, Professor. He raped me."

Professor Yang jerked his hand off of Hyon-hui's arm as if he'd been burned. "Raped you?"

"Yes," she sobbed. "I am so terrified. And ashamed. He said he would kill me. I don't know what to do. I wanted to tell you. Or go to the police. But –"

"When did he do this?"

"The day I was inducted into the Party." She shuddered, remembering the nightmare that should have been the best day of her life. "SSA men took me to his house. He hit me. And then – I am so ashamed professor. When I see him, I am so embarrassed – and terrified – and angry. And– And –" She broke down again. "I was so scared that Mitch would find out. And then he would hate me. He would never look at me again."

"You should have gone to the police immediately," Professor Yang said tersely.

Hyon-hui glanced up in alarm. "He told me if I said anything that he would kill me. And my mother." Her eyes were red and filled with tears and panic. "I believe he would do it, Professor. I believe he would!"

Hyon-hui sensed his change in tone. "Professor?"

"There is nothing I can do. There is nothing anyone can do now," he stated, looking away. "I am just a weak old man."

"You are a delegate to the Seventh Party Congress!"

His eyes flashed with anger. "*I am nothing!*" he snapped. "Nothing…"

"I need your help!" she cried.

"Help? My influence is gone. There is nothing I can do." He rose painfully to his feet and shuffled in the direction of his house.

Hyon-hui called out to him. "Professor! What am I to do?" He ignored her and kept walking. "*Professor!*" she cried, rising to her feet. Students studying nearby raised their heads. "*Professor!*" she called again. "*Professor…*" She sank back onto the bench, lowered her head, and wept.

"The imperialist American aggressors have done this to us," growled Kim Suk-won, a physicist from Mitch's Gadget Division. He pointed through the broken window of the train at denuded hills and empty fields, scarred by years of mismanagement, flooding, and drought. There had been no fuel for busses to take them back to Sagi-dong, so they'd been forced to travel by rail. The wind whipping through the broken windows filled the car with noise and dust and diesel exhaust from the old Dandong Line engine up front. The unpleasant conditions spurred the Party members on, with others picking up the chorus with charges of *yang-kee* weather control technology, accusing the Americans of using high-power microwave transmitters to ionize the stratosphere and create gigantic lenses they could then use to heat or cool certain spots and shift weather patterns.

Hyon-hui bit her lip until she couldn't stand it any longer. "Can you hear yourselves?" she blurted. "Weather control? Floods and droughts happened long before the Americans appeared, and they will happen long after the Americans are gone."

"*Yang-kee* lover!" snapped Major Lee. His amicable manner had disappeared along with Mitch and Max. "It is well known that you are sympathetic to America. Perhaps your grandfather was not Russian after all!" A gasp was heard from those watching the argument.

"My grandfather was Russian," Hyon-hui growled, her face contorted with rage. "A Red-Army Captain. His ideology was as red as yours or mine." She cast her eyes over their faces, wondering what was going on in their heads. "You call yourselves scientists," she challenged. "How can we blame Americans for a flood? Or a drought? How can they possibly be responsible for any of this? Open your eyes," she cried, pointing out the window. "Look at the hillsides. The trees are all gone and there is nothing to hold the soil in place. Go ahead, look at them! It is not forbidden to see!"

But they all stared forward, refusing to follow her finger to the same hills Suk-won showed them moments before. Shame showed in the eyes of a few, but most held nothing but contempt. And fear. Hyon-hui shook her head. Were these the same people she had worked with for the past five years? Had they always been like this? Had she?

"Open your eyes, Comrades! Look at the hillsides!" she cried again. "The trees are all gone and there is nothing to hold the soil in place. When the monsoons come, the topsoil washes away. Did the Americans do that? Our fields are over-farmed and sterile. Did the Americans do that? Our factories produce inferior products that the rest of the world doesn't want. Did the Americans do that? We cannot go on blaming them for everything or we will never fix any of our own problems. Americans are the cause of much misery, but not all!"

As her words died in the air, all that could be heard was the clacking of the wheels and the squeaking of the engine far ahead.

After a long silence, Major Lee rose and glared at her menacingly. "Who, then, would you say is responsible?"

"I don't know," Hyon-hui answered evasively. "But the answer must lie closer to home. America is so far –"

"Silence!" he erupted. "I will hear no more counterrevolutionary speech! We have scientifically proven the superiority of the Juche ideology. Whatever evil is at work here is no failing of the Great Leader's scientifically perfect system. You would do well to examine your thoughts more carefully before speaking against the Party again!"

Hyon-hui's jaw fell open. "The Party? I didn't speak against –"

"I said silence!"

"But I –"

Major Lee struck her across the face with the back of his hand. "*Silence!* Your impure blood is an affront to the Great Leader, Comrade Generalissimo Kim Il-sung, the Dear Leader, Comrade Marshal Kim Jong-il, and the Workers' Party of Korea. And you have no place in it!"

Her face stung and tears blurred her eyes, as she remember what Mitch had once told her about being beaten on the bus on the way to prison. That day he was saved by the North Koreans. She looked out the window, determined not to cry. No one would be coming for her. She had no escape.

The sun was going down when they arrived at Sagi-dong and a rapidly waning moon was rising over the mountains. Hyon-hui saw it before shuffling inside her apartment and thought about Apollo.

"Hyon-hui!" called her mother excitedly. But the smile faded from her mother's lips. "Hyon-hui, what is wrong?"

"Mitch," she said weakly and began to sob. "He is gone."

"Dr. Weatherby? What has happened to him? Was he killed?"

Hyon-hui collapsed on the couch and her mother turned on the TV, raising the volume to mask any listening devices. Sup-Suppie sat down beside her daughter. "What has happened to Mitch?" she said into her ear.

"When it came time to bow to the Grand Monument on Mansu Hill, he refused. *Refused, Mother!*"

Tears filled the old woman's eyes as Hyon-hui told her everything. She didn't say what their mission had been about, but she told her mother of how Max and Mitch had been admitted to the Party and their love had finally blossomed. About the Grand Monument and how he was taken away in chains by the SSA. She confessed her fears of the lies she'd been told and had always believed about everything from the food supply to manufacturing. Her mother patiently listened, pressing Hyon-hui's hand comfortingly in hers.

"Nothing makes sense," Hyon-hui concluded as her sobs subsided. "I should not be having these thoughts, but I cannot deny what I have seen – what is all around me. Something is wrong and I don't know what to think anymore."

The old woman sat, stroking Hyon-hui's hand for a moment until she patted it resolutely, as if having reached a decision. "It is time you knew the truth," she said simply. Hyon-hui looked up at her questioningly. When Sup-Suppie finally spoke it was with as clear a voice as Hyon-hui had ever heard from her. "I am not half-Russian, Hyon-hui. My father, your grandfather, he was an American. An American, Hyon-hui. Just like Mitch."

Hyon-hui's eyes were bloodshot but the flow of tears was suddenly staunched. "What did you say?"

"Your grandfather," the old woman confirmed with a nod. "He was an American. You and I are not part-Russian, Hyon-hui. We are part American."

It was exactly as Major Lee had said on the train! "But – but – but his picture. It is on the wall!" Hyon-hui insisted as she jumped up and pulled it from its hook. She waved it at her mother. "This is my grandfather! Sergey Ivanovich! He was in the Red Army! A Captain!" Her finger stabbed the medals on the man's chest. "He received the Order of Lenin for bravery!"

"Take it out of the frame, child," her mother urged softly.

A savage light came into Hyon-hui's eyes and she ripped the back off the frame and flipped over the photograph. On the back of the photo was a page number, half-a picture of some battle-worn tanks in a muddy field, and the first few words of a caption written in Cyrillic. It wasn't a photograph at all, but a page from some old book.

"This isn't happening," Hyon-hui said weakly, dropping to the couch. "This cannot be true." The scrap of paper fell from her hand as her mind grappled to find any shred of her life that was real.

"My uncle cut it out of a Russian history book," Sup-Suppie said simply.

Hyon-hui looked up, her eyes black pits. "Who am I?" It was a rhetorical question, but her mother answered anyway.

"You are the granddaughter of Jacob Flint, from a town called Winchester in the state of Tennessee. He was the oldest of eight brothers and sisters. We have relatives still living there, I would guess. First and second cousins. Perhaps some aunts and uncles even."

Hyon-hui wandered around the room, trying to absorb the idea that she was part of a murderous American family – the enemy! She did not notice her mother on her hands and knees until she had pried a knot-hole out of the floor, then used the hole to lift a floorboard out. From the space beneath, the old woman removed a small package wrapped in plastic and bound with a piece of red ribbon. Hyon-hui watched in horror as the plastic came off revealing a forbidden black leather book with a gold cross embossed on the cover. Her mother deftly flipped through it, her fingers knowing every page, and took out a yellowed photograph. She smiled sadly.

"Perhaps I should have given this to you long ago," the woman said as she handed it to her daughter. "But I wanted to protect you."

Hyon-hui took the picture of a happy young couple holding a baby. A Western-looking man in a suit with an Asian woman in traditional dress.

"His eyes were green, too," said Hyon-hui's mother. "Like yours. At least, that is what my uncle told me."

"How? How did this happen?" Hyon-hui demanded. Her entire life and everything she had ever known was disintegrating right before her. Unless – "He was an American soldier that raped my grandmother and left her pregnant! That is it, isn't it? Bastard imperialist jackals! I hope they killed him slowly!"

"*Raped her?*" exclaimed her mother in shock. She sat back against the couch and addressed her daughter firmly. "Look at that picture, Hyon-hui. Use your eyes. My mother was raped only once, Hyon-hui. Actually five times, but it was all at once – just four different men. One of them twice. I saw it with my own eyes." Her words were bitter. "And yes, they were soldiers. But soldiers of the Korean People's Army. Just after the war started. It was their way of celebrating."

"No!" Hyon-hui hissed, turning away from her mother. "That cannot be. That could never…" But her words strangled in her throat as the memory of Pak raping her flooded back as if it had just happened. And her face still stung where Lee had struck her. Soldiers of the People's Army could well be that cruel. She knew, first hand, that their leaders were.

Her mother continued slowly. "I never told you a lot of things, Hyon-hui, because most of them were dangerous for you to know. Your father died in a coal mine. I didn't want the same for you.

Your grandfather was a doctor. And a missionary. He didn't go around raping people like these Party cadres. He opened a hospital in Oro in 1938. Three years later, he had to leave because of the war between Japan and America. After the war, he returned and resumed his work at the hospital, treating the bodies and the souls of the people. He fell in love with my mother, whom he had led to Jesus. But the Japanese would not let her go. So when they deported him, he promised to return. And she waited for him. They were married in 1946. I was born nine months later."

"Kim Il-sung resisted the reunification of Korea under the terms of the United Nations. It was to be under his communism, or not at all. So, when I was four years old, the war began." Her eyes took on a faraway look. "I remember the soldiers coming into our village. They were so kind and polite at first, handing out leaflets and looking for young men to join a valiant cause. To join the war against the South. But no one wanted to fight. They had already lived through long years of harsh occupation. Many had been forced to fight for the Japanese. Their leader became enraged. He rounded up a dozen youths, and hung them in the town square. Then they went from house to house, breaking down the doors, taking the young men. When they came to the hospital, they discovered your grandfather was an American and hung him, too. Then they raped and murdered your grandmother for having married him. My mother's brother hid me in his grain cellar where their church met or they would have killed me too.

"My uncle knew it would be far better for me to be half-Russian than half-American. There were many Russians in the country in those days. And many children born to them. So he found this picture, made up the name Sergey Ivanovich, and put it in that very frame." She chuckled suddenly. "I still can't believe it worked as well as it did."

Hyon-hui lifted her eyes from the photo in her lap, trying to make it fit with anything she had known. Perhaps her mother was an informer for the Secret Police, Hyon-hui suddenly thought. Perhaps everything had been a test of her loyalty. Perhaps even now she was being tested. After all, how could her mother have kept these things secret for so many years?

Her eyes darted around the room and she saw cameras and listening devices everywhere. No doubt, Colonel Phoung was sitting in the hut next door, shaking his head in disgust at another failure. At any moment, he would walk over and collect the traitor. From every direction, the authorities began to close in! A knock would come at the door at any instant! When it came, she would spring from the house and race to the KWP office! She would find Kim In-taek! She would tell him about her mother. About the Bible. Everything! That was the only way to save herself!

A scream began to form in the pit of her stomach. But somewhere between her racing heart and her darting eyes, her gaze landed on the old photograph still lying in her lap. Her hands stopped trembling and the outburst stuck in her throat. For the first time in her life, the thought formed in Hyon-hui's tortured mind that maybe the secret police *didn't* know everything. And if that were true, it was possible they didn't know about *this*. She glanced over at the Christian Bible sitting in her mother's lap. A forbidden book! Had her mother not concealed her Christianity from the authorities all these long years? She'd certainly kept it hidden from Hyon-hui. Or was it all a trap?

Many times when she was young, her school teachers had sent the children home to play a game of secretly searching for just such books. Hyon-hui had always done so but never found anything. It always disappointed her because children who found books and brought them in were given candy and paraded around the room. The students always disappeared soon after and the teachers told them these children then got to go to special schools. Hyon-hui had wanted to go to one of those special schools, but she'd never been good enough. Her best friend Hea-gyong had disappeared in this way back in the third grade. She'd never even told her friend goodbye.

A new horror grew in her chest. Had those special schools existed? Or had the children been shipped to reeducation centers, or maybe executed with the rest of their family, never to be heard from again? Is that what had happened to Hae-gyong? Had Hyon-hui escaped that fate simply because her mother had hidden these facts so well?

It was a threshold moment for Hyon-hui. She knew that turning in her mother would ensconce her precarious position within the Party and almost certainly result in an early promotion to cadre. Absolute loyalty to The Dear Leader, Comrade Generalissimo Kim Jong-il, was the *only* requirement for such advancement. Outside of the inner circle, those who were the most loyal received the coveted positions. And the most loyal had invariably proven themselves in some outstanding way such as informing on a parent, a child, or a close friend. Such actions were usually the stepping stones to much greater responsibility. Hyon-hui had known people who had done this, and until this very moment, had admired them. Even envied them. Hoped for a similar opportunity. They'd had the strength and the loyalty to put aside their personal feelings and allow their loyalty to the *widaehan suryong* be their only guide.

Her entire life, she'd believed strongly and completely in the righteousness of the Juche Idea and everything it demanded: the deity of The Great Leader and his son. The theory of the *chajusong* and the socio-politically derived, eternal component of man. Juche's core tenet: man is the master of everything and man decides everything. Mitch had challenged that, yet her faith had withstood the test. But now, her mother was trying to turn her world upside down. The barren countryside bleated a different truth at her. And the words "*Made in Shanghai*" burned like a brand. Could Juche, like all of these things, be nothing more than a fabrication? Everything drawn from it, an illusion? And the proof as close as a picture hanging on a wall. All she'd had to do was look at the back.

Hyon-hui again studied the photograph in her lap. A focal point for her spinning thoughts. She looked up at her mother who sat with her hands folded atop the black book, praying. She looked around the tiny, ill-lit room. Such a contrast with the bright, modern rooms in P'yongyang. And that, an even greater contrast with the miserable state of the countryside. The crumbling villages. The haggard, starving peasants with hollow eyes. Children in schools being drilled on the techniques of hate. And everywhere, the soldiers, and the tanks, and the armored personnel carriers, and the guns, and the missiles, and the mines, and the barbed wire. And the SSA.

Hyon-hui jumped at a frantic knock on the door and glanced at her mother in terror. Such knocks simply didn't occur. Not at day. Not at night. Not ever! Not in Kim Il-sung's Choson.

"It is the SSA!" Hyon-hui hissed. Thoughts of prison, torture, and visits by Pak leapt into her head. "They had us under surveillance and they are coming to take us away!" She jumped to her feet. "I didn't do it! It wasn't me!" she called to the walls.

The knock came again. More urgent.

"It wasn't me! It was –"

"Silence child!" Her mother's eyebrows knit in thought. "That's not the SSA. They don't knock. Answer the door."

But Hyon-hui stood frozen, her eyes like those of a animal trapped.

"Do it, girl!"

Hesitantly, she put her hand on the knob and pulled it open. "Who is it?" she squeaked, staring into the gloom. A face moved into the light. Hyon-hui recognized it instantly. "Bok-won?" The soldier Mitch had saved. He had visited the hospital many times when Mitch was sick from his nighttime descent. He slipped in and they could see he was dressed all in black like he didn't want to be seen. "What are you doing here?" she hissed. "Did the SSA send you to keep watch on me?"

His face turned white. "Are they coming here?! Are they watching you?!"

"Yes! I fear that –"

"No," her mother interjected coolly. "They are not here. At least, not yet."

"I must hurry. If I am discovered here –"

"Well, what is it, young man?" said Hyon-hui's mother impatiently.

He paused and looked at the floor. "Doctor Weatherby," Bok-won said softly, leaning close to Hyon-hui. "I have seen him. And the Russian, too." Hyon-hui knees weakened and she swayed, but her mother caught her arm. They are in the prison at Yonjom-dong.

They brought them in last night and I fear they will..." He looked away.

"Torture them?" said Hyon-hui's mother.

The terrified soldier nodded his head and Hyon-hui cried out as it was being inflicted on her. "Why have they done this?" Bok-won asked. "What has Dr. Weatherby done? What has he done to deserve this?"

"He has done nothing," Hyon-hui blurted out between her quiet sobs. "Nothing at all. Nothing."

"You must go!" her mother said quickly. "Now. Before you are discovered."

"Thank you, Bok-won," Hyon-hui choked. "Thank you."

The young soldier hesitated.

"Now!" Hyon-hui's mother stood at the door, her hand on the knob. "*Now!*" She cracked it open and he slipped out, but turned back half way through.

"He saved my life. I cannot let him stay in there. Not like that." He bolted outside and disappeared into the darkness.

30

Mitch stared at the water-stained concrete of the ceiling, speckled with black spots of mildew. A naked bulb screwed into a rusty socket cast hard-edged shadows, and the walls were streaked and spattered with thick, brownish blobs. The hot, sticky air smelled like stale urine. But at least, so far, no one had done him any harm.

The police had taken him and Max to a station, then plainclothesmen arrived and took them to another station. That was the last time he had seen Max. Since then, he'd traveled by road and rail but had been blindfolded most of the time. No one spoke any English and talked rapidly, in hushed tones. He'd only caught a few words. And now he was here, strapped to a wooden board with his head in some kind of harness that kept it from turning. They were going to hurt him. That he knew. From the corner of his eye, he saw a rack holding 'tools' on the wall. Corroded and blood-stained hammers, picks, iron bars, and tongs. They were going to hurt him bad. "Please God…" he whispered over and over. "Please." But he knew it wouldn't help. This wasn't torture, it was punishment for his crime against the world.

They'd left him here for hours. Maybe even days. Or maybe it was just a few minutes. There was no way to tell and the visions of horror playing in his head turned time into a meaningless quantity. He missed Beth horribly. More than he'd ever missed her. He missed Hyon-hui just as much but in an altogether different way. The pain in his heart had him begging for death and his captors hadn't even arrived yet. Whatever they were going to do to him, he deserved it. But he didn't look forward to it.

Many times he heard noises somewhere outside his cell. Footsteps. The sound of doors creaking open and then slamming shut. And screams. The screams were horrible to hear but not as bad as the silence. It was then that he could hear the bugs. Could hear their tiny feet marching across the floor. And there was nothing he could do to stop them when they crawled over his flesh, eating him one tiny bite at a time. He saw no point in praying but that didn't stop him from begging for deliverance.

Mitch woke with a start, jerking against his restraints as a man moved into view above him. He couldn't make him out as he placed a rack with what looked like a funnel over his head. The spout pointed straight at Mitch's face. Someone put something under the board at his feet so that his body slanted downhill. Mitch felt his head swell slightly as the blood pooled.

"What are you doing?" he asked in no more than a timid whisper. The man didn't answer. "Please don't do this," he pleaded. "I haven't done anything. I helped you."

A different man's face appeared above him. And this one he knew.

"Minister Pak." Mitch's voice trembled at the cruel look in the man's eyes. "What are they going to do to me? I didn't do anything!"

"Didn't do anything?" Pak sneered. "As if contaminating your 'Sonny' wasn't enough? He was a perfectly good Party member before you polluted his mind."

"I didn't say anything about Kim Il-sung. I swear. He just wanted to know about scientific advancements. That's all I told him."

"You really have been having a time, haven't you Dr. Weatherby?"

"What do you mean? What have I done?"

"Let me see," said Pak. "Defying the Great Leader on national TV. Comrade Chun is in trouble. Four men are dead for failing to consider leap years in the construction of the Juche Tower. Their families have been sent to re-education facilities. And I don't think Max is going to live much longer."

"What are you doing to him?" Mitch tried to challenge, but it was just a hoarse choke. "He didn't do anything. I swear. All he ever did was tell me to shut up. He's innocent. Don't hurt him." Pak put his hand over Mitch's mouth.

"You should have thought about that before you filled everyone's head full of your capitalist lies." He looked up and nodded at someone Mitch couldn't see.

"Please don't torture me!" Mitch cried, straining at the straps. "I haven't done anything! I haven't done anything! Please God, no!"

Pak laughed. "We aren't going to torture you Dr. Weatherby. Do you think we are barbarians? We are at least as civilized as your own people. And Americans don't torture." He nodded to the other man again. "Do they?"

Ice cold water poured down the funnel. It gushed through and splattered into Mitch's face and filled his mouth and nose. Mitch heaved and gagged but was determined to take it. But then something happened to his body. Something totally outside his control. His body thought it was dying and activated every physiological system to try and free itself. He felt his blood pressure spike like a grenade had detonated inside his head. Adrenaline roared into his veins. His body fought to free itself from the shackles and nearly broke itself in the process. And still the water came. In less than a minute, Mitch was sobbing uncontrollably and begging for Pak to stop. Begging God to let it end. Promising to do whatever he wanted him to do.

Mitch heaved and gasped for air when the water stopped.

"See, that's not torture, is it?" said Pak. "We learned this from your country. And it is so civilized. Leaves no marks at all."

But Mitch couldn't talk. He kept choking and gagging and coughing. Pak finally dried his face with a smelly rag. "Better?" he said.

"What do you want from me?" Mitch groaned.

"Everything." He knocked on Mitch's forehead with his heavy knuckles. "Everything in that head of yours."

"You can't make me tell you anything," said Mitch, rebounding as head cleared.

"So stubborn." Pak stepped back and the water came again. They only stopped when Mitch stopped breathing. Pak screamed in rage and the torturer had to clear Mitch's lungs and revive him with mouth-to-mouth. When he regained consciousness, Pak leaned down close to him. "You died, Dr. Weatherby. I can't have you doing that yet. Not until we get everything we need. Do you understand? No more dying."

Mitch just laid there groaning. Water and blood trickled from his mouth and nose.

Screams came faintly through the concrete. Or under the door. Or however they got into the room. Agonizing screams filled with unimaginable pain and despair. Pak looked up. "Oh, that would be Max." He looked back down at Mitch and smiled. "Russians don't waterboard. They torture. You should not worry. Max understands this."

Pak paced the room, relishing this moment as the sounds of Max's agony filled Mitch's mind with despair. "You are a fool, do you know that Dr. Weatherby? You could have stayed here in Choson for as long as you liked. The Dear Leader, for some reason, was fond of you. You, a capitalist, Yankee pig! He was even going to let you marry that bitch, whore half-breed, if that is what you wanted, and go on screwing her to your heart's content." He took a claw hammer from where it hung on the torture rack and examined it. "Sometimes I don't understand him." Then he hung it up and turned back to Mitch. "But he is the *widaehan suryong,* so there it is. Of course, after Mansu Hill, he has changed his mind about all of that. I guess I get Comrade Chun now."

Mitch's eyes opened wide and he struggled. Pak leaned over him and patted his cheek. "So you can hear me now! Good. Yes, Comrade Chun will be mine. You know I had her once already. Yes, I took her the night she was admitted to the Party. Very sweet she was." Pak grunted approvingly. "The sweetest yet. Like a flower, Mitch. A tender new flower. I guess she didn't tell you? She must have enjoyed me."

Tears were streaming from Mitch's face now. His muscles were too tired to struggle anymore. If they started the water again he didn't think he would survive it. He wished he was already dead.

"But you know what is really ironic?" Pak asked, continuing his pacing. "It was I who planned the operation responsible for your being here in the first place."

"I know," Mitch groaned. "You had me abducted."

Pak laughed all the more. "Much more than that Mitch. That was the *end* of the operation. The enriched uranium the police found on your property? My men put it there, and the computer flash drive. It was my agents that tipped off the FBI." Mitch's brain went numb. "Major Lee said it would work, but I didn't believe him. I said you would figure it out immediately. But he said that Americans always blamed their own government *first*. He was right. And we never blame ours. So strange. You never even considered that it was us, did you? I see it in your eyes. Not until this minute did you see it. Even when Major Lee showed you that report on your connections to terrorism. I bet him that you would reject it. A bet that I lost! I think Major Lee deserves a medal for that one. A DPRK merit award. What do you think?"

Mitch's mind seethed as he processed this new data. His nation hadn't betrayed him at all. It had been the North Koreans all along. And Mitch fell for it. Duped because he was that stupid? Or was it his arrogance and pride wanting the chance to build a bomb? Just send more water, Mitch thought. Max would soon be dead and Mitch would join him. He'd open his mouth and let it come. Fill his lungs, drown his mind, end his miserable existence. God would then send him to Hell where he belonged. He'd made it all so easy for them. And ruined so many lives. Just pour, his mind screamed. *Please!* But there was still one thing he wanted to know.

"Why?" croaked Mitch. "Why me?"

Pak returned to his side. "We profiled a number of young Los Alamos scientists. We needed someone with a wife but no children. Someone outspoken. Convicted. Idealistic. Politically motivated. Highly religious. But most of all," he leaned over Mitch and looked him up and down as if he were an inventor admiring his greatest creation, "you had never faced suffering. Your beliefs had never been tested. But it was your outspoken letters to the editor that caught Major Lee's attention. He felt you could be broken. It seems he was right."

Mitch just stared, his mind trying but unable to shut down.

"And the bomb. The best my own scientists could do was as large as a car. Useless! We are going to miniaturize your design and put it on a missile. But that will be someone else's job. I'm going to sell the next bomb we make to Al Qaeda. Since they know it will work, thanks to your test, they've already agreed to pay me twenty million Euros and I will get out of this rat hole country." His voice had been soft, but now turned acid, filled with what Mitch recognized as Korean cursing. "I hate this place. I am so sick of communism and Juche. I'm going to live for once. I'm going to retire to Thailand like one of your successful businessmen. Ride around in a boat, play golf, and have sex with teenage girls. Maybe even try out some teenage boys. I certainly think I deserve it after fifty years in this place. And I owe it all to you, Mitch." He glanced up at his guards. "Good thing they don't speak English, huh?"

Mitch groaned and coughed again.

Pak smiled down at him and the contrast sent a shiver through Mitch. "I know what you're thinking, Mitch. You want me to pour some more water so you can breathe deep and end it all right here." The smile stayed plastered on his face. "I'm betting you can't do it. Do you think I would win that bet, Mitch? Let's find out."

He looked up and said something in Korean.

"No!" Mitch blurted. "Please don't do –"

Water gushed down the spout and into Mitch's face. He tried to scream but all that came out was a throttled gurgle.

31

"The fatherland is under threat of invasion," blared the loudspeaker. *"Your families and your children are in grave danger from imminent attack. The imperialist American aggressor never sleeps. Rise, and working together under the red-flag banner of Juche, we will build a powerful socialist nation of which the Great Leader can be proud."* Every morning of her life, Hyon-hui had awakened this way. Except last night, she hadn't slept.

It was early August and the beginning of election season in the DPRK, so this morning's announcements were filled with Party slogans encouraging everyone to cast their vote for Marshal Kim Jong-il as General Secretary of the Korean Workers' Party. After that came the militant march music and the patriotic songs.

Hyon-hui's mother was in the kitchen, cooking rice. It was all they had. When Hyon-hui entered, her mother stopped what she was doing. "Are you okay, Hyon-hui?" They both knew that the droning of the loudspeakers would mask anything they said.

Hyon-hui stared blankly into space. "I don't know who I am anymore."

"At least, you know who you're not. This places you ahead of our comrades."

"I hate Mitch," she moaned bitterly. "This is all his fault! If he hadn't come here then none of this would have happened. None of it!"

"Hyon-hui!" exclaimed her mother. "I remember the night I met Mitch. I stood in this very kitchen and watched the two of you fall in love. You spurned him for the next six months for your precious Party. What has that gotten you? What has it ever gotten you?"

Tears suddenly burst from her eyes in a flood and streamed like rivers down her cheeks. "What can I do?" Her words came as a desperate plea. "They are torturing him and there is nothing I can do."

"Control yourself!" her mother snapped. "You are a member of the Party. Use your position. Your access. With that, perhaps you can find a way to free Mitch. He is not far from–"

With a tremendous crash, the door sprang open in a shower of splinters. The women screamed as SSA men in black uniforms burst into the room. Without a word, they grabbed a trembling Hyon-hui. Mother was right, she thought to herself, the SSA doesn't knock.

"Where are you taking my daughter?" Her mother cried, beating ineffectively on them. "Where are you –"

One of the SSA men batted the old woman down. "Shut-up, hag, or we'll take you, too!"

They threw Hyon-hui into a waiting truck. Those walking to work watched from the corners of their eyes, pretending to see nothing. Hyon-hui cowered in the back of the vehicle, waiting for the turn toward Pak's house. But when it didn't, she shook, thinking of others who had disappeared like this throughout her life. She'd always thought it made sense. But nothing made sense anymore. But maybe that meant this *was* for the best. For the good of the Party.

They passed the Party headquarters, now decorated with General Secretary election posters, and continued through the gate at the edge of town, as she resolved herself to death. She'd told the professor about being raped. Professor Yang had talked to Pak. She was to be shot out in the woods and dropped in a hole, just as he had said. No one would ever know. Or care.

They stopped at a squat concrete building with a heavy, windowless door. It bore no external symbol of its function, but a malevolence radiated from it like the stench from a mass grave. Inside sat an SSA officer spinning a set of keys on a big ring. Behind him on the wall hung pictures of Kim and Kim.

"Chun?" he asked.

"Yes, Comrade Lieutenant," answered her abductor.

He lifted her dress with a billy-club and peeked at her long legs and privates. "Very nice," he said and wrote her name on a form. After copying numbers from her identification, he opened a heavy door with his keys. Behind it, a narrow set of concrete stairs led down. There was no rail and the air grew dank as they descended. It was all she could do to keep from throwing up. She was going to die down here.

At the bottom, they entered a dim hallway lined with narrow metal doors and painted with patriotic slogans. At the edge of her hearing came groans of pain and despair. The air smelled like torment. The lieutenant opened a door that was larger than the rest and pushed her through. It clanged shut behind her and she lost all hope of a quick and merciful death.

A crude, oversized table with heavy, unfinished wood timbers for its legs filled the center of the floor. It was wet with water and stains that looked black in the dim light marred its surface. On its top lay rusty manacles and leg-irons. An assortment of hammers, iron bars, chains, and other implements caked with a crumbly, black coating hung on the wall and ruddy pools from the blood of former occupants stained the floor. Hyon-hui sank into one of the corners, squeezed her eyes shut, and waited.

Kim In-taek sat brooding in the security building. When he'd nominated Hyon-hui for permanent Party status, a tiny voice in the back of his head had whispered that he was making a mistake. She had other blood flowing in her veins. She didn't belong in the Party. Normally, he listened to the voice. This time, however, he'd let her pretty face and her fervor to prove herself worthy take advantage of his better judgment and, at Professor Yang's urging, had recommended her anyway. Of course, with the exception of her genetic impurity, her credentials were good, there was no doubt about that. A long history of loyal service to the Korean Workers' Party. Never any reports of disloyalty. Even her relationship with the American had ended well.

A face appeared in his doorway. "Chun is here, Comrade Secretary," said the SSA officer.

"Unharmed?"

"Yes, sir, just as you ordered."

Hyon-hui crouched in the corner with her legs drawn up. Against her efforts, her eyes lingered on the implements of torture. Square iron bars to crush bone. Hammers to punch holes. Pliers for splintering teeth and pulling fingernails. Other tools with more horrifying uses. She thought of her mother. And Mitch. And the paintings of Americans using these tools on Koreans. And everything about the Party that she could remember. This was nowhere in it. Nowhere. Her mother had been right. Lies. It was all lies. Lies held together by terror. Held together by this room.

"Miss Chun," Kim In-taek said as the door swung open.

She lifted her head. "Comrade Secretary," she answered in a shaky voice. She rose to her feet and bowed. "It is an honor to see you."

"Leave us," he said to the officer who'd escorted him.

The door closed and In-taek motioned toward the table. "Sit down. Remove your shoes."

As she neared the table, her breathing and heart rate climbed until she was hyperventilating. She sat down on the very edge, fumbling as she pushed her shoes off. She kept her arms crossed, not daring to place them near the manacles, but failing to hold in the trembling.

"Lay down, he commanded."

She did and found herself staring at the naked bulb and the splattered stains on the ceiling.

"So, what do you think of our little room, Comrade?" he asked, circling the table slowly. "Not a very comforting place, is it?"

She tried to stammer a few words but nothing came out.

"I don't like this place, Comrade." In-taek told her. "Others do, but not me." He lifted a claw-hammer from where it dangled and looked at it closely in the dim light. It had been used before. Hyon-hui felt her heart start to race. Her vision closed in. Yet, In-taek continued speaking. "But its existence is necessary, at times, to maintain ideological purity." He hung the hammer up and picked up a nail-studded board. "And Juche teaches that ideological purity is of the utmost importance."

"Why am I here, Comrade Secretary?" Hyon-hui asked, anticipating the coming pain with every breath.

"Why do you think you are here?"

"I don't know, Comrade Secretary," she whispered. "Please tell me." Actually, she could think of a lot of things. Her outburst on the bus. The revelations with her mother. Her many impure thoughts.

"You really don't know?"

"No, Comrade, Secretary. I have never been disloyal to the Great Leader, Comrade Generalissimo Kim Il-sung, or Marshal Kim Jong-il. Never."

In-taek didn't say anything. Just stared at her with a mixture of sadness, disappointment, and contempt. After a full minute of this silence, he sighed heavily. "Do you recall, some time ago, when I visited your office and we spoke of the responsibilities of the Party member?"

"Yes, Comrade Secretary," she stammered. "I remember."

"Do you remember what I said at that time?"

Hyon-hui searched her mind but fear was clouding her memory. "You ... you said – you said that a bad apricot will ruin a good one."

He nodded. "But your actions would seem to indicate that you do not understand what it means."

"My actions?" she replied, trying to force herself to stop shaking. "Of what actions do you speak, Comrade Secretary? My loyalty to the *widaehan suryong* is absolute." She wondered if In-taek could tell that she was lying. But was she lying? Even she didn't know.

"Loyalty? That is an interesting choice of words. I didn't say anything about loyalty. I wonder why you would use it?" In-taek asked, bouncing the end of the nail studded board in his hand.

If only she could control her bursting mind, she'd be okay. Think back, she told herself, back to her ideological training. It should have been easy. She'd studied it more than she'd studied chemistry. But she was having enormous trouble recalling any of it, her mind was frozen on the board tapping In-taek's palm. Even things a preschooler could recite, like the three guiding principles of the Juche ideology, or Kim Il-sung's ten points of reunification, were a complete blank.

She took a breath and forced herself to speak. "Loyalty is all that there is, Comrade Secretary. There is *nothing* else. And our loyalty to the Eternal President, Comrade Generalissimo Kim Il-sung, and the Great Leader, Comrade Marshal Kim Jong-il, is demonstrated through our actions. I ask, which of my actions has called my loyalty into question?"

"If your loyalty is unquestioned," he continued, "and your ideology red, then why would you make counterrevolutionary statements?"

"But I have made no counterrevolutionary statements, Comrade Secretary. My ideology and my deeds are red."

He took out a sheet of paper and read from it, slowly and deliberately. "Open your eyes, Comrades. Look at the hillsides. The trees are all gone and there is nothing to hold the soil in place. When the monsoons come, the topsoil washes away," He paused and glanced up. "*Did the Americans do that?* Our fields are over-farmed and sterile. *Did the Americans do that?*"

Hyon-hui squirmed and the rough cut timbers bored into her back.

"Our factories produce inferior products that the rest of the world doesn't want. *Did the Americans do that?* We cannot go on blaming them for everything or we will never fix any of our own problems. America is the cause of much misery, but not all." He looked up again. "Do you deny making these statements?"

"I deny nothing I have ever said."

"Then how can you say that your ideology is red? These statements are not red. They are counterrevolutionary."

"How can these statements be counterrevolutionary if they are true?"

In-taek shook his head. "They are counterrevolutionary because anything that weakens the Party is counterrevolutionary. As a Party member, you should understand that. By definition: everything bad is America's fault."

"But Comrade Secretary, failure to recognize our own problems weakens us, does it not? If you were sick and went to the hospital, would you not prefer the correct diagnosis so you could receive the proper treatment. While the cure is sometimes painful, it is always preferable to doing nothing."

"Are you saying that Juche is in need of a doctor?"

"No, Comrade Secretary. Juche is perfect as it was elucidated by the Great Leader, Comrade Generalissimo Kim Il-sung and the Dear Leader, Comrade Marshal Kim Jong-il. But the people who administer it are often not. The Great Leader recognized this. He called it *bureaucratism*. And *commandism*. When it is recognized, should it not be combated in order to forge a strong bond between the popular masses and the Party?" Hyon-hui's words came to a halt and she flinched, realizing that she'd just insulted In-taek.

"*Do not lecture me!*" he snapped and swung the nail studded board into the soles of her feet, driving dozens of tiny spikes into her flesh. Hyon-hui screamed and lurched up. "*Down!*" In-taek ordered, and shoved her onto the table. "Do not force me to chain you. It is not your place, or the place of any woman, to work in the field of socialist construction, or develop your own personal interpretation of the Great Leader's monolithic ideology. The Party interprets! It is your place as a member to carry out policy of the Workers' Party of Korea. And to be loyal. Especially as a KWP member yourself. Not to 'open your eyes' and see whatever *you* want to see. What would happen if everyone opened their eyes? They would all see something different. The *widaehan suryong* opened *his* eyes and *his* sight is better than ours. Certainly better than yours! The truth can only be seen if we cast aside our own eyes, and look through his. The Party *is his eyes!*"

He struck her feet again, landing the blow squarely across her heels. The nails sunk through the flesh and Hyon-hui howled in pain. "But the Great Leader wants us to use our minds," she cried. "Juche calls us to be creative –"

"The Great Leader!" he barked, hitting her twice, "wants us to use *his* mind! *His mind! His eyes!* He established the Party to teach us how to see with his eyes and understand with his mind! He is our brain! The Party is his body!"

"But truth –" she sobbed, her feet screaming in pain.

He hit her again, squarely across the bottom of her arches. "Truth is what the Great Leader says it is! It is clear you do not see the world through his eyes or interpret it through his mind or you would know this."

"But Comrade Secretary, I –"

"If you cannot see through his eyes, you are not a true member of the Party." He hit again.

"Comrade," she sobbed. "I haven't done anything –"

In-taek stepped into the light, his face shimmered through Hyon-hui's tears as he reached down and jerked her pin off.

"Comrade Secretary," she cried, "Comrade Secretary, I am nothing, if not loyal."

"Then you are nothing! It is only because of your importance to Silla-14 that I do not have you re-educated immediately. But that cannot save you forever, so you would do well to embrace the perfectly structured ideology that you have been taught and we may be merciful!" He hit her again, before flinging the board into the wall and storming out.

The nails had only penetrated a few millimeters but the soles of her feet were covered with scores of tiny holes oozing blood. Hyon-hui curled up on the table, cradling her throbbing feet in her hands and watching the red blood seeping through her fingers. She rocked slowly back and forth, sobbing. "I am red. I am red. I am red…"

32

Hyon-hui lurched through the door and collapsed. Behind her, a black clad SSA man climbed into a UAZ and it roared off down the road. Her mother leapt up with a shout from where she'd been kneeling. The old black Bible lay on the floor opened to Acts 12. She helped Hyon-hui to the couch and took her shoes off. They were blood stained and ruined.

"What have they done?" the old woman wept. "What have I done?"

"Water," Hyon-hui gasped. "And… for my feet." Ice would have been better but no one had any ice. Or even a freezer. They had nothing to ease the pain. Her mother turned on the TV and increased the volume. The sound of machine gun fire and falling bombs from the movie about a valiant KPA unit that had fought to keep the bastard Americans out of P'yongyang filled the tiny room. Hyon-hui gulped the water down, having had nothing to eat or drink all day.

"What have they done? Where did they take you?" her mother asked, her cheeks wet with tears.

"It doesn't matter," Hyon-hui mumbled, lying back on the old couch. "I've been dismissed from the Party. Everything I worked for is lost."

"Was it because of me? Because of what I told you last night?"

Hyon-hui shook her head. "No. Someone reported to the SSA that I made counterrevolutionary statements."

"Did you?"

"I spoke the truth."

Her mother laughed in spite of herself. "Then you made counterrevolutionary statements!"

"No. *No!*" Hyon-hui's green eyes flashed. "I said nothing against the Revolution or the Party. Nothing. I merely said, the other scientists should open their eyes, look around, and not blame the Americans for everything."

Her mother cringed. "Oh, Hyon-hui! How could you have?"

"But it isn't counterrevolutionary! An honest assessment of the Party can do nothing but strengthen it!" she argued, fighting to believe that the Party she'd lived for still made sense.

"An honest assessment of the Party can do nothing but kill it!"

Hyon-hui rose onto her elbows. "But I was always taught that –"

"You were always taught that Juche respects truth. That it *is* ultimate truth. So, now that you know the real truth, you believe that Juche would be strengthened by it. Except Juche is not truth, and it has never been about truth other than how Kim Il-sung defined truth. It is Kim Il-sung – and now his son – that defines truth, and history, and even reality in Choson. Juche is a lie."

Hyon-hui recoiled as if she'd been slapped. "But it always made sense before. I don't understand why nothing makes sense anymore. It is like everything I ever learned is suddenly wrong."

"Everything you learned *is* wrong and always has been. And Juche never made sense. Never. That's why you and I argued all the time. You loved Kim Il-sung and absorbed his every word."

"But –"

Her mother cut her off with a terse wave of her bony hands. "*Nothing* is what you were taught! *Nothing*. You must throw it all away. *Juche sasang. Chajusong. Kimilsungism. Pulgungi.* The history that you thought you knew. Your view of America. Your view of the West. Of the South. All of it."

"All of it?"

"Lies!"

Hyon-hui's pupils grew, devouring her iris until all that remained was a thin emerald ring. She'd never heard her mother speak with such authority. "It is all that I know. All I have ever known. How can I go on living like this? How can I function?"

"As I have. As millions of your countrymen do everyday. You just go on."

"How can I? I shall never see him again and his torment is all my doing."

"Mitch's torment is not your fault, Hyon-hui. He stood and –"

"I should have stood with him!" she blurted.

On the television, an American had just bayoneted a Korean in the chest. The blade had passed through a photograph of his wife and children in his shirt pocket. The camera zoomed in on the image as the man agonizingly expired with his son's name on his lips. When Hyon-hui finally spoke again it was a whisper and almost couldn't be heard over the battle on the television. "Remember what you said this morning? That I should use my standing to try to help Mitch? Well, now I have no standing."

The two of them sat on the couch as the black-and-white battle raged on TV. Wave after wave of Americans charged the North Korean lines, driven forward by merciless, cigar-chewing officers. Mitch had once told Hyon-hui that very few Americans smoked cigars. Even supported by tanks, the Americans failed as the stouthearted, heroic North Korean defenders strapped explosives to their bodies and leapt onto the iron beasts. The room slowly faded from orange, to purple, to black and still neither of them said anything.

At the climax, a stogie puffing general in sunglasses gave the order. "Give 'em the gas." And howitzers manned by more cigar-chewing officers lobbed chemical and biological weapons into the city. The final scene showed masses of dead civilian bodies lying among mountains of rubble. Old men. Boys. Women. Pregnant women. Little girls in pig-tails. Women with babies in their arms. Then, onto the screen came the word, *Fight!*, and below it, the date it was made: 2010. It was replaced by a static nature scene of Mount Kumgang and with a superimposed, digital clock and soft music.

"Mitch said Americans did not use poison gas in the Victorious Fatherland Liberation War," Hyon-hui said softly and they returned to their silence. She was about to apologize to her mother for failing the Party and brining this trouble into their lives, when the older woman rose so abruptly it startled Hyon-hui.

"Mother," she hissed, "what is it!"

The old woman picked up the Bible and handed it to Hyon-hui. "This is the only thing that can save you now."

Hyon-hui frowned. "Is your God so powerful that he can –"

"No. I mean, yes, He is. But –" The old woman softened and the weariness and pain of a lifetime suddenly melted away. She nearly looked like a little girl, carefree and joyful. Smooth and strong as a young willow. Her voice changed as well, carrying a strength and conviction that had never been there before. Her fear was gone. A lifetime of keeping secrets evaporated like dew on the morning grass. She sat down on the couch and took Hyon-hui's hands in her own.

"Daughter. Beloved daughter." She smiled as if the solution were obvious. "You must reveal me."

"Reveal you? What do you mean?"

"Reveal me. As a Christian. Take this Bible to the SSA. Then your loyalty to Kim Il-sung will be beyond doubt. You will be reinstated as a Party member. Perhaps even a cadre. That is how the Party works. Then, you can –"

"Never!" Hyon-hui pulling back in horror. "Never!" She pushed the Bible away.

"You will." Her mother pushed the Bible back into her hands.

"No! Mother! No!"

"If you had found this Bible a year ago, would you have hesitated, for even an instant?"

"But – but, that was different. I did not –"

"Just answer the question."

"*Mother* – I love you!"

"You would have turned me in. I know you would have. You know you would have. And that was for a lie. You would have worked evil for the sake of a lie. Now, you have the chance to work good, for the truth."

"*But mother!*" she cried, tears gathering in the corners of her eyes. "Losing you would not be good! I have only just found you!"

"I have always loved you, Hyon-hui. And you didn't find me. It is yourself you have found."

Hyon-hui stared at her mother. "*I can't do this.*"

Her mother's voice suddenly gathered authority and she seemed to grow, filling the room. "Even though the sky collapses on us, there is a hole to escape through. You *will* turn me in, and you *will* save Mitch. The two of you will flee this accursed land, and you will marry him, do you understand me, child? Then you will have many, many children that you will teach about God, about liberty, and about freedom. And you will tell them of Kim Il-sung, and about your grandfather and your mother, and about you and Mitch. And they will despise the evil, and love truth. *This*, Hyon-hui, will be my *chajusong*!"

The Party's response was consistent with Kim Il-sung's lifelong policy of swift reward and even swifter punishment. They understood that Hyon-hui loved her mother and, while they thought that she had known about the Bible for longer than she said, they didn't count it against her. Rather, they exalted her love and loyalty to the *widaehan suryong*, demonstrated by putting no one before him -- not even her own mother. *That* was the kind of person the Party wanted. Totally committed.

She was reinstated at a higher level and given a pin with a picture of both Kim Il-sung *and* Kim Jong-il. Her food rations were increased and she received a refrigerator that made its own ice which she put on her swollen feet every night. Kim In-taek preached about her at the study session. She was lauded in Sagi-dong's Party newspaper. Written up in the *P'yongyang Times*. Called a 'Hero of the DPRK.' Recommended for a DPRK Citizens Merit Medal. Promoted to the status of cadre-in-training. Sent to Kanggae for a week of indoctrination.

Only Professor Yang, watching from afar, found her actions curious. Perhaps her accusation of Pak had been a test of *his* loyalty? But he was too ashamed to even look at her, and would never ask. Too ashamed, too hungry, and too tired. So very, very tired.

As the nation's leading nuclear explosives expert, Hyon-hui was placed at the forefront of the most important project in the DPRK: the miniaturization of Mitch's cylindrical implosion design into a weapon small enough and light enough to fit on the tip of a ballistic missile. Or carried in a suitcase. Those who watched her blossoming career wished for a similar opportunity and prayed to Kim Il-sung that they, too, might have the opportunity and the strength to do the right thing.

But Hyon-hui had discovered that the Party didn't know *everything*. They saw her actions, heard her words, but her thoughts remained her own. She had deceived them and it had worked.

Mitch scratched more words on the paper. He'd been moved to a better room in the prison. It even had a small barred window that looked out on sacred Mt. Paektu, and bookcases with physics and mathematics texts, a computer, and pads of paper. And pictures of the Kims on the wall. He was ordered to begin writing everything he knew about Atomic Vapor Laser Isotopic Separation – the technology that could purify the uranium 233 and make it safe for long term use.

He raised his pencil, trying to remember what came next. He was still having trouble thinking. After the waterboarding, he'd not been able to keep a string of thoughts going at all. And even after the memories of his torture began to fade, he was in such despair from what Pak had told him that he couldn't hold complex thoughts in his head. The North Koreans had framed him and he'd fallen into their trap. Beth, he felt, was surely looking down on him. Would she understand? Would she understand the pain her death and everything surrounding it had brought him? And what of Hyon-hui? The thought of her subject to Pak's whims drove him mad with rage and helplessness.

But Pak warned him sternly that his work would be reviewed weekly and that if steady progress wasn't made, there were ways to persuade him to be more productive. And that was enough. Mitch had nightmares from the waterboarding and woke up choking all too often. The mere sound of water made his blood run cold. Splashing his face sent his heart racing so fast he had to lie down. Perhaps he'd get better in time. But for now, the only thing that mattered was filling as many pages as possible with whatever he could remember about AVLIS. Everything unclassified that he could think of, he wrote down. Anything to take up space and give them nothing they couldn't get on the internet.

His mind balked and swirled at the very idea of telling them anything. He'd been down this path before. He was still helping them, even if the information he scrawled onto the paper wasn't classified. Why was he doing this?   Why had he done it before? Why couldn't he have just allowed himself to be killed, or even done it himself, rather than helping them. It was his fault – *his fault* – that North Korea was now a nuclear power. As much as he hated the water boarding, and as terrified as he was of it happening again, he knew he deserved it, and worse. He, Mitch Weatherby, had fundamentally changed the power structure of the planet and, now, not only was there was nothing he could do about it, he was still helping them!

He began quietly reciting the Bible verses he'd memorized as a child to calm his mind. It was the only way to find any peace. He had hated the verses when he'd been forced to memorize them. Always resisted. Now, it was his only source of strength and left him wishing he'd studied harder. He also came to an unexpected conclusion.

Pak had hoped that telling Mitch why he was really here was the worst thing he could do to him. But he'd been wrong. The injustice of Mitch's arrest and betrayal by his country had been the nail driven into the coffin of his faith. To learn that it had all been faked – painstakingly orchestrated at great expense – left him suddenly knowing that it hadn't been random at all. His government hadn't used him as a scapegoat. God hadn't punished him for some unknown evil in his life. It had been a conspiracy by wicked men with an agenda. The willful act of an evil person. Pak had murdered his wife as surely as if he had pulled the trigger himself. It wasn't God's fault. It was Pak's.

The world began to make sense again, but with it came the undeniable responsibility for his own sins. Mitch knew, just as Pak had told him, it was his own pride that had ultimately been his undoing. He set down his pencil and walked to the window, thinking of his deeds since arriving in North Korea. He given them the bomb – a betrayal of all he'd believed in – but that was just the outgrowth of something deeper. A fundamental change in how he saw his existence. He'd denied God, cursed Him, and sworn at Heaven. He'd come to believe that man was the supreme being, the same thing that Juche taught. Except Juche maintained that this concept gave man great strength. Mitch knew the truth. No God meant there was no purpose to life, no right and wrong, nothing other than survival. And when you accepted that, North Korea was always the result. He dropped to his knees in his cell in the pool of sunshine and wept bitterly, begging for forgiveness and deliverance but knowing he deserved neither.

Hyon-hui tiptoed through the darkened storeroom, scarcely daring to breathe. Rack upon rack of unused equipment, old power supplies, and test apparatus, many bearing a yellow radiation symbol, lay forgotten on the shelves. Wires dangled and protruded everywhere amid tubes, gauges, and scopes, all permeated with the pungent odor of moldy electronics.

The disassembled skeleton of the *Canglong*, Rhee Sun-yi's executioner, lay here in the last forgotten chamber of the main corridor almost a quarter mile from the entrance to the labyrinthine warren. It had taken Hyon-hui nearly a week to work up the courage to come here. A week in Kanggae for cadre training. A week to repair the damage done to her Party standing. A week to grieve for her mother. A week to ensure that she wasn't being followed by the SSA. Every week – every second – she hoped that Mitch was alive, but that brought the horrors of the pain he was probably suffering. And every day brought the Silla scientists closer to their new, smaller, lighter, more powerful weapon, a device that Hyon-hui knew she could not give them, but that she must build lest they suspect her true purpose.

She picked up the cradle that had once held the plutonium target, its resonance radiation long since dissipated. When the U-233 started arriving and had proven to be much easier to work with, interest in plutonium dwindled and the thirty or so kilograms of test pieces, enough to build six or seven of their oversize bombs, went into storage in a nitrogen filled, boron-lined cabinet in CM-Division. That was before they had left for Heard Island. As far as she knew, they were still there and, as one of the division leaders, she had access. It would just be a matter of getting everyone else out of the lab.

Now her nimble mind and steely gaze analyzed how the *Canglong* worked: a small piece of plutonium fell through a hole in a larger piece. When the two were together they became supercritical. Only for an instant, and only just barely, but it was enough to kill Sun-yi. But if the large piece were encased in a tamper and neutron reflector, and the small pieces shot in at once, and not allowed to pass through, it might be enough to generate a small nuclear explosion, perhaps equal to as much as two or three thousand tons of TNT. A few kilotons. A few, very dirty kilotons to destroy the abomination they had unleashed on the world. Several thousand tons of TNT would easily turn the entire lab to rubble.

It would be a rather simple matter to put the *Canglong* back together. Getting the plutonium would be more difficult but ideas were already forming in her head. It seemed too easy but Hyon-hui knew only too well that there were major problems with this design. Problems that kept the Koreans or anyone else from making exactly the kind of 'simple' weapon she sought.

The problem was predetonation, a result of the high neutron flux from the spontaneous fission of reactor bred plutonium. In a gun-type arrangement such as this, the nuclear chain reaction begins before the pieces are completely assembled. This chain reaction happens so fast that, if there is a high neutron flux, the entire system can heat up and vaporize while the pieces are still approaching one another. The reaction stops after just a few generations of neutrons.

Gun assembly had worked for uranium-235 because the low spontaneous fission rate of U-235 allowed for an assembly speed of just 3,000 feet per second. But for plutonium a speed closer to 6,000 feet per second was needed. Impossible then – and impossible now. Because of this, Los Alamos had abandoned the plutonium gun-assembly in favor of the much more difficult concept of spherical implosion, something at which Sagi-dong had already failed, and replaced with cylindrical implosion. But that was far too complex a process for her to do on her own.

A sliding metal sound brought Hyon-hui out of deep thought just in time to glimpse a two-foot long steel tube slip from the shelf and plummet to the floor. She lunged toward it, but missed and it hit the concrete with a clatter.

By the time the echoes faded, her heart was racing, adrenaline was thundering through her veins, and her ears alert for the sound of approaching footsteps. She put the pipe back in place and fled from the mausoleum.

33

One cool, clear Saturday morning in the middle of September, Sonny was placed before a firing squad in the field behind KWP headquarters, his hands tied, his mouth gagged with a large rock. He was condemned for collaborating with the enemy. An empty socket remained where one of his clear eyes had been. He died gazing with his remaining one at the gibbous dawn moon setting over the west wall of Sagi-dong's valley. Even at the last, he didn't understand why they were killing him. *"One small step for a man!"* he thought as the soldiers readied their firearms. *"One giant leap for –"*

The shots rang out and Sonny slumped over and did not move again.

Hyon-hui wiped the tears from her eyes as she turned and came face-to-face with a huge election poster of Marshal Kim Jong-il that spoke of his manifold wisdom and surpassing benevolence. North Korean propaganda portrayed Kim Jong-il as if he were a god, ten feet tall with a voice like thunder across a mountainside. Hyon-hui wondered how true it was.

It was only eight in the morning but the sun was already beating down. Insects screeched in ragged clumps of weeds. All around her, Sagi-dong was a dust bowl. The rains had never come. Directly ahead lay the sterilized fields of the cooperative farm. Her stomach was groaning, while a breathless narrator on the loudspeaker extolled the merits of the Juche agricultural system.

In the weeks since her secret visit to the Canglong, she'd devoted much thought to the problem of the plutonium gun-assembly but nothing had come to her. Every piece of theory she knew told her it was impossible. Perhaps if Mitch or Max were here to help her with simulation, she might be able to come up with a workable design. But of course, they weren't. That was the problem.

"Miss Chun." A voice said softly beside her, jolting her from her thoughts. Bok-won was at her side in his army uniform, carrying his Kalashnikov rifle.

"Bok-won!" she hissed.

"Keep your eyes forward," he said coolly. She focused her eyes back on the ground a few feet in front of her. "Are you alright?" he asked. "You are limping."

"My feet are still sore. I fear they will never again be right."

"I heard. I am sorry. But I wanted to tell you –" He paused, looking this way and that as if they were not engaged in conversation. "They have cleaned up Dr. Weatherby and are feeding him well. He looks much better."

"That is good news," Hyon-hui choked out, wanting to cry. Or shout for joy. "Thank you, Comrade."

"It is rumored that Pak Yong-nam intends to present him to the Great Leader, Comrade Marshal Kim Jong-il on Foundation Day."

"*Marshal Kim Jong-il is coming here?*" Her green eyes widened and more pieces of her plan fell in place.

"Yes. There is to be a celebration honoring the Dear Leader after his election as General Secretary."

"How is Max, the Russian?" she asked.

"I have not seen him in several weeks."

It was now or never, Hyon-hui told herself. Mitch had to be saved. Max had to be helped. This was twice now that he had come to her unsolicited. Either he was an SSA informer or he wasn't and she could agonize over which it was. She swallowed hard and cringed as she asked. "You mentioned when you came to my house comrade, that you might... help me to help Dr. Weatherby."

"Did I say that?" he said guardedly.

"You said you wanted to help him."

"Why would I say that?"

"*Bok-won!*" Hyon-hui hissed. "We must at least trust each other. I'm *not* an informer. I'm *not* working for the SSA. My goal is to get out of North Korea and take Mitch with me. Will you help us?" She tightened, knowing she'd just put herself at great risk.

Bok-won marched along silently for a long time until he finally said, "I want to come, too."

"We will probably be killed."

"I know."

That was enough for Hyon-hui. "I have a plan," she said.

They stopped talking and separated as a policeman came along the street and passed close by.

"I have access to explosives," she said after they came back together. "I am going to build a bomb. When it goes off, it will divert the attention of the SSA enough for us to get out of Sagi-dong unnoticed."

A slight scowl formed on Bok-won's placid face. "What will you do then? The garrison in Yonjom-dong will respond immediately, blocking any escape from here."

"They would if they were in Yonjom-dong." Hyon-hui shot a quick glance over at the soldier before revealing the rest of the plan. "I am going to detonate it during the October Ten celebration. When Marshal Kim Jong-il is here."

"*What?* But the Dear Leader –"

"Do not worry, he will not be harmed. But the entire garrison will be here in Sagi-dong, correct? They will be caught up in the surprise of the explosion and – "

He cut his eyes at her. "How big of a diversion are you talking about?"

"Large enough to create the chaos we will need to escape." They walked along in silence, drifting apart and then together again.

"What are those?" Hyon-hui asked, looking up to the big knob of rock above the entrance to the underground lair. High above on the hillside a group of soldiers were setting up some kind of large gun with a long, thin barrel. "I noticed them several days ago."

"Anti-aircraft batteries," he answered. "For the visit of the Dear Leader."

Hyon-hui had trained on an anti-aircraft gun crew in the Workers' and Peasants' Red Guard and didn't recognize this model. "It is not a ZGU-1 or an S-60. Those are the only single barrel anti-aircraft guns that are that small."

"It is some new kind of weapon," he answered. "It shoots electrical magnets. I am to be trained on it."

"Electrical magnets? That doesn't make sense."

"My lieutenant said it is an electrical magnet launcher."

"Aye!" she exclaimed. "*Electromagnetic* launcher. They don't shoot magnets. They use electromagnetic forces to launch projectiles at very high speeds. Much faster than a normal gun. They can even –" Hyon-hui froze in her tracks.

Bok-won glanced around nervously. "Miss Chun!" he hissed. "Miss Chun!" They were attracting attention. "Miss Chun?"

She nodded woodenly and her lips parted in a smile that spread across her face for the first time in weeks. The movement was so unfamiliar, it came out as more of a wicked grimace. But the emotion was pure.

"What is it?"

She looked back up at the anti-aircraft battery high above them and could see the soldiers moving about it. "I've got to go to my office," she announced and turned toward the lab entrance.

"We should meet again," he said quietly after her. "On your way to work, in one week."

Hyon-hui nodded slightly and hurried on her way.

Within a few hours, Hyon-hui had derived the basic electromagnetic equations and calculated the design parameters for a rail gun that could assemble her plutonium pit. Two aluminum rails four meters long, separated by ten centimeters, and driven by 335 kiloamps should accelerate the plutonium slug to 6,500 feet per second in six and a half milliseconds. Fast enough to get a significant yield.

It wasn't possible to simply pull 335,000 amps from the grid. The only power supplies capable of providing that kind of current in a short period of time were very specialized and only used in a few types of work – rail guns, x-ray machines, high energy pulsed lasers, and nuclear weapons. The power supplies developed for

The Silla Project's multi-lens atomic device were ideal, and now were abandoned in Hyon-hui's storeroom!

But the design was not without problems. Hyon-hui discovered that the speed of 6,000 feet per second would not be attainable no matter what her calculations required. The trade-off between current and mass simply became too high or required rails longer than she could easily acquire. But at 5,000 feet per second, a half kilogram slug could be used with a lower mass pit surrounded by a one centimeter thick tungsten carbide reflector behind a beryllium radiation shield. If this core was embedded in a six inch thick iron tamper, a one point two kiloton blast would result, more than enough to provide her with the manmade natural disaster she needed.

There was much to do and not much time. She only had a few weeks to get her bomb ready and there were parts to collect and others to fabricate. The beryllium neutron reflector would be the most difficult. And she would somehow have to get the plutonium from the Chemistry and Metallurgy Division's storage facility. Without the plutonium, her bomb, no matter how carefully designed and assembled, would be useless.

The days flew by, and on Saturday, Bok-won never appeared as planned. Nor the week after that. Nor on any of the days in between. Hyon-hui thought she saw him once, high up in one of the western guard towers but couldn't be sure. The seasons started to change and the weather turned cooler and with it, she became convinced that Bok-won was gone. All manner of possibilities raced through her mind. Had he been followed? Had he been caught? If so, did he talk? Or had he just been reassigned to another duty station? It could be anything, but the prospect of doing this without him seemed impossible.

Still, the hope of freeing Mitch, the sacrifice of her mother to give her this chance, and the atrocities of her homeland drove her beyond any limits. By day, she worked diligently to perfect Kim Jong-il's ultimate weapon so as not to raise suspicion. But by night, she put on her alternate persona, traitor to the state, well aware of the consequences her actions would bring. Foremost in her mind was the image of Sun-gun battered and strapped to a pole for only asking Mitch about the outside world. Her fate would make his look like an afternoon walk along the Taedong. But that just made her more determined to succeed. Even if she had to do it alone.

34

"Dr. Jabril has assured me it will arrive on the ninth," Professor Yang said in a strained voice. The heads from each of Silla-14's five technical divisions and POOP Division were gathered in the conference room discussing the miniaturized version of Mitch's cylindrical implosion design.

"Enough for another weapon?" Ri Kyu-jae asked. He had come from the Yongbyon College of Physics to fill Mitch's position as the technical director of the Silla Project and was already taking credit for their success at Heard Island. Every reference to Mitch had been expunged. It infuriated Hyon-hui but there was nothing she could do, and didn't dare bring heightened scrutiny on her actions if she was to have a chance to save him.

"Yes, Comrade," he answered wearily. "That will give us enough 233 for the miniaturized gadget." Mitch had always used the term gadget but it was the first time that Professor Yang had ever done so. He missed Mitch, too, Hyon-hui suspected, but she knew he would never say so.

She leaned forward in her chair. "We should invite Marshal Kim Jong-il to witness the refinement!" she said enthusiastically. Professor Yang started to protest but Hyon-hui cut him off, turning to the man in the room she could tolerate the least. "We should demonstrate what you have done here at Silla-14, Minister Pak. Show the Dear Leader how Juche has blunted the aggression of the imperialist stooges. The last RaLa tests show that my implosion system is ready for the nuclear material. All that remains to complete the dagger is refinement of the U-233, then we can plunge it into the eye of the Western dogs." A fanatical light gleamed in her eyes and Professor Yang looked at her with suspicion, but Pak smiled broadly at his new protégé.

"*Yes!*" he thundered. "Yes! Juche in action. I will show the Dear Leader exactly what kind of work I do here at Sagi-dong. It might perhaps give him a greater appreciation for the difficulties I face."

Hyon-hui smiled but not for the reason those watching her assumed. With the preparations for the October 10th Anniversary Celebration of the Korean Workers' Party, everyone was busy, keeping them far from the storeroom and her work on the Canglong bomb had been unhindered. All it lacked was a detonation timer and the plutonium. She had already acquired a programmable timer from the electronics division but still needed to wire it into her simple fuzing circuitry. Which left only the plutonium. She had less than a week to get past the guards that protected it. With Kim Jong-il's visit only days away, it was now time to check off that box.

She mentally reviewed her plans for her evening. After the meeting, she would attend her political ideology session at Party headquarters. Then she would return to the lab and retrieve the plutonium from the Chemistry and Metallurgy Division's storage facility. She went through every detail in her head. With any luck –

"Comrade Chun," Pak said for the third time.

Hyon-hui suddenly realized Pak was speaking to her. "Yes, Comrade!" she barked.

"Are you ready to come back to us, Miss Chun?"

"Yes, Comrade Minister. I apologize. My mind had wandered into an idea for more easily purifying and casting high explosives for precision lenses. The Juche way is to work without ceasing toward reunification." Her eyes glanced across the staring faces and she wondered if they could tell she was lying. "What would you ask of me, Comrade Minister?"

"I said, you will provide us with a revolutionary talk at tonight's meeting."

Inwardly she wanted to commit suicide. These talks were always filled with hatred toward America and all things not Juche, but she could not refuse. "Yes, Comrade!" she burst, and threw an extra dose of patriotic gleam into her green eyes. "I have been hoping for just such an opportunity!"

Her address that evening was reprinted widely across the DPRK and was well on its way to becoming one of the legendary speeches of the Sagi-dong Party Cell. As she recounted the U.S. massacre of civilians at Sinchon in 1950, she began to embellish more and more until she started simply making things up as she went along. Pushing the stories of rape, sack, and pillage far beyond the absurd and into the satirical, just to see what people would do. And their response no longer surprised her. Despite the fact that she was introducing new material into stories that had been recycled for over half a century, no one questioned a word. They just cheered all the more vigorously. How many of the 'old' stories, she wondered, had been created the same way? And how many of the people in there were cheering because they had visited the little room in Yonjom-dong?

With Kim In-taek's accolades still ringing in her ears, she left Party Headquarters making for the lab. It was time to retrieve the plutonium and complete her bomb. She merged with the mass of citizens headed home after a long day, and had not yet reached the guard tower when a voice whispered behind her. "Do not turn around. You are being followed."

Hyon-hui instantly recognized it as Bok-won's but turned to check anyway.

"I told you not to turn around!"

"Who is following me," she asked.

"The SSA. All day today. Yesterday as well."

Her mind reeled, trying to remember what she'd done the day before... Friday labor. She hadn't gone near the lab all day. "Where have you been?" she hissed, back. "We were supposed to meet weeks ago!"

"P'yongyang. Ideological training. Is everything ready?"

"It was about to be. Are you certain about my being followed?"

"Absolutely. I have been following you for two days."

Hyon-hui racked her brain, trying to think what she could have done to be assigned an agent. Since turning in her mother she'd been the model Party member. "Who is he? What does he look like?"

"She, in a dark blue jumpsuit, wearing a red kerchief on her head."

Technician's uniform, thought Hyon-hui. "So what do I do?"

"Shh!"

A middle aged woman was staring at them. Probably an SSA informer. It was well known that about one in four citizens were on the SSA payroll. Bok-won barked something ugly at Hyon-hui, then hurried on.

Hyon-hui was suddenly alone again, her plan aborted. There was no way she could finish the job now. All she could do was go home. But before she entered the residential section, Bok-won was back at her side. "Your diversion? Is it ready?"

"Almost," she answered.

"You are certain that Marshal Kim Jong-il is in no danger?"

"None," she lied. Everyone would be in some danger, including her country's beloved leader. Including herself.

"After the diversion, meet me just inside the main gate. I'll have a jeep and supplies waiting.

"How is Dr. Weatherby?"

"Much improved. And he is getting regular meals."

"And Max?" Bok-won's face grew dark. "What is it?" hissed Hyon-hui.

"I have not seen him." There was a pause. "You're certain about the Great Leader?" asked Bok-won again.

"Yes. But expect a very large diversion. Probably larger than you're expecting."

Bok-won looked at her uncertainly but didn't press the issue. "Just remember, act normal." He backed into the darkness.

For the three days, Hyon-hui tried to act normal, wandering around Sagi-dong and the halls of Silla-14 like a zombie on amphetamines, trying to come up with ways to finish her plan. Sleep was impossible. At times, the sensation of being watched was so intense she had to fight the urge to turn around with all her strength.

What had tipped off the SSA, she wondered. If they knew what she was actually doing, she'd already be back in that horrible room. So her plan must move forward, and timing it for when the Dear Leader was here was ideal. Most of Yonjom-dong's security detail would be at Sagi-dong, leaving Mitch and Max guarded by an unusually small staff. And the large numbers of people outside would cause mass confusion helping their escape. It had to be this Friday. But that gave her only two more days to retrieve the plutonium. And she knew that tomorrow was out – Election Day. A national holiday.

The atmosphere was electric at the Party meeting after the day's polling had closed. Kim In-taek waited on the stage as the room filled. Everyone piled in, eager to find out who had won the election. Why had Hyon-hui never seen this exercise for the scam it was, she wondered, placing a smile on her face. Kim Jong-il was the only candidate, and although there was a process for casting a dissenting vote, the two Party officials watching the casting of each ballot made that suicide. And yet, the room buzzed with excitement. How many others here were faking it like she was?

In-taek raised his arms and silenced the group. "Comrades!" he gushed. "Comrades! I have in my hands a special communiqué prepared by the KWP Central Committee and the Central Military Commission received only moments ago." He cleared his throat and started reading. "The Workers' Party of Korea, organizations of the Korean Peoples' Army, provinces, municipalities, ministries, national institutions and other bodies with the function of provincial Party organization have adopted resolutions on recommending Comrade Kim Jong-il as General Secretary of our Party with *one hundred percent* of the vote."

Cheering filled the hall. Party members jumped up and down, waving their arms as if this was some great and unexpected victory. When they finally calmed down, In-taek continued. "The WPK Central Committee and Central Military Commission solemnly declare that Comrade Kim Jong-il has been officially elected to be General Secretary of our Party." The cheering crescendoed again. "As desired by the whole Party, as he has strengthened and developed our Party to be an invincible, veteran revolutionary Party which enjoys full support and trust from all the people ..." He had to speak louder just to be heard over the growing din. "...has trained our people as an independent people with indomitable faith and will and has opened a new era of the Kim Il-sung nation's prosperity, with tireless revolutionary activities over the past thirty odd years!"

They leapt to their feet as one and shouted their approval and support, clapping and cheering, and calling for the immortality of Kim Il-sung and Kim Jong-il. Hyon-hui joined them, leaping to her feet and crying out in mock-joy.

The rest of the meeting went on to praise Kim Jong-il for wise actions and great deeds and showed a brand new documentary on his life and accomplishments. But Hyon-hui heard none of it. As the meeting drug on, she weighed her options for retrieving the plutonium and assembly her bomb. But since she was being followed, it would be impossible, and trying to lose her tail would only make the situation worse.

Hyon-hui emerged from the meeting, her head weary and her heart aching at the conclusion that she would fail. As she passed the central guard tower, she spotted a woman following her. She rubbed her arms to calm the shiver that was only partly from the cool night air. She hadn't expected to have a chance to sneak off into the lab, but the woman trailing behind her, slowing as she slowed, removed any hope. Hyon-hui turned to take the road home.

Before she'd gone a few yards, a UAZ sped up the road, jerking to a stop beside her. Two SSA thugs hopped out, grabbed her, and threw her in the back. Hyon-hui cried out for help, but nobody even acknowledged the incident. She cowered as the door slammed shut, knowing it spelled the final defeat. She was headed back to Yonjom-dong, this time to die. Max would die, too, if he hadn't already. And Mitch would spend the remainder of his life in prison. She closed her eyes, feeling the rumble of the tires against the rutted road, and waited.

The UAZ stopped much sooner than Hyon-hui expected. The door opened and she was hauled out, only to find herself, not in Yonjom-dong, but standing before Pak's house. As before, the guards shoved her through the door and slammed it behind them.

"Come in," Pak grinned with his eyes closed. He was sitting on a couch with his legs stretched out from under his bathrobe. Gentle music played in the background as he took a sip of an amber-colored drink.

Hyon-hui spun around and yanked at the door but it wouldn't open.

Pak laughed. He picked up a glass plate from the table next to him, momentarily used a razor blade to push around what looked like fine sugar, then used a thin metal tube to suck the powder into his nose. His eyes gleamed wickedly when he looked back at her. "Why don't you just stay awhile. You'll find you enjoy it. A lot of women do."

"You cannot have me!" Hyon-hui hissed, choking back fear and rage. "I am not yours. I would never be yours!"

His eyes narrowed venomously. "And whose are you? That bastard American?"

"Don't speak of him that way. Mitch treated me with respect!" she snapped, unwilling to stop the torrent of thoughts from spilling from her mouth. At this point she had nothing to lose. If she couldn't save Mitch or herself, at least she didn't have to debase herself in her failure. "Mitch Weatherby is a real man. You are not fit even to lick his shoes!"

Pak rose, a cruel smile twisted his lips. "You have not seen him as I have, Comrade Chun. Crying like a woman. Begging me to release him, promising to do anything for me. He is not a man."

She thought of Mitch standing tall at the bronze feet of Kim Il-sung, refusing to bow to what he did not believe, and a wave of bravery swept through her. "Murder and torture do not make you a man!" she pronounced. "They make you an animal! The Party is nothing but criminals and thugs." Pak took a menacing step toward her, but she continued. "Choson was once known as the Land of Eastern Courtesy. Now we are considered freaks by the world! A laughingstock!"

Pak took another step, and Hyon-hui instinctively backed away. This was going just as before, but she decided it would not end the same. "What would your precious *suryong* say if he could see you now?" she spat. "Beating up girls and raping Party members. Is that what Kim Il-sung stood for?"

"Kim Il-sung is not here," Pak lisped with a cold voice. "He is dead. And his son is a fool." He grabbed her roughly by the neck and shoved his tongue into her mouth. But this time, Hyon-hui bit down on it. Pak howled in pain, spitting blood. She kicked him in the crotch, then hit him in the face. As he staggered back, she sprang forward to attack. But he was too fast and too strong. He caught her by the throat in mid-step and hurled her to the floor, knocking the wind from her lungs. Hyon-hui's eyes bulged and she clawed at the iron-like grip but it was no use. *I'm going to die*, she thought with surprising clarity. *And I'll never see Mitch again.* From nowhere the words, "God help me…" squeezed from her lips and she knew they were the last words she would ever speak.

35

Everything was dark. Hyon-hui was groggy, her throat burned, she was freezing, and her head felt like several hatchets had been embedded into it. And it smelled… like dirt. Somewhere in the distance she could hear water trickling.

"Am I dead?" she asked herself. "Is this what it feels like in the grave?" The sound fell flat, but at least it was sound. She tried to sit up, but struggled until she realized she was laying in sand with her head steeply downhill. Rough weeds tugged at her clothing and scratched her skin. She squirmed into a seated position, brushing off the brambles which tried to hold her down. She caught her breath before carefully standing up, her legs shaking, barely supporting her.

It was utterly dark and the air felt moist. She clawed her way up the slope, stumbled out into a flat area where she tripped over a mound and fell down into dry reeds. "A rice paddy dike?" she whispered. "I must be in the collective farm." Pak must have dumped me out here, thinking he'd strangled me.

Away in the distance, her eyes detected a faint, gray glow and she groped toward it, tripping over one dike after another. Her head ached and she couldn't make out anything. "Fog," she said to herself when she figured out that the gray glow ahead was a security light on her Explosives Facility. She glanced at her watch. She only had fifteen minutes to get home before curfew.

She stumbled onto the gravel street connecting the collective farm with the central guard tower. It had taken longer to get to the road than she'd thought and she had only about five minutes to get home. She'd never make it but slipped into a trot despite the pain in her feet, with the crunch of stones underfoot breaking the complete silence of the night.

After a few steps, she pulled up short and listened. Not a sound marred the still Korean night. The woman following her was *gone!*

"Good evening, Miss Chun," the first guard said when she appeared like a ghost out of the fog. "It's almost – " His eyes grew wide but Hyon-hui knew he would not ask about the bright red marks on her face or the hand print on her throat. Fortunately, the ground was dry enough that the dust had brushed off. Everyones' clothes were smudged anyway since there was no longer water to wash anything. And her mother – the woman who did the laundry – had disappeared weeks ago.

Hyon-hui flashed the guard her lovely smile. "Have you ever fallen out of an electric car at 20 kilometers per hour?" she asked.

He just stared and shook his head.

"I was riding to our KWP meeting tonight with Colonel Phoung and Minister Pak. When the Minister – you know how he always drives too fast – turned a corner, I slid right off the seat. He had to grab me by the throat to save me!" she pointed at her throat and winced. "But it was better than falling out."

"Have you been to the doctor?"

"Just bruises. He says I will be fine."

She received the same reception at the lower desk where she exchanged badges and told the same lie. It was after ten o'clock when she finally stopped by her office. She retrieved a glass vial of bright yellow powder hidden beneath her desk drawer. To avoid being seen, she crept along little-used side passages and wandering corridors until she arrived at a duct. She could hear the cool, fresh air from the surface rushing through it. With a screwdriver, she removed a small cover and dropped the vial through the opening. It clattering down the shaft as she hastily replaced the cover and stole down the corridor.

The vial shattered on the ventilation fan and the yellow uranium-oxide powder was whisked away. Seconds later, radiation detectors exploded all over the lab. Sirens blared and flashing lights lit up the main hall with spinning red and blue beams just as Hyon-hui reached a storage closet she'd prepared almost a week earlier. She sat down in a corner of the closet, grabbing the breathing mask she'd hidden under a pile of rags. The risk of inhaling any of the powder was low, and uranium was quickly expelled from the body, but she put on the mask to be safe and checked the time on her watch.

People in offices and machine shops and laboratories ran out into the main hall, bewildered and jabbering. Soldiers emerged to direct people out of the lab. The ventilation system shut down automatically. Hyon-hui waited. She knew that in thirty minutes, men in sealed suits would enter the lab to search for the problem. Until then, once everyone was out, she would be the only person in the underground warren.

When five minutes had passed, Hyon-hui cracked the door and peered into the hall. The spinning red light was the only movement. She stole into the lab where the plutonium was kept. It took only a moment for her to replace the pit and the smaller spheres with steel impostors. If examined closely, the fakes would be discovered, but they only had to work for two days. With the plutonium finally in hand, she headed to her hidden lab where she found everything exactly as she'd left it.

36

"Speak!" barked Pak Yong-nam, leaning forward in his cushioned leather desk chair. The voice on the other end of the phone was that of his counterpart, Comrade Secretary Kim In-taek, and he sounded nervous.

"*Minister, I know you did not want Comrade Chun arrested before the visit of the Great Leader, but I have come to the unavoidable conclusion that it is absolutely necessary.*"

"Chun?" asked Pak, his back straightening more. Had someone seen him dump her body last night? No, In-taek was talking about arresting her; he didn't yet know she was dead. "I haven't seen her this morning," he said tightly into the receiver.

"*I have been having her followed for the last week. And last night, after being picked up by some of your men, she didn't come home at all!*"

Pak's mind froze. "My men?" he said slowly. "I gave no such order."

"*Logs show that she entered the lab at 9:57 last night. After the contamination accident, she was not among those evacuated. And this morning, she was seen coming out of a storage room. Now, she is in her office.*"

In her office!?! Adrenaline surged through Pak's body at those words. Chun was dead. *Dead!* There had to be some mistake. "This morning?" he said, forcing his voice to be calm, but his eyes stared out the doorway to his office as if expecting her ghost to arise there at any moment to accuse him. "Are you sure it was Comrade Chun?"

"*Yes, who else would it be? You sound surprised,*" In-taek's voice said, taking on a tone of suspicion.

"No! Not at all," Pak stammered as he recovered. If she hadn't gone to the police yet, she probably wasn't going to. She was easily controlled. Child's play for him. But if she was alive, In-taek questioning her about her actions could prove difficult. "She was probably looking for some old test equipment. We store a lot of equipment in there. I don't see why you would arrest her."

"*All night long?*" In-taek scoffed.

"Perhaps she fell asleep. People sleep in the lab every night. Comrade Tarasenko used to sleep in here for days at a time. She is helping prepare for the visit of Marshal Kim Jong-il. Our dedicated scientists often work overnight and sleep in their offices. This is not unusual."

"*I'm going to bring her in for questioning this morning.*"

"*No!*" blurted out Pak. "She is helping prepare for the Great Leader's visit. She is a division leader. We cannot have her showing up beaten to a pulp if she's done nothing! Last time your men finished with her she couldn't walk for a month! I still see her limping. No," he said firmly, then cast around for a persuasive reason. "The Great Leader – you know how he likes pretty women. I want him to see Comrade Chun. Perhaps if he is looking at her, he will not notice the collective farm. After he is gone, you can do what you want with her."

There was silence on the other end of the phone.

"I'll tell you what," Pak went on. "I'll meet you at Miss Chun's office. I'll contact Professor Yang. We'll check out this storeroom ourselves, question Comrade Chun, and find out what has been going on. Will that be satisfactory?"

"*When this is over,*" In-taek said, suspiciously, "*I want a more thorough investigation.*"

"And you shall have it. After the Dear Leader is gone." Pak hung up the phone and swore at himself. It had been stupid of him to strangle her. He knew strangling with the hands was one of the most unreliable killing methods. Better to use a rope or a belt. But he had been angry, and drunk, and high. The next time, there would be no mistake.

*

The blood drained from Hyon-hui's body at the sight of In-taek and Pak Yong-nam in her office doorway. Her face went white as putty making the bruises look all the more black. "Yes, Comrade Minister," she said weakly, then acknowledged In-taek with a shallow, seated bow. "Comrade Secretary." She was exhausted and didn't know how much more she could take.

"What happened to you, Comrade?" In-taek asked in a suspicious tone.

Hyon-hui's mind raced. She could take this opportunity to turn Pak in. It might even stick. But it might also change the order of events. Her eyes flitted to Pak, who glared at her ominously from behind In-taek's back. "A rack of lens molds fell over on me," she said sheepishly. "Last night in a storeroom."

"Lens molds? That looks more like a hand ..." In-taek started when Pak interjected.

"Lens molds. They are large, heavy, rather unwieldy molds made from ceramic. We press high explosives into them for the lens shapes."

"You should be more careful," In-taek scolded. "You look like somebody beat you up! You should go home and go to bed!"

"Thank you, Comrade Secretary. Perhaps I shall."

"But before you do, we need to walk down to the storeroom."

"*What?*" she exclaimed, losing her composure for a split second. In-taek caught it and tipped his head, his beady eyes boring in to her. "I mean, must we do it now? I am busy preparing for our Dear Leader's visit. Everything must be perfect," she added with a partial bow.

"You were seen coming out of there this morning," Pak explained. "This cannot wait."

"Yes, what were you doing in there?" In-taek asked. "And why did you not evacuate last night?"

"I already told you, Comrade. The lens molds fell over on me. I was knocked unconscious." Her eyes jumped back and forth between Pak and In-taek. It was a lousy lie and she knew it. "I can show you."

As they walked through the halls, Hyon-hui clung to the hope that neither Pak nor In-taek would understand what they were seeing in the storeroom, and that she would come up with a plausible excuse for having been there. But when they entered the room, all hope left her. Professor Yang was already inside, teetering on a cane. Their eyes met and despite the momentarily startled expression from her appearance, Hyon-hui could tell that he'd already figured out the mechanism that lay along the floor on one side of the room. Her fate was sealed. Yang would explain it to Pak and In-taek and she would be executed, perhaps not even as kindly as Sonny. Silence hung for what seemed like hours as Hyon-hui glanced between the man who had raped her, the one who had tortured her, and the one who had abandoned her.

"Comrade Professor," In-taek greeted the old man. "Have you found anything?"

There was a momentary pause. "Yes," he finally hissed, in a raspy voice. Hyon-hui held her breath. This was it. The end of everything. "A lot of junk," the old man said and tossed something to the side with a clank.

Hyon-hui quietly let go her breath. He didn't know. *He didn't know!*

"What am I supposed to be looking for, Comrade Minister?" Yang asked, making it clear he felt they were wasting his time.

Pak and In-taek moved into the room poking and prodding contraptions they had no hope of understanding. "I don't know," said Pak. "Stinks in here, like mildew."

"As I said," Hyon-hui explained, mustering her courage, "I was looking through the lens molds, searching for a promising design that we lost the documentation for." She walked over to the stand where they were piled, drawing them away from the bomb. Kneeling down she took one off the lower shelf. "I picked this one up – see, they are stamped with the lot and date – and I heard something and looked up just in time to see the entire rack fall over on me."

In-taek had moved over to where the professor stood. He was now standing right next to her bomb, staring curiously at the gantry-like contraption laid on its side. At one end was a stack of iron plates and, at the other, several thick cables were hooked to big electrical boxes. Unlike everything else in the room, it looked… recently touched. "What's this?" He asked. "It looks like it's turned on."

Hyon-hui watched in horror as In-taek bent over one of the firing sets, reaching out to touch a half-inch diameter copper rod fixed to the upper rail. At 50,000 volts it would kill him instantly. She closed her eyes tight so she wouldn't see the horror when he popped.

"I wouldn't," Professor Yang said calmly. In-taek jumped back and Hyon-hui opened her eyes. "That is highly radioactive." The professor picked up a radiation detector and waved the short, metal probe over the loaded gun. It crackled and hissed. "The remains of the *Canglong*."

"The *Canglong*," In-taek whispered in awe and inched backwards. "The machine that killed Comrade Rhee Sun-yi?"

"It is still highly radioactive. These instruments monitor its status."

What?! The world blurred out of existence for an instant as the implications of Professor Yang's statement sank into her mind. *He knew! He knew everything!* He glanced at Hyon-hui and she knew that everything was going to be alright. He knew exactly what it was and was covering for her.

"Why don't you throw it away if it's so dangerous?" Pak demanded, backing away from the device.

"Because, Comrade, we do not yet have a long term, solid waste storage facility. I have been asking for one, and as soon as it is built, this," he pointed at it contemptuously, "and a lot of other contaminated equipment will be the first things to go. It was mistakenly constructed from steel high in cobalt and now contains large quantities of cobalt-60. It could contaminate all of Lake Nangnim and foul this watershed for a thousand years. In fact, we have already been in here for too long." He turned and shuffled slowly towards the exit.

Both bureaucrats backed further away in terror. Hyon-hui would have laughed were she not so frightened herself, although for different reasons. At Professor Yang's words, In-taek seemed to lose interest and he strode off with Pak, debating about who would stand where upon Kim Jong-il's arrival the next day. Leaving Hyon-hui and Professor Yang to the contaminated storeroom.

"A rail-gun," Yang chuckled when he was sure they were gone. "You have managed to do what the most brilliant scientists of the last century could not." Hyon-hui bowed deeply to the man who'd just saved her life, as she rose Professor Yang's tired eyes examined her bruises. "Pak?" he asked, raising an eyebrow.

She held her head high, looking her colleague in the eye. "Yes, Comrade Professor. He tried to kill me last night."

"Did he… rape you as well."

"No," she said boldly. "He did not do that. I would not let him."

"Then you, as a woman, are a better man than I," he replied, his voice thick with shame. "For I have abandoned and betrayed one who I swore to champion." His eyes flitted over her battered face. "And I have helped…" he paused and looked around the room, "… with this." Before her eyes, Professor Yang seemed to slump, becoming withered and drawn far beyond his years, the opposite of how she had seen her mother expand. "I have come to find that this – that everything – was never about Choson, or Juche sasang, or even reunification." He shook his head and sighed heavily. "Pak Yong-nam and people like him are not what the Great Leader wanted. They have…" His words trailed off.

"Corrupted the Party?"

He nodded. "I am proud of you, Hyon-hui. You were the daughter I never had. But in the end, I turned out to be nothing but a cowardly old fool."

"No, Professor," she came back. "You saved my life today. You have been a great inspiration to me and to many others. Your life has been – "

"My life has been a lie," he spat. "I have always known that the cause of Choson was flawed. But I chose to close my eyes to the truth so that I might enjoy success for a season. And look where it has led us. To the brink of holocaust. We are about to unleash a nuclear weapon, not for the good of Korea, not for our people, but for Pak's personal gain. I should have never allowed this to continue. For that, I have received my punishment."

His eyes searched Hyon-hui's green ones for a moment, gathering a sense of urgency. "Hyon-hui, don't come back here for any reason. You are being followed. I understand what you intend to do, and I will detonate the device at eight-thirty tomorrow night during Pak's speech. Use the diversion to get out of Sagi-dong and out of Choson. To escape while there is time! The rains are finally on their way. The nation is out of fuel. This may be the only chance you ever have for freedom."

"No! You will be killed," she argued, her heart bursting at the sacrifice her mother had already made. She couldn't allow anyone else to die because of her. I have a timing device. All I have to do is –"

"I am ready, Hyon-hui." He smiled and squinted his heavily-lined old eyes. "And I'm dying already."

"Dying?"

"Leukemia. From all this..." he made a sweeping gesture towards the lab, "radiation. Punishment for a lifetime of sin."

"No! That cannot be. How do you know it is leukemia?"

"When we were in P'yongyang I was diagnosed by a French medical doctor. There is no doubt. And no cure."

"Perhaps in the West you could find help. Come with us!"

"Even if there was a cure, I would not accept it. For my dishonor to you and to all of Choson, it is time that I go. And I could not make such a journey anyway. Tomorrow night, you will leave North Korea. Forever. Promise me, Hyon-hui," he said with tired urgency.

"I will," she replied, then started to say something but stopped.

"What is it, my niece?"

"I am going to take Dr. Weatherby with me," she blurted. "And Dr. Tarasenko. They are being held prisoner in Yonjom-dong."

He marveled at her in wonder. "You would go to America?"

She hung her head for a moment, then lifted it with pride and looked into the professor's old eyes. Never again, she told herself, would she feel shame because of who she was or attempt to hide it. "Yes, Professor, I will go to America if they will have me. My mother, before she was taken by the SSA, she told me… She told me that my grandfather was not Russian. He was an American. I have American blood in my veins, Professor. And that is where I belong."

37

The Dear Leader Comrade Marshal Kim Jong-il seemed comical to Hyon-hui. Not like a god at all and certainly nothing like the election poster. More like a play toy. He was half-a-head shorter than her and wore a frumpie, taupe leisure suit that bulged over his prodigious belly. With his short legs sticking out the bottom, he reminded Hyon-hui of a picture she'd seen of penguins, except not as colorful. Over his eyes, he wore massive, dark glasses that wrapped all the way around his face. For a peerlessly brilliant man of wise actions and great deeds, she was unimpressed.

Behind the Party headquarters, Sagi-dong's Party faithful had been standing at attention in the sweltering sun for hours, until two black limousines pulled in, escorted by troop carriers and little motorcycles that smoked badly and buzzed about like flies. The road to Sagi-dong had been paved for his visit. Kim Jong-il emerged, and after paying his respects to the statue of his father next to the pond, he received the cheers of the Party, waved, and then headed off to a six-course lunch hosted by the Sagi-dong cell of the Korean Workers' Party. Naturally, only the senior cadres had been invited.

After a tour of the desiccated collective farm, where the Dear Leader offered on the spot guidance to improve the yield of the barren land, it was time for the tour of the underground lab. The Department Heads gathered in the main hall where Pak introduced each in turn. "Comrade Professor Yang, head of the Theoretical Division, you know already."

"Comrade Professor," Kim Jong-il said with a shallow bow. "You have served the fatherland long and faithfully. *Choson* owes you a debt of gratitude." Hyon-hui suppressed a smirk at the Dear Leader's squeaky, nasal voice.

Pak went on to introduce all the other scientists. Each, including Hyon-hui, bowed deeply and with great reverence. From a lifetime of ideological indoctrination, she found herself awed to be in the Dear Leader's presence, despite his absent charisma.

"A woman in charge of explosives?" he squeaked, then his eyes narrowed as he examined her. "You are not fully Korean, are you Comrade?"

"No, Dear Leader. My grandfather was Russian."

"Was he a member of the Communist Party?"

"Yes, and a captain in the Red Army. Before he died, he was a commissar and won the Order of Lenin for bravery." She thought about making up more but decided not to push it.

"Do not be too ashamed by your lineage, Comrade, for you are still a beautiful woman. Come, you will walk with me." She joined his side, to the obvious annoyance of Pak and Kim In-taek as they left the hall for the tour. "Were you by chance," he asked as they strolled into the main corridor, "ever on one of my father's pleasure teams?"

"No, Dear Leader." She kept catching herself staring down at the top of his head, amused to find it covered by a toupee. "I went from high school directly into Kim Il-sung University."

"An oversight," he said. "Are you now married?"

"No, Comrade General Secretary," she stammered, her blood turning cold at the line of conversation. "I am not."

The little man nodded. "Interesting…"

Pak's irritation mounted as Kim Jong-il remained more interested in Hyon-hui than anything else they showed him. He yawned through the Theoretical Division's spaces. And for the most brilliant man in all of history, failed to grasp the significance of the particle accelerators or the unique properties of the chargeless neutron. Occasionally, he gave advice on physics which his aides wrote down carefully. Hyon-hui cringed behind her smile, knowing that it would be distilled into a book and everyone would have to memorize it, even though it was wrong.

"What happened to your neck, Comrade?" Kim asked at one point, catching sight of the deep bruises. "Have you been recently injured?"

Hyon-hui heard Pak's footsteps as he padded close behind them. She could crush him here and now, with a single statement, and they both knew it. But it would risk everything she'd worked to set in motion. "I had an accident, Dear Leader, in one of the labs. It is not serious and I will be fine. Thank you."

The Dear Leader shook his head in disapproval. "This is too dangerous a place for you, Comrade Chun. Perhaps you'd like to return to P'yongyang with me? A position as a full professor at Kim Il-sung University would suit you well."

Her mind reeled at the offer. Kim Il-sung University! Professor of Chemistry! That was her life's dream! And here it was, served to her unexpectedly by this funny little man.

"Pak," Jong-il quipped over his shoulder. "Do you think you could spare Comrade Chun? She would better serve *Choson* in P'yongyang where her obvious revolutionary spirit, technical competence, and devotion to the cause of Juche can inspire the younger generation. More than anyone I have met in a long time, she embodies the true essence of the Three Revolutions Movement."

Pak had to force the stunned look from his face. "She is quite important to Silla-14. I think it might be best if *I* went to P'yongyang. I could –"

Jong-il laughed. "I am certain that we will not be able to spare you for some time to come, old friend. Not after the excellent job you have done completing the work here. All the reports I read have hailed *you* as the reason for all this." He turned back to Hyon-hui. "Tomorrow when I return to P'yongyang, you will come with me. Do you have family here?"

Hyon-hui shook her head woodenly, unable to speak. Her dreams of advancing in the Party and returning to Kim Il-sung University were blossoming before her eyes. To teach at the educational pinnacle of the world. And the Dear Leader, himself, had taken an interest in her! Once you'd caught his eye, there was really no limit to where you could go. A life in P'yongyang. A fine apartment. Perhaps even a car. And Pak Yong-nam would never again be a threat! A thrill rose up inside her such as she'd never felt before. It was the Dear Leader. This man was so great, he inspired her as none other. A broad grin spread across her face.

"Good! It's settled then," he told her. "My personal secretary will make the arrangements." The Dear Leader looked around at Pak and the scientists waiting for him. "I'm hungry," he yawned to Hyon-hui. "Let's go get something to eat."

"Comrade Secretary," Pak butted in, turning pale as he made his last pitch for Kim Jong-il's attention. "The uranium purification. We have been awaiting your esteemed presence to complete…"

The stubby leader waved his hand. "Fine, fine. Come get me when your little experiment is done." With that, Kim Jong-il took Hyon-hui by the arm and strode off with his aides, leaving Pak mouthing words at no one.

The acne-scarred scientist, who had arrived a month ago to fill Sun-gun's place, picked up a large hammer and struck the side of the still-warm refinement canister several times, then removed the top. The magnesium-oxide liner had shattered like the inside of a thermos. He looked up at the Dear Leader who had returned to the lab moments before, Hyon-hui still beside him, beaming. Wearing a pair of heavy leather gloves, the scientist turned the steel canister upside down and poured the contents into a high-lipped dish. White chunks of broken liner and pieces of gray slag poured out. Last of all, a silver disk about the size of a big cookie dropped out with a metallic ring. He picked up the hot piece of metal and plopped it into a container of clear liquid that smelled like vinegar. It fizzed for an instant, then lay quiet until it was retrieved with a set of tongs, rinsed off, and dried with acetone.

"One point zero one kilograms of 97.6% pure uranium-233," the scientist announced. "That gives us a total of twenty-four point five kilograms."

Pak turned to Kim Jong-il. "General Secretary. I am pleased to inform you that we have your nuclear weapon."

Kim Jong-il turned to the technicians. His beady eyes gleamed as he said in his squeaky voice, "Excellent. How quickly can you have the weapon ready?"

They went ramrod straight for a moment, then began milling about like minnows caught in a shrinking tidepool. "A few hours perhaps, Comrade Generalissimo," the scientists answered when Pak, who appeared to have been turned to stone, failed to speak.

"Excellent. Make it so. I will be taking it with me when I leave tomorrow."

Pak's face contorted and his knees buckled, but he quickly recovered. Swallowing hard, he turned to the technicians and barked that it be done.

Deep inside the rabbit warren of the lab, Professor Yang knelt beside the crude nuclear weapon Hyon-hui had fashioned. He stiffly folded his old legs into a position of meditation he'd not assumed since his youth, unconcerned that anyone would find him. As evening fell, everyone had gathered at the drill field behind the KWP headquarters, just as Hyon-hui knew they would. She was a brilliant girl, he thought to himself. And brave. How he would have been blessed to have a daughter like her. It was an honor to die for her, and for Mitch. He had no regrets as he lit the ceremonial candle he brought with him and placed it on the floor. First, he prayed for Hyon-hui and Mitch to the Christian God his mother had worshipped when he was a child, then made his apology to his ancestors for soiling the honor of his family and his people. At last, he asked their forgiveness and prepared himself for death. He was ready.

"Have you seen Professor Yang?" Pak's voice startled Hyon-hui as she sat in the review stand, two rows behind the Dear Leader. Never in her wildest dreams did she envision herself here – sitting so close to the man she'd worshipped her entire life. She was supposed to be out on the dry dusty field, marching past like the others. But she wasn't. In only a few minutes, simply by being introduced to Kim Jong-il, everything had changed.

And that change filled her with power, as the man who had raped and strangled her, now stood waiting for a response as if nothing had happened. She could squash him as if he was an insect and there would be no consequences. Better, there was likely to be a reward. And greater respect from our Dear Leader. Who knows where that could lead? She'd never dreamt of anything more than being a professor. Now, she might even become a delegate!

Her eyes flickered down to the fake mat of hair on the stubby leader's head. But it was all a lie, just as everything she'd ever known was a lie. The righteous Party. The agricultural perfection of the collective farm. The protection of the guard towers. The technologically advanced lab. All of them were lies. Truth or lies. For the first time in her life, she had a choice.

"Miss Chun," Pak said again. "Have you seen Professor Yang? I have Colonel Phoung and Major Lee searching for him. He was supposed to join the Great Leader and myself at dinner but he never appeared. Did he say anything to you?"

"No," she finally said, looking Pak steadily in the eye. "I do not know where he is."

So that was her decision. The honorable decision, evaporating her lifelong dreams before her eyes. But it was for her mother. For Professor Yang. For a half-century of lies and deceit and men like Pak. For Mitch. Her resolve stiffened. It was time for the lies to end. To be what her mother, and Professor Yang, and Mitch knew she could be.

The Great Leader rose and a hush fell over the crowd. At the cue, Pak scurried to the podium. Hyon-hui looked at her watch. It was 8:03.

"Tonight," Pak began with a thunderous voice, "on the auspicious occasion of the anniversary of the founding of the Workers' Party of Korea by the Eternal President Comrade Generalissimo Kim Il-sung ..." Hyon-hui fought the urge to look at her watch again, and when she succumbed, only moments had passed. She was nervous that something would go wrong, that her plan would not work, and even more horrified that it would. Pak's meaningless laudations were broken only by thunderous applause, far exceeding what would normally be expected for a gathering of only 3,000 people. They waved patriotic banners and flags bearing the symbol of the Party and of the nation. Large photographs of both Kim Il-sung and Kim Jong-il were raised high. Women swooned and prostrated themselves before the *widaehan suryong*. Pak spoke again, longer this time, then the applause renewed.

It was 8:27. Drops of sweat rolled down her neck. The second hand on her watch seemed to slow and stop. Yet, Pak droned on, citing articles from North Korean newspapers and reading dispatches from governments and political parties around the world congratulating Kim Jong-il upon his election as General Secretary. Mostly they were from autocrats, dictatorships, and communist parties across Africa, the Middle East, and Asia, but also well-wishes from France, Russia, and South American nations.

At two minutes to go, a rush of adrenaline kicked in. Hyon-hui's heart began pounding and her face flushed.

Pak reported at length on the fact that something called CNN had shown video on the evening news in the United States, presenting the information as if it were congratulatory.

8:29:30. Hyon-hui's head began to spin and she couldn't remember how to breathe.

"Mass media of many countries," said Pak, "including Cuba, Syria, Uganda, Switzerland, Indonesia, Vietnam, Cambodia, Pakistan, Thailand, Singapore, the Czech Republic and Mexico gave wide publicity to the news."

8:29:43.

"Upon hearing the special communiqué, leaders of political parties and heads of state of many countries extended the highest glory and warmest congratulations to him."

8:29:51.

"Right after the publication of the special communiqué –"

... *six seconds* ...

" – Jiang Zemin of China – "

...*four seconds*...

" – sent a congratulatory message – "

...*two seconds*...

" – to Comrade – "

... one second... Hyon-hui squeezed her eyes shut and waited.

" – Kim Jong-il. Other messages of greetings came to him from Norodom Sihanouk, Bashar Assad, Lansana Conte and ..."

Hyon-hui opened her eyes and blinked. Nothing had happened.

"Don't move, Professor!" Colonel Phoung's voice said cooly.

Professor Yang lifted his eyes to find the man standing on the doorway of the storeroom. "Colonel, what are you doing here?" asked Yang, trying to appear unsurprised and innocent.

"Why are you not at the celebration?" demanded the Colonel. He stepped into the room and saw the professor's candle, now burned down to nothing and tensed as his suspicion heightened. "What is going on in here?"

The old man struggled to his feet. "I am old. I am sick. I cannot sit out in the heat to listen to the ranting of a mad man."

Colonel Phoung removed his pistol from its holster. "I think you should come with me, Professor Yang."

Yang glanced at the makeshift control panel but the colonel caught it. "Don't even think about it, Professor."

"This is not Juche-sasang, Colonel. Pak intends to sell our nuclear weapons to terrorists and emigrate to Thailand. I am no lover of the United States, but sponsoring Islamic revolutionaries to set up religious states is not what the Great Leader, Comrade Generalissimo Kim Il-sung would have us do." He took a half-step toward the switch, a few feet away.

"*Professor!* Don't make me shoot you!"

"I have no quarrel with you, Colonel. You are an honorable man. I give you five minutes. That should be enough time. I would suggest that you not slow down or turn back."

Colonel Phoung raised the pistol and cocked it. "Comrade, I will not warn you again."

"Is this what you want, Colonel? Is this the dream of the Great Leader?" He took another half-step. Phoung pulled the trigger and a bullet slammed into the Professor's chest.

But Professor Yang didn't fall. He staggered forward, gasping as he clutched his chest. Around his hand, his shirt turned a deep red. Colonel Phoung shot again, this time hitting the professor in the arm. And still he didn't stop. The colonel bolted forward to stop the old man, but Professor Yang looked up one last time and saw him coming. He lurched forward and collapsing onto the panel.

Nothing had happened! Hyon-hui's heart galloped, threatening to burst from her chest. What went wrong? Had Professor Yang been caught? Or changed his mind? She stared at Pak, unable to hear his continued drone through the rush of blood through her ears. Mitch. What would happen…

A sharp tremor passed deep through the earth, halting Pak in mid-sentence. Silence descended and the wind could be heard rustling the dry leaves in the trees. Even the locusts and crickets stopped their song. A second later, all heads turned toward the butte above the lab as a new sound filled the air. A huge, misshapen boil expanded on the mountaintop with an indescribable creaking and popping, like a vast army of scimitar wielding skeletons rattling across a field of rocks. In slow motion, it grew as trees and boulders tumbled down its face. And the screaming began.

At the first tremor, Hyon-hui ran, ducking into the heavily-built KWP headquarters building for protection. All at once, geysers of rock blasted from the side, hurling dirt, rocks, and whole trees outward. Seconds later, the sound arrived with a mighty *whoosh* as the fountains of shattered stone grew and merged, transforming the entire ridge into a wave of devastation, accompanied by a deep rolling boom that reverberated through the canyon.

Onlookers screamed and shouted as rocks fell among them. Kim Jong-il's bodyguards sprang over him, trying to shield him from the debris but it was too late. A massive rock arced in and struck the Dear Leader in the face. His head popped like a melon. Hyon-hui screamed, and grabbed at her hair as his lifeless body crumpled to the ground. What had she done?! She stared in shock, unable to move.

A huge boulder cart-wheeled lazily through the air and hit the base of the central guard tower. It shuddered, then fell slowly over, landing on top of the police station. The entire promontory slid free and spilled into the residential section and the collective farm, taking out the transmission towers and plunging the village into twilight.

A dense cloud of dust rolled outward from the collapsed hillside and enveloped the entire valley, blotting out the sky. The public security officers, police, soldiers – everyone ran screaming in all directions.   Hyon-hui stood frozen, just inside the KWP building, staring at the Dear Leader's body, as gray dust and small rocks settled upon it. Kim Jong-il was dead. She had killed the Dear Leader.

She turned and ran. There was something she had to do. Something… What was it? Yes! Mitch. This was her chance. She'd freed her people from the man responsible for the death of her mother, responsible for torturing Mitch, responsible for allowing people like Pak to have power. This was a good thing. It had to be! She sobbed uncontrollably as she ran.

Bok-won stared in a daze through the thick dust at the slumped mountainside that covered much of the residential area, filled the failed agricultural collective, and spilled out half-way to the remains of the central guard tower. "What have you done!?" he shouted to Hyon-hui in dismay.

Hyon-hui clutched his arm and dragged him toward the gate. "I have saved millions!" she screamed.

"The Dear Leader," Bok-won cried. "Is he…?"

"He is fine," Hyon-hui lied. "I saw him. Where is our vehicle?"

"I – I couldn't find one!"

"Well, how are we supposed to get out of here?"

He couldn't answer. His mind was in shock.

Hyon-hui popped open his holster and pulled Bok-won's Makarov pistol out as they ran to the gate. "Open it!" she called to her accomplice.

"*Stop!*" yelled one of the guards, trotting up to them out of the dust, his arms waving. Hyon-hui raised the pistol and shot the man in the chest.

Bok-won stopped in his tracks. "*Are you mad?*" he cried.

The other guard appeared and Hyon-hui shot him, too. "Bok-won!" she yelled in panic over the bodies sprawled on the road, "Get it open, NOW!"

38

"What has happened?" shouted the guards at the Yonjom-dong checkpoint as Hyon-hui and Bok-won stumbled in. "We felt a tremor in the ground. It seemed like an earthquake!"

"An accident!" Hyon-hui gasped, between breaths. "Radiation! Headed this way! Run! Run for your lives!" she cried, wildly waving her arms. Behind them came a mass of people, all fleeing from the mountain. The head guard started shouting something about radiation suits and all of them scattered.

"Radiation?" Bok-won asked, with terror filling his eyes as well.

"No. Bok-won. It is just dust," Hyon-hui hissed quietly. "No radiation. Now we get Mitch!" She eyed the cinderblock building in front of them.

"Follow me," Bok-won nodded, and sprang easily away. Hyon-hui stumbled after him, gasping for breath, her feet on fire.

Just as she intended, the confusion and chaos left the prison virtually unguarded. Bok-won ran up the steps outside and through the door where he dispatched the stunned officer-in-charge with his rifle butt, then burst into the warden's office. The middle-aged man whirled around just in time to catch the butt of Bok-won's rifle in his abdomen.

Bok-won grabbed the man's hair, jerked his head back and shoved the barrel of his assault rifle into his mouth.

"*Where is the American?*"

The eyes of the warden narrowed, suggesting defiance.

Hyon-hui stumbled in and shot him in the leg. "*Where is the American?*" she shrieked.

"Second floor," he moaned through clenched teeth. "Cell seven."

"And the Russian?"

"No Russians," the man groaned.

"Maxim Tarasenko?" Hyon-hui said.

"He's not here," said the warden.

Hyon-hui struck him in the forehead with the butt of her pistol. He fell to the floor and they pilfered his keys.

Mitch jumped down from the chair he was standing on and slunk into a corner at the sound of keys in the door.

"Dr. Weatherby?" came a vaguely familiar voice.

"*Bok-won?*" Mitch questioned as the soldier's bulk stepped into the light of the dim bulb.

"Yes! Yes! We must go. *Now!*"

"What's happe –"

"No time for questions! Quick, follow me!"

Since the tremor, Mitch had been trying to see out the window. He couldn't see anything but after a few minutes, he heard the shrieks and wailing of people arriving in town on foot. There had been an accident at the lab, he concluded. Bok-won must be here to fetch him to safety. They hurried down the stairs and Mitch stumbled out into the lobby and stopped in mid-stride. Hyon-hui was standing in the middle of the floor holding an AK-47. "Hyon-hui?" he gasped. "Why are you holding a –"

She dropped the rifle and threw her arms around his neck. "Mitch!" she cried, kissing his face over and over.

Mitch buried his face in her hair, pressing her to himself. "I prayed I would see you again," he sobbed, "I prayed that you would be okay."

Bok-won pulled them apart. "No time! We must go. Now!"

They grabbed one another again and Bok-won shoved them toward the door. "No time for that! This is a rescue. Move!"

"Wait. A rescue?" Mitch snapped to his senses. He led Bok-won back upstairs, destroyed his computer and set fire to his notebooks while Bok-won opened all the other cell doors. A half-dozen prisoners wandered out and melted into the night, as the three conspirators stripped the dead guard and slipped from the prison as well.

From the shadows along the road, they saw soldiers everywhere with refugees piling up around the gate but there was no organization as yet. "Communications must be out," muttered Bok-won.

"What happened?" Mitch whispered, trying to keep hold of the uniform, the boots, and the pistol they'd taken from the guard. "There was an accident at Sagi-dong, wasn't there?"

"*Shh!*" hissed Bok-won, looking around. "We must find a vehicle or we will never leave this place."

"We have just found one," said Hyon-hui, peering into the gloom. Down the street a set of brake lights flashed, then went dark again.

"I know that car," said Mitch quietly.

"As do I," Hyon-hui confirmed in a frosty tone.

Bok-won motioned for them to stay down, before slinking across the street, where he crouched down behind the car. The door of the Mercedes opened and Pak climbed out. Bok-won emerged silently from his hiding place and doubled over the unsuspecting minister with a single blow to the gut. Mitch sprinted from the hiding place with Hyon-hui right behind him. His foot swiftly met with Pak's fleshy stomach where he crouched on all fours, but he wasn't satisfied with the minister's pained grunt. Mitch snatched the gun from Hyon-hui's hand as she reached him and aimed it at Pak's. "You're dead," he said and put his finger on the trigger.

"*No!*" cried Hyon-hui and thrust Mitch's arms up just as he pulled the trigger. The pistol barked once but the bullet sped into the sky. "We need him."

Mitch's eyes shot to Hyon-hui, wanting to tell her how much he hated this excuse for a man. But he couldn't. This wasn't the time. His finger eased from the trigger and he handed the gun back to Hyon-hui.

"Get him up," said Hyon-hui. "Where's Max?" she demanded, as Bok-won hauled Pak to his feet.

"Dead," gasped Pak.

"You bastard!" Mitch slammed Pak in the gut again, doubling the man over. Mitch jerked his knee up into Pak's face, hearing the crunch as it made contact with his nose. Pak lurched back against the Mercedes and slid to the ground with blood pouring from his face.

"Get in the car! We need to go. Now," said Bok-won, his sharp eyes checking up the road. The voices and sounds of activity were coming closer.

"I'm going to kill you later," Mitch spat. "Soon as we get out of here."

Bok-won shoved the gasping Pak into the back seat and followed him as Mitch and Hyon-hui scrambled for the front.

Mitch spun around in the driver's seat. "*Keys!*" he demanded after finding the ignition empty.

Pak just sat there, staring ahead as if no one had spoken. Mitch leaned back and grabbed Pak's ear and tried to rip it off the side of his head. "*I said, keys!*"

Pak screamed in pain and clutched at Mitch's hand, while Bok-won searched their captive's pockets until the shiny, silver keys emerged. Mitch didn't let go until Bok-won thrust the keys toward him.

"Please!" yelled Bok-won. "Go!"

Mitch turned around and smiled suddenly, staring over the illuminated gauges, massaging the wheel. Twice he gunned the motor and lowered his hand to the shifter. It had been a long time since he'd driven a car, and this was a nice one. "Buckle your seat belts."

"Go!" Bok-won bellowed.

Mitch rammed the shifter into first, gunned the engine, popped the clutch and the V-8 screamed. The tires broke loose with a screech and the Mercedes fishtailed forward. In seconds, they had set the Yonjom-dong land-speed record. The Korean passengers shrieked in terror as Mitch laughed in unrestrained glee.

"My Mercedes!" screeched Pak. "Don't hurt my Mercedes." But Mitch ignored him.

They ran down the lone guard at the gate and sped off on the newly paved road. At the edge of town, Mitch hit the brakes and spun the wheel as they careened around a corner.

"Slow down!" Hyon-hui hissed, grabbing for the handhold on the dash. "You're going to kill us all!"

"I can handle it," Mitch said coolly. "Besides, nobody else is gonna' be on this –"

They rounded another corner and came face-to-face with a huge, eight-wheeled armored vehicle roaring up the road. Everyone screamed. Mitch jinked to his right and the nimble Mercedes hugged the road like a minx. The APC jinked to its right and smashed into a tree.

"*You were saying?!?*" Hyon-hui screeched. "Please, slow down. We've come too far to die in a car crash!"

"*Sorry.* Sorry. My bad." He backed off the accelerator pedal, but just a little. "Now, where are we going?"

Silence fell over the car, and the hole in the escape plan reared up to swallow them. Neither Hyon-hui nor Bok-won had thought of how to get out of the area, let alone the country. They'd focused only on escaping Sagi-dong.

Mitch smacked the wheel. "I thought this was a rescue? You're telling me there's no plan?" he asked in response to the silence.

"I know a place," Bok-won said at last. "At least, somewhere that we can hide for a few days and figure out what to do next."

"Can we hide the car there?" Hyon-hui asked.

"Easily."

"How far is it?"

"About fifty kilometers around the lake. No farther than fifty-five."

"Thirty-five miles," Mitch mumbled, and glanced at the fuel gauge. "How far will this thing go on three-quarters of a tank?"

Pak didn't answer immediately and Mitch slammed on the brakes.

"We can't stop now!" Bok-won shrieked.

Mitch ignored him, spinning around again. "Tie his hands," he said with cold determination. "Use the seatbelt." Bok-won cut it free with his knife and started looping it around Pak's wrists. "That ain't tight enough. Not even close." Pak glanced up, fear in his eyes. Mitch met them and grinned. "Tighter!" Mitch demanded, not breaking his stare. "A lot tighter. Just like he did to me."

Pak cringed as his hands turned purple. "Please, Dr. Weatherby, I never –"

"Shut up!" Mitch snapped.

"How far?" Bok-won demanded.

"Maybe five hundred kilometers," Pak moaned, trying to wiggle his fingers. "Now untie me."

Bok-won moved to loosen the ropes but Mitch stopped him. "No!" Mitch barked. He lifted his own hands into the light showing the scars on his own wrists. "The ropes stay *on*. Now, how do I get us to this place, Bok-won?"

A moment later, they were back up to speed, but not for long. Mitch slammed on the brakes and the car skidded to a halt in the middle of a crossing road. The downhill road from Sagi-dong had run out, and Bok-won said he needed to turn here, to follow the western shore of Lake Nangnim. He backed up and spun the wheel right, dumped the clutch in a cloud of smoke, and tore off with Pak pleading for Mitch to be careful with his car.

Unlike in America, where the roads would be clogged with rescue vehicles, they passed not a single one. Eventually, they would appear, Hyon-hui opined, but they were probably having to move fuel around before they could respond. Mitch shook his head, wondering how such a backwards place could exist. But then he thought about the beast sitting behind him, and the Mercedes they now rode in, and it was all too clear.

"So what happened back there?" Mitch asked, peering into the gloom as he drove.

"Yes," snapped Bok-won. "Did you expect your diversion to be that large?"

"Diversion?" cried Pak. "That was an accident!"

"What happened?" Mitch asked again, more forcefully this time, stealing glances at Hyon-hui.

"It must have been an accident," she repeated, and Mitch saw her glance at Bok-won who looked at her suspiciously and sank back into the seat.

After several more miles, they came upon a little used dirt road that Bok-won told Mitch to take. It snaked back into a narrow valley, growing steadily worse, until they were scraping the chassis on rocks and debris. Pak whined in the backseat. After about a mile, under a waxing moon, they could see what looked like a bridge across a ravine with a railroad track crossing above. Beneath were two black arches and Bok-won pointed to the one on the right.

"That one," he said, and Mitch pulled slowly into it and shut off the motor. He turned on the parking lights and the tunnel filled with an orange glow. It had a sandy floor and there were pieces of wood here and there from high water times but other than that it was empty.

They all crawled out of the car, Hyon-hui limping across the sand, and Bok-won pushing Pak to the ground. Mitch stared into the gathering darkness outside. They were deep inside North Korea, and eventually, soldiers and rescue vehicles would arrive, making escape more difficult. They had limited fuel, and no food or water. And had only Pak as a bargaining chip. He didn't feel good about their chances, but then again, he'd never expected to see Hyon-hui again. Or the outside of a North Korean prison cell. So things had improved – for him at least. "We'll stay here for the night," he said. "Figure out what to do in the morning."

Mitch tied Pak's feet tightly with seat belts then secured him to the rear axle. Bok-won offered to sleep outside on the sandy ground and keep an eye on him through the night. He insisted that Mitch and Hyon-hui sleep in the car. Mitch tried to disagree but didn't have the strength and a wave of exhaustion washed over him and his legs buckled. Hyon-hui helped him into the cabin where they both collapsed onto the supple black leather.

"I never thought I'd see you again," Mitch croaked. He turned his head to find Hyon-hui examining him with her magnificent eyes. His throat suddenly tightened and tears flowed. "I love you," he said quietly, and she opened her arms and he nestled close to her, resting his head on her soft breasts.

Slowly, they began to talk, freely and openly for the first time. Hyon-hui told Mitch about her weapon design and that it had not been an accident. He was glad to hear that the latest bomb they had made had been destroyed, along with much of the work on how to make it. They cried together about Max and Sonny and Professor Yang. And she told him about her mother, her faith, and her heritage. Mitch remembered how his mother had cried when he prayed at dinner. It all made sense now.

"So your grandfather was an American," Mitch said in wonder.

"Yes, so perhaps, I have always belonged there," she said with a gentle smile. "What do you think will happen to us when we get there?"

"If," Mitch corrected her. "If we get back."

"No," she answered firmly. "*When*, we get to America. What happens to us, then?"

"I guess I need Pak alive, too," he said in a somber tone. "I need his testimony." He told her how Pak and Colonel Phoung had set him up to be arrested. How they'd been responsible for Beth's death, and his conviction, so they'd look like saviors to him. He cursed himself for falling for it, and cursed them for ruining his life but Hyon-hui reminded him that they had kept a nation together with such tactics for over sixty years.

"I don't know what they'll do to me back home," he admitted. "I am a convicted felon, even if I was innocent. But my explanation of what happened, and why I did what I did will mean nothing if no one will back it up. I need Pak alive. If we can get him out, it'll make my case that much stronger. I don't want to escape from prison in North Korea only to get tossed back in, in America even if it would be better than this."

Hyon-hui sat up. "You mean they will separate us?" She grabbed his hand, as her voice grew desperate. "They can't take me away from you. They'll have to kill me first. What if we're married?" Hyon-hui suddenly said. "They can't separate us if we're married."

"They can, but it might help," Mitch said slowly, then a light came into his eye. "Will you be my wife?"

"Yes," she blurted, then paused. "How does one get married in your country?"

Mitch scowled for a moment as he considered the question. "A license, I guess. And a ceremony, or at least someone who signs the license to make it official."

"A license?" Hyon-hui questioned in surprise. "Your government determines who and when you can marry?"

"No, no. Nothing like that," Mitch said with a chuckle. "You just have to fill out forms, pay a fee, and …" He paused. Seeing that part of it through Hyon-hui's eyes, it suddenly seemed odd, and uselessly bureaucratic like so many things in this country. He looked at her green eyes, steadily watching him. "That's not the part of it that matters," he told her, then smiled broadly. "You're my wife! Mrs. Mitch Weatherby," he announced. "If I can be your husband."

Hyon-hui startled in confusion. "Is that all that it takes to be married in America?"

"In Vegas, just about," he chuckled. "And I guess that will have to do, because we are lying in a stolen car under a rail trestle in North Korea. Half the KPA could soon be after me. No minister to perform a ceremony. Facing certain death. Unable to consummate —"

"Okay, okay!" she laughed. They kissed deeply then laid back down on the seats exhausted but relishing one another's presence.

"Mitch," Hyon-hui said in a cautious voice. "There is something I must tell you."

The hairs on the back of his neck stood on end from her tone, but he resisted the urge to sit back up. Whatever it was, he could feel the hesitation in her. Maybe it would be easier this way. "Okay."

"I …" She stopped as her breath hitched, not wanting to go on.

Mitch ran his thumb across the back of her hand to comfort her. "I'm your husband, now. You can tell me anything." He felt her head nod.

"Yes," Hyon-hui continued softly. "That is why you need to know." She paused again, mustering her will to speak. "I'm not a virgin," she said quietly. "Pak raped me. If you don't want to be my husband now…" He heard her choke back tears in the dark. "I will understand."

Anger coursed through his veins at the pain in her voice and the fear, but Mitch forced himself to remain calm. "I know," he said as calmly as he could through gritted teeth. "Pak told me when he was torturing me. It's not your fault."

She sat up in shock. "You don't hate me, then?"

"Of course not. It only made me love you more," he said but thought about the man lying outside the car, barely a few feet away. "But it makes it harder not to go out there and kill that son of a bitch right now," he growled, dreaming of ways to accomplish the act – with appropriate and prolonged agony. But Hyon-hui spoke once more.

"There is one other thing, Mitch." He waited in silence for whatever it was. "I… I," she stammered. "The Dear Leader, Com – Kim Jong-il is dead, Mitch."

"What?!" He jerked up straight. "But – how? When?"

"The bomb," she said, through a tortuous mask of agony and pride. "My bomb. I saw him killed."

"Are you sure? Maybe he's just injured."

"No," she said slowly. "No. I am sure. He is dead. He is absolutely dead."

"I love you," Mitch gushed, and folded her lithe body into his arms. She yielded to him and together, in Pak's Mercedes, under a rail trestle in the middle of North Korea, they consummated their marriage.

39

Mitch woke to the cheerful babbling of the stream nearby. The rains came during the night and the previously bone-dry tunnel took on a musty smell. Rivulets snaked down the walls and glistened on the chiseled faces of the stones, turning the clinging moss a vibrant, emerald green. The clock in the dash said it was 5:30. Mitch listened, marveling that, outside his prison home, the sound of water no longer paralyzed him. Hyon-hui lay next to him, her long legs stretched out on the black leather of the seat. He shivered and threw an arm over her thin body, almost laughing at the contrast – him in his lightweight prison garb holding Hyon-hui dressed in her standard Party uniform.

Mitch stared at her for a long time in the pale morning light. Even with the bruises, her face was so beautiful that it made his heart ache. She was his wife now, and he felt a tinge of guilt that didn't simply vanish. He still loved Beth. He loved Hyon-hui, too. And she filled much of the hole left when Beth died. But not all of it. Part of him was gone forever and always would be. But Hyon-hui accepted him this way. That made it okay. Each had experienced savagery.

Hyon-hui opened her eyes and gazed up at him. "Good morning, husband," she said, and pulled him down to her lips.

"Good morning, wife," he said after their kiss, as memories of the previous night filled him with warmth.

"Is it raining?" she asked. Off in the distance came the gentle rumble of thunder. "I like that sound," Hyon-hui said quietly, laying back down. "It is peaceful. The way the Land of Morning Calm should sound." She lifted her eyes to Mitch. "Did you know, this is the first morning of my life that I have not been greeted by the sound of loudspeakers? The first time."

Mitch looked away, his eyes moist, and Hyon-hui's brow furrowed. "What is wrong?" she asked, wiping a lone tear from his cheek.

"So much pain," he answered in a hoarse voice. "And suffering. So many people, abused. Tortured. Killed. Several because of me. But others, thousands before, that had nothing to do with me. I don't understand how it could go on so long."

"Fear," she answered simply. "I don't know how I could have been so blind. How could I have gone through my entire life with my eyes closed, seeing none of this? Not seeing, 'Made in Shanghai.' I feel like such a fool."

Mitch glanced out the window, cleared his throat and looked down. "We're gonna get out of here and you won't have to live in fear anymore. I promise."

"But what of my countrymen?" she asked sadly. "What happens to them when I am gone?"

"All we can do is what we can do, Hyon-hui. We can love each other. That's worth something. Last night was certainly worth something." Hyon-hui smiled and blushed, smiting Mitch's heart with a hammer blow and robbing him momentarily of speech. He cleared his throat. "And we can carry your message. Try to let the world know what's happening here. How bad it really is."

Hyon-hui lay back on the seat and placed Mitch's hand on her breast and held it there with both hands. It sent Mitch's heart racing but her next comment surprised him. "Tell me of your God."

"What do you mean?"

"My mother sacrificed herself for this God. This, Jesus. To save me. But she died before she could tell me anything about it." A darkness swept across her lovely features. "At least, I think she must be dead. You were a Christian once, weren't you? Was that the same as my mother? Why did she do that for me? Why does my country hate it so much?"

"Fear," Mitch answered, almost immediately. "None of this works unless Kim Il-sung is god."

Hyon-hui's laughed bitterly. "Well I have seen Kim Jong-il and he was no god." The bitterness turned to mirth. "The Dear Leader was shorter than me. And bald!"

Hyon-hui settled into Mitch's arms as the Bible knowledge within him poured out like the prophets of old, telling Hyon-hui of how God's people began with Abraham, and following this down through the ages until the birth, death, and resurrection of Jesus.

"This soul you speak of sounds like *chajusong*," Hyon-hui commented, when Mitch slowed. "Do you understand *chajusong*?"

Mitch nodded, remembering his discussions with Lee and Sonny. *Chajusong*, the societal memory of Party members. "I thought that, too. But they are different. The soul doesn't depend on society or other people to exist. It dwells inside each of us and lives on after our death. It's what makes us spiritual beings and connects us with God."

Hyon-hui thought about this for a moment, staring at the clock on the dash. "Well God must consider it very important if he let his son die to save it. I can't imagine Kim Il-sung would have given up his son for anything." She grew serious. "If it is *that* important, perhaps this is why everything has happened to you? So you could come here and tell me of this. There is no other way I would have ever heard."

Mitch was stunned by the enormity of her simple statement. Did God let all of this happen to Mitch to reach a single lost soul in a lost land? Was the value of a soul that great? If that was true, then Beth had died so this could happen? Part of him wanted to be angry about that, but a small, still voice told him that Beth was now with God. With Hyon-hui's mother. He grinned at the though of his dead wife and his new wife's mother talking, probably talking about him!

"What is it Mitch?" Hyon-hui asked, her eyes bright with curiosity.

"Nothing," he laughed, shaking off the revelation. The clock now read 6:45 and the sky, while gray, was growing lighter. Mitch craned his neck to see out the back window. "Better check on them," he said and climbed out.

Pak was still tied up, with Bok-won squatting beside him, telling Pak what it was like in the Army – sparing no details. The soldier rose when Mitch walked up.

"Sleep well?" asked Mitch.

"Not a bit," Bok-won chirped, seeming still fresh.

"Would you please shut this fool up," snarled Pak. "He's been babbling for hours!"

"Army stories," said Mitch flippantly. "Real life. Do you good." He kneeled down at Pak's side and slapped him irreverently on the cheek. "But I'll most likely kill you today so don't be making any plans now." Pak just glared.

"So what do we do now, Dr. Weatherby?" asked Bok-won.

"We need a map or something," said Mitch, looking around. "Anything." He stared at the trunk of the Mercedes. "Maybe there's something in there."

"Nothing," said Pak. "Just the spare tire."

"Right." Mitch got the keys and popped it open. "Just the spare, huh?" he said, lifting out a heavy duffel bag.

He opened the top and poured the contents onto the ground. The first thing they saw was food and water bottles. For the moment, they ignored everything else and wolfed down the rations. Mitch even let Pak have a nibble before turning to the gear.

"Pretty good spare," he said. There was a map, GPS unit, pistol, spare ammunition, satellite telephone, and even a few hundred U.S. dollars. Mitch picked up the thick bundle and flipped through it, amazed that it still had that money smell. "Still think you're headed to Thailand?" he jeered at Pak.

"What's this?" asked Bok-won as he lifted a black aluminum case with heavy hinges and clasps from the trunk. "Heavy," he said, ignoring Pak's glower as he set it down on the sandy floor of the tunnel.

"Let's have a look," Mitch said. Inside the oversized briefcase was a metal panel with a numeric keypad with Korean markings, an LED display, and a hole for a key. The color drained from Hyon-hui's face and she groaned in shock.

"What is it?" Bok-won asked.

"A nuclear bomb!" hissed Hyon-hui. She turned to Pak. "I didn't know it was finished."

"You would be surprised what you don't know, peasant," he sneered.

"You piece of shit," Mitch snarled back. "The nuke, the phone, the GPS unit. You were going to sell this to the highest bidder."

"I want out of this place," Pak snapped. "We can all get out together, and have money to spare. I have buyers ready to pay twenty-million euros for that."

"And give a nuke to the likes of al Qaeda? I don't think so!" Then he looked at Hyon-hui. "But maybe I can use it to buy our freedom."

"There should be a key," Hyon-hui told him.

Mitch roughly searched Pak and found it around his neck. With it, the bomb could be set on a timer, or set to self-destruct which, Hyon-hui told him, would detonate only the high-explosives without causing an implosion. It would destroy the device and disperse the uranium, but no big boom. Mitch had Hyon-hui set it to self-destruct in ten hours so that it couldn't fall into the wrong hands and be used. They'd reset it every hour and hope she was right.

"So what do we do now?" asked Hyon-hui, eyeing the bomb with unease.

Mitch looked over the equipment and picked up the satellite phone. "I'm going to call my brother," he said.

She looked at him as if he were insane. "Call your brother?" she exclaimed. "In America! Can you do that?"

Mitch couldn't get the device to work. Pak stubbornly refused to assist until Mitch buried his head in sand and sat on his wriggling body until he was almost dead. And soon after, Mitch had punched in the access code and stood at the south entrance of the tunnel to get a signal. After the phone established a link, he simply dialed 4-1-1 where he was connected with an international operator. "Hello, may I help you," she said with a lovely British accent. After two years of North Korean abruptness, Mitch nearly wept at the sound. He asked her how to dial the United States and she did it for him, then took Steve's number. The first time it rang, Mitch's heart fell into his feet. What would he say? He wanted to hang up. It rang several times and he finally heard somebody fumbling with the handset on the other end. It was only then that he realized it was the middle of the night in New Mexico.

"Yeah," said the voice, at once both groggy and anxious.

"Steve," said Mitch.

"Yeah," said the voice again, a little clearer, and a little suspicious.

Mitch swallowed hard. "Steve, this is Mitch, your little brother."

There was a deathly pause that lasted a good five seconds. "I don't know who this is," the voice on the other end said with deep anger, "but that's a pretty sick joke. Now –"

"Don't hang up!" blurted Mitch. "Steve, I swear to God it's me. You remember that abandoned mine where you dropped dad's lantern and we lied to get you out of trouble?"

There was another pause and Mitch heard Steve say something, probably to his wife. Then he heard him return to the phone. "Who is this?" he asked again, this time with more suspicion than anger.

Mitch smiled in spite of their situation. "Steve, it's me. I'm not dead. They didn't kill me on that bus. They replaced me with a double and flew me out on a helicopter."

"I knew it!" cried the voice, and Mitch could hear sobs of joy from the other end. Tears streamed down Mitch's face too, as he realized how much he'd missed his family. He explained to Steve where he was and what was happening and that he and his wife needed help getting out alive but that the government would want what they had.

"You're married?" shrieked Steve.

Mitch laughed and told him the abbreviated story of Hyon-hui. "Tell him, hi," Mitch said, thrusting the phone into her hands. He was giddy with excitement.

She refused and pushed the phone away but he kept on until she lifted the phone and shyly said, "Hello, Steve," and gave the phone back to Mitch, glaring at him.

Steve decided to call the New Mexico governor to get the ball rolling on his end. Being a DA in Santa Fe, he was well versed in the hot buttons of local politicians, and thought that the bait of a top level defector and inside information on the North Korean nuclear program would be the intelligence coup of the decade. They had no idea what the plan would be, but at least it would put things in motion.

"I'm going to call Mom and tell her," Steve said, as their conversation drew to a close. "I can't believe you're alive! God, I can't believe it!"

"No! Don't you dare tell Mom," Mitch hissed. "She already lost me once and chances are we're not going to make it out of here alive. And we sure don't want the press to get a hold of this. You've got to swear to me that if I don't get out she'll never know where I've been for the past two years."

They ended their conversation with promises and hope. But when Mitch cut the connection, the reality of his situation collapsed back in like an unstable mineshaft. They were in the middle of nowhere in North Korea with over a hundred miles to the nearest coast, and those miles were filled with guard stations, check points, and citizens eager for the chance to turn someone in to better their own fate. They would never get that far. And even if they did, they didn't have a boat to get out of this cursed country. But at least it was a destination – a goal to make their way toward. Mitch scanned up and down the coast of the map, looking at the tiny villages, when his finger suddenly stopped at one: Kumho-ri. A memory flickered, giving him an idea.

"Kumho-ri," he said aloud, and everyone looked at him.

"What does that mean?" said Hyon-hui.

"KEDO," Mitch replied with new found hope brimming within him. Kumho-ri was the site of a huge construction project funded by the Korean Energy Development Organization, a shell company established in the late nineties to manage the construction of two light-water reactors in exchange for North Korea claiming to drop its nuclear program. As far as Mitch knew, due to the starts and stops, they were probably still working on it after all these years. "There'll be Internationals there," he said. "Maybe even Americans. We can plead for asylum."

Mitch called Steve back and told him their plan. Steve had already talked to the governor and things were beginning to move, but he didn't know when he'd know more or what would happen. But at least now, there was a location to give them. Kumho-ri.

40

"Which way?" Mitch asked in a tense voice. After leaving the concealment of the rail tunnel a half-hour before, the fugitives came to the paved road at the same place they pulled off the previous night. With the wet ground, it had been much slower going. Mitch stopped not far from the intersection and the car sat idling in the darkness. Waist-high scrub brush and spindly trees concealed their presence. Drops of rain spat from the sky and dotted the windshield. It was amazing the Mercedes hadn't become stuck.

Bok-won studied the GPS unit. Mitch had showed him how to use it but he still didn't trust it. "Take a right," he said calmly. But Mitch didn't move, just sat with bowed head.

"What are you waiting for?" snapped Pak. He still didn't budge. "What is his problem?"

After a momentary pause, Hyon-hui asked, "Mitch, are you okay?"

It was a full minute before Mitch lifted his eyes back to the road. "Just asking for help. We're not going to get out of here without some." He pulled the car onto the hard-surface road and accelerated into the darkness with the lights off, straining to see the sides. Fortunately, it was North Korea and there was no traffic. None. Mitch knew that was normal but it didn't calm him.

Bok-won glanced at the GPS unit as the road began to snake back and forth up the hill. They were between the south end of Lake Nangnim and the Chosin Reservoir on the same road they'd taken out of Sagi-dong for the test. "Carefully, Dr. Weatherby. There is a checkpoint ahead." The road was now rising steeply, twisting and winding up the side of a mountain, clawing for the low point between two dark peaks that straddled the ridge line like giant sumo wrestlers. The top could appear around any corner.

"How many guards at the checkpoint at the top of the pass?" Mitch asked, knowing this was but the first of many hurdles. SSA posts were located in most of the villages and all of the county seats according to Pak's map. And even if they got past all of them, as they approached the coast there would be border patrol, a concentration of guards near the naval base only ten miles south of Kumho-ri, and, of course, police.

"I don't know. Perhaps three, maybe more. Why do you think I would know?" Pak snipped indignantly.

"There's no way were gonna get out of here!" Hyon-hui groaned. "This prison has too many guards. Too many walls."

Mitch knew they needed to stay calm, so, although his hands gripped the wheel tightly, he began describing America to his companions. Walmarts and Targets, bursting with food and consumer goods. Cars everywhere and restaurants, too.xz People from all over the world – different races and nationalities – choosing to make America their home. And with them, churches of various faiths on every corner. Pak muttered that he was lying, but Bok-won simply sighed, longing to see them for himself.

The waxing moon had slipped below the western horizon around midnight, leaving the night dark as a dungeon as they blindly made their way up the hairpin turns. At the top, the checkpoint eased into view with the dim glow from a dark, rectangular shack with a stick protruding from the side – the gate – a hundred yards away.

Bok-won peered forward into the darkness. "Looks like two of them. There will be a third inside. Back up a little." He turned to Mitch with round eyes. "I'll get rid of them."

"There's got to be another way," Mitch said. "You can't do that."

"I've seen too much," said Bok-won. "What they did to you. To Max. I can't stay here." He swallowed heavily. "In ten minutes, I want you to pull forward and turn on your headlights. Okay?"

"Roger that," Mitch answered.

Bok-won pointed at the clock, then looked at his watch. "Ten minutes from… now."

Bok-won leapt from the car handing his pistol to Hyon-hui in the passenger seat. "Keep him covered but don't shoot him. Okay?" he said, nodding toward Pak. "A gunshot will bring everything in for miles around." The big man turned and melted into the night, scrambling up the rocky slope on the right side of the road.

Hyon-hui glanced at her watch. It seemed to be running slower than usual. She glanced at Pak who was sitting behind Mitch. Then back to Mitch. "What is this KEDO?" she asked. "How does this help us?"

"It doesn't," Pak said smoothly.

Hyon-hui glared at him and her finger twitched on the trigger.

"In 1994," Mitch said ignoring Pak, "the U.S. made a deal with Kim Il-sung. It was called the *Agreed Framework*. If he shut down Yongbyon, we'd build you guys two nuclear plants, and – "

"Impossible!" she snapped.

Mitch just shook his head at the North Korean reflex to deny anything that challenged their world view. "If we make it there in one piece, you'll see. And if we don't, then it really doesn't matter, does it?" He paused for a moment before telling them some details of the agreement. When he was done, he gave them the punch line. "Now, there's a large international presence there. Americans, Japanese, French. If we can get inside the fence –"

"You will not get in the fence," Pak broke in. "It is heavily guarded. And even if you do, there is an agreement in place stating that you will be handed back over to the North Korean authorities."

"So you know about this?" Hyon-hui said, narrowing her eyes at their hostage. "It is real?"

"Yes," Mitch interjected. "It's real. And I'm fairly certain the agreement applies to North Korean citizens, not abducted American scientists." Pak tried to interrupt again but Mitch raised his voice to talk over him. "Carrying a nuclear warhead from a supposedly suspended nuclear program!"

"You can't get into the KEDO site," Pak stated flatly. "There is no way you –"

"Shut up! I know a way. I've seen it!" Mitch barked back. They both looked at him like he was crazy.

"Mitch," Hyon-hui said slowly, "you've never been there."

He shook his head at how little they understood. "Los Alamos doesn't just build nuclear weapons," he explained. "We also monitor nuclear programs. I've seen a lot of photos of that site and I know a way in." Pak demanded that Mitch tell him but Mitch refused.

"None of this matters anyway," Pak snarled in frustration. "Because even if you get all the way to America, even that won't matter!" The black pit of Pak's face was pierced by two glints of light where his eyes half-hid beneath his thick lids. "If you get out of the DPRK you will just go straight back to prison!"

"He's not going back to prison!" yelped Hyon-hui.

"He's a traitor," repeated Pak. "Of course, he's going to prison. They may even kill him."

"That's the only reason you're not dead," Mitch growled. "Because when we get out of here, and we will get out of here, you're going to tell them all about how you cooked up your little scheme to blackmail me."

"And send me to prison?" Pak scoffed. "I don't think that is going to happen."

"Oh, they won't send you to prison. You answer their questions and they'll treat you real good." The very thought of Pak avoiding the punishment he deserved made Mitch's intestines knot, but it was the only way they could get out of here and Mitch stand a chance of gaining his freedom. A fair price to pay to be with Hyon-hui.

"You may not like it, Dr. Weatherby, but I am a survivor. As long as I am in the DPRK, I will do what is necessary to survive." His snake-like eyes darted back and forth between them. "*I* can get us out of here. You and Bok-won and that telephone, there is no way."

"You think we'd trust you," Mitch said. "After what you've done? And what do you get out of this?"

Pak grunted. "Kim Jong-il is dead. I saw him killed." He paused, clearly expecting them to jump, but neither of them moved. Pak cleared his throat and went on. "His death will not be announced to the world for some time. There will be a power struggle. I anticipate his son, Kim Jong-un will succeed him. Kim Jong-un and I…" He paused and cleared his throat.

"Don't see eye-to-eye," Mitch chuckled.

Pak shook his head slowly. "I have no desire to be ruled by a spoiled brat who is the son of a spoiled brat. *I* can get us to freedom, Dr. Weatherby. And if you are captured, I don't believe you are prepared for those consequences. If you think waterboarding was bad, imagine this lovely lady hanging naked in the air by her hands, so that her toes just brush the ground, while being stripped of her flesh centimeter by centimeter, pulled from her smooth breasts like an orange peel. Have you ever seen a nipple torn off? I know men who will eat it as you watch. And you *will* watch. And you *will* hear each scream. She will not be beautiful when –"

"Okay!" Mitch fired back, wiping the ghastly image from his mind. "And what's your plan?" he challenged. "Once you get us out of here, what then?"

"We use the bomb to buy our freedom. I have the connections to do this. You don't think –"

"Never!" hissed Hyon-hui. Her eyes were locked on Pak, but she directed her next comments to Mitch. "All he speaks are lies. He thinks we will not escape and hopes to turn us in so that he can secure his place in the new order. I would rather see him a rich man in America than have him returned to any position of power over my people. If it means risking a slow and painful death, so be it! But I will not be taken alive."

"You don't have to do this," said Pak.

"Shut up!" barked Mitch, glancing at the clock as time drew near. "Does Bok-won know that Kim Jong-il is dead?"

"I don't think so," answered Hyon-hui. "And I don't think we should tell him."

Pak agreed with her for a change. "It would be hard to get out, if we were all dead. We should not mention that you killed his Dear Leader."

Hyon-hui glared at Pak, as Mitch started the engine and inched forward until they could see the checkpoint. "Now!" said Hyon-hui when the glowing green number changed. Mitch turned on the lights.

The guard jumped a foot in the air and ran to the middle of the road. Two more men followed him from inside the guardhouse. Bok-won's dark form appeared behind them and seconds later, with ninja-like precision, all three were dead.

41

"We're about 90 kilometers from the coast as the bird flies," Bok-won said, as Mitch sped the Mercedes around another blind turn, praying that nothing was on the other side. They were headed south along the winding east shore of the Pujon Reservoir, separated from the sea by the rugged Cho Gyuryong Sanmaek mountains. "But we're not a bird so it's more like 130. And the road will be worse in places. We may have to slow down."

"We are *not* slowing down," Mitch barked.

"Pujon-up," said Pak, looking at the moving display in Bok-won's hand. "There will be a checkpoint there."

"That's only about twenty-five kilometers," added Bok-won. "And there is another town on the other side of the mountains, Pukch'on. There will be a checkpoint there, too."

"So how's our time?" Hyon-hui asked with a yawn

Bok-won frowned. "Not good." He put his finger on the map at a crossroads on the other side of the mountains. "I'd say if we're not here by oh-four hundred, we will encounter more difficulty. It will be daybreak and this valley opens up. No cover. Hundreds of villages."

There was a momentary lull in the conversation. Mitch tried unsuccessfully to relax. In the seat next to him, Hyon-hui wearily closed her eyes. Pak leaned back in his seat and rubbed his face. Mitch yawned, too. Only Bok-won seemed fully awake and alert.

"Are you okay, Dr. Weatherby?" asked Bok-won from the backseat.

Mitch nodded and yawned again. "I'll be okay. It's nice to drive a car again."

The reservoir to their right fell away a half hour later and the road began to rise. Mitch knew they were nearing the next checkpoint. He glanced in the rear view mirror to see Pak snoozing.

"Wake him up!" Mitch snapped and Bok-won nudged Pak in the ribs.

"This checkpoint," Mitch said again. "Any ideas?"

"Use the American dollars to bribe him," said Pak groggily.

"Just like that?"

"Let me drive. You and Comrade Chun sit in the back. I will bribe him."

"Do we look stupid or something?"

"Do you have a better idea?"

Mitch eyed him in the rear view mirror before pulling over and switching places. Pak was now in the driver's seat with Bok-won beside him. Mitch shoved the pistol hard into the back of the seat so that Pak lurched forward.

"That's the barrel of this gun," Mitch said.

"How much you think he'll want?" Hyon-hui asked.

"We'll overwhelm him," Pak said.

"Couple of hundred dollars?"

"That would make him the richest man in the county."

This checkpoint was a narrow concrete block building with a thick, deep set window. The gate was heavy black steel, and the whole thing was sheltered beneath a high concrete portico. Mitch was reminded of a toll booth except there was nowhere to put the quarters. The place was dark and seemed unmanned, until they approached.

A light switched on and a gaunt young man, no older than twenty-one stepped into the road. He held up his hand up for them to stop and the cuff of his uniform, made for someone who ate well, slid up to his elbow. If he was surprised by the bright red convertible, his wary eyes didn't show it.

"Make it smooth and don't try anything," Mitch whispered to Pak, leaning back into shadow. His hand tightened on the *Makarov* pistol. Its narrow grip felt good. "The exit wound from a nine millimeter is about the size of a baseball."

Pak pulled to a stop and the electric window slid down with a whir. With any luck, the tinted rear windows and darkness would conceal Mitch. The guard barked a request for their papers, and sensed that something was wrong when he glanced into the backseat and saw Hyon-hui rigidly staring straight ahead. He took a quarter-step back, but froze as Pak casually held out the bills, the way he would his credentials, using the man's body to shield the money from the guard still inside.

"Annyong haseyo," Pak said casually. From his comfortable demeanor, Mitch guessed this wasn't his first time to bride a guard.

The guard's eyes danced back and forth between the money, Pak, Bok-won, and Hyon-hui. The sweat beading on his forehead told them he was probably wondering if he was being set up. Pak placed another twenty on the stack. Then another, bringing the total to $240.

The guard stared at the wad of cash. Food for his half-starved family. New clothing to replace the rags they were wearing. Medicine. A doctor visit for an ill son. A kerosene heater for the winter and fuel for it to burn. Perhaps even a television set and a refrigerator. The basic decision was really not all that difficult. He was held at bay by the same thing that drove every North Korean mad with paranoia. Was this real or a test?

The guard took the money and examined it as if it were official papers, keeping his back to his partner in the guard shack. He pretended to give them back, tucking them into the top pocket of his tunic instead, and waved them through. As they pulled from beneath the portico and headed into Pujon-up, the light switched back off.

"How do you know he won't talk," Mitch asked, looking back.

"He just became the richest man in Pujon County," Pak told him confidently. "Why would he give that up?"

Like every other North Korean town, Pujon-up reeked of raw sewage even as it was immaculately clean, with not a scrap of litter in sight. The county seat had a single, paved avenue with dirt side-streets, all lined with square, unadorned concrete buildings, none more than three stories tall. One building was marked as belonging to the Nangnim Mining Cooperative, but everything else, including streets, was blank. The only light in town was aimed at the bronze sculpture of Kim Il-sung in front of the Party building. They passed quietly through to the south side of town, reaching the shell of an ancient, bombed-out factory with a set of shattered smokestacks.

"Korean War?" Mitch asked as they passed it by.

"Victorious Fatherland Liberation War," answered Pak. "There are many such sites in Choson."

"Why don't you tear them down and rebuild?"

"And forget what the Americans did to us?"

Mitch opened his mouth to respond when another light flipped on ahead of them. "What's that?" he hissed.

"Another checkpoint!" said Bok-won.

Mitch shoved the barrel of his pistol into Pak's neck, pressing it in, just beneath his ear. "*What is this?*"

"I didn't know it was here!" he cried. "I swear! There used to be only one. I haven't been here in years!"

"It is true, Dr. Weatherby," said Bok-won. "It was not here the last time I passed this way."

"*Crap!*" Mitch fished in his pocket and came out with the rest of Pak's cash. "Eighty bucks. Shouldn't have gone so high on the last one!"

"It'll be enough," Pak assured him.

The soldier strode to the middle of the road and put his hand up. Behind a thick glass panel, they could see another guard slouched inside. Mitch leaned back to avoid the security light shining through the front window. Unlike the last one, it lit the interior, leaving him like a roach caught out in the open.

Pak stopped the car and went through his routine again, flopping the bills casually out on the edge of the door. "*He's gonna see me!*" mumbled Mitch, clenching his teeth.

The guard stooped and peered in, then made eye contact with Mitch, who swore under his breath.

"*Mee-gook-in!*" cried the guard, stumbling backward as he grabbed for his pistol.

A deafening shot rang out, as Bok-won moved like lightning. The guard flailed backwards, as the bullet passed through the open window and hit him in the chest. He collapsed against the glass, leaving a bright red streak on the pane as he slid to the ground. His comrade jumped out of his seat, frozen for a moment in shock and fear.

"Punch it!" cried Mitch.

"The gate is still down!" Pak cried.

Bok-won aimed and fired.

The bullet hit the glass leaving a small, white crushed area about the size of a silver dollar. Behind the bulletproof glass, the guard scrambled for the telephone. A knife flashed in Bok-won's hand as he cut through the convertible top and bounded out.

"My Mercedes!" shrieked Pak, grabbing for the ripped cloth of the roof. Mitch shoved the gun into the back of the seat to shut him up, before jumping out of the car himself.

In the guard shack, Bok-won sliced through the phone cord with an upswing, then dispatched the shrieking guard with a wicked downward slash that nearly cut the man's head off. An instant later, the gate swung up with a whir.

Mitch nearly drug Pak into the backseat, while Hyon-hui scrambled into the front passenger seat. Bok-won circled the car and kicked in the rear lights with his heavy boots.

"What are you doing," screamed Pak. "You are destroying my Mercedes!"

"Just go!" Bok-won shot back, as he leapt over the trunk lid and dropped into his seat. Mitch hit the gas and they roared out of Pujon.

"The foxes are out of the den now!" yelled Bok-won above the din of wind and flapping canvas.

"We're going to be captured!" cried Hyon-hui. "They're going to find us!"

"Not if I can help it," Mitch yelled back.

"My Mercedes," moaned Pak, staring at the flapping shreds of the roof. "Where will I get it fixed?"

"Which way?" called Mitch, slowing at an intersection.

Bok-won consulted the GPS unit for a split second. "Straight," said Bok-won. "In about twenty-five kilometers, start looking for a dirt road off to the right. I'll let you know when."

They tore off, climbing high into the mountains along a twisting road, slick from the intermittent rain. Long drops into a steep valley appeared first on one side, then opened up on the other. Mitch drove as fast as he dared, and perhaps a bit faster, at times nearing 150 kilometers per hour. But if they didn't escape, death by auto was far preferable to anything the North Koreans would have in store for them.

Hyon-hui closed her eyes and clutched the grab-bar above the glove box so tightly that her knuckles turned white. Pak was no better off but kept his eyes open. Both cried out each time the car slid on the wet pavement.

Bok-won was unbothered by the speed, cutting away the remnants of the top with his knife so he could keep watch out the back. "I hope it does not rain again," he laughed, throwing the last of the black cloth away.

The road narrowed at the top of the pass, then dove steeply down for a few miles, then headed up again. At the top of the next pass, they saw behind them, on the other side of the valley, a sight they had feared since their harrowing journey had started. Tiny beams of yellow light crested the mountaintop and stabbed into the darkness behind them. One set. Two. Three. Four.

Mitch applied the brakes at a turn and suddenly understood why Bok-won had smashed the taillights. They couldn't be seen from behind. "Where's that turn?" Mitch asked. "We ought to be there by now."

Hyon-hui whipped around and saw the dim, green, phosphor glow from the GPS unit reflecting in Bok-won's eyes. "We'll let you know," she yelled. "Just drive!"

"Getting close!" Bok-won announced a few minutes later. "Closer. Closer. We're here!"

Mitch slowed and looked to the right. "Nothing but rock!"

"Slow down some more," said Bok-won calmly.

"Not slow down!" Pak yelled, frantically staring out the back. The vehicles behind them continued down the valley. Visible one moment, then hidden behind a spur of the hills, then visible again.

"Is that it?" shouted Hyon-hui, peering into the darkness. She pointed to a lighter patch among the rocky shoulder.

"It isn't the same on the map," said Bok-won, studying the GPS.

"You're going to get us lost in these mountains, Weatherby," Pak whined.

"Just going to have to trust in the Lord." Mitch gunned the engine and made for a muddy, narrow track disappearing into the night. But he didn't slide onto it. He didn't want anything to give away their course, least of all, fresh dirt and gravel slung all over the road. So he stopped, squared up, then accelerated hard up the steep hill. The car climbed away from the road, but the mud became loose and the car slipped, barely clawing its way up. They all leaned forward as if it would help, and Pak whimpered like a frightened child.

"We did it!" Bok-won cried as they spun over the top.

"I'm driving German for the rest of my life!" Mitch swore. An instant later the tires grabbed onto bare rock and launched forward. He stabbed for the brakes and slid to a stop just as they bounced through a deep rut.

Pak and Hyon-hui were both thrown into the floorboards. Bok-won was still staring out the back and seemed almost nonchalant. "Not only do you shoot well," he said with admiration, "you are a good driver, too, Dr. Weatherby!"

After taking a deep breath, Mitch urged the car another hundred yards along the rutted, little-used track until the highway below was completely out of sight. They all scrambled out and hid in the brush. Mitch tried to call his brother while Hyon-hui reset the bomb self-destruct to ten hours. When the satellite lock failed, Mitch stumbled back down the dirt track to where Bok-won was hidden, peering down to the highway below them. Within only a few minutes, a line of jeeps passed on the road.

"That was close," said Mitch.

"And they won't stop looking," said Bok-won, watching the taillights disappear around the bend. "Not until they find us. We have not NATO's nighttime sight ability, but when daybreak comes, there will not be a rock that does not have a soldier standing up on it or a peasant looking beneath it. We must hurry."

They reached the small clearing where the car waited, to find Hyon-hui holding Pak at gunpoint. "He tried to get away," she snapped, glaring at him down the barrel.

"I did not," Pak retorted. "I just have to use the bathroom."

"Go over the edge," said Mitch, pointing to the ledge to the side of the worn and rutted track.

"The other one. To make dirt, not water."

"Bok-won?" said Mitch, and thumbed over his shoulder. The soldier seized Pak by the collar and pulled him into the darkness.

"So how do we get out of here?" whispered Hyon-hui when they were gone. "You said you had a way."

Mitch turned on the GPS, showing that on the other side of the mountain, the road ran down into a valley and paralleled the meandering Kumamdae River, passing through several towns before ending at the coastal town of Chunghun-ni. Kumo-ri was only a few miles east, on the other side of the river.

"Nuclear power plants require a lot of concrete," Mitch began. "The foundations and containment vessels alone require thousands of cubic yards. And the primary ingredients of concrete are gravel, water, and cement. The cement is shipped in, but the water is being pumped straight from the river, and the gravel dredged from the bottom and shipped in on a short railroad track. I've seen it on satellite photos." He and his colleagues had followed every stage of the construction, and he knew the exact location of the aggregate site downstream from Puk'chon. "All we have to do is sneak onto the train and bury ourselves in gravel," he said proudly, having never imagined that piece of information, idly gleaned from Google Earth, would someday be the difference between life and death.

"Do you think it will work?" Hyon-hui asked cautiously.

"Do you have another plan?" he asked, knowing there were a dozen things that could go wrong. But he had no other options.

42

At four-thirty in the morning, the Mercedes sped back onto concrete, a few strips of the cloth top flapping in the wind like little black flags. The eastern sky was still dark, but it was no longer black as they descended into the broad Kumamdae River Valley. A winding road ran through its fertile fields, following the river to its mouth at Chunghung-ni. Had it been lighter, they would have been able to see the ocean.

Mitch's fingers were numb as he fumbled with the heat control knob and turned it up to high. "How much farther," he shouted over the wind whipping through the car.

Bok-won studied the GPS unit, then turned back to the map. Pak helped him hold it or else the air would have stripped it from his hands. Their current road followed a mountain stream swollen with rain, until it joined with the Kumamdae-chon proper, doubling its volume. At the confluence stood a village where they planned to steal a boat and take to the water. "About twenty-five kilometers," Bok-won called.

They wound down the mountainside until, in the near dawn light, the narrow valley could be seen slanting away below them. Silver-gray fog clung to its surface and they could hear the river roaring down in a ravine to their left. Farther down, the valley flattened out and the river wound through it like a thick rope, bloated from the rain.

"Slowly," cautioned Bok-won as they rounded a low hill. His GPS unit and the map told him that on the other side, the rivers came together and were spanned by the bridge. "Stop. Let me go survey what we're facing."

Mitch brought the Mercedes to a halt and it sat idling like a steaming horse after a race. He glanced at the fuel gauge, about a needle's width above empty. "About out of gas," he said.

"Give me five minutes!" Bok-won jumped out and ran down the road about fifty yards, to where it doubled back. He left the road there and headed up the hillside, disappearing into dense pine trees.

"We should reset the bomb," said Mitch from the driver's seat. Hyon-hui joined him at the trunk and pulled out the heavy black case. It had only ticked down a few hours since their last reset.

"How long do you think?" she asked, opening the case with the key hanging around her neck.

Mitch stared into the sky. He had no idea what was going to happen next. It would be daylight and the closer they came to the coast, the greater their chance of being caught. They might need to seek shelter. It was close to five o'clock right now. "How about four hours? Should get us inside the KEDO site."

Mitch watched in awe as his bride reset the device to 3:59:59 and it began ticking down. He couldn't have ever imagined thinking such a thing, but Hyon-hui's beauty rivaled Beth's, perhaps even surpassed it. One thing about these Koreans, Mitch had learned, all the weak ones had died so those that remained were near perfect physical specimens.

She closed the case and caught him looking but he didn't turn away. "Why are you looking at me like that?" she asked curiously.

"No reason, Mrs. Weatherby," he answered with a smile, and her own grin spread even wider.

"Somebody kill me now," groaned Pak, snapping Mitch from the joy of his wife.

"Don't tempt me," Mitch growled and slammed the trunk closed. There was nothing he'd enjoy more than putting a bullet or two into Pak's brain pan, but he needed the sadistic slime.

"This is your last chance, Weatherby," Pak said cooly from the back seat. "We leave now or we'll all be dead in a few minutes. I can get us out of here. There is no way you will get through Pukch'on. No way."

Mitch didn't bother to look at him. "I have an idea," was all he said.

"We are all going to die doing it your way."

"Just you," Hyon-hui said, pressing the barrel of her pistol against his forehead. Pak glared. But Hyon-hui's finger on the trigger never wavered, waiting, until Bok-won emerged out of the woods and trotted back over to them.

"Bridge is guarded," Bok-won panted as he reached the car. He cast a glance at the pistol to Pak's head and Hyon-hui lowered it, at least for now. "Six armed soldiers."

"Six! What are we going to do?" she asked.

"I could scale the hill again," Bok-won said. "Work my way across the ravine and attack from behind as you come in from the front, like we did at the first checkpoint."

"It will take too long," Mitch said, scowling as he stared toward the bend in the road. It had grown noticeably lighter in the past few minutes. "Frontal assault. We surprise 'em, get in close, put the guns on full-auto, spray and pray."

"Do you think –" Hyon-hui started, but Pak interrupted her.

"Kim Jong-il is dead, Bok-won," he said coldly.

"What?!" cried Bok-won, whipping toward Pak in shock. "The Dear Leader?" Mitch tightened his grip on the pistol in his lap. "It cannot be!"

"He's lying," assured Hyon-hui. "You can't trust him. He raped me. Tortured Mitch. I saw Kim Jong-il standing after the blast."

A wild light came into Pak's eyes. "He's dead I say! Her diversion killed him. Hyon-hui murdered the Dear Leader! Are you going to listen to a murderer? Don't let her get away with it? I saw him! I saw him killed! His head smashed by a flying boulder from her blast!"

"And you're only now mentioning it?" Hyon-hui questioned. "Why didn't you mention it earlier."

Pak flung his hands up in frustration, but Bok-won still stood frozen. Mitch didn't want to shoot him, but time was short.

"Guys, we kind of need to get moving," he urged.

"I tell you, the Dear Leader is dead!" Pak exclaimed. "You as a sworn soldier of the Korean Peop –"

"You're trying to divide us," snarled Bok-won.

"Of course, he is," Hyon-hui cried. "He wants us to be captured!"

Bok-won remained still, looking back and forth between them, before nodding once. Without taking his eyes off Pak, he asked Mitch, "What is spray and pray?"

"Spray bullets. Pray to God."

"Spray and pray?" repeated Bok-won doubtfully. "Careful, aimed fire is always the best alternative."

"But we'll be in a speeding car. You got a better idea?"

"But the entire valley will hear the gunfire, Mitch. What then?" Hyon-hui wanted to know.

"Hop in the Mercedes, and go for it. We're out of time." Mitch pointed at the sky. It was growing steadily more light and there was no cover from here on out. It was now or never, and they all knew it.

"We are all going to die," stated Pak as if he were an oracle.

Bok-won ignored him. "Yes. We are out of time. To stay any longer ensures our capture. Yes, Dr. Weatherby. Spray and pray."

Bok-won pulled the two AK-47's he'd collected from the first checkpoint from the trunk, checked the magazines and handed the full one to Mitch, the other, almost full, to Hyon-hui. "I know Dr. Weatherby knows what he's doing." He gave Hyon-hui a questioning glance. She said nothing but pulled back the bolt and inspected the magazine. It was enough for Bok-won.

"What about me?" Pak asked, broodingly.

Bok-won picked up a rock, and slapped it in Pak's hand. Pak bristled, and threw it into the roaring river. Mitch winked at Bok-won. "You're going to fit in great in America."

Bok-won smiled back. "I want to see this Walmart you have told me about."

"They're everywhere," Mitch said, and Bok-won just shook his head and smiled as he climbed into the car.

Mitch inched the Mercedes forward to where the road curved. Around this bend, Bok-won told him, the soldiers would be about fifty yards away, at the very edge of the range for un-aimed fire, especially coming from untrained troops in a moving vehicle.

"Okay then. Everybody ready?"

Mitch punched the accelerator and the car leapt forward, careening around the corner on two tires and closing the gap with surprising speed. Bok-won stood up in the backseat, bracing himself against the skeleton-like convertible-top frame. Hyon-hui stood up, too, resting her AK across the top of the windshield. Pak cowered in the back seat behind Mitch. On the bridge, the soldiers jumped up and scrambled to bring their weapons to bear, Mitch turned on the high beams to blind them.

Bok-won and Hyon-hui opened up and the rattling of their guns filled the valley. Soldiers fell and dove for cover. Rocks in the bridge sparked and splintered. Bullets striking their vehicles lit up like tiny fireflies, winking on and off.

Mitch heard a distinctive popping-crunching sound, and the radiator erupted in a spout of steam. Hyon-hui screamed but kept firing. The windshield cracked and filled with little pockmarks. Someone grunted in the backseat. Mitch slammed on the brakes and they skidded to a stop only yards away. He leapt out and shot a struggling soldier with his pistol. Another one moved and he shot him, too.

And it was over. They stood panting as the sound of the battle echoed off the hills. Dead and dying men lay scattered about the bridge. Bright green radiator fluid poured hissing from the Mercedes, mingling with the blood oozing from the soldiers. A dog barked. And below, the river roared.

"Mitch!" cried Hyon-hui.

He spun around and there was Bok-won, sprawled across the trunk. A bullet had passed through the windshield and slammed into his abdomen. He lay there, groaning in pain, his blood almost invisible against the car's red paint.

"*Bok-won!*" Mitch yelled, running wildly around the wounded auto to reach him.

The soldier opened his eyes and grunted, "Go, Dr. Weatherby. *Go!*" On the hillside, doors slammed and voices called out.

Mitch jumped back in the car. "Pull him in!"

He pressed onward, knowing that they wouldn't make it more than a few miles before the engine overheated. When they reached the valley floor, the hissing was almost gone and the temperature gauge was dropping. Mitch knew exactly what that meant; almost out of water. But they were out of the mountains.

The road flattened out and Mitch brought the car up to 100 miles an hour. Muddy fields whipped by on either side. A boat ramp flashed by on their right, reached by a quarter-mile track through a muddy field. Mitch slammed on the brakes and the Mercedes skidded nearly a hundred yards. He turned around and sped back to the access road.

"You'll get stuck!" cried Hyon-hui.

Mitch set his jaw and floored the accelerator again. "Don't fail me now," he muttered as the sports car left the paved road. The tires spun and flung mud and the engine shrieked, but the indomitable Mercedes moved forward, making it to the pitted concrete of the ancient boat ramp, where the rattling and knocking motor told Mitch that it was over.

"Everybody out!" he ordered. Just yards away the taupe water flowed swift and strong.

The engine heaved one last time and died. They pulled Bok-won from the car and laid him in the mud as it started to rain. His skin had grown the color of wet concrete. His dark eyes, staring into the gray sky, were mere slits. "Spray and pray not good," he groaned.

Mitch knelt at the stricken soldier's side. "Bok-won!" he cried. He cradled the dying man's head in his lap, leaning over him to keep the rain out of his face. Hyon-hui knelt down next to him and took the young soldier's hand. Even Pak edged in to watch. Blood mixed with the mud and formed a red-brown pool.

Bok-won's eyes opened further and looked up. "Dr. Weatherby…" he said weakly. "Kumho-ri… Get there… Get out… Get Chun away…"

"You're gonna' be alright," Mitch said instinctively. "You're gonna make it." He searched the man's face, watching the life drain away like the water dripping off his face.

Bok-won mumbled something weakly.

"What?" Mitch asked, leaning over and put his ear to the dying man's lips.

"Walmart. I would have…" came the words again. One hand squeezed Hyon-hui's, the other clutched a handful of mud and it squeezed out between his fingers, then fell limp.

"What did he say?" Hyon-hui asked, shielding her face from the rain with one of her long hands. Mitch just shook his head and squeezed tears from his eyes. She felt for a pulse, then looked up at Mitch and shook her head. "His soul is gone."

Mitch bowed his head. He thought of Beth. He thought of Max. And Sonny. And Professor Yang. The soldiers at the bridge. Now, Bok-won. How many more would die before this nightmare was over? The pain, the frustration, the profound loss rose up, overwhelming him until a guttural roar burst from his throat.

Hyon-hui took his hand and as the sound died, letting Pak's hysterical ranting intrude.

"…you think you're going to get out now? Now that you've killed all those soldiers. It's too late!" he said shrilly. "Too late, Weatherby! We're dead. All of us! You've killed us!"

Mitch ignored him and knelt down by Bok-won in the drizzle. He put his hand on the dead man's forehead and said a silent prayer. "I'm sorry, my friend," he whispered as he pulled Bok-won's eyes closed. "Fubar," he whispered.

"Well?" Pak said impatiently. "How are you going to get out now? You should have listened to me."

"Shut up," Hyon-hui snapped.

"Now it's too late! You've killed the Dear Leader. You've killed us all."

"I said, *shut up!*" Hyon-hui shrieked through her tears.

With one last look at the man who'd given his life, Mitch rose, determined to make sure that sacrifice at least was not in vain. He emptied the trunk of the automotive carcass. "Help me get him in here," he said, placing his hands beneath Bok-won's shoulders. Once the dead soldier was inside, Mitch slammed the trunk shut. Bok-won deserved better but this was the best he could do. He released the emergency brake and stood back as the Mercedes rolled down the ramp toward the seething brown water.

"No!" Pak wailed. He rushed forward and grabbed the bumper, pulling with all his might, but on the slick, wet concrete, his feet could find no purchase and the car inched slowly toward the water. As the current grabbed the once beautiful convertible, Pak had to let go,wailing as the water sucked it under. "Now what do you –" he began blasting, wheeling around toward Mitch, and found himself staring down the barrel of Bok-won's Makarov.

"It's gone," Mitch said evenly, not wavering with the gun.

"*Jon-cha!*" Hyon-hui yelled, pointing down the road.

From the direction of Pukch'ong-up came four huge iron beasts from the Soviet era. Eight-wheeled, armored personnel carriers, their tires roaring over the pavement, throwing waves of water off the road.

Pak lifted his arms to wave to them, but Mitch struck him on the back of the neck with the pistol, buckling his knees, then dove forward and drove him the rest of the way down. Hyon-hui flattened herself beside them, and they waited. After minutes that seemed like a year, the drone of the motors had died away. They'd not been seen.

"We gotta get out of here!" Mitch said, raising his mud-smeared face. "We'll have to float for it."

"Float?" Hyon-hui questioned, eyeing the muddy current in the hundred yard-wide river. She turned pale and trembled. "I thought… a boat. We should use a boat!"

Mitch looked in both directions. "Do you see a boat?"

"I cannot swim, Mitch. Not at all."

"You won't have to," he answered, pointing at a log floating not far from the bank. "Wait here." He shoved the pistol into her hands. "And keep your eyes on Pak."

Mitch sprinted toward the river, and launched himself off the bank, disappearing into the murky, brown water. He resurfaced almost immediately and swam madly toward the tree. It was several hundred yards downstream by the time he reached it, stretching to a good quarter mile when he'd finally towed it ashore. Mitch stumbled, shivering, onto the bank and collapsed.

On the launch ramp, Hyon-hui pointed the gun at Pak, motioning him to lift the bomb, while she grabbed Bok-won's pack. With another gesture from the pistol, they trudged off across the mud that climbed over Hyon-hui's feet with every step. Her shoes were sucked off to remain captives of the wet land. She wiped the sweat from her face and kept going, following behind Pak with her head down. Up on the road, a police car sped by with its lights flashing. But its occupants didn't take notice of the two downtrodden Koreans wallowing through the sticky brown goo in a scene repeated endlessly across the Worker's Paradise.

Mitch was kneeling beside the salvaged log, breathing hard when they reached him. His face was pale, and the swim had left his flimsy prison garb and hair slicked down.

"Are you okay?" Hyon-hui asked.

"I don't feel too good," he said shivering with the cold.

Hyon-hui reached down. "We must keep going, Mitch. Cannot stop now or it will be too late. Come on. Come on!"

He took her hand but groaned as he rose. He swayed for a moment with his eyes closed and rubbing his forehead. "I think I'm gonna' throw up."

"No time to throw up!" Hyon-hui commanded firmly. She grabbed his shoulders and turned him toward the water. "C'mon Pak!" she called over her shoulder, but there was no response. Hyon-hui spun around to find him trudging determinedly across the muddy field, hauling the bomb on his shoulder! "*He's trying to get away!*" she shrieked.

Their hostage was already twenty yards away but he could not run. The weight of the bomb sank him in the mud up to his ankles with each step. Hyon-hui pulled out the Makarov and fired.

BOOM! "You bastard!" she screamed, as the round went high, slapping into the rice paddy on the other side of the road.

"*No!*" Mitch shouted, snapping out of his stupor. "It's too lou _"

She pulled the trigger of the nine millimeter again. "I'll kill you!" She broke into a stream of Korean that needed no translation.

Pak dove, landing face first into the ooze. Only inches away, another round slammed into the ground and sprayed mud and sand into his face so hard it stung. His bowels went limp and his pants filled with the waste he'd been unable to rid himself of with Bok-won watching. He crawled ten yards on his hands and knees, then leapt to his feet and started running again, leaving the heavy bomb behind. Two more bullets zipped by, emptying the pistol. He glanced behind to see Hyon-hui raising Bok-won's AK-47 to her shoulder. He ran faster, never looking back again.

Hyon-hui's finger barely squeezed the trigger of the assault rifle when she heard a grunt from behind her. "Mitch!" she cried, spinning around to see him clinging to their 'boat' as it attempted its own escape. With one last look at Pak, Hyon-hui threw down the rifle, and joined Mitch pulling the log back to shore. She retrieved the bomb from the mud, dragging it back to the river bank where Mitch lashed Bok-won's pack to it and draped them over the log. Once convinced the bomb was secure, they shoved off into the freezing water, lying safely atop the broad trunk.

"Pak is gone," Hyon-hui said as they floated downriver. "That is not good."

"We'll get out," Mitch assured her as best he could. "It's not far now."

"But you said you need Pak, at home, in America. You need him to say why you are here."

"I know," Mitch confirmed, willing himself not to think of it now. Pak's testimony would have helped him a lot, but they weren't going back for him now. "With what you know – the things you can confirm – maybe they will believe me."

The river moved at a steady clip south between low mountains on either side, carrying them past the fields at their feet. They glanced at the shore as the town of Pukch'on approached. Unlike an American city, the buildings – low, colorless structures – were built on an elevated rise a quarter-mile back from the water's edge. In the distance, three big hillside slogans made from colored rocks proclaimed Juche in Korean script.

The long span of a bridge emerged from the fog, reaching not just over the river, but across much of the floodplain on either side of the main channel. There was no one on it yet but Mitch could see people ashore. Whether they were farmers getting ready for the day or soldiers mobilizing they couldn't tell but, to be safe, Mitch and Hyon-hui lowered themselves until just the tops of their heads were poking out of the water until they passed beneath the span.

"Is the g-g-gravel site m-much f-farther?" Hyon-hui stammered when they emerged downstream. Her teeth were chattering and her lips were blue. The first stages of hypothermia. Mitch was cold too, but Hyon-hui was smaller, losing heat much faster.

"Close now," he assured her, having no idea where the gravel quarry was relative to where they were but he needed her to hang on.

When he could no longer see the bridge behind them, Mitch pushed himself up on the log. Barely visible through the morning mist, the top of a tall steel crane emerged, maybe a half-a-mile away. "I see it! I think we found it!" he said excitedly and lowered himself back into the water to be ready to paddle to shore.

Around the next broad bend in the river, the entire site was visible. The crane was sitting on a barge in the middle of the river and on the right bank rose a high retaining wall of logs. Atop it sat gravel sorting machinery and just beyond, the railroad tracks Mitch had expected, with two hopper cars and a diesel engine. But the entire area was crawling with people arriving at work. Dozens stood along the shore, exercising to stay warm in the dawn chill.

"We're t-t-too late," said Hyon-hui, and they again lowered themselves until just their heads showed, and floated on past. "What do we do?"

"I don't know," Mitch said quietly. That train had been his only plan. He had no other, and downstream, he saw only more drab river banks and fog.

"Mitch!" Hyon-hui hissed again. "What is your plan?"

"I know, I know!" he shot back. It had all seemed so possible and now he had nothing. Just like that, it was gone. The aggregate site faded into the morning haze and they were still freezing in the water. He had no backup. Nothing.

Swept along by the river, the mountains that rimmed the north side of the valley gradually receded into barren fields. To their right, steep, rugged hills dotted with short pine trees marched closer. The cold seeped through them, and it was getting harder to grip the log. They'd come so close, Mitch groaned inwardly. So close. He mumbled a dozen frantic prayers but didn't feel like he was connecting.

"What are we going to do?" Hyon-hui stammered, near tears. "We cannot float all the way to the sea."

Mitch looked at his wife's blue lips and the graceful, graying fingers that clutched to the log. He wanted to curse himself for bringing her to this – only to watch her slowly fade away before him. He closed his eyes tightly. This couldn't be how it would end. Just get Hyon-hui out of here, he prayed. He didn't care what happened to him, as long as she was safe.

A low, brick structure appeared on the right bank. Beside it sat a large, cylindrical fuel tank surrounded by a chain link fence topped with curls of razor wire. A concrete boat ramp led down to the water and a half dozen men meandered about, waiting for the work day to begin. But on the boat ramp sat, of all things, a yellow hovercraft almost exactly like the one they'd used down at Heard Island.

"KEDO!" Hyon-hui exclaimed excitedly as they drew closer, reading the stencil on the large hoop that encircled the stern-mounted fan. "I almost didn't believe you."

"It's the pumping station," Mitch commented, trying to remember where it had appeared on the satellite photo.

Hyon-hui looked at him suddenly with wide eyes. "Mitch!" she hissed.

Mitch smiled and nodded. "Exactly what I was thinking." He glanced at Bok-won's pack where the barrel of his rifle poked through a fold in the cloth. No one on shore was armed.

43

"Comrade Captain!" recited the patrolman, snapping to attention as he entered the border guard station. "We found –"

"*What are you doing back here?*" demanded the green-clad captain. "You just left!"

"He found me," Pak announced, stepping around the guard. He eyed the shabby receiving room with its few desks. A map of the area, in addition to the obligatory pictures of Kim and Kim, hung on the wall, and the balding captain rose from his chair.

"Who are –" the man began to ask.

"Pak Yong-nam. Minister of Atomic Energy Industry and delegate to the P'yongyang Party Assembly."

"His papers," said the border guard, handing them to his superior.

After scanning the documents, the captain raised an eyebrow at the bedraggled stranger and crinkled his nose at the unmistakable odor he brought with him. "What happened to –"

"Traitors carrying stolen contraband took me hostage," Pak answered firmly. "I only just escaped with my life. They are attempting to flee the country. It is imperative that we apprehend them and return this property to Marshal Kim Jong-il."

The captain nodded and picked up the phone but Pak placed his hand on the cradle to stop him. "No, Comrade Captain. This is politically sensitive and could embarrass the Dear Leader. I know where these traitors are headed and how they can be apprehended." He strode over to the map, ready to muster a search, when he realized no one had followed. In fact, the patrolman had moved the other direction, away from the stench of human waste. Pak's jaw set, as he addressed the captain again. "What are your –"

"Comrade Minister," interrupted the captain suspiciously. "It is standard procedure that I alert Central Military Command and –"

"Captain," said Pak quietly. "If you ever interrupt me again, I will have you shot. Do you understand?"

The officer pulled up short. Something was wrong. They were already on alert, and regardless of his titles, the captain suspected that the man standing before him, dripping wet with pants full of his own waste, may know something about the attack on the military patrol at the bridge. At the very least, Pak wasn't telling everything. This could be a set up, or worse. His eyes flitted to the patrolman who'd joined two of his colleagues, trying to look unnoticeable on the side of the room. Witnesses to whatever response he made. He needed to play by the book. "Comrade Minister, with all due –"

"Arrest this fool," Pak snapped to the patrolmen. At the order, they glanced uncertainly back and forth. "Arrest him!" Pak cried with mounting furor.

Haltingly, the patrolman moved toward the captain who stood motionless, staring at Pak with a mixture of fear and loathing. "You're making a mistake," the captain said to his men. "I don't know what's –"

"Handcuff this traitor, gag him, and throw him in your cell!" The captain didn't try to resist as his men restrained him. Once bound, Pak looked him in the eye. "Tomorrow morning, you will be shot."

Within minutes, Pak and his three new subordinates, eager to show their allegiance, were staring at the map. Pak fingered the spare key to the bomb he had kept in his pocket. Something had told him to bring the extra key and now he was glad that he had.

"What are your assets," Pak demanded to know.

"Under our direct command, Comrade Minister, we have three patrol cars, a helicopter, two shore patrol boats here, two at Chunghung-ni, a coastal defense ship at Tanchon-up. The other border guard locations in Pukch'ong County are under our jurisdiction as well and have –"

"Recall the cars you sent north."

"But the Sojangnae-ri bridge was atta –"

"Do you want to join your captain? Make your wife a widow like his will be?"

The frightened man bowed repeatedly. "Accept my apology, Comrade Minister!"

"Leave Sojangnae-ri to the Army. Have the helicopter fueled and placed on standby. I may need it. See that both patrol boats are manned and ready to go, as well as the coastal defense vessel. Call in all border guard personnel in Pukch'ong County and place them on alert. Give them strict orders to keep the operation silent, then seal the county border."

"Central Military Command has far greater assets, Comrade Minister," the older patrolman offered. "Shall I –"

"Do you want to be arrested, too?!" Pak shrieked. "Can you not follow simple orders? Perhaps I will suggest that the Dear Leader visit this station and teach you all some respect!"

The man lowered his head, his jet black hair shining in the dim light.

"How about the rest of you?!"

They, too, stood silent and submissive.

"Do not question me again!"

Pak paused, calculating his next move. "Tell the other stations to detain any Westerners they find, along with any vehicles they may be traveling in. But do not conduct any searches. They are to call us here, and we will conduct the searches when we arrive. Is that clear?"

"Westerners, Comrade Minister?"

"Do you have a problem with that?"

"No, Comrade Minister."

"Then why are you standing there, you fool? And get me some dry clothes. And some breakfast!"

The telephone rang and Pak's new second in command answered it. A second later he lowered the receiver in astonishment.

"Well," barked Pak, "What is it?!"

"An American man and a woman just stole the KEDO hovercraft at gunpoint!"

*

"You didn't have to lock them all up!" Hyon-hui said for the tenth time.

Mitch and Hyon-hui were in the enclosed, truck-like cockpit of the hovercraft. Mitch had only just begun to get a feel for the controls. Hyon-hui was at his side. "What was I supposed to do?" he said back. The roar of the huge, ducted fan mounted at the stern was just a faint hum with the cabin door closed. "They've probably already busted out and called the authorities. So you're right. I shouldn't have locked them up. I should have killed them."

"Mitch!" Hyon-hui exclaimed. "And what would your God think of that?"

Mitch shook his head, thinking about the last two years of his life. "I don't know, but you'd be surprised what God is willing to do when he wants something."

Speeding down the river at a healthy thirty knots, they hadn't reached the sea but the blank horizon told them it was there. Farms were everywhere beside them, filled with well-tended crops ready for harvest. Here, next to a river flowing through the most fertile land in North Korea, even the Juche system of agriculture couldn't fail. A sandbar cropped up in front of them, and Mitch tried to swerve to avoid it, but failed. Yet, the hovercraft slid right over it without so much as a ripple.

"How much farther to the coast?" he asked.

Hyon-hui studied the GPS unit. "About six kilometers. This is an amazing device Mitch."

He glanced at her and smiled. "In America, everyone has one of those these days. Even kids."

She examined the clunky, mil-spec device in shock. "Like this?"

"No, actually it's a lot smaller than that. About like a pack of cigarettes. And it also has a camera, a calculator, a television, intern – you don't know what the internet is, do you?" She shook her head in the negative. "Oh, and a telephone. You can take with you anywhere."

"Anywhere?"

"Even in the grocery store," Mitch laughed, thinking about how people abused their technology by talking loud in the produce aisle, taking the convenience entirely for granted. He prayed to have such minor distractions once again as he scanned the river in front of them. He couldn't believe they were going to get out of here uncontested but, so far, they were alone. Even the people on the last bridge had barely noticed them, obviously being used to the strange vessel going back and forth on the river. "Check behind and see if anything is following us," he asked Hyon-hui.

She opened the rear cabin door and stepped into the twelve foot-long well deck behind the cabin. The drone from the massive propeller and the hiss of the wind drowned out everything else.

"Nothing," she shouted, scanning the horizon as she shielded her eyes with a slender hand. She came back in and shut the door. "What do you want to do with the bomb? It's been at least an hour since we set it before the checkpoint."

"See how much time is left on the clock."

Hyon-hui opened the case, lying on one of the rear seats of the cabin. "Less than I thought. Only about two hours."

It was getting dicey, Mitch thought. He wanted to cut it close so in case they were captured the North Koreans would not have enough time to deactivate it, but enough time that Mitch and Hyon-hui would have a chance to reset it if they needed to. At the moment, it looked like two hours might be too much time. "Why don't you set it for an hour. We're getting closer to the coast. We'll reset it every thirty minutes."

Hyon-hui stooped to perform the reset as Mitch scanned the river in front of them. It was widening rapidly now into a broad, flat sheet of brown, reflecting the morning sky, so he knew they must be getting close to the river mouth. The GPS unit showed that the natural mouth of the river was a half-mile wide, but that the exit to the sea was only a few hundred feet wide at the most. Either the action of the waves or a stream of North Korean dump trucks, had walled off most of the opening with a narrow sandbar. It looked natural but, either way, it left a very narrow gap through which to make their escape.

Hyon-hui appeared beside him, pale as a ghost. "What's wrong?"

"The key," she asked slowly. "Do you have it?"

"You mean to the bomb?" Mitch questioned. "I thought you had it!"

"I can't find it anywhere. It must have slipped off in the river!"

Mitch blurted a string of curse words, his stomach tightening at this new twist. No matter what happened now, he would not have the bomb. Which meant... he needed Pak all the more. No one was going to believe the wild story of lies and deceit based solely on his wife's corroboration of minor details. Not without some physical proof.

Hyon-hui was bowing and profusely apologizing, but it wasn't her fault. Mitch couldn't even remember who had been carrying the key. He assured her that, somehow, it would be okay, but she apologized again, only to cut off in mid-sentence.

"Mitch," Hyon-hui said, pointing off the port bow.

It was exactly what he had been fearing. Two boats rapidly approaching. A glance at the GPS confirmed his suspicions. They'd come in from the narrow channel to the sea, now only about a mile away, and were blocking their exit. Their only options were to turn around, ram the boats and destroy themselves, or run aground on the wide sandbars blocking them from the ocean.

"That's it. We can't get out," Mitch said numbly. "All this way and we can't get out!"

"Mitch," said Hyon-hui.

"I can't believe it," he went on. "Even after finding the —"

"Mitch!" she said a second time. "It's a *hovercraft*! You can go right over the sandy parts."

Mitch eyes sprang open and he let go of the wheel and kissed her, then seized it once more and veered to the right. With any luck their pursuers would follow them, boxing themselves in.

At first, Mitch wasn't sure they were going to respond, but after a half a minute it was clear that they had changed their course to follow their hovercraft into the aquatic cul de sac. Mitch looked up at the sky and muttered, "Thank you, Lord," before giving Hyon-hui a big smile. "We might get out of this yet, baby."

Her brows came together in a frown. "Why do you call me a baby?"

Mitch laughed. "It means, I love you,"

Hyon-hui found binoculars in the glove box and watched the two vessels come around. They were small runabouts no longer than twenty feet in length. And while they knew their hovercraft could go places the surface boats could not, the border guard craft were much faster. They closed, but before they were trapped, they turned in arcing loops to head back the way they had come.

"They figured it out," Mitch muttered as he pushed the throttle to full. "They're going to try to cut us off on the other side."

"At least no airplanes," said Hyon-hui trying to be upbeat. But the words had no more left her mouth than a thumping sound roared through the air. A helicopter flew over, barely fifty feet high, sending Mitch and Hyon-hui instinctively ducking below the dash.

"No, airplanes?" Mitch cried. "Just helicopters!"

The helicopter hovered off their bow and matched their course. They faintly heard a voice over a PA system. Mitch opened the door. "… is impossible! Bring your speed to zero immediately or you will be fired upon!"

"That's Pak!" Mitch said, trying to see up to the helicopter. "I know it is!"

Hyon-hui stared out the side windows through the binoculars. "It is Pak! This means he has not notified the military!"

"He wants to catch us himself and take the bomb," Mitch agreed.

"Yes, but it also means we will not have ships out here trying to stop us!"

That was better than Mitch expected, but it still left a problem. "We still have a helicopter and two patrol boats. That's not a lot better."

The sandbar, no more than a few feet above the water, was rushing toward them fast. Beyond it, a bright blue sea was dazzling, even on the cloudy morning – a striking contrast to the murky, rain-swollen water of the river.

"Brace yourself," Mitch barked, and Hyon-hui clutched a grab-handle tightly. But it wasn't necessary. The transition from water to land was almost imperceptible. The sun came up, shooting through a gap in the clouds as they sped over the flat, smooth sand, and in less than ten seconds reentered the water. The world filled with a blinding golden light. Mitch felt a rush as the hovercraft bumped over the breakers that rolled in from the sea. They were out of North Korea! Against all hope, against all odds, they were outside the wall.

"Something is different," Hyon-hui said, staring strangely toward the open sea. Mitch felt it too, as his skin broke out in goosebumps. "It is like we have been in a cave, and here, there is suddenly light and color."

Bathed in the sun's warmth beaming through the windshield, Mitch gazed at Hyon-hui. Tears were brimming in her jade eyes and rolling down her smooth cheeks. She was right. Mitch remembered the darkness that enveloped Kim's statute that day in P'yongyang and knew that same darkness permeated the entire country. And now, it was gone – from the glistening sea before them, and from his own soul. He inhaled deeply, feeling a great weight being lifted. Hyon-hui touched Mitch's face and her hand came away wet. Mitch took her slender hand, squeezed it lovingly and kissed it.

Spray from machine gun fire hitting the water just in front of them covered the windshield, jerking them from their thoughts.

The helicopter overshot them and whipped around, throwing the tail high in the air, before roaring back, machine gun fire blazing from the side. The water alongside the hovercraft erupted in a line of white geysers. They could see Pak on board waving his arms and screaming as he grabbed at the gunner.

"Weave!" Mitch barked to Hyon-hui as he left her to the controls.

"Weave? What does that mean?"

"Serpentine. Like this." Mitch sliced his hand through the air making a series of tight, S-like turns.

"Oh! Okay! To make us harder to hit."

"Exactly. Pak doesn't want to sink us. He just wants us to stop." He scrambled out of the cockpit and into the open well with Bok-won's AK. Flipping off the safety, he readied himself for their next pass. But the helicopter remained behind them, waiting. "I don't like this," shouted Mitch, fighting to keep his balance against the waves and Hyon-hui's meandering path. "He's waiting for something. Go ahead and straight –"

"Mitch! Get up here!" cried Hyon-hui.

Joining her in the cockpit, he saw why. Two boats were headed down the coast, either the same ones as before or ones just like them, moving to cut off their escape route.

Mitch pointed at the shoreline. "It's a hovercraft," he yelled. "Use it!"

Hyon-hui turned their vessel back to shore, as Mitch ducked back out to keep an eye on their pursuers. But back wasn't the way they needed to go. She scanned across the sea, and quickly turned back toward the path of the patrol boats.

"What are you doing?" Mitch cried. "They're gaining!"

Hyon-hui was making for one of the gaps in a string of rocky islets. The tallest plug of black stone rose over a hundred feet from the water. At its crowned summit, an old Japanese lighthouse stood alongside a North Korean radar site. On its seaward side, separated by a hundred feet of frothing, white water, was a much smaller shoal, less than twenty feet high. Smaller, shorter islets, tending to mere rocks strung out in a line beside them.

"*What are you doing?*" Mitch screamed, rushing back into the cabin.

"It's a hovercraft!"

"But it can't fly!"

Their pursuers were closing quickly, only a few hundred yards behind as they reached the string of islets. They could hear the sporadic stutter of automatic weapons, as little geysers erupted around them. As they entered the shoals, the border craft veered to the right to race around the plug and meet them on the far side.

"When you get through the pass," Mitch yelled into the wind, "whip it to starboard and cut power. We can't outrun them so I've got another idea!"

"Starboard?"

"The right! To the right!"

"The right?"

"The right. The right," he yelled, motioning in that direction.

Mitch returned to the well deck, checked the magazine of the Makarov, and stuck a spare in the waist band of his pajamas. The islets loomed up on either side of them. The black, moss-covered cliffs of the taller one teemed with sea birds and the echoes of waves. To the left, the rocky shoals of a tiny beach. Between them, surf tossed, splashed, and turned to foam on the sharp, barnacle encrusted boulders.

Hyon-hui gritted her teeth, preparing for a bumpy ride. "Hold on!" she yelled to Mitch. But they roared over the shoals with barely a ripple.

In the middle of the channel, Hyon-hui turned the rudder hard right and cut power, taking them dangerously close to the cliff that rose straight out of the water like some kind of colossal tree stump. The sound of their pursuers disappeared as they drifted around the back side of the rock. For a moment, all was peaceful. All they could hear was the low rumble of the diesel, the slap of the waves, and the crying of seabirds wheeling above. For an instant, Mitch thought what a beautiful place this was, then stood up and aimed the rifle at where he expected their pursuers to emerge from behind the rock.

The first boat flashed out in a burst of noise and spray. Mitch pulled the trigger, eating up half his mag and but only hitting around the craft sending it into a chaotic dance. The second one appeared an instant later and roared past the hovercraft. They noticed their error and tried to turn, but it was the wrong thing to do. The boat slowed, leaning hard to port, which gave Mitch a big, slow target. Mitch drew a bead and unleashed a hail of lead into its cockpit. Heavy black smoke poured out and bodies crumpled.

"Punch it!" yelled Mitch. With a whoosh and they surged forward, throwing Mitch backwards, into the heavy wire mesh that protected the fan.

With the remaining boat still giving chase, Hyon-hui had no choice but to head to the beach. She raced along in the surf, crashing through the waves half in, half out of the water. Mitch looked into the cabin from his crouch in the well deck and saw the wipers going. For some reason it seemed humorous.

"*Dug!*" Hyon-hui cried from the driver's station.

"What?!" yelled Mitch.

"Pier! Bridge! In front of us!" She pointed to a jetty of concrete and stone, reaching out to the sea. They were too high for the hovercraft to mount, but even if they made it to the other side of the first one, the patrol boat could easily trap them in the artificial bay they formed.

Mitch crawled into the cabin as Hyon-hui swerved right and pulled up onto shore, flying across the sand. A dump truck flashed by and workmen dove out of the path of the on-rushing hovercraft. Ahead, a sandy hill rose gently from the beach forming a bluff. At its foot was ocean with no beach at all. To the right, trees bumped up to the base of the hill. Behind them, the helicopter shadowed their every move.

"Where does this go?" Hyon-hui yelled, steering the hovercraft up the hill.

"The wrong way!" But there was no other way to go and they were already ten feet above the waves and rising. Glancing out the window, they were clear of the bay formed by the jetty, but the remaining boat had pulled even with them, her crew staring up in amazement.

Mitch seized the wheel and pushed Hyon-hui out of the way, jerking the rudder to the left. "Hang on," he cried.

"*You said it can't fly!*" Hyon-hui screamed, as they shot off the edge of the thirty foot embankment.

And they flew. It was more like riding a sheet of paper to the ground, and with the rear fan still blowing, to the astonishment of all – and especially to Pak, watching from his vantage in the helicopter – Mitch steered the hovercraft with surprising agility and settled it down squarely on top of their remaining pursuers. A single burst of automatic weapons fire came from below, punching a line of holes through the open deck, followed by a horrible crunching sound. The hovercraft shook and vibrated and clanged like a lawn mower in a field of rocks. Suddenly, the ride smoothed out and ran steady, with only a slight flutter. Behind them, all that was left was a bit of flotsam and the dark outline of their pursuer's craft just below the white froth of their wake.

With a snap of his wrist, Mitch pointed the bow out to sea.

"What happened?!" Pak screamed, staring down at where the border guard patrol boat had been but an instant ago. "What happened?!"

"We must go pick up the crew of the other boat," said the pilot, swinging the chopper to the right. "There were injuries."

"*No!*" Pak ranted. "Follow them! I order you to follow them!"

"We can't, Comrade Minister!" replied the pilot, holding the controls firmly. "We don't have the fuel."

Pak slapped the seat hard in frustration. "Radio ahead. Have your ship at Tanchon-up steer an intercept course. We will rendezvous with her and you will drop me off."

"Me? I don't have that authority!" cried the pilot. "I'm just a pilot!"

"Do it," Pak ordered. "Or you will die."

44

Mitch stepped out through the cabin door into the wind and noise. The fan at the stern droned like a B-29, and a row of ragged holes glared from the yellow fiberglass deck, eight black dots in a neat line about six feet long. The wind whipped by at thirty knots. With the throttle pushed to the stops, the craft should have been moving faster, but it had been fast enough. The shoreline, twenty minutes back, was nothing but a thin white line on the horizon, and no one was in pursuit.

The sun shone down on him, as he punched in the code to check the timer on the bomb's self-destruct – 2:15:50… 49… 48… 47…

Hyon-hui stepped into the sunlight as well. "Do you think your brother has been able to do anything?" Hyon-hui asked, voicing the fear that festered in the pit of his stomach.

Mitch peered out, squinting into the glare. "It's only been a few hours. This would travel up the chain pretty quick. But it's still only a few hours."

"Have you tried your brother again?"

Mitch shook his head. "Can't get a satellite. Your people might be jamming the phone."

"They're not my people anymore," Hyon-hui replied. "With my mother gone, there is nothing left for me." She looked back toward land. "I wonder why they don't send aircraft or helicopters to stop us."

"Pak hasn't told them we're here," Mitch muttered. "He'll do anything to get this bomb for himself so he can sell it. With Jong-il dead, he's no better off than we are."

"We cannot let that happen, Mitch."

"No, we can't," he agreed. He glanced into the cabin at the short-wave unit in the dash. "Maybe I should use the radio. Send out a mayday."

"But it will give away our position. And if they don't know where we are –"

"I know, I know. We'll be in international waters soon, if we aren't already. But if there isn't anyone around to claim us, lot of good it's going to do if the bad guys find us first."

While they were talking, he took the magazine out of the Makarov and looked at the top.

"What is it?"

"Just making sure there's at least two bullets left. Just in case." Hyon-hui stiffened at his words. Mitch's mouth twisted in a wry grin. "You know, Max said it would end like this."

"End like what?"

"He and I were talking one day – it was on the bow of the *Mikisan Maru*. On our way back from Heard Island. It was the night we found out we were going to P'yongyang and all of you guys got medals." She nodded, remembering. "I told him that I was in love with you, and he said situations like this always end up like *Romeo and Juliet*."

"Romeo and who?"

"You know, Shakespeare?"

She shook her head. "No."

Mitch shook his head. It didn't even surprise him. "No, I guess you probably don't. It's a play. It's probably the most well-known literary tragedy of all time. At the end, Romeo and Juliet kill themselves."

"I haven't heard of it."

"You're livin' it." They retuned to the cabin and rode in silence while Mitch searched the horizon with the binoculars. "So much for luck," he mumbled after awhile, staring through the glasses to the north. "There's a ship."

"A ship?!" Hyon-hui said hopefully. "What kind?"

"One comin' this way. From the west. That would make it North Korean." Mitch sat down and stared at the radio again. "Won't make much difference at this point." He fiddled with the knobs, picking up the microphone when it came on. Not knowing what else to say, he keyed the mic and spoke into it. "To anyone in the sound of my voice, *mayday*, *mayday*, *mayday*. I am an American being pursued by hostile North Korean forces. My current position is approximately twenty nautical miles due east of Kumho-ri in the Sea of Japan. Please respond."

Nothing.

Hyon-hui looked down at him. "There's no one out there, Mitch."

"It's all a matter of time, Hyon-hui. I promise you, the Americans want us. Badly. You and me. For what we know. We have formidable forces forward positioned in Japan and Korea. Everything from aircraft carriers to jeeps. If someone can make a decision and get the word up the chain. If they can get to us in time, they will." He stared ahead, squinting into the morning glare. "They just have to find us. It's a very big ocean and a very small hovercraft." He paused thinking as an idea came to him. "Wait a second," He mumbled and disappeared out to the deck. A moment later, he returned with the GPS unit. Once it initialized, he rebroadcast his mayday with a noticeable lift in his voice. "*Mayday*, *mayday*, *mayday*. This is Mitch Weatherby being pursued by hostile North Korean forces twenty miles due east of Kumho-ri in international waters." He included their exact coordinates, speed, and heading, and repeated it twice then hung up the mic and checked the horizon as if he expected to see ships and planes appear in the distance.

After several more minutes of waiting, Hyon-hui let go of the wheel and turned to him. "I don't think anyone's coming, Mitch. It is like you said. Not enough time." She wasn't panicked or even scared. Just disappointed. Covered with dirt and grime, her clothes soiled beyond recognition, her eyes still sparkled like emeralds. They peered back out the window to the pursuing ship that couldn't yet be seen with the naked eye. When their eyes met again, both were moist with tears.

"I would have liked to grow old with you in freedom," Hyon-hui said, brushing the dried dirt from her face so her tears wouldn't turn it to mud. "And I would have liked to look better for you at the end."

Mitch held her tightly and smiled as best he could. "We're not dead yet. Until then, there is always hope. Can you believe how far we've come? I choose to believe that God is part of this." He squinted at the ship again, and scanned the eastern horizon. By his estimation, it wouldn't be much more than half-an-hour until intercept. Suddenly, his eyes stopped roving along the horizon and held fixed. A look of hope sprang into them. He glanced at Hyon-hui.

"What is it?"

"I got an idea," he said and darted outside.

He rifled through the storage lockers next to the engine compartment and came across six lifejackets, a fire extinguisher, a flare gun, and a small first-aid kit. He tossed them aside before rushing back into the cabin to check under the seats. "*Ah-ha!*" he exclaimed and lifted out a bulky, orange bundle. "This has got to be it!" He hefted it outside and unrolled it. "Yes! A life raft. Slow down!" he called into the cabin. "But keep your heading."

Hyon-hui backed off the throttle and the wind in the open well deck died down.

"That's good. Hold it there." Mitch pulled the inflation ring and in seconds it expanded into a puffy orange rectangle. "That'll do nicely," he remarked, grabbing two life jackets. "Shut us down."

Hyon-hui cut power and as soon as the skirt deflated, settling them down onto the water, she helped Mitch heave the raft into the water, and move the bomb, Bok-won's pack, and all their firearms into their new vessel.

"*Mitch?*" Hyon-hui called after she climbed in and saw him heading back into the cabin rather than following her.

"Don't worry. I'm not gonna be a hero."

He rebroadcast their mayday three times and followed up with a hearty, "*Geronimo! Geronimo! Geronimo!*" hoping they would interpret it as bailing out. After clicking the microphone back into place, he said a silent prayer that someone other than the North Koreans had heard it. He scanned the eastern horizon one more time, pushed the throttles to the stops, and jumped off the side, hitting the water with a smack. He tumbled and when he righted himself, turned and watched their transportation glide off across the waves.

"And what did that do for us?" Hyon-hui asked, as the hovercraft roared into the east.

Mitch climbed over the side and lay dripping in the floor of the raft. "It bought us some time. I hope."

The hovercraft continued east, pursued by a 75 foot, Sin Hung class Patrol Boat. On the bridge, the captain, dressed in the white tunic and hat of the North Korean Navy's summer service uniform, paced nervously and kept one eye on his passenger. He looked ridiculous wearing a heavy, yellow life-jacket, and he smelled horrible, but his political authority was formidable.

"How much longer to intercept?" growled Pak Yong-nam.

"About fifteen minutes, Comrade Minister."

"Can't this thing go any faster?"

The captain glanced at the engine indicator. "We are ahead full, Comrade Minister. Fifty-three knots."

The yellow speck drew imperceptibly closer until, at two thousand meters, Pak's patience was at an end. "Fire a volley across her bow," he demanded.

"It is still two kilometers away, Comrade Minister."

"Fire a volley!"

The captain sent a message to the sailor manning the bow gun. "Fire a volley across her bow."

The sailor directed a burst from his gun a hundred yards ahead of the racing hovercraft. Pak Yong-nam watched the bullets disappear into open space. Seconds later, spray rocketed into the sky in front of the KEDO vessel.

"Again," Pak ordered.

"Again!" barked the captain into the intercom. "Closer this time!"

"Comrade Captain," said a seaman on the bridge, peering through a set of large, pedestal-mounted binoculars. He wore a white sailor suit and hat and looked a bit like the Cracker-Jack kid. "There's no one on board, sir!"

"*What?*" cried Pak.

"I don't see anyone on board, Comrade Minister. She appears to be abandoned."

"Let me see!"

The captain was bending to take a look but Pak muscled him out of the way and stared through the twin lenses, twisting the focus knob back and forth to get a clear picture. It was difficult to fix on, but the sailor appeared to be correct. He stepped back, puzzled, and the captain checked it next.

"Continue on intercept," he ordered. "Bring us alongside and hold at twenty meters." Pak paced the bridge until they'd drawn within a hundred yards when he stepped out and stared into the emptiness of the open hulled craft. Rage crawled up his spine.

The captain hailed a burly marine sergeant up to the bridge with an AK-47 and ordered him to disable the hovercraft.

They pulled alongside, paralleling the hovercraft's course, both ships doing thirty knots. The sergeant aimed and fired several short bursts until thick black smoke poured from the engine vents. The hovercraft deflated onto the water as its big Deutz diesel sputtered and died, trailing a multicolored oil slick. The ship circled back to where it lay drifting.

Three sailors went over the side, but all they found were a pair of binoculars and shiny brass shell casings rolling around on the yellow, fiberglass deck.

"Check for a raft or life boat," called the captain, with Pak spluttering in rage at his side.

"If there was one here, it's gone now," the men called back.

"They must have dropped off somewhere between here and Kumho-ri," the captain said to Pak.

"Sink it," Pak ordered.

The captain looked at him. "I was going to have it towed –"

"You heard me, Comrade Captain, sink it. Sink it now. Then we will make for Kumho-ri. As you said, they must have dropped off . And they can't get far paddling with their hands. Now move, you idiot!"

*

Smoke rose over the horizon. Floating low on the water, Mitch and Hyon-hui could see only a few miles and they'd lost sight of the patrol boat long ago. And their hovercraft before that. But the distant column told them their decoy was gone. It had bought them time but the eastern horizon was still empty. Mitch stared at it without blinking though the glare of the sun pained his eyes. He knew his brother would die trying to get them rescues, if necessary. But there just hadn't been enough time.

"Now," said Hyon-hui, as the puff of black on the horizon grew more faint, "they turn and head back this way."

"Yup," Mitch replied heavily. "No one knows we're here." He glanced at the display on the bomb. "Forty-five minutes. You want to die by plutonium laced explosion, nine-millimeter bullet, or torture. Or we could just drown ourselves."

"Bomb," Hyon-hui answered solemnly. "Quick. Painless. It requires us to do nothing."

The raft rocked gently, back and forth on the swells. Blue water stretched from horizon to horizon in all directions. Mitch leaned against the gunwale and Hyon-hui lay back on him and together, they waited. It was quiet and peaceful. The morning sun shone down on them, and a gentle breeze cooled them. Screnc. As if everything Mitch needed surrounded him. A pleasant way to spend the last minutes of his life. He – the man who had unleashed an unspeakable power into the world – would die in the arms of the woman who ensured the knowledge to use it had been lost. Better than he deserved, he thought. But the rays of the sun on his face and the love of the woman beside him said otherwise. All was right with the world. Things were exactly as they should be.

Mitch shifted and checked the self-destruct timer again. Fifteen minutes. He gazed at the ocean, where the PT boat was visible again. He watched it tack back and forth, searching for them, coming slowly closer.

"We could climb out and float in the lifejackets," Hyon-hui suggested, shielding her eyes from the sun. "They would not see us that way."

"Neither would anyone else," Mitch pointed out. "And there are sharks."

"We wait, then, for the bomb to self-destruct."

But ten minutes later, the vessel was no longer searching. Instead, it had turned straight toward them and was closing fast. They had been spotted.

"So much for the easy way." Mitch took out Bok-won's Makarov and checked the magazine again. He slapped it back in, then cycled the slide, feeding a round into the chamber. He looked at Hyon-hui, exhausted and ready for this to be over. "I'm sorry you got sucked in to this, Hyon-hui. If I hadn't shown up, you'd be advancing in the Party right now. Making a name for yourself. Now you're going to be dead. I'm sorry for ruining your life. I really am."

She smiled softly with the look that melted his heart every time. "You didn't ruin my life," she said and kissed him. "You gave me a life. If you had not come I would have never known kindness. Never had a husband. Never known love. *That* would have been a wasted life."

Mitch looked up again with tears in his eyes. He tried to smile but failed. "You're so beautiful, Hyon-hui." His emotion overflowed and he broke down. "I don't understand how a woman can be so beautiful. I just don't see how it's possible in this universe. And I can't believe that I –"

Hyon-hui kissed him gently on the lips, her green eyes sparkling with tears. "I love you, Mitch Weatherby."

He sniffed and wiped a hand across his eyes, and the two of them looked out at the patrol boat headed their way.

"Hyon-hui, this is my fault, so I'll kill you first. Then, I'll kill myself."

"No. I'll kill *you*," Hyon-hui replied solemnly. "Then, I will kill myself."

"Uh-uh, I'm not going to lay that burden on you. Not when this is all my fault."

"No, Mitch." Her voice was quiet in a determined, impossible-to-refuse sort of way. She reached out and put her hand where he held the weapon. Her touch was as warm and stimulating as it had been that night so long ago when she'd fixed him the toughest chicken he'd ever eaten. "You've already watched one wife die. You're not going to watch a second one." Hyon-hui looked out at the patrol boat, now just a few minutes away. "They are almost here." She gently pulled the gun from his grip. "Please, Mitch. Let me kill you."

He hung his head, and agreed. She was right, one per lifetime was more than enough. And after all, he thought, Romeo did die first, then Juliet awoke and killed herself.

"I would trade nothing for last night," she whispered, moving her finger to the trigger. They could hear a dim rumble from the engines of the patrol boat.

"I love you," said Mitch.

"I love you, too," said Hyon-hui.

Mitch folded his hands in his lap in resignation, and looked at the sky, searching for some kind of meaning in all of this. He didn't find it, but he knew, now, that didn't mean it wasn't there. His eyes were closed and he said simply: "I'm ready."

Hyon-hui raised the black pistol to Mitch's forehead, gripping it with two hands to stop from shaking. This gun was made for larger hands and she had to stretch to reach the trigger. It was cold, with angular edges.

Mitch sat in front of her, breathing gently. She studied his face. Peaceful, but at the same time, empty. She wasn't sure she could do this, but then thought of Sun-gun and the torture he'd obviously endured. She thought of Pak's threats of what he would do to them. She would spare Mitch that pain. Only love could make her pull the trigger. And after killing Mitch, doing herself would be easy. Natural even.

Her brain sent the order to jerk the trigger but her finger balked. Her eyes rose back to the nearing patrol boat, as she used all her mental will to force her finger to squeeze the short metal lever. It started to move. The hammer lifted slowly off the firing pin, tension building in the spring that would drive it forward and ignite the primer as soon as the trigger engaged the sear.

And she froze.

Mitch sensed it and opened his eyes. Hyon-hui was staring past him toward the horizon, eyes wide in wild disbelief. She let go of the gun and pointed east, toward Japan. He turned and saw nothing but the looming PT boat, until he followed her index finger and saw ... something. They both lifted a hand to shade their eyes from the blinding glare of the sun. There, low on the horizon was a cluster of tiny, black dots.

Hyon-hui swatted at the air to convince herself that they weren't gnats a few feet away. "*Bee-haeng-gee*," she said transfixed.

"Planes," Mitch mouthed and began a frantic search for the binoculars. "*Crap!* Where are the binocs?" Mitch rifled through the pack but didn't find them. "Must've left 'em on the hovercraft!"

"I can't hear them," Hyon-hui said, confused. "They cannot be airplanes."

"Supersonic," Mitch replied excitedly. "C'mon, c'mon," he urged, watching the dots rapidly grow.

Hyon-hui turned to him quickly, the color draining from her face. "Mitch, the bomb!"

He flung up the cover and punched in the code. "Three and-a-half minutes! We gotta get it out'a here!" Together they muscled it over the side, Mitch nearly falling out after it. The large suitcase and its deadly contents dropped into the water and sank like a stone. "We need to get away from here!" he said, pulling himself back in. They both knew the plume from the explosion would be laced with radiation, and hacked at the water with their arms to get clear.

On the ship, Pak watched them through a set of binoculars and laughed coldly. "Fools! They're trying to outrun us in a life raft! They should know when they're beaten. Captain," he barked. "Whatever happens, I want them *alive!*"

"Keep paddling!" cried Mitch, as he hung his legs over the back, kicking madly. He glanced back to see the the sailors on the bow of the warship, braced against the wind. Just behind the ship, coming up fast, were the black dots, now clearly airplanes – eight of them. Still there was no sound other than the PT boat's thrumming engines and the sound of Mitch and Hyon-hui hacking at the water with their hands and feet.

"Mitch, I can't go anymore," cried Hyon-hui. They stopped a few hundred yards from where they'd dumped the bomb, panting heavily. Mitch looked at Hyon-hui and their hands clasped.

The ship drew closer. They could see a man on the bow with a rifle. The curved magazine told them it was an AK. The sneer on his face told them he was North Korean. It also told them he had no idea what was behind him.

Pak licked his thick lips. His quarry was in sight. He could see them clearly on the raft. Weatherby and Chun. He smiled as he thought about how he might torture them, the fun he would have watching their agony. He would stay in North Korea for that simple pleasure. And then, he would take the bomb and be gone.

The F-18s overtook the Sin Hung Class patrol boat at Mach 2. In a perfectly timed maneuver, four of them pulled back hard and went straight up, directing their afterburners down at the ship. The roar and the 176,000 pounds of thrust from eight massive turbofan engines and the shock wave from the sonic booms converged upon the unsuspecting warship, turning the surface of the ocean white, shattering windows, and driving her crew into a cataleptic state.

The other four came straight on, splitting into two groups after passing the raft, and banking hard left and right. A half-second later, the roar and the sonic boom blasted the tiny raft.

Mitch thrust a fist into the sky and howled with delight.

"*We cannot fight imperialist warplanes!*" shrieked the captain of the PT boat, his eyes wide in terror. "We are in international waters. We must break off or we will be destroyed!"

"*No!*" yelled Pak, still dizzy from the overpressure of the sonic booms. "Shoot them down!" shrieked Pak. "Kill them all or I will have you shot!"

"We have no air defense! We have no way to fight them."

"Kill them! For the good of Choson, they must die!" shrieked Pak and lunged at the sergeant, clawing for his rifle. But he was no match for the powerful, agile athlete who stepped to the side and brought the butt of the rifle down on Pak's back. The big man crashed to the deck with a grunt.

"Sergeant, arrest the Minister!" ordered the captain. "He is insane!"

The aircraft that had gone vertical established an orbiting position at 25,000 feet providing fighter cover. The others burned off speed and went subsonic, circling only a few thousand feet above the water. Unseen but backing them up, the ships and planes of the U.S. Seventh Fleet painted the sky with electronic sensors and identified every target and threat from the mouth of the Tumen to the DMZ. Korean speakers got on the radio and, on North Korean channels, advised against making any moves against the rescue operation being conducted in international waters off of Kumho-ri.

Mitch whooped in glee and slapped his hand on the water as the PT boat, just a few hundred yards from them, turned hard to starboard. Hyon-hui sat in stunned disbelief, elated, and at the same time horrified. She'd very nearly shot her husband in the head. If she had been facing the other direction...

Suddenly, there was a dull rumble as the the bomb went off in the deep water between the ship and the raft. The gas bubble burst through the surface, and a sailor manning the stern machine gun on the PT boat panicked and cut loose. The volley struck the water near the raft and launched a plume of water into the air. Mitch and Hyon-hui screamed and dove into the floor of their tiny craft.

An instant later, a missile roared across the water with an ear-splitting shriek and slammed into the North Korean vessel amidship. With a flash and a tremendous *boom*, bodies flew in all directions, and in the space of a few heartbeats, the 75 foot-long craft was gone.

45

Mitch and Hyon-hui sat staring at the placid blue water that had so unexpectedly swallowed their pursuer. Around them circled the planes that had saved them. Approaching zenith, the overhead sun beat down, warming their tiny raft. Exhaustion and overload set in, leaving them dazed and mute.

The soft breeze blew them into floating scraps of wreckage from the patrol boat. A scorched canvas deck shoe drifted by. A bit of wood. A sailor hat. Bits of insulation and other unidentifiable flotsam. A body. Then another. It couldn't be long until sharks arrived for an easy meal.

They found him, bobbing through flotsam and dead bodies. He alone had been wearing a life jacket.

"Weatherby," he called out weakly.

"Well, well, well," Mitch gloated. "Look what the cat-fish dragged in."

"Pak?" Hyon-hui said in a combination of rage and elation that she would get to deal her revenge. "Pak Yong-nam!"

"Help me," he begged. His voice trembled with terror, his eyes darted about in fear. "My arm. It think it is broken." His eyes once so filled with hate were suddenly docile and pleading and he begged Hyon-hui in Korean. But Hyon-hui had seen those eyes in ways she could not forget.

Pak flinched at some unseen movement beneath the surface. "*Weatherby*. Pull me in!" He flailed at the water and started whimpering. "I'm sorry. I'm sorry for everything that has happened. I'll do anything you want. Say anything you want. I may even be able to get your mother back. Anything. Just, let me get in your raft!"

"I know in my heart she is already dead," Hyon-hui scoffed. "You will join her soon!"

"Bet there's a lot'a sharks out here with all these bodies," said Mitch, peering over the rubber gunwale. "I've heard they always go after your feet first. They're drawn by splashing sounds. Like this." He reached over the side and smacked the water with the palm of his hand. "They think it's a fish in distress. Now you try." Mitch splashed some more. "It's fun!"

Pak's eyes filled with terror. "Weatherby, *please!* This is not a joke."

Hyon-hui lifted the pistol and pointed it at his head, wondering at the bullet that just minutes ago had been meant for her husband but would now serve justice upon a monster. "Don't worry," she said. "You'll never know they are here."

Pak's eyes grew wide. "They think you're a traitor, Weatherby," he stammered. "I – I – I – could tell them what happened! That I tortured you! Forced you to work for us!"

Mitch gave him a lopsided smile. "You mean tell them the truth?"

"The spy! The spy at Los Alamos! I could give you her name! You would be a hero."

Mitch laughed and shook his head. "Nice try. You already told me you killed her."

Pak's eyes opened ever wider. "Everyone else is dead! You need me. I could tell them. Tell them the whole thing was a set up. The flash drive. The uranium. All of it!" The breeze was pushing them slowly past Pak but he was afraid to move his legs or splash with his arms.

"Let me kill him, Mitch," Hyon-hui growled. "Please."

"Weatherby," Pak screamed. "You need me. You need me. I'll tell them about the 235 uranium! I'll tell them I put the 235 in your house. Just please don't leave me here!"

"Mitch, please. For this," Hyon-hui urged, pulling her shirt aside so he could see the bruises on her neck. "And for you. And for Beth. And for Max. And for Sonny. And my mother. Just one bullet in his ugly, fat face. Just one."

"Weatherby," Pak groaned. "My wife. My children… Think of them. Don't leave me to these sharks! *Weatherby, Please!*"

Mitch stared at Pak. He had dreamed of this while lying on the floor in his cell. He would bear scars for the rest of his life. He thought about bringing it up, but Pak knew all these things already,and delighted in them.

Something swished the surface not far away. Mitch's eyes followed a dark, torpedo-like shape as it descended into the gloom.

"Weatherby!!! Comrade Chun! You have to help me. You can't leave me like this!"

"You know, Hyon-hui," Mitch said, " I didn't go to Terminal Island but I still spent the last year and a half in prison. There were times I wasn't worth saving. But look at us now." He pointed at the planes orbiting them. "Things can change quickly."

"What are you saying?!" snapped Hyon-hui, her eyes growing wide. "You're going to save him?!"

A million thoughts, spun through Mitch's head. Stories from real life and from fiction throughout the ages were filled with this exact scene. The movie going public loved to see the villain die in the most creatively gruesome fashion that the director and his staff could come up with, and Mitch had dreamed of this moment a thousand times. But staring at a man and deciding to kill him, in cold blood, was another thing entirely. Even a man who'd done you wrong. He turned to Hyon-hui and said, "Where would Frodo have been if Bilbo had killed Gollum?"

"What? What are you talking about?" Her voice was shrill and her face a storm. "Who's Frodo?"

"We need him, Hyon-hui."

"Yes! Yes!" cried Pak. "Or you will go back to prison."

"The only thing we *need* is to kill him!" Hyon-hui fired back. "The sharks need to eat, too! Please Mitch. For all that he has done to us."

"When I was in his prison," Mitch replied, still staring at Pak but speaking to Hyon-hui, "I thought I'd never see you again." Mitch caressed the stock on the AK-47. "Nothing would give me more pleasure than putting an entire magazine in his head and watching the sharks have lunch. I'd even stuff his screaming head in their mouths to have that pleasure." He shifted his eyes to Hyon-hui, who was staring at him like he was the monster North Korea propaganda painted all Americans to be. "But I don't want to take the chance of being separated from you. Having you, trumps killing him."

Hyon-hui's eyes softened. "But..." she groaned. "Everything he has done... To us!"

"I know." Mitch looked back at Pak and the man was crying, kicking gently to keep up with them. "I know. But this is what I *should* do. The last time I had this choice, I didn't do what I should have done and gave the world a nuclear North Korea."

"Please, Mitch," Pak whined. "I only want to live. I will do whatever you say."

"He can't hurt you again, Hyon-hui. But killing him can hurt us. God didn't give me another chance, didn't show me mercy, only to have me withhold it. I've learned my lesson." He paused for a moment, and handed her the AK-47. "But I can't tell you what to do."

Hyon-hui took the rifle, uncertain if Mitch wanted her to kill Pak or truly wanted her to choose for herself. She weighed the rifle in her hand then sighted down the barrel at Pak's head. For so long, killing him was all that she had wanted. The man who had raped her. The man who had tortured Mitch. But now, as he bobbed only a few feet away, defenseless and cowering, all she could see was a pathetic, weak man. And he was apparently the only thing that could guarantee that she and Mitch would be together.

"You know, you already killed the big fish," Mitch told her, as she struggled to make up her mind. "This," he pointed at Pak, "it's a minnow."

The distinctive beats of a helicopter drifted to them across the ocean. Out to sea, they saw two dark shapes approaching across the water, still some miles away.

Hyon-hui sighted down the barrel again and pulled the trigger. The water a few feet to Pak's right erupted in a geyser. Then the water on the other side. Pak screamed and sobbed, certain he'd breathed his last. But as the spray landed, Pak opened his eyes slowly to find that he was still alive.

Hyon-hui lowered the rifle and handed it back to Mitch. "If it means losing you, or even the chance of losing you, it is not worth it."

"Yes, yes," Pak bubbled with submission. "That is a good decision. You need me. I'm your man. I will say whatev –"

Mitch pointed the AK back at the floating figure. "Shut. Up. Don't say another word until they pick us up. Understand?"

"Yes, I underst –"

Mitch shot next to him again, and Pak clamped his lips tightly together.

"Understand?" Mitch said again, and Pak nodded vigorously.

Together, Mitch and Hyon-hui paddled the raft back to where Pak was floating in the water and carefully hauled him aboard. He groveled on the rubber floor, clutching his obviously broken arm and bowing profusely.

"America must be a wonderful place," Hyon-hui said, holding the gun on Pak, "if everyone is a Christian and is so merciful."

Mitch leaned back against the rubber hull and laughed. "I never said that, Hyon-hui. We have our Paks, too. And some people treat Christianity more like the Party."

Hyon-hui's eyes flashed, and she kicked at Pak. "The Party?" she spat, snatching off her pin and tossing it into the water. "I will not go back to the Party!"

A connection came together in Mitch's head at the sight, and it made him smile. "I have to think that Kim Il-sung was trying to make a difference when he started the Party. I think he wanted a better life for the Korean people after the Japanese occupation. It just got out of control. *Waaayy* out of control. It always does. Hitler. Lenin. Jim Jones. Personality cults always end badly. People take advantage of them. People like this piece of work." He nudged Pak with his foot. "They use it for personal gain. There are people who say they are Christians who are no different. They take advantage of those who show mercy or are trusting. Or they just want to be in charge. Or they just use their connections to try to extend their business. Sound familiar?"

Hyon-hui nodded, but her brow was furrowed. "You opened my eyes to the Party, and now you want me to go back?"

The helicopters were coming closer. Mitch could tell now that one was a twin-rotor Chinook and the other a Seahawk. The sweetest sights he'd ever seen. They'd be boarding in a few minutes and heading back to the United States. Mitch anticipated that his conviction would be thrown out and the three of them would be debriefed extensively. He and Hyon-hui would probably get new identities and disappear into some Federal disappearance program. This nightmare was finally ending.

He looked at his wife, and wanted to sooth the concern on her face. "No, I never want you to go back to anything like the Party. It isn't about parties or institutions. Think about it. Professor Yang was in the Party and neither of us would be here, about to be rescued, without him. Sonny was in the Party, too. It's no different with Christianity. There are people who say they are Christians and then there are people who live like it. It's really not very hard to tell the difference." Hyon-hui's face twisted more with fear, and Mitch realized, how could she not be afraid? She was facing an unknown after a lifetime of indoctrination and terror? "It will be okay," he assured her. "You will see."

Hyon-hui shook her head tightly. "What if they won't let me in?" she asked, through clenched teeth. "It took me years to get into the Party. And then when I finally did –" she cut her eyes at Pak and he cowered in the raft. She raised her pistol again and pointed it at his head, her thin arm shaking with the desire to end his existence.

"It doesn't work like that," Mitch said softly. "It's between you and God. Not ass wipes like Pak or some committee."

Pak nodded profusely. "Yes, I am an ass wi –" He clamped his mouth shut when Mitch and Hyon-hui both pointed guns at him.

Mitch longed to put a bullet in Pak's head and was already regretting his decision. "But I'd still like to blow you away," he said matter-of-factly. "And I know my lovely bride would just as soon cap your ass as yawn." Hyon-hui nodded viciously, though Mitch suspected she had no idea what he'd just said. "And if you ever try to harm Hyon-hui again, in any way, I will kill you.

Because citizens of the United States can own guns and protect themselves. And that is what makes us free. You, comrade, are not a citizen. And I can shoot a gnat off a fly's back from a hundred paces. Do you follow?"

The story of Mitch's shooting skills had circulated widely and Pak's head bobbed rapidly.

Mitch raised an arm to wave at the big helicopter with the magnificent white stars on the hull. The emblem of his homeland. A shining star in a dark world. He had been right, the United States wasn't what he'd thought. It was better. Far better than he could ever imagine.

As the Chinook drifted in gently to set down in the water, he leaned over and kissed Hyon-hui. "And now," he told her, "they live happily ever after."

Let the **world** know what *you* thought of *The Silla Project.*

Or visit this page at

http://johncbrewer.com/?page_id=1823

to leave your feedback.

Other Books From
PlotForge, Ltd.

by

Terri-Lynne Smiles

Foreseen
Book 1 of
The Rothston Series

and coming soon

Choices
Book 2 of
The Rothston Series

Sarandipity
a Science Fiction Saga

www.PlotForge.com

BIBLIOGRAPHY

What follows is a partial list of books, articles, and other materials used in the preparation of this novel. It is by no means complete and does not include scores of short articles and documents by individuals, corporations, and government agencies, as well as anecdotal accounts and personal interviews. For those interested in layman's technology of nuclear weapons or the Manhattan project, see those items marked with the symbol '*'. For those interested in learning more about the DPRK consult those items marked with a '†'. All technical information in *The Silla Project*, is public domain or derived from declassified government documents.

Allison, A.G., Nadler, M.R., "LA 1133: Production of Crucibles for Melting and Casting Plutonium and Uranium-235," *Los Alamos Technical Reports*, Los Alamos, NM, 1950

Baker, C.P., Holloway, M.G., "LA 618a: Critical Masses of Enriched Uranium Hydrides and Some Related Measurements," *Los Alamos Technical Reports*, Los Alamos, NM, 1947

Baker, R.D., "LA 412: Chemical and Metallurgical Operations Involved In the Fabrication of Uranium 235 For Use In Nuclear Weapons: Part III Reduction of Uranium Tetrafluoride to Metal," *Los Alamos Technical Reports*, Los Alamos, NM, 1946

Baker, R.D., "LA 472: Preparation of Uranium Metal By the Bomb Method," *Los Alamos Technical Reports, Los Alamos*, NM, 1946

Bakker, Paul, "North Korea: March 1995," *World Wide Web*, Australia, 1998

Beal, Tim, "Photos from the DPRK: April 1998," *World Wide Web*, New Zealand, 1999

†Belke, Thomas J., *Juche: A Christian Study of NK's State Religion*, Living Sacrifice Book Co., Bartlesville, OK, USA, 1999

Benedict, Manson, "Developments in Uranium Enrichment," American *Institute of Chemical Engineers*, New York, NY, 1977

†Bermudez, Joseph S., *North Korean Special Forces*, Janes Publications, UK, 1988

Bethe, H.A., Christy, R.F., "LA 11: Los Alamos Handbook of Nuclear Physics," *Los Alamos Technical Reports*, Los Alamos, NM, 1943

Bloch, F., "LA 17 A: Fission Spectrum," *Los Alamos Technical Reports*, Los Alamos, NM, 1943

†Bone, Simon, "Life After Tyranny: Happy Birthday Korea," *World Wide Web*, 1998

Bunge, Frederica M., *North Korea: A Country Study, 3rd Ed.*, The American University, Foreign Area Studies, Washington D.C., 1981

Burke, J.E., "LA 37: The Formation of Uranium Hydride," *Los Alamos Technical Reports*," Los Alamos, NM, 1943

Callow, R.J., *The Industrial Chemistry of the Lanthanons, Yttrium, Thorium, and Uranium*, Pergamon Press, Oxford, London, Edinburgh, NY, Toronto, Sydney, 1967

Choe In Su, *Kim Jong Il: The People's Leader*, Foreign Languages Publishing House, Pyongyang, North Korea, 1985

Focus on Korea, *This is KOREA*, Seoul International Publishing House, Yongdong PO Box 629, Seoul, Korea 135, 1986

Friedlander, G., Spence, R., "LA 140: Gamma-Ray Sources," *Los Alamos Technical Reports*, Los Alamos, NM, 1946

*Groueff, Stephane, *Manhattan Project: The Untold Story of the Making of the Atomic Bomb*, Little, Brown & Company, Boston, Mass., 1967

Halberstadt, HansU.S., *Navy SEALS*, MBI Publishing Company, Osceola, WI, 1993

Hamza, Khidhir, *Saddam's Bombmaker*, Scribner, New York, NY, 2000

*Hanson, Chuck, *US Nuclear Weapons, The Secret History*, Aerofax, Inc., Arlington, TX, 1988

Hawkins, David, *The History of ModernPhysics: 1800-1950*, Tomash Publishers   Los Angeles, San Francisco, 1983

*Hoddeson, et.al., *Critical Assembly*, Cambridge University Press, Cambridge, NY, Melbourne, 1993

Kang Sok-ju, Gallucci, Robert, "*Agreed Framework Between the United States and the Democratic People's Republic of Korea*, United Nations, Geneva, 1994

Kewish, R.W., "LA 1652: The Preparation of High Purity Uranium Metal," *Los Alamos Technical Reports*, Los Alamos, NM, 1954

†Kim Jong Il, *On The Juche Idea*, Foreign Languages Publishing House, Pyongyang, North Korea, 1989

Kim, C.I., Koh, B.C., *Journey to North Korea: Personal Perceptions*, Institute of East Asian Studies, Berkeley, CA, 1983

Klema, Ernest D., "LA 188: Fission Cross Section of 23 [U233] From 30 KeV to 3 MeV," *Los Alamos Technical Reports*, Los Alamos, NM, 1944

Knox, Donald, *The Korean War: Pusan to Chosin*, Harcourt Brace & Company, New York, NY, 1985

†Korea Central News Agency, Various Articles, World Wide Web, P'yongyang, DPRK

Korean Energey Development Organization (KEDO), "The Nuclear Round Table," New York, NY, 1995

LaMar, Lawrence E., "LA 1474: RaLa Process Research," *Los Alamos Technical Reports*, Los Alamos, NM, 1952

*McDonald, C., Brown, A, *The Secret History of the Atomic Bomb*, The Dial Press, New York, NY, 1977

Murray, Florence J., *At the Foot of Dragon Hill*, E.P. Dutton & Company, Inc., New York, NY, 1975

Northeast Asia Peace and Security Network (NAPSNET) Daily Reports, DPRK Reports 1996 – 1999, KRB-ICIP, Moscow, 1996-1999

†Oberdorfer, Don, *The Two Koreas*, Addison-Wesley, Massachusetts, 1997

Paxton H.C., Orndoff, J.D., Linenberger, G.A., "LA 1159: Oralloy Hydride Critical Assemblies," *Los Alamos Technical Reports*, Los Alamos, NM, 1950

Perlman, M.L., Weissman, S.I., "LA 33: Preparation of Compacts of High-Density Uranium Hydride," *Los Alamos Technical Reports*, Los Alamos, NM, 1943

Pike, John, Federation of American Scientists, World Wide Web

Richards, H.T., "LA 60: The Fission Spectrum of 25 [U235]," *Los Alamos Technical Reports*, Los Alamos, NM, 1944

Richards, H.T., "LA 84: Fission Neutron Spectrum of 25 [U235] and 49 [Pu239]," *Los Alamos Technical Reports*, Los Alamos, NM, 1944

Richards, H.T., "LA 200: Neutron Spectrum for Fast Fission of 25 [U235]," *Los Alamos Technical Reports*, Los Alamos, NM, 1945

Rossi, Bruno B., Staub, Hans H., *Ionization Chambers and Counters*, McGraw-Hill, New York, NY, 1949

†Savada, Andrea M., North *Korea: a country study, 4th Edition*, The American University, Foreign Area Studies, Washington D.C., 1994

Scholte, John W., "LA 1268: RaLa Process Testing, Final Report," *Los Alamos Technical Reports*, Los Alamos, NM, 1951

*Serber, Robert, *The Los Alamos Primer*, University of CA Press, Berkeley, 1992

Serber, Robert, "LA 1: The Los Alamos Primer," *Los Alamos Technical Reports*, Los Alamos, NM, 1943

Shroyer, Jo Ann, *Secret Mesa: Inside Los Alamos National Lanboratory*, John Wiley & Son's, New York, NY, 1998

Snyder, T.M., Willimas, R.W., "LA 102: Number of Neutrons Per Fission For 25 [U235] and 49 [Pu239]," *Los Alamos Technical Reports*, Los Alamos, NM, 1944

*Sublette, Cary, "Nuclear Weapons FAQ version 2.22," *World Wide Web*, 1998

Taschek, R.F., "LA 211: Radioactive Threshold Detectors for Neutrons," *Los Alamos Technical Reports*, Los Alamos, NM, 1945

Korea Tour: DPR Korea, National Tourism Administration DPRK, P'yongyang, NK, 1997

Villani, S, *Topics in Applied Physics V 35: Uranium Enrichment*, Springer-Verlag, Berlin, Heidelberg, NY, 1979

Williams, J.H., "LA 520: Fission Cross Sections of 02, 23, 25, 28, 49, B10, and Li6," *Los Alamos Technical Reports*, Los Alamos, NM, 1946

Young, Dwight S., "LA 1487: Neutron Distribution Measurements at Pajarito By Means of Photographic Emulsions," *Los Alamos Technical Reports*, Los Alamos, NM, 1952

KOREA: Its Land, People and Culture of all Ages, Hakwon-Sa, Ltd., Seoul, Korea, 1963

Author Bio

John C. Brewer grew up the son of a naval aviator and has lived in Canada, Florida, New Mexico, Washington State, Virginia, and Alabama. At Auburn University, he earned a B.S. in physics and an M.S. in aerospace engineering. He lives in Huntsville, Alabama with his wife April and his three sons, and is working hard on his next book. To learn more about John and what he is doing please visit www.JohnCBrewer.com.